RODGI

WII

A HARLEY DODGE NOVEL

K. L. Metzger
2Fish Tales · Virginia Beach

This is a work of fiction. Similarities to real people, places, or events are entirely coincidental.

RODGER-DODGER, WILCO OUT

First edition. November 13, 2020.

ISBN: 978-1393369080

Written by K. L. Metzger.

Also by K. L. Metzger

Harley Dodge
Dodged the Bullet
Rodger-Dodger, Wilco Out
Dodge Central

Watch for more at https://kathiemetzger.wixsite.com/
klmetzgerauthor.

Table of Contents

For all the Miss Surelee's of this world.

Chapter One: A Charming Spectacle

When I was five and the youngest of three (Derby and the Halvsies being the exception), mom drove us kids to Barney's Alter Ego to pick out our annual Halloween costumes. Naturally, my oldest brother, Rob-Bob went cowboy while my other brother, Rodger-Dodger set his sights on being Batman. Not knowing any differently, I wanted to be his sidekick, Robin. I mean, Robin wasn't as tall or as brave or as cool as Batman is but that didn't matter much because he was a superhero after all; a superhero with lots of cool superhero gadgets and gizmos who got to kick ass, nonetheless. Besides, costumes gave you the chance of being somebody else, not somebody you were.

Mom being the voice of reality, said no. Little girls didn't wear little boy costumes. Little girls didn't wear capes and black eye masks. But back then it was the seventies, so what did she know? She eventually talked me into a Tinkerbelle replica complete with wings, tutu, tights and magic wand. Now being the Dodge that I proudly became today, I waited until everyone was fast asleep, yanked off those glittery wings, ripped away the itchy tutu and snapped the star clean off the plastic magical stick. Tossing most, I fashioned my own version of a superhero, complete with glittery mask and see-through cape with five-pointed star. I thought my version was way, cooler looking than all the costumes rounded up at the Ego.

Yeah, mom had a conniption the very, next morning.

You could say that pretty much sums up my unique view of the world and why today, now more than ever, I, Harley Dodge resurrected that sidekick of hillbilly stubbornness, put my booted foot down on Aunt Bertie's well-worn, wooden floor of her older-than-dirt, Victorian, refusing to budge one inch. You know...just in case she was on potty break.

"Ut-uh, no way, you can't make me do it," I cried for all that is Boolee to hear.

Having taken in my fourteen-going-on-thirty-year-old daughter and me, so we wouldn't have to sleep in the bed of Red's older-than-dirt, holy, flaked and faded red '72 Dodge (now my new loaner) dusty Rusty, should have been enough of a warning for her to keep from pushing any more of my buttons. It should be, but it wasn't.

"I'm sorry dear, but I'm way behind as it is," Bertie said with all her two-hundred-and-twenty-pounds of towering, feminine, pokerfaced charm. "And, dear, if you happen to run into Rodger, please let him know that Reynold is looking for him."

Ah...nope.

Aunt Bertie was behind, but not in the rear. She may have the coolest little shriveled up nuttier companion in the world, Mr. Willoughby or be Red's older sister with a better vocabulary and softer demeanor and the only other person aside from Barbarilla who can put the brakes on damnation by calling Red by his real-real name, but that doesn't mean

I'm not fearful of a Dodge. She could still whack me across the head with a wooden spoon if the situation warranted or, if I pouted or stomped my boot a second time.

Today might not be one of those times to test out Aunt Bertie's patience, though. The weeks leading up to Halloween were her busiest (second to the month after hunting season) for her elusive hobby-turned-cash hauling trade of petrifying road kill for all to admire, indefinitely. She was mad-crazy swamped. But hey, seeing how her hobby was the whole point of my protest, and the only reason I was glad to be a Dodge, I didn't care, threw caution to the wind, and stomped the other booted foot regardless.

She ignored me. Naturally.

Aunt Bertie wasn't caving to my tantrum especially since she knew why I was vehemently protesting the idea of delivering a stuffed and petrified cat to the owner of a newly opened shop in town because, well, firstly, she knew of my freak talent. Secondly, she knew I needed the money—A.S.A.P. It didn't matter that I still had five hundred dollars left of that finders' fee over that damn bullion. (Okay, I'm now down to a quarter of that no thanks in part to my daughter's new school year wardrobe, books, and supplies). I was hoping for more. Like all of it. Enough to upgrade from dusty Rusty to something assembled this decade so I could haul ass to oblivion and never return. Alas, it wasn't enough, because my life mirrors Rusty's uphill sputtering with sporadic buckshot thrown into the mix. You know, just in case I wasn't reaching my heart palpating, caffeine induced, redlining, thrill, for the day.

Therefore, I threw hands to the air and whistled steam.

She gave me a Dodge's infamous stink eye before saying, "Is that what you're wearing?"

Laney's newly acquired midnight, fur covered pet slinked into the kitchen as it gave a quick scan of his surroundings and then, with an innocent glance my way, mewed in agreement.

My stink eye toward Bandit fell two carbs' short of anything truck-worthy.

I turned back to my Aunt Bertie with a frown before saying, "What, I'm dressed, aren't I?"

Aunt Bertie only harrumphed.

I glanced down at my faded blue jeans, a threadbare and washed out heavy metal concert t-shirt from several decades ago slipped over a long sleeved thermal, and of course, my Harley Davidson, black leather motorcycle boots with balding tread. Annoyingly enough, there was Bandit, cuter than sunshine sporting a harness so Laney could hook on a leash in a most humane way, now rubbing up against my right boot. I ignored the urge to drive Bandit to the shelter the next county over, shrugged then furrowed my brow, just for my Aunt Bertie's sake. In my mind, I looked just fine to sit around, nursing my wounded heart (and depleted bank account), from here to eternity. No reason to dress all fancy-shmancy for that. Unlike Aunt Bertie who wore dresses year-round, except in the case like today, when she was working. She aptly covered up in t-shirt and blue jean overalls, rubber boots, rubber gloves, with her silvery stands braided up to the top of her head like the *Swiss Miss* girl.

I shrugged my shoulders a second time.

"Suit yourself, dear," she said, peering over the tops of her half-moon spectacles, a twinkle to her periwinkle colored eyes.

Two can play...

"Hey, where's Tucky," I asked, with a smirk, arms crossed.

Tucky and his dumber half, Boomer came by once a month to groom Aunt Bertie's' overgrown plot of rolling twenty acres. By the jungle state of things, he was a month overdue. He also was the one who moonlighted for Boolee's only cemetery (managed by our mutual cousin, Walt Jr.) that saw more action in one day this past July/August than it has all year.

She flashed me a fully loaded, double barreled stink eye.

I snickered. I knew damn well, where my cousin was: upstate at *WV Community* renewing his license. I could have cared less where Boomer was. I just couldn't resist pushing her buttons.

Tucky or rather, Kentucky was one of my twenty-something cousins on Red and Aunt Bertie's side of things, grandson of Leonard 'Leo' and Margaret Dodge. Great Uncle Leo, the youngest of nine children and brother to my (rest in peace) Pawpaw, Elmer Dodge, was Bertie, Walter and Red's Uncle Leo and something of a reformed criminal. Margaret was born a Spigot. And not someone you messed with either. However, Margaret, being a Spigot, having married a Dodge and settling to Boolee, was a bit of a scandal and I'm not talking the running around kind; I'm talking, get-your-shotgun, feuding kin kind of trouble with an underscored Kentucky, exclamation point and something about a foot and a pig thrown in for the fun of it. This might explain why Tucky's' parents' skipped town the day he was born, why they named him after the state he was from, why Tucky never married, rumored to have spawned four bastards and has a lazy, wandering eye.

But today isn't about family no matter how much I wish I wasn't related. So, I maintained the course and kept at my irritation by huffily saying, "I don't care if it was a rush job, I'm not setting one foot in that place!"

Spooked by my outburst, Bandit darted out of the kitchen to begin his personal game of hide-and-seek.

Someone should tell him I'm not playing.

I slumped to one of the wooden, ladder-back chairs at the far end of the farmhouse styled, wooden table, and sagged all of me. I averted my attention from the sunshine yellow painted cabinetry to my ragged cuticles and dug in, refusing to budge another inch.

Aunt Bertie wouldn't budge either, having been born and raised a Dodge, in Boolee. Surviving the Great Depression like it was an afternoon stroll amongst the ribbits. She could outwit/outwait a snail without breaking a sweat.

A moment later, Aunt Bertie aptly placed the statuesque vermin on the table along with the shop owners' address then headed for her makeshift taxidermy shop: the converted dining room. Then, to drive the point of her knife deeper, she gave off a hearty laugh and said, "Yes you will."

Crap. She was going to be a tough nut to crack.

I glanced up from my hands and took stock of the well-organized and spotless surroundings of the kitchen settling last looks to the stack of newspapers that is the nasty result of my Aunt Gladys' *Redlight* business: unsubstantiated gossip. Aunt Bertie had them stacked to the farmhouse styled wooden table, presumably to use as catchall for road kill entrails, rather than have them carted off to Red's recycling plant, formally the ozone contributing, Mill. Personally, I thought Aunt Gladys' rumor mongering pages belonged in the landfill instead, but that's just my one-track mind of an opinion.

The top paper had an article that luckily wasn't about me, or my bizarre life as a Dodge. Shocker. But there was mention of Letty Spigot Dodge suddenly widowed, unflattering black and white picture accentuating her crinkled expression as the spitting, albeit slightly younger image of her mother, Margret. Not wanting to fill my head with stupid thoughts, I skimmed down to the bottom of the page and felt my heart give a thump in my chest. It was about Rodger-Dodger's life-long friend, Junior Pensky, about his tire and lube business going up in a blaze of glory this past Thursday. There were no injuries because his shop had long since gone out of business and sat vacant for nearly a year. Hope that joker had insurance.

I sighed and turned my attention back to the petrified Siamese. Aunt Bertie's hobby-turned-profession of taxidermy didn't creep me out, at least, nowhere near the creepy crawly effect it had on my daughter, Laney. Yes, I'm snickering here. She'd pinch her nose at every one of them. Aunt Bertie was an expert and not one of those dang frozen lumps of vermin ever smelled (unlike Bandit if Laney didn't get around to changing that litter box of his). You know it'll probably be me doing the change out, right? No matter, I've lived my entire youth around Aunt Bertie's statues, so I'm well used to them like my Dodge heritage. Or, maybe I'm just nose blind. More importantly, I have nothing to fear touching one of those long dead, well-preserved fuzz balls of road-kill either. Gratefully, my burdensome talent has no effect on them.

That doesn't mean I'm happy about it, though.

Enter one antiquity shop chockfull of the lingering dead. You heard right, *antique* shop. As in, my reason for "sweating bullets" about my daily existence due to one left handed will of its own; something that I'd do anything—with a capital yikes—to avoid visiting at all costs. I might as well run naked at high noon through the cemetery, or, better yet, call up my ex-Trolloping, Dickie (from where ever in the hell he'd slithered off to) for a let's-make-up-and-forget, reunion.

Up until recently (thanks Gladys), only two people knew of my freakish talent: Detective Pine and, my Aunt Bertie (Naturally). The third person wasn't talking, literally. Pumped so full of Thorazine she'd be lucky if she remembered her name: Derby Dodge. She was one of my twenty-something cousins growing up until two and a half months ago, when she graciously clued me in on the fact that she and I have the same momma. We also shared Dickie with a third: jailbait Brandi with an "I" and one of those stupid hearts dotting it as if she was in love with herself. Somehow, she conveniently managed to disappear as well. Good thing I didn't legally marry that Dick breath. Thanks to that debacle back in July/August, the whole town now knows of my freakish talent. Wish they'd forget about it instead.

Maybe if I sit here long enough, Aunt Bertie will forget all about me too.

"Better get a move on," said Bertie from the other room. I cringed. Guess she wasn't giving up. "Smells like rain's coming and you'll want to make it back in time for supper. I'm making lamb chops."

I sniffed the air. I closed my eyes and drooled. She had a pumpkin pie baking in her pioneer-days-type oven for dessert. Oh, how fitting. I can't believe she just yanked my guilty chain. Sucking me in with the promise of my favorite food was an all-time low. Okay, whom am I kidding? I can believe she wasn't above blackmail. Food is my ultimate favorite type of food. Especially the kind that magically appears, steamy, glistening and smelling as if I didn't have to lift one finger to order takeout. Dang, Aunt Bertie was hitting below the fan belt of my iron stomach. I bet you she's making them with stewed tomatoes and tiny, roasted potatoes with a sprinkling of garlic and rosemary. Ah, damn. My stomach just protested my stalling. Aunt Bertie just hook, line and lamb chopped me.

I'd better skedaddle before I get pie in my face.

I gave a hearty sigh to the inevitable, pushed away from the table, stuck my tongue out at fraidy-cat—the petrified Siamese—then scooped it and the address up and headed for the door. Aunt Bertie's rotary styled telephone rang as I snagged my purse and fleece hoodie off the coat tree next to the front door. I didn't dawdle. I had no reason to believe that call was for me and even if it were, I was much too petered to care differently. Besides...my arms were inaccessible, loaded with petrified cat.

I stomped out of the old Victorian and climbed into dusty Rusty. With a shiver from the morning chill I shrugged into my hoodie then shook some more, desperate to keep my toes from petrifying on their own. A moment later, I glanced at the address, mentally placed its location, and geared Rusty up for action. I flipped the wipers once to scatter the sprinkling of pine needles and decaying leaves that accumulated overnight and with my last will of defiance, I appropriately spun the tires as I floored Rusty and drove away from my temporary home away from home.

I headed down the dirt packed and unpaved, winding county road R, lined with trees bursting with sunset orange, blood red and gilded golden leaves, following the bend to the left. I startled just a bit when I didn't even have a body spasm or pass out as I sped past the fork, ignoring the shoot off to the right. I did however get a second shiver. It could have been coincidence or it could have been the fact I can't bring myself to roll the window all the way up and keep the near freezing temperatures from airing out Rusty's cracked and faded interior. It still smelled terribly sour from years of permeated sweat, grease and road-kill that no amount of bleach would ever dissolve. I'm pretty sure, however, that my chill had a little something to do with my crossing that fork in the road and not stopping for all the chocolate in the world. You may call me crazy brilliant, but I am *NOT* with-a-capital-Sane stupid enough to find my way going down that road again. That one led to hell. That one led to my childhood home. That one led to Red and Barbarilla's funhouse of flames.

I cranked the heat to high, nevertheless.

Rusty sputtered along Main Street catching all green lights, rumbled beyond homes and stoops littered with carved pumpkins, the doors and windows sported cardboard ghosts or witches on broomsticks and storefronts painted with spooky slogans as I urged him two blocks past the Piggly Wiggly and hooked a left at the west end of the town Square, headed toward Sycamore Court. I put as much of my one-hundred-and-twenty pounds' worth of muscle as I could muster into the turn, because Rusty did not back then, nor now, come with power steering. Rusty looked like a refrigerator and cornered worse. Oh well, at least I was getting some exercise.

I needed more warmth so I slapped my palm to the dash panel as I drove four more blocks of stop and start traffic south. The heat wasn't cranking out fast enough and no amount of abuse would change that. I needed something else, like a new identity but that wasn't going to happen for me this side of my thirty-fourth birthday. I thought, hey yes, I know what will do the trick—coffee!

A quick in, quick out and I was idling in the parking lot at the corner of Sycamore and Summit, snuggling up to a cup of heavenly warmth, wishing I could curl up into a ball and pretend I had not woken up today. I took a deep breath of the eye opening, freshly brewed Columbian aroma, hoping to spark some morning bravado. It worked, somewhat because thank gaud for Quick E Stops! I was oozing euphoria over its' heart-stopping warmth and stuffing my face full of a glazed, round sugar bomb, delirious of the short-tempered passerby's' around the packed parking lot; oblivious to the pre-winter chill in the air and doing my best to ignore the radio announcement that Dickie Trollop's ex-partner, Arnold Hibbard was dead—as in: found murdered in his multi-million-dollar Amarillo, Texas mansion five nights back, his wife, Loretta Hibbard, suspiciously missing. I only met Arnold once and I was just as unimpressed then as I am now. Sucks to be him, I guess.

Cripes. My day just nosedived into ill-fated territory at buckshot speed. Okay, I might be just a little freaked out over the knowledge that someone (possibly dipshit) sought to end Arnold's illegal activities, permanently with a twenty-two. But at least I know it wasn't moi who pulled the trigger. I shuddered nonetheless, hoping to scrub that thought away while I slurped at my cooling cup of java.

Quick E Stop coffee is *okay* and I could have, just as easily filled up a to-go mug of Aunt Bertie's morning brew to get me through the day. However, if I really wanted a great cup of coffee that brought me one step closer to the gates of heaven then I should have ordered a Javalot special. Nothing ever comes close to Javalot's swirling cups of caffeinated magic. And I mean NOTHING! But well, Javalot was at the Square and the Square was in the opposite direction. Now that I think about it, I should have ventured a detour just to keep Rusty and me from the inevitable of delivering one of Aunt Bertie's road-kill specials to an eagerly waiting, antique shop-owning customer.

Okay, you caught me...I'm stalling. Time to get this errand done and over with I suppose...

Oh, my lucky stars, someone is waving at me, adding to my need to stall such a horrifying delivery. Oh, crap, I think she's flagging me down. Nope, she's waving...nope, she's (definitely) flagging me down. It was the wife of my second-hand-past ex-boyfriend, a one Mrs. Detective, Sally Pine. Back in late July, I got, suckered into subbing for her down at Red's Mill while she anxiously awaited the arrival of ankle biter number three. Looks like she's still convalescing. Sally and I went to school together and were only two months apart in age but today she looked years older and carrying several extra pounds around the middle. Trotting toward me and Rusty, a splotch of something greenish-yellow on the lapel of her well-worn coat, dishwater blonde hair disheveled, dull brown eyes bugging out, cell phone in hand frantically waving while the other, clutched at a near empty baby bottle. She looked a fright. I swear, if she's still pregnant I'll ditch Rusty and flee the country right now!

"I'm so glad I caught ya," she said, near out of breath. "But I'm in a bit of a state."

This could mean anything...

I shoved the last of my donut to my mouth and stared on.

Sally muttered something about Rodger-Dodger and the Volvo, glancing over her shoulder then back at me with pleading eyes.

I swallowed; fighting back the urge to roll eyes heavenward but blew out a sigh, shut down Rusty before begrudgingly angling down from the bench seat. I slammed the door shut and followed her across the parking lot back to her family wagon. The wind picked up. I huddled deep to my hoodie, peeked into the back of her Volvo, and understood the state of her frazzled appearance. Nestled between two belted in but wiggly boys, strapped and sleeping in a pink carrier, was the cutest fluff ball of wonder; Jasmine Pine and the girl Sally had always wanted. Jasmine had her daddy's looks from what everyone says which, in my opinion isn't much of a compliment. But according to gossip (thanks Gladys) she is the sweetest and the best-behaved newborn anyone could beg for, seeing how her two older brothers were a handful.

Just wait until that little angel turns thirteen.

However, this wasn't Sally's dilemma. Seems she had a flat tire from running over a galvanized nail. Ouch. Unlucky break there. Unfortunately, with no way of knowing how to change it, she proceeded to explain how her cellular phone had powered out of juice, with no help from her eldest son, Todd or the other spawn who took it upon themselves to scramble the internet trolling for *Sesame Street* videos. And naturally, payphones went extinct somewhere back when Nixon skulked out of his embarrassing Presidency. She had no way of calling someone up for help.

Yes, I'm giggling...inwardly, of course.

So, after ten minutes of trying to flag someone down for help (most of whom were young woman and were just as inept at tire changing), she was ready to give up and walk the five blocks home when I came strolling on up for a cup of Quick E Stop's underrated finest. I should have faked being in a coma and stayed in bed or at the very least, offered her the use of my cellphone.

Twenty minutes later, I had Sally up and running (sort to speak) with her rambling on about something charming...an unexpected invite to dinner...something about bringing

Laney over...seeing Jasmine...blah, blah. I was in neutral but ever so grateful; she just helped me to stall further yet!

Our goodbyes said, Sally and her brood on their way to school then home, I huddled within the swanky seventies-styled interior of Rusty, desperate to warm my chilled bones, for one reason or another. The heater and the coffee weren't doing the trick. The sooner I get this dammed errand over with, the sooner I'd be back within the cozy embrace of my home away from home, warm, dry, and sedate after consuming half a rack of lamb. My stomach gurgled, fully agreeing.

Relentlessly, I skimmed the address a second time. I sort of knew where I was going, and as it turns out it was only a block away. I pulled out of the parking lot and drove that miserable block south into the heart of one of Boolee's Suburbs of clapboard and split-level styled homes that have been around since Lincoln's Presidency. One truck per drive, two-point-five kids to their five-rooms of worn carpeting, basements filled with games, boxes stuffed with unused clothes or childhood memories and somewhere, a family dog, roaming, sniffing, and pooping to their modestly medium-sized, chicken wired, fenced-in and muddied back yards.

I cruised past the building, rounded the block when I had to break five times so I wouldn't bumper car several distracted drivers. This time of day, kids were at school, wives were busy about their kitchens and husbands were working to bring home the bacon. So, what's with all the traffic around here?

Frowning, I rerouted. I dug in my boots, gritted my teeth, and drove past a second and third time when I finally managed to spot a parking spot on the opposite side of the street near the end of the block. Sheesh, I should have just left Rusty back at the Quick E Stop and hoofed it from there. Sighing, I shut down Rusty and glanced to the front of the building opposite where I sat. I noticed the shiny, hand painted sign, swinging on the pre-winter breeze. I'd found the store after all but it didn't set my heebies at ease.

Nestled on the North side of one of Boolee's suburban streets between brick and stone-block, vacated and boarded up buildings sat a red brick and mortar, two story broom-closet with angled, tarred roof that has been around since Boolee's founding (lucky me). Mind you, it is now a newer version of its ghostly past. Meaning, a long, long time ago, a Blacksmith owned and operated it. Then, it became a feed store. After that, I think it was a bookstore, a glassware shop, a pet store, a vision center, a woman's hat boutique, a shoe place when finally, it sat vacant for ten years. No part due, I'm sure to the recently renovated town Square. A month ago, some poor schlep decided to buy that cursed shop and turn it into something Boolee was in no need of needing: antiques. Junk from the attic is how I see it. The owner went with a more fitting sign, calling the shop, *Treasures of Days Forgotten*. Forgotten is how most of it *should* stay.

Then I noticed something else: people. Lots of them, coming and going from that cursed shop. More precisely: every single woman known to the greater tri-county area; women who looked primped, primed, and ready for some heavy-duty flirting and possibly, some after hours, heavy breathing.

Whatever...

I blew out a sigh. I can't stall any longer. I'm all out of excuses and I had a job to do.

Taking a deep breath, I hitched my special edition, leather purse to my shoulder (oh you know I wasn't leaving that behind in the mausoleum, blood, or no blood), snagged fraidy-cat and started across the street cautiously, feeling the sweat tickle my brow. Okay, now I'm just being stupid. Had I'd gotten this over with twenty minutes sooner, I wouldn't be dodging the misting sprinkle. There goes my already, overly frizzing, rusty colored, untamable hairdo.

"Checking out the goods, there, Harley?" came a voice of my second-hand, past partner-in-crime that jumpstarted my heart and nearly caused me to pitch fraidy-cat to the heavens.

"Oh! Uh, hey there Marty," I said, my voice ratcheting up several notches, eyes darting all around as I fumbled fraidy-cat beneath my hoodie. I was hoping for a quick in/ quicker getaway, with none of Boolee the wiser. No such luck. All two-hundred-and-sixty pounds of lean muscle, a gleaming and freshly shaven head and a smile seen from space was flashing me his goldenrod eyes in a way that said he knew what I was up to. He was after all Boolee's newly appointed Lieutenant and Detective Pine's Thursday night, poker-pal. Not to mention, someone I've known since birth and may once or twice have considered dating. Seated next to him was someone with hazel hair and hazel eyes and matching blue and grey Wannabe uniform; someone I've only seen once or twice; night duty, I think. He flashed me an encouraging smile.

Swell. My stealth-like visit to one of the last places I cared to visit was going to be a front page, headliner. Who needed the *Redlight* (sorry Gladys) when my ex was sure to get an earful before I made it across the street? No doubt, Marty Smarty, and the rest of Boolee would spread this tidbit of gossip for all to hear. Sigh. Such the life for being born in Boolee; no one can stay tongue-tied.

Oh, who am I kidding...neither can I.

"Hey, what's with all the traffic," I said, keeping a two-person distance from his blue and grey, county issued crossover, but held a breath out of reflective instinct, nonetheless. No, not because I was afraid that he might taser me (Newbie, rest in peace) but because he never got the memo that Bruit aftershave went out of fashion like smog, or coal burning and refused to tone it down. I can't believe he has nose hairs left after whiffing that for nearly sixteen years. Blah!

"You all ain't heard?" he said, his uniformed chest heaving to the tune of a chuckle and threatening to pop a button or two. Then he cast a curious grin toward his hazel-eyed partner. The partner just frowned and glanced away.

"This isn't funny, smarty-pants," I barbed. (Nope, this was not at all that funny).

"No?" he said, turning back to me eyes crinkling with laughter.

"No. Not since everyone around town now knows about my freak talent, you can see why I'm nervous here." Yes, pun intended.

"What—about the Treasure Shop," he asked.

"Bingo!"

Marty roared with laughter. Or what might pass for laughter smothered beneath a rumbling of snorts and hiccups. "Seriously Dodge, I think the trip inside will be worth it!" and with that, he popped a stick of spearmint gum to his mouth, turned on his blinker, powered up his window and motored around the block, leaving me to shiver and choke in his county issued, crossover's wake.

As an added insult, the sprinkling turned into a downpour.

You see? That is why I should have stayed in bed this morning.

The bell obscurely hooked up to the glass front door of the forgotten junk store, loudly announced my drowned and squishy-heeled arrival. The smell of musk and dust hidden beneath a smothering of perfume stank assaulted my sensitivities at once. My eyes watered as fifty pair of eyes rounded on me, scanned my wilted and grease smudged attire, some frowning, some of those greenies, narrowing, pinched lips following suit until no longer perceived as a threat and all three hundred women went back to their stalking.

Okay, maybe it was more like thirty women loitering, sauntering, swooning...

What. In. The. Hell?

I know a new store in Boolee is like accidentally coming across a secret stash of chocolate and salt the day Aunt Flo decides to visit, unannounced. Nevertheless, even that rush of sweet and bitter addictive goodness grows stale after three days of binging. So why is this place still vibrant with activity; womanly activity; scheming, conniving, drooling and hot-flashing activity?

I glanced about then fumed. Oh. I see. I suddenly understood why Aunt Bertie was interested in having me upgrade my appearance. I must have forgotten to change the oil in my brainpan because I just spotted the reason behind the front counter, ringing up a flushed, ninety-three-year-old, Angus Barker. Oh. Now I really see. The man flashed a heavenly grin Angus's way, handed her, her change and purchase then turned to the next person in line. He moved like a fluid dream; like a tall, exotic, mysterious, dreamy shot of *Jack Daniels*. So, this is who the owner was. The reason for the sudden rush of shoppers; the reason for Marty's laugh, his partner's frown, Aunt Bertie's scrutinizing eye and scheming mind because by the looks of the steam rising on up in here, I'd bet my left boot this antique shop owning god of a man who looked like he was near my age group was single.

Ut-oh, I think my body is doing the female version of a hard on. Sha-wing!

Now I really was having flashback sweats and not because the owner was gorgeous or because he was not from around these parts. I realized I was the only one here who didn't show up to check out his goods. Yes, pun, visual and heavy sigh intended. I instead, was on a mission and I needed to deliver, speedily, stealthily, and most importantly, untouched by anything haunting, but how? The shop was wall-to-wall of tittering woman looking to get lucky. Should I wave? No, I'd better not because one of the Bennet twins (a.k.a., the Snot Sisters) might misinterpret and set their claws on me. Should I wait out the crowd? No chance in Red's hell. These hyperventilating women had their heels dug in and could wait out a fire sale on Black Friday without breaking a sweat. Besides, most of them were Dodges or related to a Dodge. That figures...I'm going to have to inch my way up front, liberate my jangled, shaky nerves of fraidy-cat and haul my dampened bones back to Rusty, incident free.

And I would have made it out of there inconspicuously had someone not just bumped into me, causing me to stumble and plow straight into my Aunt Letty's elephant sized backside which in turn caused me to spin around and plow straight through Regatta Miller's lingering cloud of something musk and rose scented.

"Ah-choo," I said. Shit, I just inadvertently touched something I knew better than being within a missile range of.

Cue the nosedive and watch as the floor greets my face.

Freakin' allergies...

Five minutes later, I came too. I looked...well, I'd like to tell you I passed out with the grace and style of a Kardashian, but no such luck by the looks of womanly scowls hovering. I took out two end displays (which only added to my freak talent) and gave myself a bloody nose. When I blinked away my pain I just wanted to seep into the cracks, forgotten.

Stranger-Danger was getting a front-row show to my less than stellar, well gossiped about, shenanigans. I suddenly remembered my swan dive, closed my eyes, and shuddered. They sprang open at once. I needed to keep them that way because closing them only revived images of Arnold getting a blow job while gun pressed to his nose. It wasn't something I cared to know or keep seeing.

But I had a better reason for keeping my eyes open because, I couldn't stop staring. The antique shop owner, hunk of a man, with eyes bluer than the purest waters of the Caribbean was grinning down at me. Graciously he overlooked my recklessness and reached out an un-calloused hand, smiled devilishly then said, "I like the boots. You must be Harley Dodge".

I think I might have peed just a little.

Chapter Two: Hill-Billy Hell

To the heated stares and even angrier blather of the shamefully flirtatious woman shoppers (who bitterly gawked at me rather than help me up), the junk-store owner, effortlessly lifted me to my feet and led me down the furthest isle and toward the front counter, ignoring everyone but me. I mumbled some worthless apologies while I hugged fraidy-cat and my shoulders closer so I wouldn't have another unexpected, freak-show mishap.

Or, accidentally wrap my lips around his.

I quickly glanced about my ghostly surroundings. I sure hope the shuffling of onlookers overlook me. And then I noticed Letty high-tailing it for the exit. See ya, wouldn't want to be ya!

"I'm Billy. Please, allow me," said Stranger-Danger, his breath smelling like cinnamon and mint. He stood nearly half a foot taller than me as he leaned in and gently pressed a cotton handkerchief to my nose that he magically produced from behind the counter, thumb gently brushing my chin, eyes locked on mine, fully forgiving (or ignoring) of my destructive-like prowess. I helplessly sighed and nearly swooned.

Several women huffed or foolishly giggled or stormed out of the store to my Aunt Letty's wake. The dwindling of them laser-locked Billy's every move.

My face flushed but not from his attention.

Okay, maybe just a little so I squirmed and looked away. His eyes left me breathless, not to mention, that side of dimple to his left cheek. I was a sucker for dimples. But those eyes...they were like kryptonite! They had a way of making me loosen all inhabitation and ponder the fantasy of doing his licking—I mean, bidding.

Okay, that thought was embarrassing if word got out but no one noticed. Instead, my face grew red over the one stupid thing I was hoping to avoid at all costs (such as, paying the devil himself to disinherit me as a Dodge); I had touched something this-way-wicked west of the Appalachians. Ugh. Now I'll never get that image of Arnold scrubbed from my brain. Just like the one running irresponsibly about my daydreams of Red hugging Barbarilla as if she were Agnus (his trusty shotgun).

"No damage done, Boots. I think your nose will live to sniff another day," he said grinning, voice smooth like a fifth of one of the Whiskey Barrel's five-year finest...eyes blind to his dismantled glass shelving, crinkling around the edges...kissable lips...curling...puckering...

CRACKER JACKS AND PEANUT SNACKS, I'VE LOST IT!

I think I smacked my lead filled head harder than I thought because this man has me thinking things that I haven't had the time or need to daydream about in over three years. Yikes! I need to peel rubber and flee, A-SAP!

Sensing something, probably the opposite of what I was thinking, Billy leaned in. My heart skipped a beat. The skies parted. All movement ceased. Then my heart beat on. He just relieved me of fraidy-cat, exclaiming (exaggerating rather unnecessarily, I thought) "She is a beauty! Miss Beatrice's talent surpasses her greatest fan."

Her 'greatest fan' being all that is Boolee, West Virginia. No surprise here. He was preaching to the rusted-over hubcaps of my pathetic sized chest. I already knew Aunt Bertie had talent. Hell, even two counties over was well-aware. That wasn't what had me reeling in my tongue, clamping my mouth shut, contracting my lids, and finally seeing this so-called demigod with a heavenly use of the English language for what he really is: a *stranger*. A stranger that suddenly only had eyes for me (and my psych ward appearance) and at the present for, fraidy-cat.

I may have mentioned once or twice before that nobody moved here on a whim or a dare. You'd have to be plastered-out-of-your-mind, lost to find yourself stuck like a muddied stump with no growth imminent and possibility, no chance of making it to the pulping plant. Sigh. Such is Boolee. It sucks you in before you realize why. Which is why I'm having trouble escaping the hills, or why I'm having trouble understanding why this live and in person, Michelangelo replica found himself upping Boolee's population by one.

"Ope, nope. Already done-did paid for," I quipped, waving off his wallet in hand. I cringed. This stranger and his shop had me wound tighter than a rubber band propeller on a paper thin, pinewood airplane. So much, that I'd just reverted to Boolee speak. Something I'd pay anything to take back from the cosmos of the universe of me having said. Hell, I'd rather brag about being a Dodge.

I did a mental head thunk instead.

No time to remove my boot from my mouth, I blinked stupidly and did a one-eighty for the door.

Ut-oh, my feet just failed me. I'm peddling like *Fred Flintstone* but going nowhere, fast.

Oh. I guess Billy the new in town, shop owner wasn't through with me yet. Guess he remembered my cluster-fucked-up swan dive when he gently grabbed me by the crook of my arm.

I gave up (temporarily, of course) on my less than graceful getaway and spun around to face Billy. My hand slapped at his forearm (accidentally, you know). Sparks shot up, the Angels went into chorus and I melted. Oh boy, I didn't want to yank my hand clear. So naturally, I did what every other woman in this shop only wished they had the courage to do: I allowed it to stay put and squeezed. It was after all, the most action I've had in years. Shameless, I know. One of my many Dodge inherited flaws.

Touching his forearm was like caressing carburetor steel. Roused by this—and the fact that several more icy-eyed gawkers just stormed their way past—I allowed my eyes to wander, freely as they pleased. Up those steel cables they went, past his taunt biceps, lingering over his sturdy and expanding shoulders that framed well maintained, six-packed-abs, (I'm only guessing here because I couldn't spot a beer gut bulging beneath his neatly tucked, *Loony Tunes* t-shirt) when my eyes caught wind of what I was inadvertently thinking and wandered south of the border. Damn his dark denim jeans fit nicely. Not too loose, but not too tight, either. Just the right amount of snugness...

"What," I slurred out, stalling on coherent thought, fully forgetting where I was or that I was a Dodge, or the fact this grown ass God was wearing a shirt you'd see on one of Laney's youthful admirers, rather than someone our age.

I suddenly remembered what I was wearing and snickered, inwardly.

He flashed me another one of his knee-weakening smiles, only this one quizzical.

I quickly pulled my hand back.

With a jerk of his chocolaty, silky hair covered head, he repeated, "Follow me."

Abso-freakin-lutely!

"Hold the peaches and cream, mocha latte dream-team," said a rather feministic, yet robust voice that I knew like the tread marks of my Dodge riddled life. "Not so fast!"

I reluctantly turned away from said dream-team and spied a blur of a pasty, trunk load filled blob of courage. I watched as she bobbed and weaved, pushed, and bounced her way clear of the onlookers and right up into my face. Okay, not literally. She was a good ten inches shorter, so she had to stand on her stiletto clad and perfectly painted tiptoes and look up at me from her recently, gone under the knife, nose. A second later, she smiled.

No really. She smiled. Then she scooped me up into a great big squishy bear hug. Um, is that Bruit aftershave I smell lingering? Ugh. After which, she released me and gushed, "What up, girlfriend!" as only a one-hundred-and-eighty-pound (I think), couture wearing, white man with an angled cut, bubblegum colored pink weave, knew how. Today, she didn't disappoint, wearing a

Vera wrong number, which looked better on her than it ever will on me with my misplaced curves.

Gawd I've missed her...or rather, *him*...Lee Harvey DůVough; Miss Surelee to the rest of us who knew her back in Texas. Miss Surelee after she left her naturally blonde roots and steely jewels somewhere deep in the heart of the Bayou.

"What are you doing here," I said, totally stunned, totally pleased because she wasn't a native and I was a thousand percent certain, she wasn't a relative either.

Miss Surelee took a step back and pursed her lips. She perched one neatly manicured hand to her elephant shaped hip and snapped the other across her face twice. "You don't know how glad I am to see you, Sweetness," she said taking a moment to take in her surroundings of the antique shop. "Whew! You weren't kiddy when you said this place is a snoozer—but look at you!"

Yep. Look at me, you, haters...

"Anyhoo, heard about that business with Richard, thought I'd pop on over, give you a wave and from the looks of things, a touchup of that ratty do can't hurt none."

"Um..."

"Whatcha been doing to it?" she said, pointing, gaping, groping and thus, causing the last of the lingering single women to do the same. "Good thing I'm here, Sweetness, I can have it whipped back to shape in two shakes of a tiny-hinny!"

"Um..."

"I know, I know...I look swank, right?" she said, because she caught me gawking back. "I've lost five more pounds! Look out Broadway, here I come!"

Where she lost those five pounds was a mystery to me. She had no waist and looked a hundred pounds heavier than I last remembered seeing her.

As a beautician, Miss Surelee has dreams of becoming a Broadway star from as far back as I've known her. Aside from her other delusions—like her thinking she's a well-poised, beautiful black woman as Shasta the Fashionista proudly paid for several years back—I believe Miss Surelee might have a shot. Or the very least, whip up a killer wardrobe, complete with perfectly styled hair and flawlessly applied makeup.

"You all do hair?" asked Regatta Miller in her two-pack-a-day, gravelly voice, fully forgiving of Miss Surelee's peculiar presence and that she wasn't a native a natural woman or a threat.

Miss Surelee whipped her stylish head back and forth until she spotted the face that asked. That's all it took. Miss Surelee was in her element and shot off like a jacked up funny car.

Not one to unriddle the peculiar, I turned back to Billy, hiked my purse up my shoulder and gave him a pathetic looking smile with a half shrug of an apology for both interruptions of Miss Surelee and my unbridled talent. Billy smiled once more, eyes gleaming; this time, fully forgiving then nodded toward the back a second time. He led me, willingly down a short, narrow, unlit hall and to the second door off the right, opposite a set of heavily traveled and unpolished built in wooden stairs. Those probably led to the upstairs apartment. Probably where Billy shrugged his manly scented attire and strutted about his hillbilly abode waiting for some hot young thing to pounce. All he needs to do is ask...

Billy jerked me free of my delusions the second he flipped on the light switch, just inside the first-floor, office door. It caused a rather unflattering flicker from a ceiling suspended florescent to stutter then hum to life. I squinted against the morgue-like glare and glanced around. Hunh, sparsely furnished. One bare topped, scratched and dinged up, wooden desk with leather chair took up most of the room while two faded upholstered, armless chairs for visitors or loiters flanked the front of it. To my left, a fichus plant that was fake and drooping from a heavy layer of neglected dust was next to a rusting metal filing cabinet, probably helping to keep the tree-like plant upright. The opposite corner, crowded with unpacked cardboard boxes. No pictures neatly lined the faded and graying, wallpapered walls, or clustered about his desk. No other manly junk seemed to jump out at me either. So, either Billy was still settling in or he was simply—*gasp*—boring and didn't take to collecting such trivia as the rest of us predictable grownups have learned to do with our many otherworldly interests other than work. Oh, who am I fooling, I don't either. I trashed my collection back in Amarillo months ago.

He motioned toward the plush, real-real leather office chair that could swallow me whole, set fraidy-cat down on top of his wooden desk and then excused himself. Slipping my leather special free, I dropped it on the floor beneath the desk, sank to the confines of that cushiony seat and closed my eyes, pretending to be snug in my bed while trying to ignore the images of my less than stellar agility. Having to relive a nightmare is just one of my many rewards of living like a Dodge, gifted to me by my left-handed curse. Thanks Mom. Other than knowing with pathetic certainty, I'll never wrangle my way free from Boolee or my relation, either. Thanks again, Mom. Therefore, when I closed my eyes, I saw hell for what it truly is and I just wanted to go AWOL. Permanently, pretending I hadn't just encountered a ghost of the forgotten past, because it had something to do with Arnold and he was dead. Then Billy re-entered his cozy little office with another flash of his gleaming smile and I tumbled back to earth.

I peered out from lowered lids.

Dang he's gorgeous.

"I closed up for the day," he said, perching his lengthy, athletic sized hands to his slender, huggable hips that I would kill to wrap parts of me around it instead. Oh man, I'm losing it. "I can call up the medical center. Have them take a closer look at your head."

"Been there, done that," I said before I realized I'd spoken aloud. "I-I mean, ahem...that this...crap, well, this isn't the first time I've tripped."

"Looked to me like you passed out," he said rather stoically.

Rut-row, I think he might not be a stranger after all and quite possibly knows one of the Wannabes over at Detective Pine's lock-U-up weekend getaway.

"You have you another one of them spells," Miss Surelee asked from just outside the door, sounding expectant.

Billy stepped aside and nodded her in.

"Thanks, darlin'," she said, eyes lingering on all of Billy as she powered into the room.

I patted once at my crusting up, bloodied nose before I shot Miss Surelee a look that suggested she might live to see tomorrow if she dropped the subject of my freakish ability altogether.

Nope. No such luck. Subtly sunk to the depths of her manly wiles, forgotten.

"Sweetness there must have had her twenty of them dizzy-dives for all the time I've known her," said Miss Surelee.

"You don't say," said Billie, his voice sounding indulgent.

I sighed inwardly and slumped down further. It was only twice.

"Oh, uh-huh, I do say," said Miss Surelee, plopping down on the nearest seat, rather unladylike and feeling right at home. She rooted about her Birkin, came up with a nail file and proceeded to shape her fingernails. "Thing is, it ain't whatcha think it is. Mmm-hum. It's something, *special*, like whizzy oz special. Sure is."

Oh brother.

"That's, Wizard of Oz," I said on a sigh.

"That's what I said," Miss Surelee said, frowning.

"No matter...look, Billy, what Miss Surelee is trying to say, is that you'd know what just happened back there if you happened to read one of my Aunt Gladys' articles in the *Redlight*. (Or knew my history), you can't miss it if you haven't read it yet."

Nobody missed it. My Uncle Branson's widow, Gladys plastered a rather unflattering picture of me at the top of the article. The one taken of me all teary eyed, snot nosed and shaky when the EMT's were helping me down from the cab of Derby's bashed in bad boy Chevy. The truck I hated to crash. The truck that dipshit decided to make his getaway in with me as his hostage, at gunpoint back around August. Yeah, I couldn't have looked any worse.

Although today makes for a close second.

"My apologies, but I am not captivated by tabloid gossip," said Billy.

My heart did a tap dance of delight. Yes! That's two things we have in common.

"No biggie, it's a boring read (like his office)," I said then fumbled from that comfortable chair, ready to bolt back to the Victorian. I inched my way around the desk, saying, "Thanks for the, uh, you know..." My nose finally stopped bleeding so I handed back his bloodied hanky. He waved it off. Not one for an encore, I shoved it down my front pockets and headed for the door. "Well, I hope you like fraidy-cat...got things to do...gotta go..."

"Oh, no you ain't," said Miss Surelee, pocketing the nail file, slinging that car priced handbag over her left shoulder. She too, stood up, now blocking my only escape route with all two hundred pounds (still not sure) of her prefabricated, feminine ways.

I started to protest when there came a rather abrasive pounding of Billy's store front door. If that person didn't let up, they might shatter the glass.

"Wait here, I'll be right back," Billy said and headed that way.

Miss Surelee and I exchanged curious glances. Being the cool-like, grown women we were born to be, we naturally did the opposite, hightailing it from Billy's office and lingered in his woodsy smelling wake. We watched on as he peered past the shade, nodded once, lifted the shade, and unlocked the door. I spotted the problem at once and instantly wished I could shrivel up, liquefy, and seep into the cracks.

I threw up in my mouth instead.

The devil himself, Red Dodge thundered past a poker-faced Billy and in three strides had his Mack truck face inches from mine, peering down upon me, fuming. No Joke. His face was turning redder than the color of his shiny, new, big boy truck.

"Where is he?" he roared.

Hello to you too. "Who," I said, with as much enthusiasm as I have for my trolling ex-dipshit-of-a-lousy-husband, Dickie Trollop; because this was Red Dodge; the Devil's right-hand man and once-in-a-blue-moon, my Dad.

"You all know ding-dang well who-zit I'm askin' 'bout!"

Cripes. That was a loaded statement. Not only that, but lick-my-lips-Billy was getting both an eye and an earful today. Not only does Appalachia talk sound twangy—like someone strumming a banjo—but as everyone around these parts is clear about, is that we Dodges have only one volume when we speak: loud and sometimes, louder. And, as everyone else is well-aware of is that Red is the only one who gets away with the loudest setting of us all when he is pretending to be anything other than my dad.

Unfortunately, today is one of those days. Welcome to the hillbilly hell of Boolee, West Virginia, Stranger-Danger man.

Not one to be, outdone, I perched hands to hips and leaned in saying, "Get to the checker flag, Red, who?"

Red sprouted a set of horns from his full head of salt and pepper colored hair, puffed up his barrel chest and spat out a name that had me hearing crickets and nothing else: "Rodger-Dodger, dang-it!"

Uh...

Red was talking about one of my older brothers, Robert Dodge, affectionately referred to as, Rodger-Dodger. Last, I'd heard, he was happy to be wasting the start of his pre-midlife crisis years, working away as the first-shift foreman at Red's recycling plant. Since my glorious, week and a half stint there back in August, covering for a very, pregnant Sally Pine, I've never looked back. The last I'd seen of Rodger-Dodger was sometime back in the eighties. "Uh, why would you think I know where he might be? Wouldn't the drones at the Mill or Shelly know better," I said, sneaking a peek of Billy's unreadable expression and glancing foolishly toward Miss Surelee for an escape clause.

"Cause—"

"Now hold on," Miss Surelee interrupted. Priceless! Red looked like he was about to blow a gasket. "Who are you, and why you barging in here like yous own the place? I thought that fine drink of water was the owner. You see what I'm saying?"

I glanced over at Billy. Apparently, he wasn't overly concerned that a giant of a man looking like a distant relative to Paul Bunyan just stormed into his place of business, hell bent on delivering some whoop ass my way. Because, apparently, he was more aware of his magnetic manhood than the fact that I was blood related to Red, for he nodded once Miss Surelee's way, producing a wink and half a grin instead. Then he flashed his baby blues my way, daring almost, expectant for the conclusion of this unexpected Dodge intervention.

Unt-uh, no way! Someone other than me deserved Red's wrath; I'm not diffusing that explosive ticker as I crossed arms over chest and stared on.

Aaaand Red was off from the starter line and rounded on Miss Surelee with a look reserved mostly for me until confusion set in and he frowned. Me thinks Red's little brain is spinning, trying to decipher what his eyes are telling him. He opened his mouth about to speak, thought better of it (or lost the thought altogether) and spun back towards me.

Ah, lovely...

Red repeated his wrath. "Gone and done-did flew the coop and yoot who-zit done-did saw-em last," he managed to choke out.

What? "Who spread that load of sewer stank?"

The four of us shot looks to the front door.

Oh, that figures. It was she-devil, Barbie Bublouskie, a.k.a., Barbarilla and one of the reasons I scheme at night.

Barbarilla stood in her pink riddled getup, smiling, and foolishly waving when her eyes landed on Billy. I think Red just grunted his disproval of wife number two. Goodie. She may be married to Red but nothing, and I do mean *nothing* gives me more pleasure then someone, other than me causing Red to get indigestion. Righteous! Not waiting for an invitation to our roundup rodeo, Barbarilla giggled once, fluttered her fake, glued on spider length eyelashes, and tottered past the door. I guess she was hoping to impress the newest edition to Boolee (who hasn't?) when one of her Pepto Bismal colored stilettos snagged on the front door runner and flung her sideways into a different end display of forgotten junk, her wolf-like shriek, followed in her wake.

I should have seen this one coming, but life is stranger than fiction, I guess. Funnier too!

Yes. I am laughing. And no, I'm not trying to hide it.

Barbarilla deserved payback for the way she treated me all those many forgotten years ago and this was as good a start as any of what she had coming her way. And, no, being married to Red didn't count.

Everyone but me scrambled to help her up, lower her flowery pink embroidered woolen skirt past her pink, polka dotted, panty-covered crotch, righted her fuzzy, pink cardigan and pat at her frou-frou fluff of bleached out, teased out, hair sprayed stiffened hair.

It looks like Stranger-man was oh-for-two in the accident department today.

Yes, I'm still laughing.

Everyone rounded on me.

Not one willing to give up a spark plug, Red opened his cakehole and grunted, "Git on widit missy—spill it!"

Barbarilla took in a deep breath, unable to keep from staring at Billy and said, "Reynold, please, the poor girls' been through enough! Harley," she finally peeled her fake lashes away from sexy man and shot me a pathetic attempt at a cordial smile then concluded with her worthless thoughts saying, "I'm sure you wouldn't mind telling your father and I, anything you might know of Robert's whereabouts, hmm?"

Sure, I would, if I could, but I don't, so I won't. She-devil's sugar laced tongue might work wonder-bread on Red but it has the opposite effect on me. I shrugged my reply instead.

Red clenched. Probably from the backed-up colon he's keen on packing with twenty pounds of cooked beef. Probably because he finally realized what he married the second time around. Mostly because, he's fighting back a steam powered shout, my way, of course.

"You mind cluing me in on this Roger-Dodger," Miss Surelee asked, pretty-as-she-pleased.

Spectacular! Red just flat lined, shaking his head, running a meaty, calloused hand partway down his face. He was all out of brimstone.

I knew Miss Surelee and I clicked for a reason. Who knew that today it would come in handy?

"Rodger is my older brother," I explained. "He works first shift up at the Mill; Red's Mill." I pointed for added emphasis.

"So, let me get this straight," she began; collective sighs from the peanut gallery. "You, (she pointed at Red) are Harley's Daddy? And you (she beauty-pageant waved toward Barbarilla) is her step-monster? (Priceless!) While, you, (she swooned in Billy's direction) are lovely, but not important at present, and Rodger-Dodger is their son?"

Everyone except Billy nodded.

"Does he have a sort of gingerbread color, sasquatch-like facial growth?"

"Oh yes, that's him!" cried Barbarilla, expectant to hear more.

That was mindboggling. Miss Surelee just described about ninety percent of my Dodge relation.

"Well, shoot, honey, that's part of the reason why I came here looking for you," Miss Surelee said, directly to me.

"You know Rodger-Dodger," I asked, totally stunned.

"Can't say for sure but no, I came here needing a ride, Sweetness."

"Ah, I think I'm going to regret this, but how exactly did you get here from Amarillo?"

"Well shoot, girl, I drove!"

That tells me nothing. Miss Surelee owned three stunners. How she afforded them on a beautician's salary was beyond my reasonable understanding. Still, her cars were beauties so I took a stab in the dark.

"You drove the Porsche," I cried, clearly my concern misplaced.

"Don't-cha know it, Sweetness, candy is the fastest," she replied, clearly just as proud to think only about the superficial things in life too. She's right though, that cherry red, zippy little number of a ride is blazing-hot fast!

"Where is your car now," I asked, surprised, worried...*jealous.*

"In a ditch, back that-a-ways, I think," she said nonchalantly while nonchalantly waving to the whirlwind of mass confusion about us.

Now, if it was I, who'd just ditched an awesome, rather expensive car, as the one I've seen Miss Surelee drive countless times I wouldn't be so blasé about my ride stuck in a ditch, especially with the likes of the ones around these parts. They're ten feet deep. Nope. I'd be hand flapping and shouting up a storm for justice and a chocolate bar.

"What happened," I gasped, hearing the same words echo off Billy's lips in unison. Spooky.

Barbarilla foolishly giggled (sounding more like a gurgle) while Red stared on, flustered, mumbling something incoherent. Fantastic! I love it when someone other than me, spins Red's gears recklessly, or needlessly.

"So, there I was, following Drake's honey-do voice (her GPS) when a monster came out of nowhere, swerving and honking and fishy-tailing all over that barely-there road!"

"Then what happened," I asked, since (from the looks of opened mouths or blank stares) I was the only one who understood and followed through.

"Whew-we, girl, it was like something from one of them horror flicks you know I'm too delicate to watch, so I covered my eyes," she said. I nodded, fully understanding. I too sweated like a menopausal woman at night if I foolishly took in all that nail-biting gore. "Then before I knew it, I was blowing a rubber and ditched Candy off route fifty-two. I had no chance to save her! That's when I found myself hooking (her word for walking), looking for you. Good thing peach fuzz came along when he did."

"How in the heck did you know where to look," I asked.

"Oh, I can answer that!" chided Barbie, Red's bitter half. "I rang up Beatrice."

Okay, that made sense, but—"How did you get *her* number," I asked Miss Surelee, indicating toward Barbarilla.

"Easy, I rang up the only spare you ever gave me." Miss Surelee turned toward Barbarilla with a warm smile. "Precious there was kind enough to tells me you were on an errand for your Ladybug (my Aunt Bertie)."

I cringed both inwardly and outwardly. A little over fifteen and a half years ago, I skipped my high school graduation, ran off with dipshit and settled to the big city distraction of Amarillo, Texas. A month later, Miss Surelee and I became friends. Being that I knew of no one else, I gave her my only emergency contact number: Red Dodge. I never thought I'd find myself back in these itty, bitty parts, so I never imagined anyone outside of Boolee would ever need to dial up that number. Who would have guessed that today of all days, someone would? I just got Dodgeballed.

"Wait, why didn't you just call me on my cell," I asked, riddled.

"I did," she said, mouth puckering into a soured frown. "Check your messages once in a while, girlfriend."

Oh. Needless-to-say, I fished my cell from my back pocket and instantly knew my mistake. I powered it up and a few seconds later, it dinged twenty times. Swell, all nineteen voice messages were from Miss Surelee, himself. I'll give you one guess as to who the twentieth message was from...

"Mmm-huh," she said, looking at me as if I'd lost all coherent functioning.

Had Miss Surelee been around two and a half months ago, she'd understand my need to slip under the radar and only turn my cell on during power outages. I wasn't in the mood for any more surprise text messages from you-know-slimy-who.

"Wait, what does that have to do with Rodger-Dodger," I asked latching on once more, to the Dodge loop of my bullet riddled life.

Barbarilla nodded with earring studded ears bobbing, expectant. Red gathered all six feet of his mountain-like self into a cross-armed stance. Billy remained motionless, expressionless.

"Well shoot, Sweetness, I think he was the one driving that runaway beast!"

Shit.

Red flew into a rage and stormed out of the junk shop, fully forgotten. Then Barbarilla giggled once more, curtsied toward Billy (no idea why) and waved goodbye. She carefully made it past the front door runner without tripping a second time (darn it) and right on out into the icy air of damnation's big boy truck.

"I think I had better call up the police," said Billy.

I shuddered and frowned. Why spoil the party and bring them into it?

I hated to admit it though, but Billy was right. From the sound of things about Rodger-Dodger and Miss Surelee's intertwined problems, someone needed to call the cops whom I affectionately refer to as the Wannabes. I shuddered a second time because knowing what I know and seeing Billy fumble with an antique, one-inch thick phone book had my eyes rolling backward to last year; I knew it was going to be me doing the ringing up; because, it was *his* number that I had saved to my speed dialing queue.

Sighing, I waved off Billy saying, "No need," and tapped at the first number for a one, Detective and ex-boyfriend, Brentwood Lewis Pine.

Chapter Three: Suck it up, Buttercup

I STORMED AWAY FROM the treasure trap, slipped behind the wheel of dusty Rusty and coaxed him to action. He found a gear and sputtered to life. Brent wanted my partner in crime and of course, me, down at the precinct, "pronto", to give our statements. Yeah, right, as if I had anything to do with Miss Surelee or Red's predicament. I was a not so innocent bystander, don't you know? Brent didn't care, though. I'm sure this was his twisted way of paying me back for whatever second hand past, we shared.

Good thing the rain finally tapered off.

No matter, I warmed up Rusty's interior as best as it would and was ready to do my civic duty when Billy shrugged into a plain navy-blue colored hoodie and climbed on in after Miss Surelee. I gave him a quizzical look, Billy, not Surelee. He flashed me his superman grin then quickly explained his truck was temporarily out-of-commission. I forgot that I was still breathing and did not question further his need to tag alongside us. I wish I could say it was exciting having Billy in the loop, but it wasn't. Not today, of all days, no. Alas, I sucked it up like the adult that I pretend to be and played along.

We drove my vehicle from Billy's locked shop the three blocks north and out of what passes as the suburbs in the hills of holler. Two blocks west past three-story, brick apartment complexes, seven blocks north beyond a community park and two-story rentals and half a block east all because Miss Surelee's rocket powered sportster sat ditched somewhere and conveniently enough, Billy's was in the shop getting new shocks. Yet, if Miss Surelee hadn't had an accident in the first place, we wouldn't have found ourselves, huddled to Rusty's swank interior on our way for a pit stop at the pokey. We also decided to drive Rusty because it was too cold and dreary to walk and my boots haven't now, nor ever will, go "hooking". Besides, from the looks of Miss Surelee's heels, I would bet my last pair of clean undies that she'd rather ride an elephant through the jungle than hoof it one more step either. Rusty looked like a chariot compared to the alternatives.

Speaking of...

"Did you walk all the way here from route fifty-two?"

Miss Surelee sniffed once at the ice-cold cup of stale Quick E Stop java in my cup holder, shuddered once before saying, "You needing one of them earwax specials?"

No. My hearing was just fine. "So, how'd you get into town?"

"Like I said, there I was, tapping you up, when I got through to Precious. She was kind enough to jingle the station for me. I caught a ride from that fine, peach headed officer, Martin," she said.

"Ah, okay," I said. That explains running into Marty Smarty at the most inconvenient time in my life.

"So, where's Beauty?" asked Miss Surelee now settled upon the vinyl bench seat, smack dab between Billy and me, hesitant to touch anything. "You set her up at the spa or something?"

"No, she's...history," I sighed the kind of sigh you sigh when longing for a chocolate covered cookie, followed by a tub of rocky road ice cream during the height of diet season while recovering from a breakup. Or, as in my case: for some one-on-one time with Stranger-Danger-man. "Rusty is a loaner."

"No, not Beauty!" she shrieked. "Girl, what happened?"

"Don't ask," I said through gritted teeth, white knuckling Rusty's' cracked and faded steering wheel, praying he wouldn't backfire the entire twelve and a half blocks there. I also noticed to my chagrin that traffic had significantly lightened, not that we usually have heavy traffic around here. Still, I wasn't happy to have to stop for every one of those intersections. I blame the civil engineering idiots over at City Council for thinking Boolee needed a stop sign at every available block.

"Oh well...this one's...cute," she said, sounding polite while fighting back something less cute to say, unsure if she should pat Rusty, dust Rusty or keep clear of him altogether. She opted for the latter, keeping both hands clutched to her purse strap.

Billy had bravado and fisted the dash. I nearly jumped the curb. The glove box popped open. "Sturdy," he said, reaching out with a cobra-like aim, slamming the glove box shut. Without a second thought, he perched his elbow to the doorframe, allowing his hand to rest against his kissable lips.

"You know it," I replied to those two jokers while I cringed inward. Rusty wasn't cute, but he was sturdy, way too sturdy for my taste or liking.

Rusty sputtered and choked as I nosed him at an angle in front of Boolee's lock-U-up, tourist trap. He backfired once then died with honor. Face flushing, I hustled from Rusty and on up those wide birth cemented steps pretending I was auditioning for Homelife's Funniest Pranks rather than accept the reality that is my life. See, I was fast making the wrong sort of irresistible impression on freakishly handsome, freakishly calm, Stranger-Danger man. I had pictured our meet-and-greet going a different route, in a different state, of a different lifetime. Nevertheless, my luck like my life sucks so it wasn't having any of it and took a detour.

Naturally, it only went downhill from there, the second we pushed past the inner set of glass enclosure, double doors to my second least favorite place that inexplicably graces Boolee's (invisible) maps. Not to mention, the place I knew like the back of my hand during a blackout. We stepped forth and rounded on the front desk attendant, seated behind a pane of bulletproof glass. Good thing the florescent bathed, three-chaired waiting room was wait free. We were first in line.

The man sporting three-inch graying stubble that on better days would give him bragging rights, stopped scratching, and glanced up, shoving his brown, rectangle glasses back up his pudgy nose. He took a one-second look at me, grinned, slowly shook his head then shouted to the

Wannabes over his left shoulder saying, "Pay up guys, she all's back!" Swell. It was Joe-Bob Connelly, one of my once removed, twenty-something-or-other, cousins (by way of marriage to my actual cousin, Cynthia Waverly) and not to mention, Boomer's father (previous marriage). It looks to me like he just won a bet. Joe-Bob was a gambler and found it difficult to pass up the tiniest or innocent of bets (sort of like me with chocolate); a bet that somehow involved a one aptly humiliated Dodge. Double swell.

"Is he ready," I said to the round, metal vent, keeping my cool as I watched several boys in blue and grey uniforms frown their way past Connelly's desk and slap a greenback to his fat knuckled palm. Even Reeva Rosenbaum the dispatcher and general office manager got in on the betting action with a wink and arthritic thumbs up my way.

Connelly pocketed the money, flashed his pea-sized eyes between the hallway door and me, sweating hot under the collar. "Uh, yep, sure is, but...you all might wanna take a seat," he said, rather nervously, suspiciously.

"Hold the phone, sweet-pea," said Miss Surelee and causing every one of those Wannabes to stop and stare her way. "I needs me a ride, not a ride. See what I'm saying?"

Nope, blank stare. No one understood what Miss Surelee was saying, not even me.

"Uh...is... *(that)* with you," Connelly asked, half whispered my way.

Yuge mistake...

"What'd you call me? That? THAT!" she screeched and rounded on me. "Did you hear what cookie doughboy called me? Don't he recognize a full-figured gal when he sees one?"

Then Miss Surelee shoved me aside and pressed her puffy face right up against that bulletproof shield. Something of a talent for her to master seeing, as the bottom of the glass was nose height to her. She banged twice and said, "Do I look like a 'that' to you? Hmmm? Well, do I?"

Buckets of sweat poured down Connelly's face. He looked like he might shake his head no or nod yes until he haplessly gave up with a lumpy gulp and gave another shove of his glasses. His eyes roved all about, helplessly weighing his options, seeing that a four-inch thick piece of glass wasn't the protection from the needy as much as he once believed. However, being that he continued to flick glances from her, to me and back along the hallway, his face a deep shade of pomegranate, I was certain he was considering buzzing us on back. Then again, I think not. I think he felt cornered. He sure looked it because no matter which decision he chose, it was destined to be the wrong one. Lucky thing he won that bet though...

Okay, clear out the drunks, I know a setup when I smell one. "Red's back there, isn't he?"

"Yes," he said hissing air, curtly nodding which, caused the eyeglasses to slip to the bottom of his nose while his whiskered double chin, wobbled rather abruptly, eyes sunk deeper into that toady-looking face of his.

Swell. This is my lucky day times twenty. Speaking of, I wish someone related had let me in on that bet.

Not one to let the devil slow me down, I hitched up my pride and said, "Buzz me back, Cuz. My problem and his are connected."

"You all are admittin' he all's relation?" replied Connelly, readjusting his glasses, eyes popping visible once more.

On better days... "I mean for my reason to speak with Brent!"

"I've me a crisis, sweet-pea, let me pass," Miss Surelee cried, completely unaware that Connelly couldn't stop staring or the fact that Marty just reared his Bruit smelling Gerber baby mug. Two seconds later, Miss Surelee gasped then gave Marty a finger wave. I guess she noticed him after all.

Marty inconspicuously slipped Connelly a five-spotter, settled his curiosity on Miss Surelee while saying to me, "Happy to have you all back, Dodge." Then he noticed Billy hugging my right shoulder and grinned—hugely, spryly—devilishly. "I see you all visited the latest addition to Boolee."

Miss Surelee suddenly giggled. It was weird. I had no idea why. Sheesh, has the whole world gone nuts? Okay, I know Stranger-Danger man is off-the-charts, lick-chocolate-off-my-lips, gorgeous, but Marty too...smitten? Because I think he just shot him a wink. To make matters worse, Billy obliged with a pert nod. Miss Surelee huffed.

"Hee-llo-o... Marty," I said, waving my hand, snapping my fingers to bring the attention back where it was needed most. "Buzz me back, okay?"

"Yeah, sure," he said, cool as ice, pressing the button to release the automatic lock. "It's your party."

Miss Surelee and I did a mad scramble beyond the door. Billy patiently waited for us to shuffle beyond before he passed through. Miss Surelee and I then jockeyed for a place behind Marty. She won with Billy bringing up the rear as we silently fell in line behind Marty while he led us on back past the rustling sounds and wafting smells of Boolee's Wannabes busy faking work, slurping coffee, inhaling donuts, and playing a card game or two of solitaire on their Neanderthal-like computers. I spied the near empty box of heaven from the Piggly Wiggly's bakery department and managed to snag a chunk from a mangled jelly on my way past. Not a single flunky noticed. Guess that's why they became officers of the law. Guess that's why Billy isn't one as he lightly chuckled behind my back while I licked the evidence clear of my sticky fingers.

Enjoy the levity now, Stranger-Danger, because I promise you it will be, sucked from the room when we cross the threshold of hell.

"Oh jeezus," Detective Brentwood L. Pine muttered the moment I poked my ever-popular mug shot past the doorframe.

"Hello to you too, Brent," I replied with a mile-wide grin and a spring to my rubber clad step.

Red shot up from the pleather chair like the Judge he thinks he is and rounded on me with his inherited way of hillbilly enchantment. "That—thar—see-it? Tellin' you all missy done-did do it!"

Did not! I think.

"What's he barking mad I did this time, Brent," I huffed, easing my way clear of Red's flame and slipped to a spot on my left standing between filing cabinets and a pleather chair overflowing with Barbarilla. Not that she'd stand up for me, block one of Red's buckshot burst of vocabulary, or claim to know me, but I'd rather be within breathing space of her perfume stank than subjected to one more Red-riddled insult that is my relation. Besides, Red was blocking my path to Brent's protective custody within this claustrophobic shoebox size of a room. This spot was the furthest away without crossing state lines.

Detective Pine waved Red back to the pleather chair. He hesitated. Naturally, because, Billy and Miss Surelee brought the train wreck of our caravan to a complete stop and pumped this Dodge party up into overdrive. Not one for invitations, Miss Surelee plunked down to Red's abandoned chair without a second thought. Barbarilla swooned and foolishly, finger waved toward Billy. Red however, suddenly remembered Miss Surelee and sprung into his twisted-up version of events.

"That-a-one thar," he began, uncertain but once he turned back to Brent he refocused and concluded saying, "Saw-em and I no wanna no-none a that-thar tiddle-tart!"

"Say what," Miss Surelee said leaning back from her chair with a squint Red's way, somehow sensing that yes, he had just insulted her. Most days, she sensed it. Most days, she chose to be oblivious, Connelly being the exception. "Is that some sort of new-fangled, fancy-to-do language I'm always hearing about?"

Everyone turned her way and stared. It was like looking at a car wreck. You knew it was awful, knew it was something you couldn't forget, but you couldn't look away either. It was just too intriguing not to do otherwise. Same could be, said of Red too.

I caught a twitch of Brent's upper lip. Then I noticed the mangled wreck smudged across that twitchy upper lip, skidding to a U-turn about his barely there, flattened chin. Ugh. The overgrown worms beneath his bulbous nose were bad enough, but somehow, somewhere, someone had convinced him that a goatee was a good look on his hairline receding, ruddy and pockmarked face. Bet it was his wife, Sally the valley. Somehow my eyes wandered on over to Billy, along with my thoughts, and I was girlishly glad to see that his face was cleanly shaven and he only had one chin attached to his square jaw. Not that a six o'clock shadow wouldn't look bad on him. Hell, I bet there isn't anything that would look bad on him, but damn, he sure looks sexy wonderful all baby smooth like that.

"What...," I stupidly slurred. Crackerjacks and peanut snacks, Stranger-Danger man is crossing my wires...and my toes...and my...

"What," I cried a second time, desperate to refocus on my reason to visit the pokey this side of never.

"Get on widit, missy!"

Ah, no thanks and decided to sit this round out. I reached across Barbarilla to Miss Surelee and tapped her shoulder, nudging her on. Eager for the spotlight, she smiled to the party crowd and began her performance about her side of things. Everyone stared on, speechless. I snuck a glance Billy's way and matched his sly little smirk. His expression may have mostly read, unreadable, but I'm thinking, he too was having fun with this little round up of DNA doo-doo. I know I am.

"Alright-e then, let me get this straight," Brent began, cautiously, steely eyed, cop-mode. "You all got run off the road by Rodger-Dodger?"

"Oh yes!" added Barbie as if the car wreck had happened to her. As if, anyone cared.

Brent shot her a puzzled look, knew better than to crack open that can-of-stupid and resumed his questioning. "Now, Miss Surelee, yes?" he asked. She nodded. He continued, professionally unfazed as to her identity crisis. "Are you all sure it was Rodger-Dodger driving?"

Miss Surelee nodded yes, and then turned her attention to her manicure.

"Miss Surelee knows Rodger-Dodger," Brent asked to the collective room of Dodges.

Red crossed arms, shook his Mack truck head and grunted once. I shrugged. Barbarilla foolishly nodded. Barbarilla didn't know. Barbarilla had no clue. Barbarilla was clueless. Yep, she was even worse than me, if you can believe it.

He flashed a curious glace Billy's way before he turned his full attention upon me. "Did you happen to notice who all was drivin'?"

Hunh? "Why would you think I would know," I asked then realized Brent was laser locked on my bloodied hoodie. Oh. Damn. I can see where he might think... "Bloody nose, I wasn't in the car. I tripped. It's nothing."

Brent's latest, updated 'stash did a funny little twitch before he pressed on, turning once more to Miss Surelee. "The vee-hicle in question, you all happen to notice what it was? What make, model or colorin'?"

Miss Surelee pressed a finger to her pursed lips and squinted off into the wild invisible yonder. A minute or two ticked by and she was still thinking. Barbarilla sighed, Red grunted. Brent clicked his pen once and shot me a squint with one arched eyebrow. Talented. I quickly averted my eyes and allowed them to land on the only thing worth looking at in this miserable, tick of a town: Billy. His expression stoic, stance calm, hands stuffed to his snug fitting denim pockets despite the fact he was standing in Red's hellhound shadow.

"Oh yes!" Miss Surelee finally said, breaking up the tedium, giving everyone a jumpstart of heart attack fun. "It was one of them trucks with tires the size of U-F-Oh's. Mmm-hmm...it was a *monster*." Miss Surelee shuddered as if she just stepped in dog poop and realized it wasn't coming off.

"Colorin'," Brent asked by way of a huff.

"Oh, uh-huh, it was dark."

Brent waited a heartbeat before asking through gritted teeth, "Black...green...brown...blue...red... which one?"

I snickered. It was fun witnessing this side of teeth pulling crazy, me out of the hot seat. Yep, it was truly funny. Brent shot me a look that suggested it wasn't funny and pressed Miss Surelee for an answer.

"I can't say for sure," she said, frowning. "It wasn't like I had time to fish my glasses from my purse and put them on and have a closer peek, you see."

Silence.

Brent flashed a look that hinted to his state of utter confusion. Maybe that was a look of frustration. Yep, I would say it's the latter by the way he's massaging throbbing temples. I bet you a ten-spotter he was wishing he were dealing with me instead. Love it!

Marty Smarty just upped the tension and entered the room. That man is so steely jeweled. I wonder if he walks barefooted over hot coals for fun and relaxation.

"Just heard back from Stan (another one of my twenty-something cousins)," he said to Brent's bowl blocking scowl. Yikes! I think he's been hanging around Red a bit too long.

"And?" asked Brent, huffily.

"Got Miss Surelee's vee-hicle back to the garage, looks to be nail punctured. Should have it all patched up by mornin', but them other repairs gonna take a week, at least," Marty said, unfazed by the ten-degree downshift in room temperature when he set a Louis Vuitton luggage piece slightly larger than the size of Miss Surelee's purse to the overly waxed, fifties-styled, faded and scuffed up blue and white, square-tiled floor.

"Oh, bless you, sugar," said Miss Surelee, clutching a foam enhanced chest while waving a sly gesture Marty's way.

"Da-nada," he said then turned to Billy concluding, "Stan got you all fixed up. Pick it up anytime you all want."

Billy gave a slight bob of his dreamy-looking head.

"Is that it," Miss Surelee cried. "I've me five more!"

Marty shot Brent wide eyes and arched eyebrows. Brent turned to Miss Surelee and asked, "You all got more than one suitcase?"

"Oh, uh-huh!" she said on a tight nod.

Marty's face relaxed with understanding before saying, "Check with Connelly on your way out."

"So that it? I'm free to abscond?" said Miss Surelee, hugging her overly priced piece of luggage protectively.

"Ah, Detective," began Marty, unsure if he should say anything else but Brent nodded him on with an impatient look. "Right, we got another fire called in five minnis ago at Valentine and Ridgewood Drive. Old man Johnsons' place."

"Christ," said Brent frowning. "Take Norway and Jacobs with ya," he said, as he nodded Marty off. After which, he turned back to Red and asked, "About Rodger-Dodger...you all say he's been missin' since Sunday?"

Red grunted. Barbarilla nodded.

My heart sank a notch. Today was Tuesday. Missing...as in, gone-gone? "Wait—what? So, it's true, Rodger-Dodger really is missing?"

Red grunted. Barbarilla nodded.

"Did anyone think to talk to Shelly," I asked, hands perched to hips. If anyone knew where Rodger-Dodger might be, it would be his wife, Michelle Winters.

Red grunted. Barbarilla nodded.

"Harley," cautioned Brent.

I ignored him and gunned the pedal to the metal, hands flying toward the heavens, saying, "Why didn't anyone think to call and tell me this?"

Red shot me a glimpse of hell. Barbarilla frowned.

Oh, right, they think—"Hey! I know you think I was the last one to see Rodger-Dodger but you're wrong! I only talked to him by mistake, and that was two days ago!"

Flat out stares.

A second later, Brent asked, "You talked to him?"

"Not really," I said. "He butt-dialed me, I think."

Brent wasn't thrilled with that explanation. He shook his head once and turned back to Red. "He dint tell you all he was maybe taken a vay-kay-shun?"

"No," Red said by way of a grunt.

"You all dint forget that maybe he might a said he was takin' time off for anythang personable?"

"No chance in hell!" roared Red.

I snickered to my hand. Miss Surelee shot me a questioning look. Billy stared on, expression, expressionless.

Brent leaned back in his creaky, wooden chair and released a heavy sigh, eyes roaming the five of us. A moment later, he turned to Miss Surelee and said, "I'm assumin' here, you all are stayin' in town while your vee-hicle is bein' tended?"

"Oh, uh-huh, with Sweetness," she said with a wave of her hand my way.

Uh...this was news to me!

Brent shot me raised eyebrows, mustache following suit. I rolled my eyes to the angels on potty break and finally hissed out a, "Yes."

"Good. Now, Miss Surelee, if you all remember anythang else helpful you all have Dodge give me jingle," he said, a bit too happily.

Swell. But we were free to go!

"Oh, and Dodge," he said, causing my innards to squirm. "Don't-cha think I ain't through with you all."

Double swell. I shot him a stink eye that did little for my delicate nature. So, I switched gears saying, "Roger-dodger and Harley, out," ending with mock salute. This managed to put a twinkle in one of Billy's baby blues while an airy chuckle escaped his lips. *That's* the thing he notices about my stellar personality? Cripes...

I motioned to Miss Surelee to follow me as I high-tailed it for the exit. Billy nodded his parting and followed Miss Surelee and I free of the pokey, parting gifts aside, Miss Surelee the exception. Freedom was all the present I needed at this lousy juncture in my truck stop of a life.

Silence flooded Rusty as I drove Billy back to his newly acquired, trunkful of junk then asked the one question I knew I was better off hiding. I felt guilty, you see.

"No thank you, Boots but it'll give me something to do," he said. (Hooray!) "Besides, today was the most fun I've had in a while. (No, it wasn't.) You however, look like you could use a hot bubble bath."

Care to join me?

I grinned. I was off the hook of having to set one boot back in that little shop of horrors and waved him goodbye. Hope he enjoys fraidy-cat. With Miss Surelee riding shotgun, I floored Rusty and hauled us on back to my temporary home away from home, backed up to the heel of West Virginia, snug about the Appalachians.

"Isn't he something," Miss Surelee said as I led her into Aunt Bertie's' weathered, older than dirt, Victorian, aptly dropping her overpriced luggage set and handbag to the foot of the stairs and causing Bandit to dart free of his latest hidey-hole. Miss Surelee startled, hands to gaping mouth she turned my way, questioning. I waved her off. There will be time enough later to explain Laney's sneaky way of acquiring a sneeze-inducing pet.

"What's that, dear," Bertie asked from the kitchen due to her radar-like hearing and the fact the walls of the Victorian were, efficiently cramped and paper-thin.

"Tall, dreamy and dangerous," replied Miss Surelee sounding as if she surrendered to her thoughts or, maybe curious to learn more about my Aunt Bertie's petrified critters.

"Who," Bertie asked. Her surprise fell two pistons short of an electric-powered, sportster.

Oh, she knew darn well, whom Miss Surelee was talking about because Aunt Bertie knows all; the whole town of Boolee did. Thanks for the under fueled priming.

"She's talking about Boolee's latest shop owner, Billy," I replied rather flat, loosely crossing my arms, leaning against the arched entry to the kitchen, eyes narrowed with Aunt Bertie in my crosshairs. "Thanks, by the way."

"Oh, uh-huh, him too," Miss Surelee said as she clutched at her smoothly-shaven cheeks.

I shot Miss Surelee a curious look. Whom else was she thinking about in a town full of hillbillies?

"I see," said Bertie.

"Why, you must be Ladybug! I'm Miss Surelee, from Amarillo," Miss Surelee said, plying herself into Dodge country as if she had roots and marched on up to my Aunt Bertie. She gave her a hug, shocking us both.

Dodges are not exactly huggers. Don't get me wrong, we can do emotion so long as it's' the deflective, snarky, yelling kind then we're all for it. Hugging is like asking a Dodge to part with their shotgun. Nope. Not happening. Not even on our deathbeds.

Parting, Miss Surelee added, "I see where you get your looks, Sweetness."

Gush.

"I take it the delivery went off without a hitch," Bertie asked fully recovered from the unexpected greeting, going back to marinating lamb chops before popping them back into the fridge.

"Maybe," I said, licking my lips, going back to narrowing my lids, Aunt Bertie back to my crosshairs. "Thanks again for the heads up."

She shot me a double loaded, stink eye.

"Sure, looks like you're cooking up something fancy," Miss Surelee said, plopping down to one of the ladder-back chairs, across from Aunt Bertie's startled look.

"Oh yes, lamb chops. Isn't that right, Aunt Bertie," I said with a smirk, knowing I was about to pay her back for this morning.

I unfolded my arms, pushed off from the doorframe, crossed the room and surveyed the cooled down, whipped cream topped pumpkin pie perched to the laminate countertop. I snuck a swipe of that fresh cream and popped it into my mouth, hoping my actions went unnoticed. Aunt Bertie swatted my second attempt away with the back of a wooden spoon just in case I overlooked her frown from my first attempt then scuttled the pie free of my grabby paws and locked it down to the refrigerator.

Miss Surelee whistled before saying, "Thought I was fast with the nips."

Aunt Bertie stared on.

"She's a hairdresser," I explained, licking the last of the cream from my fingertip. "And by the way, she's staying for dinner...and the night, possibly a week—gotta run—need a shower—change of clothes..."

"Freeze," said Bertie.

I flinched on my way to freedom. I slowly turned and faced the music.

"Care to explain?"

Not really. Boolee came loaded up with a years' worth of gossip already. Did they honestly need to hear more? Sigh. I guess they do... "Miss Surelee stopped by for a quick visit on her way to New York. But her car got a blowout, ditched it off Route fifty-two. One thing led to another and Brent might have hinted to Miss Surelee staying a night or two or more, here, with me until her car is, fixed. Whew, I'm kind of beat. I'd really love to get out of these damp clothes."

"Bloodied too, I see," she said, pursing her lips, tucking in her chin to peer down the bridge of her bony nose and over the tops of her half-moon spectacles.

"MOM. I'M. HOME," came the fruit of my womb, Laney, front door slamming in her wake, saving me (if only temporarily) from the inevitable explanation of my latest shenanigans.

"Bluebird, honey, is that you," Miss Surelee called out.

"Miss Surelee?" said Laney, her voice switching gears from dreaded dislike, spiking five octaves higher over the sight of some semblance from a life she once knew. She unwrinkled her nose and unwound her pout as her jacket and backpack slipped from her shoulders and fell with a swish and a thud to the middle of the hallway floor, while her blue-black hair hung freely to her waist. A second later, she rushed past me without acknowledgement and gave Miss Surelee a welcoming hug, crying, "Oh, it's really you!"

"How's life on the farm," Miss Surelee asked as soon as Laney released her death grip hold.

Life on the farm, yeah, right. I flashed a slight, closed lipped smile and lightly shook my head. Okay, I know Boolee is a bit secluded from normal civilization, but it wasn't as if we lived out in the middle of Iowa or something. Boolee has standards. We choose to eat the hogs, not raise them.

Laney turned her sourpuss on me with a puckered-up frown, flipped that curtain of shiny, sleek hair over one shoulder, rocketed out a blue jean covered leg, perched one hand to her sweater covered, not yet there, hip and sighed, dramatically. Oh sure, now she notices me. Sheesh. It was short lived because she turned back to Miss Surelee and proceeded to explain how her life was miserable, the weather was miserable, school was miserable, the boys were miserable, the town was miserable and the Wi-Fi was miserable. Other than that, she was just "peachy keen".

Teenagers.

Miss Surelee giggled, nodded, understanding.

"Are you staying for dinner," Laney asked expectant.

Miss Surelee nodded. Laney squealed her delight then yanked Miss Surelee by the hand, bouncing on the tips of her size nine tennis-shoed feet. "Let me show you my room!"

I happily let them have at it as I gave Aunt Bertie a questioning look of my own, hoping to flee the coop.

"After dinner, dear," she said in her motherly tone. "You can tell me all about what's really going on then, hum?"

Swell.

Shoulder's sagging, I reluctantly nodded, yes, then headed for the steam room of forgiveness at the top of the stairs, second door on the right, stripped bare and scalded my body of its recklessly, inherited shame.

Chapter Four: Dumb and Dumber

"Shoot. That sure was something," said Miss Surelee in a food coma, smacking lips, sucking on a toothpick, lounging sideways on a beanbag chair that Laney was gracious enough to lend. She had since swapped out her pink weave for a foam roller infused, brunette wig. Whatever. She was however, dressed in some of Red or Walt's hand-me-down pajamas, legs and sleeves rolled at the cuff five times, because apparently, Miss Surelee slept in the nude. Not in this house, darling. A not-so-discreet burp, escaped her lips. She giggled to herself and went back to her perusal through one of Laney's dogged eared Teen read magazines.

"Uh, yep," I snapped back as I finished changing the sheets on the bed and turned to Miss Surelee, flushed with my own little pouch of surliness. Perching my fists to my pajama-clad hips, I pinched my lips tight, narrowed my lids and sublimely tried drilling holes into the back of her head, hoping for food poisoning. Not because she had the contents of her luggage strewn about like the aftermath of a tornado, but because she up and did the only thing, I have trouble forgiving: She got the last lamb chop. As if, she needed it. Not. I subconsciously licked my lips in longing. I had been looking forward to that heavenly meal all day. I however, got three-day-old meatloaf and rubbery, fried potatoes instead. My stomach grumbled its' disappointment.

Whoever made up that rule that guests should get first crack at food is stupid. They should get last crack, if you know what I mean.

Oblivious of my need to whack her into next Tuesday, Miss Surelee flung the four-month-old magazine aside, struggled to right herself, plastic scrunching to her effort, cranked her neck my way, skewing that wig off-center to further stoke the flames of my annoyance, saying, "Who knew you had relation that can cook? Thought you said you didn't know how?"

"I wasn't joking, I really can't cook," I said through gritted teeth and went to the hall closet opposite the bathroom, leaving her to arm-wrestle with the beanbag. I think she lost.

"Yigh," she said, giving off a powerful yawn when I reentered my temporary, room away from abnormal. I grinned. She was struggling to climb free. "Well, no bother, you've other qualities for snagging a man."

Wait, what? "Oh, unt-uh, I'm done with that part of my worthless life!"

"Wolf...Lordie I'm overcome with the lassitude," she said, stretching her arms wide before she asked, "Where do I bunk?"

She ignored the steam escaping my flared nostrils or the fact she just let off a squeaker of a fart. In the barn, if Aunt Bertie had one. "Right here," I said instead, biting my lip, doing my best to suppress a sigh or a buckshot worth of snark, releasing a fresh pillow to the newly made, twin-sized bed. "I'm surfing the couch."

"Oh no such doing, Sweetness, I can sleep down there, that okay?"

Better than okay! "No, Miss Surelee, you're my guest," I said, hugging a pillow, flannel sheet and quilt to my ketchup-stained, t-shirt draped, barely-there chest. "It'll be fun." And stink-free because that squeaker was beginning to fester.

Laney called out with, "She can sleep in my room!"

Not happening.

"Sleeping arrangements have been decided, Daughter. Besides, you have school in the morning—good night, everyone!"

A disappointed huff escaped Laney's room. I smiled to myself. I just love making her day, by making her day, you know what I mean?

I trudged down the creaky stairs, hooked a left and another immediate left and came to an abrupt stop in front of that fourth-generation, hand me down sofa. I glanced to the other one flanking the doily topped walnut coffee table and sighed. I really didn't properly think this one through.

"I see what you mean by fun," said Miss Surelee, zapping my heart, and causing me to jump a mile. Those peanut sized feet of hers were stealth-like.

"What are you doing down here," I hissed once I got my runaway heartbeat to stall and my breathing back to somewhat normal.

"Don't feel right putting you out like this," she said, hugging a pillow, plopping right down to the middle of that ghostly filled cushion. "Besides, your cell jingled. Who's

Gee? He sounds horny," she said, then waved my cellular my way.

I stiffened with an all-that-is-unholy gaze locked upon Miss Surelee's outstretched palm.

"Um..."

"Shall I send him an emoji back accepting his booty call?" she asked, wiggling her thinning eyebrows, clueless.

"No," I cried, breaking free of my trance and snatched the cell phone like a hot potato clear of her misguided thinking.

"Humph! You don't need to shout, I can take a hint," she said, jutting her bottom lip.

No, she can't. "It's not what you think," I said. Even if it was, I'm not one for booty calls. I nodded her clear of that dreaded sofa.

"No really, I can sleep down here," she said, refusing to move, testing out the springs, "Looks like this gone-with-the-wind-facsimile is too short for those stilts of yours anyways."

Imitation, my ass...if Miss Surelee only knew...

"No can do, Miss Surelee, that's not how we do things around here," I said. Nope, especially if you're a proud, Protestant or Catholic, Boolee born and raised woman or the wife of a native. It's sacrilege otherwise, just like buying pie or cake at the Piggly Wiggly and passing it off as homemade. I never bragged I was a native or religious or even a Dodge, however, so I think I'm the exception. I hope.

"I can sleep down here, mom," said Laney, cradling Bandit causing me to re-think the idea of straddling her too, with a cowbell necklace. That girl can slap wood with her size nine feet without even trying. Who knew tonight she figured out a way to tiptoe through the Victorian just as stealthily as Miss Surelee can? Laney gave off a one-shoulder shrug and half yawned, adding, "I don't mind, it'll be like having a slumber party."

Uh-huh. Her last slumber party upped the Victorian's occupancy by one, even if it's a fuzz ball the size of her foot. No sooner I say yes and she'll never go back to sleep and maybe, figure out a way to adopt a squirrel. I was certain of this because Laney and Miss Surelee were like a couple of sugar-hopped teenagers on spring break whenever those two traitors got together. Not-to-forget, that Miss Surelee is a 'he', gay or otherwise.

Nope, unt-uh, that is never going to happen.

I took a breath, about to break up this gathering when someone else decided to crash the party and keep my hammering heartbeat going strong. The tiffany lamp snapped to life, bathing us in a psychedelic glow of sun setting pinks, mustard yellows, and pea soup greens.

"What in all the stars is going on down here?" said Bertie, hands perched to her housecoat-covered hips, silvery strands unbraided and flowing freely down her back. Naturally, she was looking at me through squinty eyes as if I were the ringleader of this mash up of partygoers.

"I just love what you did with the place," said Miss Surelee, waving about the parlor as if swatting away flies or rather, slinging dung. "It's so authentic!"

Aunt Bertie rounded her squint on Miss Surelee. Righteous! "Thank you dear. It's been in the family four generations, now."

That is, if she meant the one going back to my late mother's side of things, stolen out from under them by the Dodge side of the crooked tree; the one she tried giving back to me upon my discovery via my left-hand talent a few months back, then yes, the Victorian was that old.

"You don't say," Miss Surelee gushed, pinching her face with both hands, oblivious to the fact she was sitting on an antique or that her wig was on backwards.

Not one to piddle around the track, Aunt Bertie gave us a lecture: "Listen, the three of you (a waggling point of her finger our way), I've me a truckload of deliveries this week and that one (jerking a thumb toward Laney) has schooling in the morning so I'm not above putting down the law (pointing to the floor). Don't get me wrong (waving to the heavens) but I've never closed my door to a stranger in need (giving off a stiff nod Miss Surelee's way). However, if the three of you (a wave about the room) can't figure out your sleeping arrangements and stick to them (stabbing a finger once more, to the floor) before the rooster crows," hands back to her hips, eyes narrowed, she took a deep breath, concluding through pressed lips, "I'll consider putting someone up for adoption."

That 'someone' she was referring to as being a one, Harley Dodge.

"Yes, ma'am," the three of us whispered in unison.

Two seconds later, Aunt Bertie had shooed sourpuss hugging Bandit, back upstairs, helped me spread out the sheet over the upholstered rosewood Victorian, forgoing the mahogany empire-styled one and had Miss Surelee settled in. She reached over to the end table and snapped the lamp off, turned back to me then steward me off to my room.

"Did you honestly think you wouldn't have had a mishap sleeping down there?" she asked, lingering in my doorway.

I blank stared her back from the side of my bed with a two-shoulder shrug, fiddling with my cell phone.

"Harley, listen," Bertie said on a sigh and I snapped to attention. She rarely calls me by my name, except in the event of an emergency. "I think you need to start understanding your gift; embrace it, dear. It's a part of you and you can't go through life avoiding it, skittish of when it might spring up. Just think about what happened today if you need more convincing."

Swell. I knew I shouldn't have told her about the incident at the treasure shop, conveniently omitting the part about the horse statue and its' obscured connection to a previously living Arnold. I was trying to forget. "I didn't ask for this," I mumbled.

"Figure out a way to coexist. Now, good night, dear," she said, flipping the wall switch to off and headed on back along the hallway to her room with Mr. Willoughby.

Nope. I'll never figure out my freakish, left hand talent and I damn sure won't find a way to embrace it. I'm freaky unlucky as it is without it, Dodge, or no Dodge.

Speaking of which, still no word on Rodger-Dodger's whereabouts to which, only led my already swirling thoughts down a dusty road of slimy, three timing stank. I suddenly remembered the text message from dipshit and swiped through the glowing screens. I'm only guessing it was my ex-husband, Dickie. I tried calling it back once last month, just for shits and giggles, but it went straight to an automated voice mailbox instead. Therefore, to keep from accidentally deleting or misplacing those messages, I had tagged it with a capital letter G. Those off kilter messages could just have easily come from someone associated with the Giovanni 'fam' as well. Regardless, the messages were just as ominous and not something, I cared to take on lightly, either. This latest one was no exception:

MEET @ TREE W/KEY @ 3

Yikes! Déjà vu!

Naturally, I powered my cell down and buried myself deep under my freshly laundered covers, hiding; forbidding my thoughts of runaway haunts. Don't get me wrong, I wasn't procrastinating. Procrastinating meant I was going to deal with it later, *eventually*. Nope. I just wanted it to go away, indefinitely. Denial was the way to go. With denial, I can pretend he doesn't exit; I can believe that part of my life never happened. I can convince myself that those text messages meant for someone else. Yes, denial was the way to go because I was all peed out of anything else. Besides, visions of Billy graciously took over all rational thought and flooded my dreams with drooling and flirtatious behavior as I happily escaped to la-la land. I had no time to be side tracked by worry or anything less pleasing.

The next morning, the Victorian was alive with startling activity and the heavenly aroma of blueberry pancakes, pepper scramblers, fried potatoes with sausages. My stomached roared to life. I startled and flailed about, breathless, desperately trying to prop myself up on elbows but something snagged my progress. Oh. It was Bandit, hogging my pillow and now scraping his sandpaper tongue against my ear.

I heard Laney squeal. Miss Surelee's voice drifted forward, sparking another round, of Laney's giggling from somewhere below. A second later, a horn honked, Laney yelled, "Bye," slamming the front door in her wake and rumbled off with her latest jail baited chuffer, Leroy Watkins. I released a pent-up breath, relieved to know I was *here* at the Victorian and not mistakenly, *there*, at hellhound central. Still, I woke up rather grumpily. Bandit just wrapped his belly over my forehead.

I rolled eyes upward in the direction of Bandit who in turn, licked at one of his paws. Sighing I closed eyes, caught my breath, and waited for my heart to downgrade to normal before I managed to kick the tangle of sheets free of my legs in frustration for being awake. Dang it, I was just getting to the good part of my delicious dream!

I glanced beyond the windows and involuntarily shuddered. The sky gunmetal grey and overcast was threatening to grace Boolee with yet another soggy day. Prickling bumps rose up on my exposed arms and feet. I shivered and hugged myself. The central heating was a bit of a challenge in this house. Whoever said heat rises sure-as-hell never spent the night in Aunt Bertie's older than dirt Victorian. It was cold up here, except for my forehead where Bandit commandeered. I thought about hibernating until spring. I shivered again, but for a much more intrusive reason than the crisp, autumn air, whistling beyond these paper-thin walls.

"You up, Sweetness," Miss Surelee asked poking her perfectly made up face beyond the wood trimmed doorway.

Bandit and I startled, in unison. He was the only one smart enough to dart past the door and beyond view, though. I eventually peered at her through a half-opened eye. She was sporting aqua blue jogging pants with white stripe down the sides and matching zip up hoodie, the words, "JUICYLICIOUS" embroidered in white, glittery letters across her well-endowed, well-faked, chest. Cleary unfazed that this look went out of fashion somewhere back in the nineties or that she was four decades too old to be wearing such an outfit. She topped this inappropriate look off with a lemon-yellow beehive doo this fine, depressing morning. Sighing, because I don't remember her sneaking in here earlier to change, I waved her my reply by way of a limp hand.

"Good, I've got good news and I've got great news," she said, plopping herself down at the foot of my bed. The springs creaked in her wake, sending a wiggling wave up my back, further adding to my crankiness. "Which do you want to hear first?"

Knowing Miss Surelee as I do, I think maybe I should change out of my pajamas and stuff johnnycakes in me before hearing her out. I needed sustenance to see me through, because she conveniently left out the part about 'bad news', as a choice because as everyone knows, news is not good or better. It is either good news or bad news, or both.

"After," I said as I swung my legs over the edge of my bed, sat up, stretched, and yawned then stood up and padded over to my dresser rather quickly. I felt like I was tippy-toeing across blistery cold, petrified wood. I rooted around, came up with my last pair of clean undies, an overstretched bra, a long sleeved, pea green Henley and my last un-faded, un-ripped, un-mangled pair of blue jeans. Swell, I was out of socks. No matter, my boots would keep my feet cozy and dry.

"Yeah, but—"

I shot Miss Surelee a well-rested, fully loaded, double-barreled stink eye.

Miss Surelee shrank three inches. Sweet, my stink eye was back in the game!

I think.

A moment later, Miss Surelee had moved on from glimpsing a sublevel of hell, composed herself to say, "Okay, Sweetness, I don't mind keeping dream-team entertained. You go on then, best to get yourself all dollied up."

Hold the, everything with everything! "What's going on?"

"Tall, dark and dreamy is down in the parlor, Sweetness," she said, matter of fact, batting her fake eyelashes. "That's the good news."

"Who, *Billy*," I asked on a whispered breath as I shifted my gaze downward, thinking I might see him through the woodwork.

"Oh, uh-huh," she said, eyes softening while she gently patted a nail polished hand to a flushed cheek and lightly swayed from side-to-side.

"Okay, what's the better news," I asked, eyes narrowed her way.

Miss Surelee jumped to her child sized, wedged heel tennis shoe, clutched her clenched hands to her recently shaved cheeks and squealed, "I landed you a double date with me!"

I shot daggers her way as I shrugged into my change of clothes at lightning speed. I had no qualms changing in front of 'her'. Miss Surelee may have been born a 'he', but 'she' was whom I was going to pummel to the ground for her latest round of her so-called, 'better' news. I had huge problems with her latest bit of news and I think she knew this. Then again, I think she didn't care for she just flashed me a frown, one hand perched to hip.

"I can't take all the credit, Sweetness," she said. Sheesh, the nerve of her expecting a thank you! "Bluebird helped, too."

Perfect.

I yanked my rat nest of rusty colored frizz into a ponytail, smartly ignoring my puffy nose and the half-moon shiner to my right eye, stuffed my feet to my boots, pocketed my cell to my back pocket and lead footed it down the stairs, rounded the corner and plowed right smack dab into a brick wall. That is, if a brick wall smelled like camping deep in the woods; was wearing a long-sleeved button down beneath a V-neck cardigan sweater, tucked smoothly into a pair of button-fly jeans, a pair of blue suede Vans size twenty (not sure, could be smaller) to finish the look. The brick wall, sporting a halo of silky chocolate was flashing me a heavenly smile. His baby blues twinkled my way in greeting.

I melted on the spot.

Bandit rounded his midnight mane with a gentle purr Billy's way. Yeah, he has that effect on me too...

"Oh good, you found him," said Miss Surelee, snapping me free of my drooling fog.

"What are you doing here," I asked, looking up, still crab sitting upon the wood plank flooring, eyes bugging, gaping mouth unable to clamp shut.

Still smiling, Billy reached down and helped me up. He then cleared his throat once before producing a one, blood smeared, special-edition leather special.

Oh, my crapadoodle luck—I'd forgotten all about my purse yesterday, after...yeah...after all *that* happened to me.

"Thanks," I said feeling my cheeks grow warm as I relieved Stranger-Danger man of my purse.

"Say no more," he said, perfectly calm, perfectly at ease, his eyes dipping to my Harley Davidson styled, motorcycle boots then back to my flushed face.

At least my nose wasn't, bloodied, anymore.

"Wait, how did you know I was staying here," I asked, riddled.

"Your drivers' license," he explained.

I cringed. Last month, I finally got around to swapping out my Texas license for one registered in Boolee. Don't misunderstand; I was hoping for the opposite but unfortunately had to change it out of desperate, hopeless necessity. My picture reflected my less-than-pleased look. If looks could maim, he'd be looking battered because my picture was as unflattering as one could get. And right now, so were my thoughts. Desperate to think of something else, I suddenly remembered Miss Surelee and Laney's latest scheme and blurted rather, unnecessarily, "I uh, I'm flattered and ran out of excuses over those two jokers' years ago, but I'm sorry to disappoint, I'm not looking right now."

Billy arched a single, perfectly groomed eyebrow.

All-righty then...

I gunned my mouth and explained further, "I'm not ready to date."

"Good to know, Boots," he said, turning his stoic expression Miss Surelee's way and arched the other perfectly combed eyebrow.

Miss Surelee giggled, grey eyes flicking all about, saying, "I think she's having one of them low sugar spells...poor girl don't know what she's saying," she said and quick to action, she shuffled Billy toward the front door and thanked him for his kindness.

A parting nod and a simple, "Thanks for the coffee", Billy retreated to the crisp morning air.

Bandit joined me as I rammed my puffy nose to the screen door and watched opened mouthed as he climbed into a dark-tinted windowed, shiny black, Chevy SUV. Is everyone's ride better looking, better smelling and just better overall than Rusty? Taillights beyond my blurred vision, longing for them to turn back, I scooted Bandit clear then closed the door, deposited my purse to the coat tree and rounded on Miss Surelee at once, claws to the ready. "Spill it, why am I suddenly diabetic?"

Miss Surelee gave up a nervous giggle, eyes darting back and forth, shoulders scrunched to her earlobes, palms facing me in a back off gesture and then she shushed me.

Oh. I must have had an out of body experience, because I suddenly remembered the other vehicle side parked to Aunt Bertie's drive because it wasn't Rusty or a mint green Ford, which is now suspiciously missing.

I yanked open the door and frowned. I knew that truck. It was a Dodge make and model, two doors, raunchy window clings, sun-faded bumper stickers that appealed only to stupid, beer-guzzling hillbilly men, dents all around and jacked to the heavens with tractor-trailer sized tires. A three stacked, chrome bumper shielding the front end with a matching chrome safety bar sprouting from the bed close to the back of the cab; both loaded with fog lights. A five slotted, fully loaded gun rack to the back window of the cab, three coolers, two travel gas cans, five fishing poles and some other worthless junk piled haphazardly to the bed of that dog poop brown colored truck, a trailer heavily loaded with landscaping machinery and equipment hitched to the rear, finished the visual. No surprise there; many people around these parts drove Dodge trucks. Hell, just look at my family if you need any convincing. It wasn't the truck, which had my head pounding, stomach clenching and fighting back a dry heave, however. It was, instead, the person whom was, said owner of that crappy Dodge that had my head rotating as if possessed and ready for the loony bin, one-way ticket, all expenses paid.

"Okay, spill it—what's really going on?"

Aunt Bertie just exited the kitchen, flashing me a knowing smile, snatched a sheet of paper next to the telephone stand before she headed for the basement stairs. I must have missed a gear because she was halfway down before I heard her belly laugh rumble my way. I shoved Miss Surelee aside and rounded on the kitchen at once.

My stomach bottomed out the moment my delicate sniffer smacked a hovering mixture of urine and gasoline, halting my forward progress. I spotted the smelly source at once and bit down acid flooding my throat. The older, skinnier, and blonder of the two greasy, hair receding, mullet sporting, wife beater t-shirt wearing, hairy armed and booger picking idiots, leaned his chair back on two legs, and, while sucking his grimy fingers clean, opened his cakehole to mumble, "Cheese-it, your granny sure can cook up a spread!"

Fuck. I'm going to stroke out I just know it. I thought about driving the Dodge off a cliff with that idiot strapped to the grill, Miss Surelee riding shotgun. Okay, that's an everyday fantasy of mine, reserved for someone else more deserving as I remembered we don't have any canyons free of trees or anything worthy of skydiving and Dickie was unfortunately on the run. I involuntary shuddered and did a mental head shake instead. Not only was I staring into the wandering eye, belonging to one of my twenty-something cousins, Tucky Offnutt Spigot Dodge, but I was now suddenly aware that he and his sidekick, Boomer just scarfed down the very last of my Aunt Bertie's fabulous morning spread.

What the fuck! "What the heck, Tucky, I didn't eat yet!"

His chair tipped forward with a thud. He glanced down to his plate and studied the crumbs, head tilted, eyes narrowed, one of them wandering away. A second later, he flashed me the same dull, glazed over look, void of recognition. Tucky looked confused by its function or uncertain of our relation. Either that or he was dumber than rat shit. I'm ruling on the latter.

His partner in stupidity, Boomer Connelly, noisily sucked the last of his chemically enhanced, caffeine fueled can of soda dry, crushed it to his forehead, belched a greeting my way, bloodshot eyes lingering south of my navel before he turned to Tucky, punched him in the arm and said, "Told you all she all'd get mad."

"Isn't he something," Miss Surelee cooed a good two-foot distance behind me.

I spun on Miss Surelee so fast she became a blur. When the room stopped spinning, I snapped back with, "We'll discuss this later." She smartly kept quiet.

Doing my best to overlook Boomer's grossness or that I stupidly went on a blind date with him back in high school (back then we weren't related), I glanced at Tucky. I was really doing my best to look anywhere other than at his wandering eye, downgrading my snarl to a scowl to ask, "What are you doing here, don't you have class?"

Tucky shrugged, belched loudly that rattled my withering bones, pushed off from the table with a scrape of the chair, stood up, hiked his loose and wrinkled jeans to his sagging belly, scratched twice at his puny manhood then said, "Gotta get granny all trimmed up." After which, he shrugged into a long-sleeved flannel button down shirt. Boomer, being somewhat better mannered, chose to omit a second burp, scratched at his wide set, blue jean covered bubble butt (or pulled a wedgie free. I can't and don't want to say with any certainty), struggled into his matching flannel, tossed his crushed soda can over handed across the kitchen table to widely miss the trashcan at the far wall and clatter loudly to the marred wooden floor. Ignoring his mess, he then followed Tucky out of the kitchen.

"See you all at three," he said in passing with two clicks of his tongue directly to my boobs, shooting them a wink with a double-handed imitation of six shooters.

I stiffened with alarm. What did Boomer mean? Was he the one who's been texting me?

My mouth fell open but nothing came out. No snark, no hiss, not even a sigh as I watched those two idiots cruise on past the dining room and beyond the back porch; stop, stare, spin around, clomp back inside, scratching their head or ass as they made it out the front door instead.

"Catch you later, sweet-cheeks," Miss Surelee said in a singsong way while finger waving the air.

I suddenly found my identity and aptly replied toward dumb and dumber with a fully loaded, double flip of the bird.

My salute went unnoticed. Naturally.

Moments later, I heard those two idiots shouting to each other, a rider lawn mower powered up, then a weed eater buzzed to life and they were off, 'giving granny a trim' about her woodsy, ten acres.

Did I mention that Tucky is really, *really,* slow? Otherwise, he'd know that dear, sweet, patient filled 'granny' is really his 'Auntie'. We've only reminded him of this about a hundred times now. I suppose though, it wouldn't make a difference if he did.

I slammed the front door shut, stomped back to the kitchen, stomach roaring its' protest and stared, dumbstruck about the dirty and scattered remains of cast iron pans, stoneware, utensils, drinking glasses and coffee mugs. Unt-uh, no way am I cleaning that up until I've had something to eat! I rummaged through the icebox and came up with the last piece of crusty meatloaf, the heel end, no less. Now sucked dry of its reason to nourish, I trashed it to the garbage can, cruised blindly past the dismantled kitchen (ignoring Miss Surelee's existence as well), grabbed my purse, my coat, key to Rusty and high-tailed it out of Dodge country without a second thought.

"Wait for me, Sweetness!" Miss Surelee huffed, scattering two feral cats, several crows and a couple of squirrels, marching band stepping/running her way down the drive, arms madly pumping with purse swirling along one arm. She finally caught me at the end of the drive. Because I had slowed down, staring back utterly speechless. That girl can plow fields when she set her mind to it and never once, knocked that beehive lose. Sighing, I shifted Rusty's steering column gear shifter to P until she had herself settled to the cab.

"Whew, what a rush—breakfast and a workout, so where we headed, Sweetness, I'm starving."

I flashed a look her way that was a cross between curiosity and the devil itself. I think. I was desperately running low of everything.

With Rusty back to a sputtering gear, I floored it for the Piggly Wiggly, fallen leaves, pinecones and pine needles scattering in my wake. I don't even remember passing the fork in the road as I swung Rusty into a parking spot of the mostly deserted macadam lot, closest to the front doors. I left him idling, with Miss Surelee keeping guard as I did a quick in/slower out because this was my reason for breathing in the morning. Loaded up with a half a gallon of chocolate milk, a box of ho-ho's, two microwaved breakfast burritos now steaming hot, four bags of chip samplers and the latest edition of Cosmo, I slipped on up into Rusty and zoned.

"Sure, gotta lot of stuff here," said Miss Surelee, eye balling everything.

I tossed her the magazine and sampling of chips and dug on in to my first meal of the day. A half hour later, I was back on the road and parking in front of the pokey.

"What we doing here? Is candy ready to go," asked Miss Surelee, licking at orange covered fingertips.

"Nope," I mumbled around half the chocolaty ho-ho sticking out of my mouth, slamming Rusty into park, keeping him idling. "Stay here, this won't take long." I hope.

I had one leg out the door when Miss Surelee was by my side. Damn she's quick. I gave her a flat-out puzzled look, slipped my cell from my back pocket,, and dropped it to my purse. I shut down Rusty, snagged purse to shoulder then slammed the door. I swallowed the last of my chocolaty treat and trudged on up those cemented steps, hell bent on blowing off some steam. What better place to snip and snarl then at the pokey, directed at a one, Detective Brentwood Lewis Pine?

Besides, it would make his job easier if I suddenly blew a gasket and offed Miss Surelee when she was looking.

Chapter Five: Denial is the Way to Go

"It weren't my idea, I swear it!" cried toady-faced, Officer Connelly with arms up and palms out the second I flashed him my puss face this side of bulletproof glass of the pokey's waiting room.

"Oh really," I said with little fanfare and hiked my purse higher on my shoulder. I slowly crossed one arm over the other, smacked out a stiff leg, narrowed my lids and locked him in my crosshairs. I was ready to get him back for yesterday's' bet, amongst other things.

"What's he mean, it weren't his fault? Yous understanding this?" whispered Miss Surelee.

My knuckles turned white as my fingers dug into my arms and I refused to look away from Connelly. Miss Surelee might have overlooked the steam rising from my head or she chose to pretend otherwise because she kept right on talking, her voice only getting louder.

"He's kind of cute when he's by his lonesome...what's he doing now? Is he having an episode, 'cause I don't know the cee-pee-are and I don't do the spasms, either! I can do mouth to mouth, know what I mean? But that other thing ain't my thing, you see what I'm saying? Oh Lord have mercy, is he gonna live?"

Connelly glanced over his shoulder then back to me then behind me to Miss Surelee. Sweat beaded his face as it sunk back in on itself and I think he forgot to breathe. His arched, wispy eyebrows faltered and frowned; whole face sagging, hissing air before turning his tiny peepers back my way once more. He reached a shaky, pudgy finger up and righted his glasses with a wobbly push back. His fishy lips flapped open and shut several times, before he managed to sputter, "Wanna deal on Stingray tickets?"

"Hell no," I hissed. "Buzz me back."

The door clicked open before the last word snapped free of my tightly pressed lips.

The Wannabes were out patrolling or snoozing because the open plan of on duty desks were mostly off duty. One or two of them eventually glanced up from their coffee and donuts, gave off a slow headshake, pretended to look busy or looked away altogether. I blew past without a second thought. Detective Pine is whom I came to see. Anyone else would have just tripped me up. Miss Surelee two stepped it to my wake. Seeing that I was the daughter of the devil himself, I needed no invitation, pushed past the frosted paned door, and entered Detective Pine's office.

"Whew-we, Sweetness, are we done running a marathon? You know I've gots to take me five of them steps to match one of yours," said Miss Surelee, bent at the waist, panting. When she finally caught her breath and righted, she flinched at once and with an unexpected shriek, her purse flew off over her head backwards while she sidestepped to her left like a grasshopper to my shadow, face draining of all made up color. Then she swayed once before falling flat on her ass in a dead faint.

Who knew today I'd get chocolate and a show, all before noon? Priceless.

"Christ Harley," Detective Pine said hello by way of swearing low and slow. "What now?"

The freakishly, disproportionately oversized man seated on a pleather armless chair next to the filing cabinets, slowly rotated his white, sandpaper stubble and leathery skin covered, rounded jaw and cleft chin my way, his movements like a jungle cat stalking its prey. I shuddered. He could give Red a run for his hellfire chill. Being within breathing room of this party crasher was spooky so I squirmed, unsure of where to look. He however, looked unfazed by Miss Surelee and my sudden interruption of their short arm of the law, get-together. I double shuddered.

The stranger didn't sport a police-issued uniform (probably couldn't find one big enough to fit him), nor did I spot a badge, but I knew he was law enforcement. Even if I had managed to overlook the bulge beneath his left arm sport jacket, I couldn't help but recognize his crisp, white shirt, corded tie, pressed and creased tan slacks, sparkling turquoise and silver belt buckle, gleaming snake skinned boots and spotlessly white, pinched cowboy hat with a thousand percent certainty as those worn only by a Texas Ranger. I suddenly remembered that little no-no piece of treasure junk I inadvertently touched yesterday morning and cringed. No idea why, but that miniature, hand-carved wooden horse statue with marble base reminded me of him, or rather, someone's Texas-sized, wide brimmed ego.

"I swear, I didn't do it," I said, emanating Connelly's earlier rant, the words flying free automatically because our staring contest was stabbing my stomach like a hot poker, certain it was giving Ranger-man wide access of my soul. So, I averted my eyes, foolishly scrunched my shoulders, and gave off a nervous giggle.

Yeah, I looked guilty as hell. No idea why.

Ranger-man turned back to Detective Pine with the same amount of stealth-like precision, uncrossed his arms, removed his left leg perched across his right knee, stood up, all eight feet and three hundred pounds of solid muscle, buttoned the only button of his sport coat then tipped his hat once. Brent nodded once and Ranger-man turned to leave. I glanced up and up and up but only saw my reflection. Those peepers of his hidden behind mirrored shades, were unreadable, but I shivered with certainty; I had a sharp, twisting pang in both head and stomach that they were taking a snapshot of my very Dodge riddled existence. Ranger-man then took a step over Miss Surelee's fallen shape without a glance her way and disappeared down the hall.

With Ranger-man gone, I quickly regrouped and roused Miss Surelee back to the land of the living.

"What happened," Miss Surelee said, sluggishly coming around and getting to her feet. She glanced about, snatched up her purse before stumbling to a pleather chair, breathless. She fanned at her wildly flushed face while adding, "Am I dead?"

"No," said Brent.

I snickered. Brent didn't. Miss Surelee's beehive was tipping like the *Tower of Pisa*.

"What's with the intrusion, Dodge?" Brent asked, face stoic, forearms pressed to the top of his metal desk, hands interlaced, dangerously going white, cutting off all circulation to his clipped, square fingernails. Not that I'm concerned or anything...

I found my bravado hiding beneath my underwire and switched gears, asking instead of answering, "What's a Ranger doing in Boolee?"

Miss Surelee sucked air.

Brent remained stoic but I think I heard knuckles crack.

Okeydokey...so I downshifted.

"Hey, Jasmine is a cutie," I said, taking a seat in the other armless, stiff-backed, pleather chair. I crossed legs and slouched, slinging one arm over the back, feeling right at home. "Looks like you got your work cut out for you when she learns to drive."

"You'd seen her?" he asked, eyebrows arched, caterpillar 'stash and mangled goatee following suit. A second later they relaxed with Brent saying, "Oh right, my Sal the other day."

"Yesterday, and yes, you're welcome, Brent," I said with a wide grin.

"Thanks," he replied through gritted teeth before he managed to unlock his fingers, sighed, and then leaned back in his creaky chair. His face downgraded from detective mode to dad mode. Yes! The only thing missing from our unannounced visit is a bottle of whiskey. Unfortunately, he had to go and ruin my moment of reminiscing about the past by mumbling something about a funeral for my Aunt Letty's husband, "...next Wednesday at two, if you all ain't heard."

Miss Surelee sucked air while she avoided my stare by suddenly finding the worn-down, blue-and-white floor tiles, interesting. Not one to unriddle the questionable that is Miss Surelee I turned back to Brent. Of course, I hadn't heard. It was news to me because I refuse to get my gossip via the *Redlight*. Even if I had known (which, I had, I just purposely forgot), I wasn't planning-on paying my respects to that side of my Dodge relation because most days, Letty pretended to be anything other than Tucky's mom and truly, I forgot she was married or that she ever resided from Boolee. Much like me! Letty is a Spigot by birth so enough said.

I just shrugged but it went overlooked. "So, Jasmine," I U-turned with wiggled brow, expectant for Brent to pick up the slack.

"Jasmine...who-dat?" said Miss Surelee, glancing about half expecting another person.

I'm happy to see that she fully recovered from her earlier state.

"Oh, that's his latest addition to the pinecone of ankle biters he has growing back home," I proudly spoke up, like the Dodge that I am. "She's two months old."

"Going on three," Brent said, interlocking his hands behind his buzzed haircut head with equal amounts of pride and worry; probably his pride being different of my pride because I'm not especially proud of my own said ankle biter-turned-soul sucker.

"They sure are a handful," Miss Surelee added as if she had an inkling of what child-rearing entails. She was childless, as far as I knew. Nevertheless, all three of us gave in to a round of understanding nods.

A second later, Brent sat upright, smoothed a hand down the Dodge wreck he calls a goatee then turned and punched a code into his left-handed, upper desk drawer. I arched an eyebrow over this newest upgrade but once more, my curious actions went overlooked. He then reached in to the drawer and removed a handgun, checked the clip then re-inserted it, closed the drawer, resetting the lock, stood up and slipped the handgun to his holster, strapped across his plains clothed shirt.

Miss Surelee flung her hands up and immediately shrieked, her purse sailing off once more and bouncing off one of the framed pictures on the wall to her right.

Brent flashed her squinty eyes, shook his head then said with a huff, "Put your hands down." He snagged a Boolee County police issued windbreaker from the back of his chair, shrugged into it, and rounded his desk.

Miss Surelee put her hands back down, hugged herself then slowly rocked back and forth, humming.

After a moment of awkward staring he asked me, "Is she all for real?"

All I could do was scrunch shoulders to ears.

"I don't do guns, see what I'm saying? They give me the heebies, they do," Miss Surelee said on a shudder.

I smiled inwardly. Boolee is the last place you want to be if you're allergic to buckshot and steel. Having lived over twenty years in Texas I'm surprised she hasn't considered carrying concealed.

Brent scooped up the purse, handed it to her and looked past the truck wreck that is Miss Surelee to plant a hard stare my way. "Gots me a lot of errands, you all mind tellin' me why you all here?"

Oh, right! I shot to my feet. "Yes, someone has been sending me some freaked out text messages and I think it might be, ah...Boomer," I said, fishing my cell from my leather special. "Look, see? Last one sent last night."

Detective Pine frowned over the message before handing me back my phone. "Who's Gee?"

"That's who'd I'd like to know too," said Miss Surelee, smiling, expectant to hear more.

"I thought it might be Dickie or, you know, *them*, the ones looking for him, so it was just easier tagging that number so it wouldn't get lost in the shuffle."

Miss Surelee frowned.

"But you all think this is Boomer's doin'?" he asked, sounding puzzled.

"Well, he showed up at Bertie's with Tucky this morning to do the landscaping and he said he couldn't wait to see me at three."

"Of course, he can't wait, Sweetness, he's your date!"

Shoot. Me. Now. Please!

Brent's steely eyes suddenly twinkled as he rocked back on rubber soled heels. He knew about my blind date with stupid back in my youthful gullibility. Hell, all that is Boolee has yet to forget because Boomer is Joe-Bob Connelly's son from his first marriage. He may be my second cousin or other in a roundabout way but that doesn't mean I like the little turd. Hell, I'm not especially fond of my blood relatives. Now Brent and I have learned that I have another date with that idiot. Freaking lovely...

I flashed Miss Surelee a loaded stink eye that fell five carbs short of anything Dodge worthy. I turned back to Brent but he was already on his way out the door. I sprang past the door and hustled right on after him, back along the hallway with Miss Surelee bringing up the rear.

"So, Brent, are you going to tell me what's up with Ranger-man or do I need to ply it free of Connelly with a five-spotter?"

Brent came to a sudden, squelchy shoe stop. I bounced off his saggy butt but lucky for me, Miss Surelee's gut bounced me right back. Cripes. I felt like a pinball in a human pinball machine. When my jangled nerves stopped jiggling, Brent turned on me at once. "Christ Harley, you all like wanna them ding-dang rashes that keeps on comin' back!"

Hmm, I wonder if he's speaking from personal experience?

"Am not," I shot back like the Dodge riddle I am.

"Lis'en, the both of yous," he began, finger pointing my way. "This ain't nutin for either a you all to worry 'bout, so drop it, got it?"

I gave off a half shrug and averted my eyes. Nope. No way was I going to forget that encounter. Miss Surelee however, looked as if she couldn't comply fast enough with Brent's request, taking it to heart, with zealous sincerity. She nodded as if she were a bobble head doll, nearly knocking that beehive free, eyes the size of goose eggs, looking like an animated cartoon character straight out of Walt Disney's nightmare.

"Christ," he hissed with a small head shake, resuming his lead beyond the graveyard of Wannabes, mumbling, "I should a stayed home."

He led us right on past a suspiciously missing toady-faced Connelly and his front desk duty, past the closet-sized waiting room and out into the grey, blanketed skies, which is Boolee in the fall. "I mean it Dodge, let it go," he repeated to the tune of some distant thunder. The three of us glanced to the horizon, all signs of life, hesitated. A moment later, Brent shuffled away and settled himself behind the wheel of his county issued, V-8 truck. I guess County upgraded him from the crossover. I watched him power the Chevy up, back away then swing it wide to the left, heading the opposite direction toward Pineville and company.

Dang diggity, I forgot to ask him about the progress of Rodger-Dodger's disappearing act. I hugged my zip-up hoodie closer. Sheesh, where's Marty when I needed a snitch?

I quickly ambled off toward Rusty and settled in behind the wheel. Miss Surelee had her door slammed shut before I even had the key stabbed to the ignition switch. One of these days, I'm going to figure out how she can get those runts of hers to move faster than mine do. She slipped a hand to the half-empty box of ho-ho's and found her calling. I mentally shook my head and understood how she managed to pack on an extra hundred pounds, however.

I fired up Rusty, waited for a gear to grab and then backed away, turning the opposite direction of Detective Pine's getaway. I thought about being a snoop by following him, but I knew it would only lead to his split-level home. Not much to see or gossip about in the family-hood, anyways.

"Now where we off to," Miss Surelee asked, perching to the edge of the vinyl bench seat, legs crossed at the ankles, swinging forward while she glanced expectantly beyond the windshield and passenger window as if she were on a site seeing tour. This must seem like a vacation to her now that I think about it. I wish the same were true of my daily existence, however.

"Home," I said, sounding less-than-thrilled.

Miss Surelee pursed her lips. "Been there, done that," she said then sucked some air as a passing, scaled-down version of a Ford SUV buzzed past and nearly took off Rusty's duck-tapped side mirror. I glanced to rearview mirror, narrowed my peepers over the driver's one-finger salute. If I wasn't already in such a tizzy, I'd make a U-turn and welcome my Aunt Letty back, Boolee style. After all, it's not my fault she forgot how to drive in the hills. I mentally shook my head of all thoughts 'Spigot' when idiots number one and two headed back to town, apparently finished giving 'granny a trim', sideswiping Rusty a second time. I glanced to the dash clock. Hunh, it usually takes those jokers four hours to landscape her land. I wonder how they managed to do it in only one.

Miss Surelee giggled over the sight of those two jokers before saying, "What about candy? Can we swing by and check on her progress?"

I broke from my fog, spent two seconds thinking that through before saying with the excitement of a rock, "Yeah, sure."

I yanked the wheel to my left, U-turning this time, close to the Whiskey Barrels' parking lot and headed west along Main Street toward the far end of town. We caught all five stoplights as we cruised past gawkers, jealous of Rusty toward the west end of town. I stopped at the twentieth stop sign looking for stragglers then turned right at the juncture of Joplin and Main that is Boolee's borders. If we continued west along the curve to my left beyond Forest, we'd catch Interstate 77. I shuddered over that memory from last August. Today isn't about escape, however, so I followed the northeasterly hilly and snaking road along Joplin for ten minutes when something flashed in my peripherals about a half mile down on the upcoming crossroad.

Miss Surelee noticed too, gave off a shriek crying, "Monster!" and smacked hands to her eyes.

I slowed Rusty as I approached the intersection of Joplin and an unmarked county road, watching as that beast of a truck with tinted windows wasn't planning to stop, squelched the turn and headed my way, south, fishtailing and honking back along Joplin. The driver of that jacked up demolition derby, four-wheeled drive flashed by in a blur of midnight blue and sparkly chrome nearly ripping Rusty's side mirror free of its hold for the third time today. Dang it, I need to get that fixed. I had no idea who that monster, Ford truck belonged to, but I knew the driver the second we sideswiped each other, leaving me flushed, my mouth yawning wide, praying to Jesus and the Angels that Red was nowhere in sight. It would be my luck he'd blame me for this near-death run in because I saw who that driver was when I caught his startled look over the top half of the parted window and it was none other than my brother Rodger-Dodger.

Unbelievable, Miss Surelee was right.

Even more unbelievable...Batman was riding shotgun.

I slammed on the brakes, bringing Rusty to a skidded sideways stop in the middle of Joplin, bouncing Miss Surelee off the glove box and slamming her back against the bench seat (Righteous). I righted Rusty, turned him around and we raced on after Rodger-Dodger and that runaway monster.

"Whatcha doing?" shrieked Miss Surelee, hand gripping the seat for dear life, the other hand doing its best to keep the glove box lid shut and its cluttering of contents from spilling out.

"I'm following them," I said, the voice of a hunter.

"Don't do that—Drive away—Drive *away*!"

"But that was Rodger-Dodger," I cried back with equal amounts of adrenaline filled words.

I chased him all the way back into town but found myself two vehicles between me and one of my reasons to turn for the interstate and kept on going. I honked Rusty's horn just as recklessly, waving the sightseeing drivers clear of my need to catch up with my brother. Rodger-Dodger took us on a chase, ignoring every stop sign or reason to slow down by turning one block west, two blocks south, two blocks east, one block north, one block west then turned left and headed back along Joplin going south once again beyond a deserted and abandoned strip mall, dilapidated and abandoned motels and flat roofed row housing that once sheltered coal mining families that have long since been vacated.

"I don't feel real good," said Miss Surelee, hugging her stomach with one hand, keeping hold of that yellowed beehive with the other.

I smirked. It serves her right for that hiccup this morning, not to mention, her calling first dibs on that rack of lamb last night. Yep, I'm still steamed about it. Suck it down girlfriend.

I mashed the pedal down. Rusty sputtered but managed to close the truck length gap between us when a roll of toilet paper flew past my visual. It bounced off Rusty's windshield twice before soaring off into oblivion. A second later, a can of oil careened past, thankfully missing Rusty by a good three feet. Unfortunately, a gallon of paint hit the windshield dead center. Several more things went sailing past while I peered through smacking wiper blades and smeared paint but I wasn't going to let it distract me or slow me down. I gripped the steering wheel, tongue wagging, squinting beyond the rust-brown colored smear, feeling delirious that we were nearly to the monster Ford's bumper when the steering wheel gave a shudder and we suddenly found ourselves fishtailing and thumping along Joplin. I let off the gas pedal, eased Rusty into an abandoned parking lot onto an equally abandoned and boarded up strip mall that once housed thriving businesses for flooring, movie rentals, a drug store, a twenty-four-hour locksmith, and a swimming pool supplier. It was rumored these vacated shops might be, turned into storage units. I didn't have anything to store so I didn't care one way or the other what Boolee chose to do with this graveyard. Sighing, I shut down Rusty then slumped head to the wheel. I knew it before I saw it. Rusty got a flat.

"Fancy driving, Sweetness, you kept him from the ditch and I didn't even break a nail," said Miss Surelee, thinking most about her own safety, forgetting the fact we were ten miles away from the nearest ditch.

Or, that Rodger-Dodger and that mystery monster truck were long gone pointed towards the Pink Squirrel or dead ending at the county fairgrounds. I can't see Rodger-Dodger visiting either place as I kept my head slumped forward. Five minutes later, my head bounced off the steering wheel the second I heard the rap at my window. Miss Surelee squealed once then foolishly giggled. See, this is my lousy luck—it was Stranger-Danger man, Billy. Sighing, I exited Rusty with the excitement of a rock.

"Everything okay here, Boots?"

"Everything is better with you here," I said before my mind registered that I said that thought aloud. I cringed inwardly to his ever so slight, grin. I quickly rerouted saying, "I got a flat." I said this with equal amounts of less than thrilled excitement.

Billy quietly followed me as I circled around, inspecting, my head full of questions and whiny thoughts. I came across the last tire, located up front, passenger side, sunk to pavement, resting on a rusted rim as the one damaged. Swell. I had run over a nail and punctured a rubber. I jogged back to the bed, released the tailgate, climbed up and yanked the jack and skinny spare free and wrestled them toward the tailgate. Billy reached up, relieved me of the tire and jack before effortlessly hauling both to the front. He proceeded to change the tire. I watched on. I could have easily done the swap out no thanks to Red for the practice because changing a tire is the only thing that I am mechanically inclined at doing. But since Billy already had the flat free of the bolts why should I butt in now? Naturally, the sky rumbled low, parted, and brought forth the *Seventh Plague of Egypt* in response. Thanks again, Red, I murmured bitterly to the earth.

Thirty minutes later, skies clearing, Billy driving away, I a bit bruised and soaked to my shaky bones, Miss Surelee all toasty and dry and licking the last of the chocolate from her thin lips, had us back on the road. I headed north along Joplin once more, this time, at a slower pace, eyes peeled through paint smears for Rodger-Dodger. I drove about a quarter mile past that monster sighting when the junkyard emerged beyond a patch of untouched, densely packed forest to my right. I slowed Rusty, parallel parked him in front of the locked and rusted chain link fencing, on a patch of muddied, urine colored grass and shut him down. I blew out a long breath, finally unclenching my jaw and gritted teeth.

"What are we doing here," Miss Surelee cried, voice sounding like nails scraped across a chalkboard.

I flinched and stuck a finger in my ear, hoping to stop the high-pitched ringing. "I need to switch out that tire I just changed. Besides, you wanted to see candy," I said, sloshing to the ground, removing the nail-embedded blowout from the back of Rusty and half-rolled, half-shoved it past Rusty's tailgate to stand next to a push button, call box in front of some rusting chain link fencing.

"I thought Martin said they took candy to a garage?" she asked, hands perched to her waist, eyes roving about, taking it all in, not knowing what or where she should look first. "I don't see no garage, Sweetness, do you see a garage?"

I snickered. She flashed me a frown. "This *is* Stan's garage." And his towing and salvage lot (double snicker). Suck it up Miss Surelee this is the way of Boolee. "Besides, Junior Pensky's shop went out of business a year ago. This is the only garage left."

The whole area of Stan's place of business looked like he wished to keep everyone out, 24/7. Surrounded by fifteen feet high, rusted and haphazardly leaning corrugated aluminum panels between an intermittent of equaled height, loose-fitting, chain-link fencing, was the teaser. All of it topped off by razor laced, looped wiring as the main deterrent. But if you were like me and threw caution to the wind and pressed forward, then there were several red and yellow, rectangle postings throughout, enticing us daredevils to a thousand volts pumping metal and possibly flesh, Dobermans on the premises, while the perimeter remained under constant supervision via vision cam that patched straight through to the lock-U-up station. Stan protected his auto/junk yard with the same type of sincere precaution as *Fort Knox*; junk parts highly regarded around these parts like rare jewels—especially the Dodge kind and probably cost as much too. Still, you'd be a fool to burglarize this place.

Good thing I'm not easily discouraged as I leaned the tire against my leg because forty minutes ago, my last pair of spotless jeans were feeling left out of the dirty pile so one more smudge of dirt wouldn't matter. I pushed the button on the call box and then I gazed off towards space and waited.

Miss Surelee continued to frown.

Five minutes later, an amplified voice crackled across the oblivion, echoing all about us saying, "Wha."

The voice belonged to Stanley Dodge. As middle child to Uncle Walt and Aunt Doty, late thirties or early forties, Stan had no time for speaking, let alone grunting, as most of we Dodges' do with Boolee pride.

"Came to check on Miss Surelee's car, plus I got me a flat," I said to the box then turned and grinned, giving a one-finger wave toward the vision cam.

Thirty seconds later, he buzzed us past the front gate. Two seconds later, it rattled shut.

Miss Surelee gave a shudder and hugged herself tighter.

Since I grew up in this worthless town, related to half, I knew where I was going and strolled and rolled my blowout deeper into the maze of stacked cars, tires, mufflers, rims, seats, and various other decaying parts to my right. Even though, I was certain that three quarters of these artfully located piles came donated by most of my living relation, I still wasn't taking any chances and was careful to keep from accidently touching anything Dodge worthy this side of my left hand. Miss Surelee hustled close at my heels. She too hesitant as she looked like she was slinking down an alley at three in the morning, eyes flicking about like a seizure, flinching and shrieking to every sound, wondering how she ever got there, let alone how she was going to make it out, alive. Priceless, I wasn't the only one with fears embedded to my DNA. Self-preservation can be either helpful or dead weight. It looks like in our situation it's undoubtedly, the latter.

Just wait until those Dobermans catch her in their colorblind visual.

Yes, I'm snickering, inwardly, of course.

I leaned the busted tire against the rusted sheet metal, ten-by-ten-foot sized building, one lopsided front door, one paint-peeling back door, one crackerjack-sized window to its bare existence. This was Stan's office, detached and several yards away from his three-lift garage. I motioned Miss Surelee up the two, sagging wooden steps, entered, and huddled to the middle of that overcrowded, hoarded recordkeeping disaster area.

Miss Surelee gave off a low whistle before I could stop her.

Bud and Hemi reared their pointy ears, wet noses, and slobbery traps from just behind the mountain of file boxes, piled sporadically along the far wall. Before she knew what was happening those two mutts were inching closer, teeth bared, growling.

"Don't move," I muttered from the side of my mouth, standing statuesque. "They're harmless."

Miss Surelee did the opposite. She grabbed at the first box closest to her and threw it in their direction with a shriek. The box bounced off a different grouping of boxes haphazardly piled up at the far wall and toppled. Naturally, Stan's guard dogs thought it was a game, following the path of the strewn contents, glanced back her way then pounced. It was over in five seconds of rapid blinking disbelief.

A tall, slender, and knobby-looking man with full-on grizzly, rusty colored beard just entered from the back door. He noticed the commotion, gave me a headshake then stuck two, grease covered fingers to his lips and gave off a well-practiced whistle. The Dobermans froze, yanked their heads toward whistle blower, expectant. He yelled, "Git", and without a second thought to Miss Surelee, the dogs bounded away behind their master and from view.

I helped a violated Miss Surelee to her feet. I even helped her right that beehive of hers before I introduced her to my cousin Stan.

All she could do was smack hands to eyes.

The man wearing a grease smeared black t-shirt with a faded picture of a hemi complete with Dodge logo, unzipped grease stained grey colored jumpsuit, gnarled hands smeared with more grease swiped at an equally greasy looking rag stood motionless before he flashed us a gapped-tooth smile in return.

"Dang Har," he said by way of a greeting, shaking his squirrelly looking head, looking like he wanted to high-five me or disinherit me altogether.

I'm game for either because I wasn't the only one known to spring a prank. Because my cousin Stan was the top prankster, back in the day at Boolee High. I heard rumors but that's all. Nothing to substantiate concrete evidence that he was the one to let loose a squirrel with lit firecrackers tied to its tail about the girls' locker room (perhaps on the goading from my oldest brother, Rob-Bob). I'm happy to see my cousin upgraded to dogs.

"Put your hands down," I said to Miss Surelee before I explained the tire, conveniently forgetting to explain away Miss Surelee's spooked behavior.

Stan said, "Third-um this week," then explained Miss Surelee's parts weren't due for delivery until next Monday. She went into a rant, hands waving, her mouth shrieking dislike. With half a shrug, unfazed, Stan said it was the earliest they'd arrive because they came shipped from New York. Because, no one had spare parts lying around that could match a Porsche's expensive control and framing—no one. He suggested her buying a truck; a Dodge make and model, no less.

"Same I told that-thar other feller," he said.

"Who," Miss Surelee and I asked in unison.

"Struts," is all Stan said. Truck speak is his first and preferable language.

"Ah, Billy, the new shop owner," I said on a nod.

"If you all says so," replied Stan with another shrug of his bony shoulders.

"Hey, do you happen to know what's going on with Rodger-Dodger?"

Stan merely stared back.

"Red seems to think he's missing," I continued. "He hasn't been to work this week, but I just saw him driving through town."

"Seen-em poker night," said Stan, looking unconcerned.

That was last Thursday night and Rodger-Dodger wasn't missing before Sunday, I thought frowning. "What about Junior? You think he knows what's up with my brother?"

Stan shrugged his bony shoulders a second time before saying, "Get you all traded?"

Twenty minutes later, Stan had me switched out with a discounted tire that would make even Red proud. Another ten minutes later, we were on the road, narrowly avoided the arrival of Tucky, dropping Boomer off for his second job as one of Stan's junkyard helpers as we drove back to my home away from home. No time to socialize with stupid, I floored it for Dodge country.

I had questions swirling about my dampened head when I spotted a cowboy hat wearing stranger, sitting to the cocoon of a tan, unmarked car at the parking lot of the Whiskey Barrel, watching. Watching for who or what was unclear. His mirrored shades weren't telling. But my shaded heart was for it thumped and rattled about my chest all the way past the fork of the road and into the drive of my home away from home.

"Is it safe," Miss Surelee asked, as she slowly inched her nose past the dash and glanced about.

I snickered. She had spotted Ranger-man too and aptly chose to duck for cover until the skies parted and blessed our passing to Aunt Bertie's protective custody.

Chapter Six: Stranger than Fiction

After all that happened yesterday with my mishap at the antique shop and my unexpected encounters with both Red and Stranger-Danger, no way in Red's hell was I going to let loose the Rodger-Dodger or Ranger-man sighting that Miss Surelee and I had witnessed this morning. Nope. Besides, I had a truckload of questions now more than ever, and not one of them cared to give me a convincing answer. Before entering the Victorian however, I instructed Miss Surelee to keep quiet all the same.

"Zipped, locked and give you the key," she eagerly said, mimicking with pinched fingers of someone sliding a zipper across her lips, turning a key, and holding out for me to take.

I gave her empty, upturned palm a slap back instead.

We headed to the kitchen for a fun filled sampling of nitrates and triglycerides. Or rather, I did while hogging the last of my chocolate milk. She picked at the butcher bologna, mushy white bread, and greasy potato chip crumbs as if it might bite her back before we headed upstairs to my room.

During the morning rush, not only had Aunt Bertie managed to put her kitchen back to its squeaky-clean perfection, she had restored my room to a manageable order and had done up a full load of my laundry as well. Guilt washed over me for all but two seconds; I had planned-on cleaning up the kitchen but wait a minute—I didn't even get a crumb, let alone cause any of that mess, so no, not going to feel guilty. Besides, I have never now, nor been all that domesticated. Why start now?

I turned to those neatly folded piles of sweet-smelling softness and greeted them with glee. I was on my last pair of undies, you see.

"Thanks Aunt Bertie, you are the best-est," I shouted down below as I headed to the bathroom.

"You're welcome dear," she replied from her makeshift workshop.

That wasn't the only thing I noticed about my neatly cleaned and straightened room once I returned from the bathroom wearing a fresh pair of sweats, complete with ground in burger grease stain across the crotch from five years ago. I deposited my, seen better days, rain-soaked jeans to the hamper, allowing my boots to fall where they may when I caught site of something else, I'm better off avoiding. Looking like a cross-section of a stale, moldy and forgotten ho-ho sat a faded tan colored mattress, sandwiched between spotted metal. It was Uncle Walt's old Army cot. Swell. He never got rid of that rust bucket because we Dodge's sure know how to horde like doomsday preppers. Aunt Bertie may not want me near the downstairs sofas but she had no problem leaving this piece of history within arm's reach. Double swell. Regardless, I wasn't going near it with all the radioactive gear in the world.

"Thanks, Aunt Bertie," I muttered under my breath as I turned to Miss Surelee, splayed out on the beanbag like an overturned water bug, breathing sluggishly heavy. "Looks like your sofa surfing days are over," I said with a wave toward the corner and that portable bed just in case she had tried to overlook it as well.

She glanced its way once then gave it a squint before saying to me, "How I'm supposed to sleep on that?"

"It folds flat," I said on a heavy sigh, taking my pile of clean clothes to the dresser, and deposited them neatly away. Oh, okay, that was a lie. I shoved them to the drawers haphazardly as if I was stuffing trash. I've never claimed to be perfect or even a Dodge, you know. Besides, they'll only end up wrinkled the second I put them on.

In less time it takes me to inhale a chocolaty ho-ho whole, Miss Surelee had that cot unfolded flat, lounged across it, one arm hanging off the side, drooling and snoring. Sheesh, I can't believe she found the time for a snoozer.

I turned back to my sock and undie pile and froze. I noticed the stark white hanky at once. It wasn't mine and I'm almost certain it wasn't Mr. Willoughby's either. Then I remembered yesterday morning. Oh, right, the antique shop. It must be Stranger-Danger-mans', now freshly washed clear of his woodsy scent and spotlessly, blood free, traces of my freakish ability gone. I gently unfolded it and rubbed it along my cheek dreamily when I noticed one of the edges raised. A closer inspection yielded a strange symbol, resembling a fishhook or possibly an anchor with horizontal pitchfork or it might have been a replica of *Poseidon's* trident, embroidered with white thread to one of the corners. Huh. I wonder if this hanky belongs to Billy, was his daddy's or some other relation he wasn't keen on giving up. Oh geez...a girlfriend's, perhaps? Oh crap, was it an antique from his shop? Nope. It's not an antique because touching it with my left hand wasn't giving anything else up, either so I settled it to the top of my dresser next to where my singed, Texas license plate once sat, like a prized procession instead. I need to figure out where that and Black Beauty's key fob ran off to.

I finished putting away the last of my laundry when Miss Surelee gave off a powerful snort followed by incoherent mumbling. I stiffened because I distinctly heard the words, "Dick" and "Arnold" flap their way free. A heartbeat later and mumbled out she gave a twist of her body, beehive askew then settled once more to the land of sand.

Bandit slinked in, gave a glance Miss Surelee's way then pounced to my bed instead, kneaded at covers before he curled tail to feet as he commandeered my pillow and purred.

I left them to it and snuck off downstairs.

I wandered past the kitchen and into the dining room. A long, long time ago, about a century since past, this room once used for entertaining people, not critters. Most of the room overpowered by an antique, oval walnut dining table that Aunt Bertie had topped with a stainless-steel cover sometime back in the seventies. The far wall hosted wall-to-wall, wooden built-ins that protectively cradled and displayed china and silver. Now they housed murderous looking utensils, rubber gloves, stacks of newspapers, bowls, tubing, bottles of chemicals and formaldehyde and a plethora of glass eyeballs, electronic devices, wood stands and more while the open, upper shelving displayed stuffed and petrified road kill. The wall next to this was only an arched opening, leading to the parlor, back porch or around the corner to the main entry. The entry between this room and the kitchen once closed off with sliding pocket doors, now permanently recessed. The corner wall door was in working order. It leads to the basement or known back in the day as a cellar. Barely the size of the dining room and kitchen combined, walls made of rounded stone packed into earth, the cellar currently houses a washer and dryer, single sink basin, a wall of shelves for her canned vegetables and jellies, and one industrial sized, top of the line subzero. This is where she kept her critters chilling until the day came for their magical transformation like the one Aunt Bertie was presently finishing.

I hovered about her right shoulder, gave a squint and watched as she stitched with a surgeon's precision the last hole of a recently pickled raccoon. "Where's that one going," I asked just to have something to say. I didn't really care which hillbilly had purchased said road kill. I was, bored. I needed the stimulation.

Aunt Bertie hesitated. I think. Maybe she hadn't heard me. No, not a chance because I know her hearing is better than Laney's is. I opened my mouth to ask a second time when she finally hissed out, "Margret."

Ouch. "That's gotta hurt", I muttered, reverting to my hillbilly roots. Great-Aunt Margret may be family and all because of her marriage to Leo but that does not mean she's well-liked around these parts, especially her side of things. It's a wonder their grandson, Tucky is, tolerated at all. Let alone, allowed to keep breathing because he is firstly an Offnutt, Spigot second, and lastly a Dodge. I wonder if Aunt Bertie left Margret a nasty surprise inside...

"Stop glaring at me like you wish me an early death," said Bertie, breaking me free of my devious thinking.

"Sorry," I said, adverting my eyes, my face and body altogether.

I went to the shelving, slid back the recently added glass doors that housed the assortment of statues protectively. I snickered to myself over that upgrade. Because the upgrade came a month ago, courtesy of Bandit poking around where he shouldn't have and caused three of Aunt Bertie's vermin to topple to the floor. Aunt Bertie was madder than most days I've seen Red get, and that's saying a lot, considering she is usually calm, cool, and collected, more than most any other Booleeite related to a Dodge. Naturally she was more upset over that addition to the built-in cabinets, than the fact that Laney never asked her if it was okay to keep Bandit as a pet. Naturally, because my sourpuss pointed accusing fingers my way, saying "Mom said it was okay." Naturally, I had, because Laney had told me that Aunt Bertie had said it was. See why I'm thinking of ditching my heritage altogether? So, I did the same as that fuzz ball and went poking a finger at one of the stuffed squirrels poised so that its miniscule, clawed hands could hold a candy dish, or more appropriately, a nut bowl. It wobbled, started to tip but I caught it just as it nosed, head over feet over the shelf and kept it from becoming road kill a second time on the Victorian's waxed, wooden floor.

"What's going on, dear," said Bertie on an impetuous huff. I heard her chair slide back an inch on the wood plank flooring. "You want to talk about it?"

No, I thought, quickly setting nutterbutter back to his place amongst the other stuffed critters and slid the glass door closed. "You going to the funeral," I asked instead.

Aunt Bertie gave off a second huff, this one filled with irritation as she slapped down the lengthy tweezers and curved sewing needle to say, "Now, what do you think?"

Yeah, I knew it before I asked her; Dodges are known for many things, skipping out on a funeral isn't one of them. Therefore, I kept at my perusal of petrified art.

Just in case I might have forgotten I was still a Dodge however, Aunt Bertie reminded me by saying, "Does your frown have something to do with yesterdays' reawakening?"

Maybe...

"Accidents happen," I replied with one shoulder hunched instead. Nope, no way was I about to let her rope me into a deeper explanation of what I may or may not know about someone getting his brains rearranged.

"Coexist, dear," she said, sliding her chair closer and going back to stitching up the raccoon.

"Is Mister Willoughby around," I asked sounding equally bored to know otherwise.

"No," she replied flatly.

"Not down visiting the ribbits," I pressed.

"You know darn well that it's too cold for his knees to be wandering down along the crick."

"So where did he go?" I know...curiosity and the cat...

She turned and gave me a murderous look then snapped, "He's running deliveries."

Oh, right. After yesterday's doo-doo of fun at the treasure trap I had refused to be, wrangled into any more of Aunt Bertie's road-kill deliveries. It didn't matter that she paid me fifty dollars per delivery or that she tried bribing me with a chocolate drizzled, peanut butter pie of my very own, I refused to cave to continue that temporary line of employment.

Now, had she offered me a plate of chocolate-covered fritters, I might have reconsidered.

Not likely.

I came around the table and sniffed the air, humming with anticipated eagerness, "Umm, spaghetti?"

"No. The gravy is for Lasagna for tonight's dinner," she replied.

Dang she was good. Speaking off—"I will get first dibs, tonight."

"Guests first, dear," she said.

Not on my watch.

"What will it take for you to hold back a piece, just for me—laundry...dishes...cooking?"

Aunt Bertie released a snort of a laugh before saying, "You haven't done a lick of that kind of work since the day you were born! What makes you think you can start now?"

Well that was unnecessary. "Forget it, I'm beat. I'm taking a nap," I said with a last glance her way. Aunt Bertie kept at her never-ending job of tending road kill but acknowledged my departure with a nod, nonetheless.

When I rounded my room, I was, startled to see Miss Surelee, fully rested, perched to the end of Uncle Walt's cot, dressed in a ruby colored Donna Karen wraparound, knee-length dress with matching heels, beehive swapped out for a Farrah Fawcett replica made famous back in the seventies. She was tapping a powder poof to her nose.

"Going somewhere," I asked, my curiosity piqued.

She gave me a flat-out stare before saying, "We". Two seconds later, I remembered her 'better' news.

"Forget it, Miss Surelee," I said, slumping to my bed. "You're on your own with that one."

"No can do, Sweetness, the invitation is for two," she replied, slipping her compact to her purse.

"If you think for one stupid minute that I'm tagging along with you and those two losers then you're loonier than I thought," I barked to my room.

"But I already accepted," Miss Surelee said, face slacking of excitement. "A lady never goes back on her word."

Uh-huh.

I lifted my head and flashed her my, *are you freaking kidding me*? glance before saying, "Unt-uh, nope, now way, no-how. Forget it. I am not going down that twisted road again!"

"But I need someone to chaperone," she said, going to my dresser. Standing on tiptoes to stare into the wall mirror while plying a moist layer of berry colored lipstick to her thin line of lips and before I could stop her, blotted them to Stranger-Danger's spotless hanky. I did a mental head shake. When she finished, she adjusted her wig once and turned back to me, plying me with a look of utter contempt.

"Don't care," I said, leaning back on my bed, one arm draped over my weary eyes.

"But what if he wants to get fresh with me?"

Uh-huh. "Then let him," I mumbled, turning my head toward the windows, relieved to see the day was half over.

"Please," Miss Surelee said, hands pressed in prayer.

"No," I said on a powerful yawn. The car chase and weather may have worn down my radar but her pleading wasn't helping. I was growing beyond cranky and I really needed to start looking for a job.

"I'll tell Ladybug about Rodger-boy," she said, sounding evil-like.

I sprang to my feet in one second flat and shushed her, hands, palm side down waving. "Don't do that—please! It'll only rain down a load of hell, and I don't mean the afterlife kind."

Miss Surelee perched hands to hips and gave me a squint. "What you saying, you want me to lie to your Ladybug?"

"No, no, just, ah, just don't say anything until I've figured out what is going on, okay," I said, eyes pleading for her to agree while shooting worried glances toward the door.

"I might be inclined to forget if you be willy to escort me and sweet-cheeks to the picture show," she said, sounding like a Ford-in-Dodge packaging.

Not above blackmail, eh?

I know I'm going to regret this, but I gave in, closed eyes, pinched at my nose while all of me drooped. I nodded with a regretful sigh.

Miss Surelee squealed right on cue before saying with puckered mouth and squinty eyes, "You might want to change first, Sweetness."

Needless-to-say, I did not change out of my man repelling attire. I slipped my sock covered feet into my boots as the only means of spiffing up. If someone had made a repellant that kept men away, I would have bathed in it. I wasn't in the mood to give cross signals Boomers way, let alone, any hint that I purposely wanted to be stuck sitting next to that joker or his delusional hero, Tucky.

Yep, you guessed it: I drove Rusty. Boomer no longer owns a truck or a vehicle of any kind, somebody saying something about a drunken night of poker. Whatever. Naturally, Tucky's truck was, loaded down with landscaping and man junk so it made sense to take my loaner instead. No worries because I wasn't keen on riding along in Tucky's pile of stank either. I wasn't happy about Rusty's less than pleasing aroma however, but decided it was a risk worth taking, regardless.

I skirted Miss Surelee out the front door, called back a "see you later," to Aunt Bertie, closed the door before she caught wind or before dumb and dumber had a chance to scarf down another freebie meal. I white knuckled the steering wheel as I drove toward the town Square like a woman possessed, wishing I had tossed those three jokers to the back end of Rusty. So, I parked at the Piggly Wiggly and made us hoof it across the street to the Square instead.

I startled when I passed the granite statue, tree fountain set to the shadows of a by-gone, civil war era statue of a Union Solider with sudden panic: Did mystery texter refer to this spot to meet up? No... couldn't be, could it? I quickly scrambled after the others without wasting another thought on dipshit or whoever was crazy enough to be texting me mysteriously, coded messages.

Tucky had his and Miss Surelee's tickets purchased and waiting in line at the snack food counter the moment I entered the theater's main entrance. I stood two feet wide of Boomers wide butt at the ticket counter, tapping my foot, waiting to get this show done, buried and over with. I nervously glanced about, hoping I didn't recognize anyone, wondering what was taking idiot number two so long. I had no choice and glanced his way. Boomer stupidly stared off into space picking his nose.

I did an involuntary shudder, steam escaping my unpicked nose. "Fine," I said through gritted teeth, slapping plastic to the counter. "You're springing for the popcorn and soda."

Loaded with a buttered trough of her own I watched as Miss Surelee and Tucky ducked to theater room number two in this two-room building. Tickets in hand, I started to follow saying and not caring if he heard, "I'll just look for a seat."

Unfortunately, Boomer grabbed me by the arm saying, "Not hap'nin, babe."

Steam escaped my flaring nostrils and ringing ears while hellfire flashed all around me.

Ten minutes later, my plastic with a nosebleed of its own I had my arms loaded with a bucket of popcorn, a gallon of something carbonated, three varieties of king-sized chocolate covered candy bars, one box of chocolate covered raisins, a bag of chocolate covered peanuts and a package of cherry licorice. I preferred the black licorice but they were all sold out. I haplessly followed in Boomers wide berth to the middle of that dimmed theater. I plunked two seats down on his right, setting my haul and purse to the empty seat between us. Boomer frowned my way. I ignored the troll and quickly glanced about, hoping that no one noticed my arrival, let alone my stupid tagalong. I squinted into the shadowy abyss until I finally spotted Miss Surelee, five rows down and to the right, snuggling up to Tucky, sharing a bucket-sized container of something frosty. The opening credits began to roll so I slouched down even more, you know, just in case someone had spotted me sitting within the vicinity of Boomer after all. I wouldn't want someone jumping to conclusions that'll never happen. I slipped down my seat the rest of the way, perched crossed ankles to the empty seat in front of me, closed my eyes and prayed that the two-plus-hours of hell would be over in a flash.

Five minutes later, I was plowing through my tub of popcorn, the bag of peanuts and half a candy bar contemplating suicide by fake butter and sodium when I realized what movie they had suckered me into seeing. Something about reviving aliens. Ugh. It was a monster-slash-movie. Crapola, I don't sleep well on thoughts of shocker gore. Nor Miss Surelee I thought, fuming, sending subliminal messages of the runs her way.

Miss Surelee gave off a squeak. I sat up straight. At first, I thought I had discovered I have powers of ESP! No such luck, I realized as Tucky hooked an arm around her. Apparently, she was shrieking at the screen and Tucky was trying to be gender biased. I shuddered. I'm going to have to burn that dress of hers when we get back to the Victorian. Hunh, Tucky just gave her a kiss and neither one of them fizzed or melted. If things work out, maybe Tucky will follow

Miss Surelee to New York. Doubt it, though. I think Tucky will head for the blue state hills once he discovers 'she' is naturally a 'he'. I snickered to my grease and salt covered hand. Tucky was in for a shocker if things went that far south. But I was suddenly worried about Miss Surelee's state of things for when or if it ever did. I liked her, a lot and she was my only sense of normal after leaving these parts far behind. It's because I like her as if she were the family that I wished I had that I was praying she'd find a reason to ditch Tucky before her delicate nature and plastic nose got, violated from a balled-up fist. I do not wish to see her hurt. She deserved someone much more understanding, worthy and obviously gayer than Tucky can ever be. Tucky deserved a one-way trip to Red's funhouse of flames, all expenses paid by me of course.

Speaking of, I think someone besides me is giving him the stink eye. I turned my head just enough to see who it was. Sure enough, I recognized the chunky, plainly dressed, plain featured woman as Penelope Constance but we just called her Penny or Con for short. Other than being short, she was weirdly different than most of us natives (yep, even more so than me), by always slinking around locker rooms, hiding behind her books or her curtain of greasy locks or just sulking behind the football field bleachers, watching. Who would have thought she managed to catch Tucky's eye her senior year? Guess I'm not surprised; look who he's on a date with now? He ended up dumping Penny though, two months pregnant for a shot at knocking up pizza faced, braces wearing, Averleen. That one only lasted four months before Tucky moved on to bigger and dumber I suppose.

Penny's sister-in-law, Andrea Rosenbaum with bottled rose colored, pixie haircut identical to her mother's, seated to her right, equally pissed off and staring down front. Both now at the edge of their seats, eyes like scopes, judging the distance between them and where Tucky and Miss Surelee sat pressed together, two rows down from them.

I thought Penny had long since gotten over Tucky? Especially since I learned from my childhood friend, Rinna Mathers and now my cousin-in-law by way of marriage to Mason Waverly that Penny upgraded to Andrea's older brother, Kevin Rosenbaum one year after that and settled down with him and his collection of action figures about his five-star-wheeled accommodations over at the Cedar Park Trailer community at the southwest end of town, pumping out three more ankle biters.

Ut-oh, this doesn't look good. Penny and Andrea just slipped down a row closer, both clutching cans of shaving cream.

I nearly flung my buttered and chocolate covered goodies as I scrambled to my feet and started down my row to my right, amidst heated stares and muttered insults for interrupting their viewing pleasure. No time to judge, or care because I needed to head those two girls off at the Kentucky pass.

"Don't forget the juju's, babe," came Boomer's voice from behind, bouncing off my ears and skyrocketing to oblivion, forgotten.

I was nearly to the walkway between sections when I spotted someone else, inching their way down the opposite isle, sighting up Tucky in his smug-ugly-mug. Of all the dumb, strange luck that is me...is that who I think it is? My heart thumped once, jumpstarting my feet in the opposite direction and back along the way I just came. More angry looks, more tittering, one hand on my ass—hey! Yuck. It was Boomer. I slapped his hand free and I was clear of stupid to chase down dipshit himself, my ex-husband, Dickie Trollop.

Did I mention that three-timing ratfink tried to set me up for tax fraud and murder and now wanted by Boolee's flunkies as well as the FBI? Never mind the syndicated Giovanni crime family wanting blood either, because it looks like I'm first in line to that hundred-thousand-dollar reward. What sweet fabulous blessed turn of luck!

Dickie was going down.

The following fifteen minutes happened in a blur, but went something like this:

Tucky suddenly sprang from his seat, Miss Surelee squealed, wig askew, popcorn bucket and soda cup sailing off in different directions; Dickie slammed across Tucky, arms and legs flailing; Andrea put Miss Surelee in a head lock while Penny started for Tucky, shaving cream can to hand raised overhead while yanking at Dickie with her free hand. Movie goers scrambled out of the way, some remained, yelling or cheering, it was difficult to be sure. I finally caught up to the wrangling of fun and lunged at Dickie but somehow ended up tripping then skidding on a puddle of something warm and sticky, taking out Penny, Andrea, and Miss Surelee in the process. Police sirens careened in the background; the movie flickered then stopped, house lights raised, people booed; management and attendants came streaming down both isles, hands waving, voices shouting for us to break it up. I squished one eye closed because someone just elbowed me; then someone slipped hands under my armpits, hauled me to my feet and separated me from the rest of the group. When I finally composed myself, I opened my watery eyes to stare into a bushy, untamed goatee.

"Christ Harley, what's goin' on?"

No time for pleasantries, I glanced wildly about. "Where is he," I cried my voice manic, right eye still brimming with tears.

"Who," Brent asked.

"Dickie," I hissed.

"He all was here?" he asked, suddenly glancing to his left then his right, nodding once over my left shoulder.

I turned but only caught a blurry version of someone headed back up that isle and out of the theater. I couldn't say with any certainty if it was a Wannabe or perhaps Ranger-man. I'm just saying that my eyes wouldn't stop watering for me to clearly see.

"Stay," Detective Pine ordered as I watched him head toward the Tucky gathering of idiots, Marty and some other Wannabe keeping a one-foot distance, watching, ready to spring to action should Penny or Andrea go after Miss Surelee or Tucky a second time. Naturally, I didn't stay put and inched closer, swiping my eyes dry. Marty noticed and flashed me a grin, small shake of his head. I think the hazel-eyed partner of his was coughing (maybe snickering) to his hand.

"You all mind tellin' me what this here all's 'bout?" asked Brent, hands perched to his off-duty belt, glancing from one food covered face to the next.

I grinned gleefully. At least I wasn't the only one food bombed. But I was the only one prepared for just such emergencies by having worn my previously grease-stained sweat pants.

Everyone shouted their misguided version at once. Two seconds in, Brent held up one hand as if he were practicing to be a traffic cop, halting the mashing of voices. Then he pointed at Tucky and said, "Go."

Tucky shrugged causing his eye to go wandering before saying, "Can't help it, dude, I'm like God's gift or sumpin."

Ah...*not*.

Penny shot him daggers while Andrea set off a round of belly laughter about the theater. Brent wasn't laughing, instead, scraping a hand down his face before he motioned for silence. After which he turned to Miss Surelee. Naturally, she was just as unhelpful saying through tears and butter smears, "I-I was just enjoying my date...s-she came at me then my s-sweet-cheeks here, like s-she was p-possessed!"

That part was true but still, explained nothing.

Brent shot a frown toward Penny and she matched his frown upping him a smirk (shaving can, conveniently missing). "That one's lyin'. Me and Andrea just wanted a word with the little turd alone is all."

"Is that true?" he asked of Andrea.

She nodded then added, "Yeah, the stupid jerk is one months' late with child support, girl can't survive without it. Little snake outta be ashamed takin' another girl out—even one lookin' like *that*—when he gots obligation back home, ain't that right, sheriff?"

"Detective," said Brent, straightening his back. "Reeva know you all here?"

"Whatever," said Andrea ignoring his inquiry of her mother to add, "We all would a got-em talkin' if that one hadn't stuck her big butt where it dint belong!"

Who me? Shucks. I'm honored to be the butt of this joke.

Brent looked my way, shook his head once then turned back to the pack asking, "Any you all seen the other one?"

Everyone stared back blank faced; Miss Surelee suddenly farted, her face turning an unflattering shade of pea green.

Clearly, that wasn't the answer Brent was searching for because he swiped at the air once, indicating for Marty to clear out the troublemakers. He and the other Wannabe escorted Penny and Andrea back up the aisle and out of the theatre; Tucky and Miss Surelee motioned back to their seats. Brent turned back on me and repeated his concern, "You all really done-did seen-em?"

"Yes," I said with a capital, yikes! "He's the one that tackled Tucky to the floor then Penny got in on the mix. She saw him, I'm sure of it!"

Brent pinched at the bridge of his nose before looking up, fixing a hard stare over my left shoulder. I turned just in time to see Stranger-Danger man, dressed to break hearts in washed-out denims, worn down, suede boots, daffy duck long-sleeved t-shirt pushed to the elbows, saunter down the aisle right behind Boomer who was hugging my tub of popcorn. My brain stopped spinning while my legs turned to jelly and my belly went all squishy. That's what kind of effect Billy has on me. Wish it didn't or I would have noticed

Boomer's arm now slung over my shoulder, copping a feel of my left boob. Billy grinned. I broke free of my stupor and found my tenacity. I slapped Boomer's hand away and gave him a three-foot shove. "Stay away from me!" He hovered for about two seconds before he headed down the aisle with my bucket of buttered popcorn and plunked down next to Tucky.

"Everything okay here, Detective," asked Billy.

I melted on the spot. His voice like the rest of him was so heavenly...

"Wha," I slurred, fully forgetting.

Billy glanced up from my boots and just shook his head once. I glanced back to Brent, but I think he noticed my brain fart for he shot Billy a quick nod and cruised on past us and out of that theater of gore. Moments later, patrons resettled, house lights lowered, people cheered as the movie resumed.

"Let's get you out of here, Boots," said Billy.

I gladly followed then jumped, turning back the way we just came. "Miss Surelee," I said, regretful. "I'm her ride home."

Billy graciously took the lead, sauntered down several rows until he located Miss Surelee, had her by the arm, escorted back my way and back on up the aisle. I snagged the box of raisins, the bag of licorice, the last two candy bars and half a bag of the chocolate covered peanuts and shoved them all inside my purse. Billy chuckled. "I paid," I said as if that explained today's picture show of stupid.

Billy waited until a shaky Miss Surelee settled to the passenger side before, he rounded my side of Rusty, pausing to inspect the paint smeared windshield. His face may have been stoic but I think I saw his baby blues twinkle once. He came to my window and rested an arm, lengthy fingers innocently draping the doorframe to linger lightly on my forearm before he asked, "Your date won't mind you taking off like this?"

What. The. Hell?

"No, he wasn't with me," I lied through my teeth, unable to stop from thinking about his fingers touching my skin. "Wish they'd stroke something else."

"I beg your pardon?" he asked, looking unfazed by the fact I just up and spoke my X-rated thoughts aloud once more.

"Uh…I mean…nothing," I said, averting my eyes, hoping he hadn't noticed the flush to my cheeks. I guess it worked, because Billy just flashed me another grin.

"You ain't from around here, are you?" said Miss Surelee, stating the obvious.

He flashed us both a pleasing smile before saying, "Chicago, originally," then with a parting nod, he headed across the street and rounded the corner.

"Shoot, that man is so steamy fine," said Miss Surelee, fanning her face. "I nearly had me a dizzy-dive."

I nodded in agreement then stiffened; Aunt Letty just popped up behind the fountain and gave me the bird. What the fuck? A second later, she was scrambling down the sidewalk and rounded the corner from view. I shook my boggled mind free of that stupid and rolled up my window then fired up Rusty and pointed us home. I would have made it there without further disturbance if it weren't for Rusty's choking. I glanced to the dash and realized I was near empty.

I swung Rusty into the two-pump gas station at the corner of Canton and Main, sidled up to an available pump, shut down Rusty and went to the panel of choices. I removed the cap, selected a handle, and gave Rusty a drink. I let my thoughts and eyes wander to no man's land after I did my best to scrape paint smears from the windshield eager to get this day tucked behind. That's when I spotted Ranger-man and his unmarked vehicle parked a block and a half southeast to the parking lot of the kiddy park, staring back. Stiffening, I suddenly got a stomach spasm and silently whispered for Rusty to hurry up with his fill. Windshield still smeared and eighty dollars' worth of guzzling regular, I was back on the road, flooring it for Dodge country, refusing to look back or stop for stragglers until I had Miss Surelee and I safely tucked away behind the older than dirt Victorian, scarfing down lasagna and lemon meringue pie, before we settled off to dreamland.

When dinnertime reared, Laney immediately asked how our 'date' went. I thought my food stained clothing said it all but I flashed her one of my stink eyes, nonetheless. Aunt Bertie and Mr. Willoughby aptly kept their heads down, eating their fill of lasagna and tossed greens. Miss Surelee hugged robe about her pajamas but kept suspiciously quiet, sighing off to the setting skies, appetite apparently slacking. Good thing too, because I got a second helping.

Half way through dinner, dumb and dumber showed up, courtesy of some other Dodge I've no business related to, to collect Tucky's truck before he and Boomer drove away.

Figures, those two idiots waited out the rest of the slasher movie before coming back for Tucky's truck. I plied Miss Surelee with a hard stare, fork pointed in emphasis saying, "Stay away from those two dummies, got it?"

Miss Surelee just nodded.

Feeling oh-for-three here, I asked Bertie for a slice of pie.

Needless-to-say, I didn't get pie but neither did Miss Surelee.

Chapter Seven: Alter Ego

Thursday came and went in the blink of an eye. I am happy to say that no one tried to sock, sucker, or set me up. Yay me!

No, not really, but a Dodge can dream.

After Wednesday's debacle at the movie theater, I tried my best to block out Thursday's existence from my grey matter (among other things) but suffice it to say, this afternoon had me seeing Red. Literally, because he just stormed the Victorian. Had Red been five minutes later (and Miss Surelee five minutes earlier), I would have missed him and my need to flee and take shelter at the Piggly Wiggly rather than duck and cover within my home away from home, sneaking back upstairs the way Bandit was acutely aware of doing.

Clutching the pages of my Aunt Gladys' gossipy *Redlight*, Red looked around and instantly zeroed in on me half way up the stairs, desperate to avoid any more of his hellfire. "What'd you all done-did ta ol' red?" he quizzed, motioning beyond the door to where Rusty was usually parked.

"Wasn't my doing," I said on a shrug. I wasn't sure if he was referring to the recent blowout, the paint smear, or the fact Rusty was gone while clearly, I was still here. He had no reason to know I loaned him out to Miss Surelee. Besides,

I thought the paint smear gave Rusty an upgrade. Red was still glaring at me so I rethought following in Bandit's wake, shifted gears, and snapped, "Don't you have a Mill to look after?"

Red waved a ham hock to the air, shook his Mack truck head once and while waving the *Redlight* my way he said, "Git it up, missy and tell-zit where Rodger-Dodger done-did run off-ta!"

Rodger, I should have known. Of course, he wasn't freeing his meat hooks of that forty-year-old riddle. But why ask me? It's not as if I'm the first in line to anything gossip-worthy. Heck, I'm not even welcomed at the Dodge convention. So, why hasn't Red consulted the slimy pages of my Aunt Gladys' tattling tabloid, clutched to his grizzly paws, or found the need to go browbeat someone else into telling him where Rodger-Dodger's run off to? Miss Surelee and I couldn't be the only ones who've seen him since Sunday. I suddenly remembered that I wasn't. Didn't Sally say something on Tuesday morning about seeing him? I narrowed my lids and felt steam percolating beneath my scalp. I resent being the only one sighted to Red's crosshairs. Even if I did know where my brother was, Red had no business threatening it out of me.

So, no, I'm not going to say, because I really didn't know.

I stared back, arms crossed, feet firmly planted and dangerously holding ground. I suppose my bravado might have had something to do with being, surrounded by the Victorian, or the fact Aunt Bertie just came up from the cellar that had me thinking I could stand up to Satan himself. I was a woman with Marty's steely jewels and wasn't about to chuck them to the wind for all the chocolate in the world. Besides, Miss Surelee just came back from whatever errand she and Rusty ran earlier this morning because she was feeling restless. I thought she looked the way I felt: spooked, but what do I know? The moment she set foot back in the Victorian however, she was back to her normal self, fascinated beyond reasonable thinking and came to my rescue.

Well...sort of.

"You got no sense of respect," she said, hands to hips, eyes all squinty, lips curled back baring a nice set of perfectly straight, not-quite-white teeth. "See here? You come in barking like a pitty, expecting an answer. No good, see what I'm saying? Disrespectful, he is."

Red stared back without understanding of what she just said or possibly, of what she was wearing. She was, dressed like *Wonder Woman*, if Wonder Woman were a five foot, two-hundred-pound white man with ebony wig.

I say they both just tied in the crazy department, but what do I care?

Not only that, but I suddenly realized Red wasn't perfectly-dressed either. He dressed the way I always knew him to look: tired, saggy, beat up, wrinkled and grease stained denims, equally wrinkled and stained white undershirt peeking from underneath a red and white checkered flannel that for some reason or other, was, buttoned askew, tanned boots scuffed with worn down heels. He looked a mess. Ever since hooking up with Barbie Bublouskie his clothes were always spotless and neatly pressed.

Oh, my lucky stars—did Barbarilla up and leave him?

"Reynold," said Bertie. Red rounded on his older sister with a look that was a cross between hellhound and buckshot crazy. She overlooked his many flaws and said, "You mind telling me what is going on here?"

Miss Surelee and I turned back to Red, expectant.

Naturally, he swung his hellfire my way saying, "That-one-thar done-did see Rodger-Dodger; that-one-thar done-did talk-it to-em; that-one-thar done-did went after Tucky—put his momma in a state!"

"Who the hell told you that load of bullshit crazy," I said, stomping down the steps but deep down, I knew he was right. Gossip rocketed faster than the speed of light around here. The crème-de-la-crème of Harley chatter went nuclear. Besides, he was still clutching the pages of the *Redlight*—dead giveaway.

Aunt Bertie turned my way. I shrugged then hugged myself, adding to it, a crooked smile before my eyes wandered about. She heaved a sigh before asking Red and I to join her in the parlor and sit down. Red and I promptly refused. My refusal had to do with one hand-me-down antique; Red's was more out of stupid pride. Aunt Bertie overlooked this and said, "What is really going on—no, dear, no more excuses or halfwit comments—just say it, dear."

Miss Surelee came to the foot of the stairs and gave me a questioning look before she nodded over her shoulder.

"No, Miss Surelee, its fine, I'll tell them," I said on a sigh and drooping shoulders, dragging bootless feet down the last of the steps before I finally explained. "I really don't know why Rodger-Dodger hasn't been to work. I don't know why he didn't say anything to anyone. No, I did not see him until yesterday—no! He was driving south on Joplin; we tried to follow, got a flat and had to abandon. Besides, he was long gone at that point."

"That ding-dang jingle," Red huffed, wisps of steam sifting away.

"Like I told Brent, I answered, but no one talked. I think it was an accidental call," I said, shrugging.

"What was Rodger doing," asked Bertie.

I shrugged once more. "I don't really know, but it wasn't his truck he was driving. It was a newer modeled, navy blue Ford, jacked up to the heavens with monster tires, just like Miss Surelee explained to Brent."

She and Red sucked air and exchanged worried glances. I've no idea why, considering what Aunt Bertie drives but I guess driving anything, less of a Dodge is sinful. Good thing I kept the Batman-riding-shotgun to myself.

"Don't sound no nutin like me boy. Nope," said Red.

I hated to agree with the devil himself, but Red was right. Rodger-Dodger's been known for many things (one of our many Dodge inherited traits and all) but sporadic, secretive behavior is not one of them. Rodger-Dodger kept his life simple and routine, a wife, two daughters and twin sons, weekly job at the Mill, Thursday poker nights with Stan and the gang and Sunday dinners at Hell Central and not to mention, he drove a Dodge make and modeled truck. Yep, his recent behavior was certainly out of character, even for my brother.

"What's this about Tucky," Bertie asked me, rather than try to un-riddle Red's dilemma.

I shrugged a second time. What's to tell? Idiot number one and his sidekick got, kicked to the curb by two kickass superwomen! No, not really, but it sounded better than the truth. I glanced to Miss Surelee but her eyes wandered south, unwilling to add to this roundup of fun. Therefore, I thought it best not to say anything either, and especially, not say anything about the Dickie sighting as well. Besides, Tucky was unfortunately born a Spigot; thought that said it all.

Speaking of the Spigots, Mr. Willoughby just returned from delivering a recently embalmed raccoon to my Great-Aunt Margret. He wandered on in about the foyer, glanced up and startled. Miss Surelee jumped back a good foot, giving his unique but pungent aroma a wide berth even though she was already ten feet away. At first, he looked like he was unsure of his surroundings, patting at his satellite dish-sized hearing aid until he spotted Aunt Bertie and then me. He sucked once at his dentures then shuffled right on up to me. With a goofy-wide grin, he handed me a four-inch nail then turned and shuffled off toward the kitchen. I stared down at it as if it was frogspawn. Then the nitrous kicked in and I realized Stan must have given it to him. I showed it to Red as if that explained everything.

Nope he wasn't having it and opened his cakehole to shout, "Gots me 'nuf trouble kickin' the wind—where in jeez-us H. Christmas is he?"

Needless-to-say, Barbarilla did not leave Red or Boolee for that matter, because she was the one who just called Red's cell phone to my relief and sensitive ears. A moment of grunts later, Red flew out of the Victorian without explanation or with any more of his useless brimstone, leaving the rest of us staring after his smoldering wake with headshakes and frowns. Taillights fading, I turned to Aunt Bertie with a stiff arm, open hand, refusing to answer any other questions she may or may not have, motioned Miss Surelee to the stairs and retreated to my room.

I deposited the nail to the top of my dresser and closed the door behind me even though Laney was still at school, the rest of the second floor vacant. I had questions for Miss Surelee that I was positive neither one of us wanted overheard. I waited for Miss Surelee to plop down on the beanbag, arms splayed before I said, "Miss Surelee, you saw my idiot ex too, didn't you?"

Miss Surelee stiffened and a squeaker of a fart escaped. Her eyes went wide, her face eerily still before she nodded once.

I heaved a sigh and sat down on my bed, facing Miss Surelee, arms perched to knees. We stared back at each other for a heartbeat before she looked away. I still had more questions but thought, given the state of these past two and a half days, they could wait. At least until this Rodger-Dodger mystery solves itself.

"What's with," I began, uncertain, foolishly waving a hand to all that is Miss Surelee. "What's with your outfit today? Aren't you cold in that?"

Miss Surelee perked up at once, all trouble aside, struggled with the beanbag and said, "It's a test drive. I was thinking of wearing it to the party! You like?"

Ah, okay... "And what party would that be?"

"Say what?" she cried, nearly capsizing sideways and onto the floor next to the door.

"Enlighten me," I asked.

"Shoot   girlfriend...and   you   calls   yourself   a representative," she said, lower lip jutting, doing her best to keep the beanbag from sliding any more south.

"Ah, nope", I said. I am the first one to claim I am not a native of Boolee and all that it inhibits. I shook my head for added emphasis.

Miss Surelee mistook my meaning and fully explained saying, "The Boolee Ball, Friday next."

Shit. She was talking about the masquerade made famous by Boolee for the scariest night of the year. I cringed; how did she find out about that? The ball was just one of the many things from my past I've purposely blocked from existence. Or, at least, I tried to until someone had to go and remind me. "Does that mean you're sticking around town after your car gets fixed?"

Miss Surelee gave off a small shrug.

"Then don't think for one minute that I'm going or anything."

Miss Surelee frowned but went on to say, "But it'll be fun!"

"You are on your own with that disaster of a roundup," I said. "And don't you dare promise me as your plus-one!"

Miss Surelee started to protest. I held up a hand to interrupt, went to my closet, struggled beyond the pileup of Miss Surelee's' overpriced luggage set and toward the back wall, rifled about some old boxes and came back with a half-inch thick book. It was my senior class yearbook. This being the only time I was glad Aunt Bertie salvaged my past before I fled Boolee and all its ghosts. I flipped through several pages until I found what I was looking for. I turned the opened book Miss Surelee's way and pointed to one of the four, black and white pictures taken around Halloween given the state of streamers, ghosts and carved up pumpkins lingering in the background. This will explain better than I care to remember.

Miss Surelee took the book from me and squinted. "Is that one of Ladybug's creation?"

I nodded.

"Is that your leg?" she asked, sounding intrigued.

I nodded a second time, this one lacking enthusiasm.

"What's that goop all over your hair and face—is that spaghetti?"

I could only heave a heavy sigh.

Five seconds later, she was snapping the book shut.

"Shoot, girlfriend," she said, head cocked to one side, one eye squinting my way. "That was ages ago. Besides, ain't no one gonna know it's you underneath a costume!"

Ah...nope, not with my shit luck.

Miss Surelee and I spent the rest of the day, squirreled away to my room, snickering at old yearbook photos, playing board games, eating toasted cheese BLT sandwiches, splitting my last overpriced, movie theater candy bar and box of chocolate-covered raisins and doing our damndest to ignore the outside world.

At four-thirty-three, it came crashing through my bedroom door.

"Miss Surelee, I got a date to the Boolee Ball!" squealed the soured fruit I sometimes call my daughter. "Oh. Hi mom."

Lovely.

Miss Surelee squealed back and gave Laney a hug. Parting, she said, "Me too!"

Oh brother... "How was volleyball practice?"

"I like the look, Miss Surelee," said Laney, going back to ignoring me. "But won't you get cold in that?"

Miss Surelee pressed a finger to pursed lips and nodded. "I was thinking the same thing. It's on loan, as it were but thought maybe I could talk your momma into trying something on before the store closes."

"Oh yes, mom, can we?" said Laney, dropping her backpack to the floor, eyes expectant, hands clasped. Uh-huh, now she's happy I'm her mom.

"No," I said, rounding the door, and heading downstairs. Naturally, those two jokers nipped at my heels so I added, "And neither are you, Daughter."

When we reached the kitchen, Laney rocked a leg, perched a hand, and modeled a pout and slitty blue eyes my way. Right, like that has ever worked on me before today. I don't care how much she resembles her father Dickie Trollop no way was I caving. I headed for Aunt Bertie's workshop leaving sourpuss and Miss delusional to huddle at the kitchen table, sulking or more appropriately: scheming.

"What's for dinner...*gizzards*," I asked my Aunt sounding like I was gearing up to go dumpster diving in the middle of a heat wave.

Aunt Bertie's face shot up from the rattler she was presently gutting. Eyebrows scrunched into a V, frown lines deepening across her freckled forehead, lids narrowing as she peered down the bridge of her nose.

"What," I stupidly said.

"You're on your own tonight, all of you," she said, planting her focus once more to that limp looking snake. "I've no time."

I startled. Did I just hear her right? I gave her a second glance but she wasn't taking the bait and kept at her vermin degutting. If it's one thing I've known my entire existence is that Aunt Bertie cooks, homemade, from scratch, always. Never has she ever said she didn't have time to cook. That's like saying I was a Trollop; a total lie. My stomach grumbled right on cue, adding to my angst. Did I mention the only cooking I know how to do is by dialing up the nearest delivery?

I turned back to the pass through between kitchen and workshop, dazed. Miss Surelee and Laney jerked their heads back at once, scrambling their ladder-back chairs in place the moment I passed the opening to the kitchen. That woke me from my coma. "What's going on?"

"Nothing," the two conspirators replied in unison.

Uh-huh.

Seeing how the only place around town that delivers food or anything for that matter, is Ordello's, I figured I'd be better off going there in person. This way I could get out of the Victorian if only long enough to stuff my pie-hole full of sauce and cheese. I gave up a sigh, pinched the bridge of my nose and said, "Looks like we're headed into town for supper."

Naturally, those two sprang from their chairs, coats in hand, beyond the front door and nestled to Rusty's interior all before I could remind them that we didn't need to leave for another half-an-hour. I thought about leaving those two jokers to figure it out, but then my rational thinking took over and I had my purse to shoulder and key to hand. I yanked on boots, shrugged into my zip up hoodie, gave a shout to Aunt Bertie that we were leaving and that I'd bring back leftovers (maybe) and headed out into the chill of the setting grey skies that is the hills in Fall. I slid on up into Rusty but something stopped my progress. Oh right, the steering wheel column. I shot Miss Surelee a frown. She giggled and glanced out the windshield. Several tries later, I managed to get the bench seat shoved back (naturally, those two remained seated on it, slowing said progress). I slid behind the wheel, fired up Rusty and we were hitting the back-county road in dusty Rusty style.

"I want McDonald's," cried Laney.

"Unt-uh, Mickey-Dee's gives me the runs. I say taco's...you gots Mexican way out this a way?"

"No and no," I said. I knew without a doubt, that Boolee didn't have the golden arches within a fifty-mile radius. Unfortunately, there was a second-rate Taco Shell somewhere about the Square in the center of town but even I had standards and wasn't about to bring up that greasy bit of information for all the cheese in the world. Hopefully, Laney would overlook this too.

"But mom—,"

No such luck.

I cranked the Rusty tunes, drowning out my daughter's whine and rounded the fork. I floored Rusty, sending him sputtering on down Main Street, catching all the green lights toward the Piggly Wiggly and turned right at Canton. I continued north beyond several mom and pop diners that looked like they served up samplings of E. Coli, beyond dilapidated government subsidized housing and turned left, headed to the only reason those two jokers got to tag along in the first place: Ordello's Pizza. I pulled into the nearly deserted and recently patched up potholed and faded blacktop parking lot, parked one spot over from handicap and shut down Rusty.

Ordello's' was a rectangle, glass enclosure, red-roofed building that looked better than most businesses sprinkled around Boolee. It was well-maintained by one of the only Italian families trapped to Boolee and operated from 10 a.m. to 10 p.m., deliveries during lunch hours but did most of their business after six and on the weekends. Since we were too early for the dinner crowd, we had first pick of parking.

Laney clapped and squealed. What teenager doesn't like pizza?

Exactly.

Miss Surelee however was frowning.

"Don't tell me...Italian gives you gas," I asked.

"No," she said, still frowning but glancing down at her barely-there attire exposed beneath a lime green, goose down sleeveless ski jacket.

Ah. I see the problem here.

"Why didn't you change?"

"I was hungry," she said, giving me a sheepish grin; Laney giggled to her hand.

"Did you leave your clothes there," I asked.

Miss Surelee gave off a small nod.

Sighing, I fired up Rusty then backed out of the lot and heard tires squawk to a stop. Oh. My bad. That was me. I nearly rear-ended a miniature Ford SUV that wouldn't have lasted five minutes if I had allowed Rusty to have his way. If I had had ESP after all, I wouldn't have locked brakes. Instantly a one finger salute popped free of the drivers' side window, tires squealing as my Aunt Letty floored it for the outskirts of town. Laney covered hand to face and slipped to floor mats. Miss Surelee frowned. I however gave a laugh, a honk of my horn and a salute of my own before we resumed this never ending, tick of a town, tour.

"Where we headed to return that," I asked, sitting at the intersection of Scranton and Pine watching a couple lazily lead their golden retriever to the other side of the crosswalk headed north along Scranton. I strummed fingers to steering wheel, expectant, impatient.

Miss Surelee perked up, fished about her purse, came up with a hand-written piece of paper, slipped glasses to the tip of her nose then said, "Barney's Alter Ego."

Well, duh. I did a mental head slap. I'd forgotten that it was the only costume shop in town, or rather, just assumed a shop around the Square offered up better and more tasteful attire, such as Almonds Clothing. I snickered to myself; Laney and Miss Surelee shooting me quizzical looks, clueless to my inside joke. Yep, it sure was fun being five...

I turned south and headed for the southwest part of town. I cruised past box shaped clapboards the size of closets, single stoop, black shingled roofs, detached garages, one vehicle to cemented drives, most vacant this time of day and found the costume shop at the corner of South Joplin and

Valentine, two blocks south, one block east of yesterday's blowout. I snickered a second time to my own private joke, ignoring Laney and Miss Surelee's curious stares. I curbside parked Rusty illegally and shut him down, frowning. This side of town used to be thriving but I guess over the years, businesses folded, people moved and now most of it sat deserted, and eerily quiet with *For Sale* signs sprouting everywhere like dandelions. There was parking around back of the Ego, across the alley to a dimly lit, cratered, cemented rectangle lot, littered with empty plastic shopping bags, hypodermic needles, candy wrappers, a bent-up and rusted shopping cart (stolen from the Wiggly) and half-taken over by bomb-proof weeds. But I wasn't about to park there. Especially since, it just started to sprinkle and I wasn't keen on getting soaked, three days in a row now. The three of us hustled on up the single sidewalk to the glass enclosure door of the two-story cinder block, flat roofed building of funk and sass and pushed on inside.

I Think Barney's Alter Ego has been around for as long as we Dodges, maybe longer, because it sure smelled like it. Oh, crap, I hope Barney isn't relation. As it turns out, we are. Not Barney, I mean. He died a decade ago. The latest owner who is a Dodge by birth, decided to keep the name. Go figure.

"Harley? Is that really you," said a squeaky voice, ten pistons short of a Dodge worthy carburetor.

"Hi there, Ginger," I replied, giving her a quick wave as I headed on up to the back counter where she stood behind a cash register. Laney and Miss Surelee curiously followed.

Ginger Dodge is my Uncle Walt and Aunt Doty's fifth child. They have seven, by the way; the youngest are a pair of fraternal twins. It used to be eight when they adopted Derby but she now resides at County Correctional Institute, all expenses paid. Growing up, most Booleeites regarded Ginger and me as sisters, rather than cousins. I couldn't see the resemblance now, so it's mindboggling how anyone thought this before. Ginger is three years older, ten pounds heavier and broader in both butt and shoulders than I (hopefully) am and sported tan eyes nearly as big around as Laney's are but wider set, giving off a bee-like look to her freckled, porcelain features. She may have married Dennis 'Bubba' Dennisy right out of high school, spawned two beanpoles that might someday, make it to the NBA and a daughter that is slower than molasses but there was no mistaking that rusty colored rat nest as a Dodge trademark, marking us as relation.

"Who's this?" she asked, with delightful curiosity and rounding her eyes on the soured gift that came from my neither-regions.

"Laney," devil-child replied with equal amounts of spunk and sass.

"Hunh, those two could pass for sisters, don't-cha think," Miss Surelee whispered my way.

Perhaps, in another lifetime...

"She's mine," I replied to Ginger on a sigh, "My *only* child."

Ginger perked up even more, asking, "Have you all met my boys, Tommy and Tyler?"

Laney just shook her head, uncertain.

"Keep a look out for them all," she continued to say. "They all're seniors this year."

Because I was feeling uncharacteristically obligated, I asked about Ginger's husband, Dennis, "How's Bubba?"

"Oh, he's great! He all just left; missed him by a tick. Headed home to set up for poker night; his turn holdin'," she said, fumbling with a box from underneath the counter. "You all wanna come by later?"

No. "Thanks all the same, but Miss Surelee needs a different look and her change of clothes back, then we're headed back to Aunt Bertie's with a super-extra-large Ordello's special."

Ginger nodded knowingly lifting a bag with Miss Surelee's previous attire, sprang from around the counter and hustled them to a picked-over rack of costumes hanging from hooks off the far wall. Laney joined them. I turned back to the counter and browsed the interloping pile of brochures left by solicitors of the usual: health insurance, life insurance, dental insurance, car insurance and one for a timeshare in Florida. The timeshare brochure looked promising.

A moment later, Ginger asked my way, "There ain't much left but is this one lookin' too?"

I tossed the brochures aside and turned back. Laney glanced my way, holding a breath, fingers crossed, expectant. With a sigh, I finally gave in and nodded. Laney squealed and shot off like a starter pistol toward the mannequins up front. I turned along the sparsely filled racks clustered about the middle of the store and absently perused. Slim pickings, I thought. Not that I'm planning-on going to that freak, showstopper next weekend, but when in hell—

"Hey babe," said Boomer, clicking his tongue, shooting my boobs a wink.

I jumped a mile, hand to heart before saying, "Go away!"

I think it worked because he strolled on over to where Ginger was lingering in front of a single stall dressing room door, arms loaded with ten varying costumes. She turned at once to Boomer's shoulder tap and gave him a frown.

"He all ain't here," she said sounding annoyed.

Welcome to the club, cousin.

Boomer leaned in and mumbled something I couldn't hear which caused Ginger's face to go rigid and draining of all color. Then as if flipping a switch, her face flooded with color, brows creased and eyes narrowed before she hissed back, "Go ahead—see if I care!"

Boomer turned to leave but Ginger suddenly stopped him, flung the armful of costumes over the dressing room door, and practically dragged Boomer by his hairy arm to her right and beyond a narrow corridor. Five minutes later, Boomer came bounding up front shaking his head, Ginger struggled with a portable television set that had seen better days. They were arguing over the portable; Ginger trying to dump it to his hands while Boomer refused out of repulsion. Ginger finally released the portable to the counter, sighed and nodded. Boomer cocked a grin, pointed a finger gun her way, clicked his tongue and turned away. Ginger smartly gave his back the middle-finger-flip in reply. Righteous.

"Goin' to the ball...wanna be my date?" idiot number two asked of me.

Hell. Fucking. NO! "You do know we're related now, don't you," I said, avoiding eye contact with Boomer, which was easy to do because he was shorter than me. I scrambled about, looking like an interested shopper.

"So," he said, following me like a lost puppy that had worms.

"Go ask your boyfriend and leave me alone."

"Tucky? Mans, gots hisself a date already," said Boomer, scratching about his body that I'm better off not knowing about.

Oh. No. She. Did not! I shot daggers toward the dressing room hopeful Miss Surelee found her strength to keep clear of that idiot cousin of mine.

"Hey, don't go gettin' your all panties in a wad, I'm free."

Not even on my deathbed.

I did my best to pretend idiot number two didn't exist but he kept inching closer until his breath was at my neck.

"Go away or stop breathing, it's your choice."

"You all on a rag or what?" he said.

That did it. I swung wide and gave him a guttural growl that'd make Bud or Hemi envious.

"Okay, jeepers. Women," he said on a headshake, before wisely stepping aside, turned on his booted heel, exited the costume shop and rounded the corner from view. That's right idiot-boy, do us all a favor and keep right on trucking all the way to the county landfill. Ugh. That was a truckload of stupid.

I went back to my mindless wandering when a second later Ginger called me back to the counter, dropping handheld to the cradle of the store telephone.

"What's up," I asked.

Ginger nervously glanced about, hands ringing before saying, "You all don't mind watchin' the place for me? I need a run an errand—won't take me but half an hour."

Hmmm, what's in it for me, I thought eyeballing, the portable. Ginger noticed and quickly inched it my way. "It's yours and... and any costume you all want! Just a half hour, please?"

I thought I wasn't the kind of person so easily bought but seeing how that teevee might have Laney admiring me in a new light, I thought it couldn't hurt. I shrugged and said, "Yeah, sure, can't be that hard, right?"

Ginger's face relaxed, a smile spread and she quickly went into a five-second rundown of cash register etiquette before she snagged her purse and coat from the back room and slipped out the back door.

I leaned back against the counter and contemplated what toppings I was going to order on that extra-large Ordello's special. Five minutes later, my chin sunk to hand while imagining how that Wonder Woman wow-zer might look on me. Ten minutes after that, I was considering that Hostess Twinkie costume in the corner up front. Another ten minutes later, the bell above the front door jingled and saved me from slitting my wrists. Frowning, I glanced up, expecting to deliver good on my earlier promise of shoving Boomer to an early grave. But wait a minute! Do my eyes deceive? It wasn't Boomer who'd just entered, not that I'm complaining here. It was Stranger-Danger man and he noticed me right away, drooling, dreamily smiling his way.

"Good evening, Boots," he said, closing the distance between us in five graceful strides.

"Uh-huh," I foolishly slurred, stirred then unfurled my curled toes, calmed my squishy stomach, and unscrambled my brain. I stood upright, at his attention to say, "What are you doing in here?" Boy that came out all wrong. It had sounded much more alluring in my head before my mouth had to go and muck it all up.

He just chuckled.

"I-I mean, are you here for a costume too?" I asked, my heart doing a pitty-pat of desire.

"You know it," he said.

Dumb, dumb, dummy, my mind screamed. Of course, he is. I rolled my eyes before I could stop them.

"You work here?" he asked.

"No! I-I mean...I brought Miss Surelee and my daughter shopping because Miss Surelee was wearing a costume and had forgotten she had left her other clothes here when we were on our way to get pizza from Ordello's because my Aunt Bertie is too busy to make dinner because of her petrified critters and I don't know how to cook and that's when my cousin Ginger needed to step out. I'm the stand in. She'll be back shortly," I said doing a mental head thunk against brick wall because I don't think Stranger-Danger needed so much information and for some reason, I couldn't get my mouth to stop talking.

"Then I'll see you at the Ball?" he asked, curiously still watching me with a charming grin.

"Uh-huh," I said before my brain caught up. Shit! Did I just accept an invite?

"Awesome," he said then set about the shop in search of something worthy with me watching his every move. Five minutes later, he thanked me and I nearly fell off the edge of the world while he grabbed his purchase of the Batman costume, complete with codpiece and utility belt and sauntered on out into the fading evening light.

Crap. Where's a cat suit when you need one?

I suddenly found myself searching for Wonder Woman, size five instead.

Okay, stop nitpicking...size *nine*...sheesh.

Hey...is that smoke I smell?

Laney and Miss Surelee were plowing toward me with worried looks, waving their bundles, shouting something I was unable to hear over the crackling of flames and smoke-alarm buzzing. Oh, my dumb, crap luck. The Alter Ego was on fire, started somewhere from the back-room office. I coughed and broke free of my confusion, quickly shoving Laney and Miss Surelee toward the front door while I went for my purse. In hindsight, I probably should have forgone a second trip back inside to rescue one portable teevee. Laney's happiness wasn't worth it. But on the other hand, Billy had miraculously appeared through the curling curtain of charcoal smoke to yank me free of that suicidal mission, just in time to see the roof cave in. I guess that might have been worth it after all.

I stood curbside of the Ego, both arms cradled a portable while my purse slipped down my shoulder and swung heavy on my shaky arm. It took all my strength not to cry, or whine or run back to Texas. My hair was, charred, my clothes smoldering, equally charred and my eyebrows singed to thin lines of unattractiveness. At least they distracted from my fading shiner. I glanced around for my spawn and misguided friend. I was relieved to see Laney and Miss Surelee nearby, hugging their bundles closer, both unscathed but shaken, nonetheless. I might have noticed an additional Twinkie-shaped costume clutched between them but I didn't dwell; I had bigger problems than the Booleeite Ball.

I inwardly sighed and stared on in disillusionment while the fire department did their thing, pushing Rusty beyond the intersection to rest at the curb at Valentine so they could hook the truck up to the only fire hydrant. Five seconds later, the right rear tire on Rusty hissed and sank to curb. I whimpered right on cue.

"You okay, Boots," asked Billy, startling me from my pity party.

"N-no," I squeaked out while two tears popped loose and slide down my cheek.

"What's wrong," he asked, taking an un-calloused thumb to gently wipe one of those tears away.

My body shuddered as if I had no reason to function. Billy's touch had my flesh melting faster than the Ego's rafters.

He was still eyeing me with concern. I eventually gave off a wimpy cry saying, "This is going to look bad on a resume."

"Are you looking for a job?" he asked to an unexpected rumble of thunder before the grey blanket above parted and the skies rained forth.

I heaved a sigh, readjusted the portable and purse beneath my hoodie before I finally said, "No. I'm auditioning for a new life."

Chapter Eight: Hit-and-Runaway

"Oooh...I don't feel real good," said Miss Surelee, hugging her stomach and rocking back and forth on the beanbag, green tinge around the edges of her jaw and cheeks.

It was half past six on a Friday night. The sky was clear of clouds, no hint of rain, sun setting beyond rooftops and highway markers, porch lights, streetlights and partygoers gearing up for action, a crisp air settling about Boolee, vigorously. Miss Surelee and I arguing over tonight's line up of double dating pleasure, due to show up in an hour, because, it'll be the first time we set foot out of the Victorian since last night's unexpected, never ending game of fun.

After yesterday's roundup of Boolee's Wannabes, EMT's and firemen and Rusty getting a second flat from yet another, construction-type nail, we decided it was best to hunker down at the old Victorian and spend most of Friday playing cards for pretzels and pennies, denying our thoughts of our dumb, shit luck. I lost ten out of ten. Thankfully, Mr. Willoughby drove us home after the Alter Ego incident and gratefully, Aunt Bertie called and had Stan deliver Rusty back to the Victorian as well, cleaned, patched, lubed, and geared for action, free of charge. You got to love family. Still, Miss Surelee and I weren't ready to leave the Victorian as we racked our brains for something to do to help pass the time quicker before our dates arrived this evening to escort us to the fairgrounds for food, games and Boolee's infamous, haunted hayride.

Now, seeing, as I am the good little Dodge that I hope to become one day, I snookered Miss Surelee into helping me clean out the refrigerator, wipe down counters, dust lampshades and furniture and sweep up floors. It was the least I could manage since Aunt Bertie's been rather distracted, not to mention, I wanted to prove to her that I could be a domesticated person when I put my mind to it. Not really. I was doing all that so I could distract my thoughts from winding their way back to all that's been going on in Boolee. I would have asked Laney to help but she was at school. This morning I had suggested she stay home from classes for different reasons other than cleaning. Aunt Bertie thought otherwise. Laney had nothing to say on the matter one way or the other which totally surprised me as I found myself checking her forehead for a rise in temperature. I was checking because I thought for sure after handing over that boxy, portable, black-and-white television last night that she would rather stay home and veg. I was sure, because I live to complicate her life and thought she'd jump at the chance to pay me back. I was mostly certain she would stay home and hide out until graduation after narrowly escaping inhaled smoke from a preplanned firebomb. I know I would have if I was her because that is exactly what Miss Surelee and I have been doing all day, today.

Miss Surelee groaned a second time. I thought her intestinal problems might have been due to that second helping of pecan pie last night that I managed to get Mr. Willoughby to detour a stop at the Wiggly on our way back from Ordello's after our unexpected luck at the Ego. Don't bring up my incompetence now. I never claimed to be a native and learned how to bake anything. Miss Surelee's groans could have easily been from that fifth slice of Ordello's specialty we ate cold from the box, hunkered down about the kitchen table this afternoon. We needed it though. Especially after, Miss Surelee, Laney and I nearly escaped the Alter Ego, toes intact. After a twenty-minute investigation, Uncle Walt discovered the source of the fire. Someone decided to lob a gasoline infused cocktail through the back window, causing it to burn to the ground. I think whoever did it was hoping we went up right along with it. Sheesh.

I gave Miss Surelee another glance and pondered: Could it be Ranger-man's appearance at the Alter Ego bonfire that has her turning green? And, the fact he only questioned her, leaving me to twist in the wind? Could it be that I tried to siphon off information from Brent and Miss Surelee but both remained tightlipped even though Ranger-man had no authority? Or, could it be the Dickie sighting at the movie theater instead? Because if that were the case, why doesn't she just say so instead of faking a stomachache. Then again, if I were in her place instead, I probably wouldn't breathe a word of it either and hibernate until my fiftieth birthday, my singed eyebrows and fading shiner the inspiration. Ranger-man's creeping about Boolee along with the dipshit sighting and Gladys' recent article, highlighting my destructive-like powers has my stomach doing summersaults as well. Not only that and aside from Rodger-Dodger missing a week of work, Ginger had gone missing as well. And of course, I was the only one, other than Boomer, Laney, or Miss Surelee to see her last.

Yeah, Brent had a field day over that one. Therefore, I told him his facial hair looked stupid.

Still, I wasn't going to ride solo or cancel tonight's festivities until I knew why. "What are you crowing on about?"

"You go on without me, Sweetness," she said, swiping at her pale and sweaty forehead.

What? Oh, unt-uh! "That's not going to happen, Miss Surelee," I said, frowning.

"Ooh...I think it's that time of the month, know what I'm saying?"

Um...

"Miss Surelee," I began, blasting her full on with a motherly expression. "I love you like a sister and all, but even I know that's not possible."

"It could happen," she muttered.

In someone else's lifetime.

I took stock of Miss Surelee's appearance: a red-red weave of braided locks, rolled to the top of her head like cat ears; beaded zebra striped scarf looped over a designer lime green shirt; pleated leopard print skirt that dropped to her cankles with sock covered feet stuffed to beach sandals that looked manly over feminine. Not only this, but Miss Surelee wasn't wearing a drop of makeup. Miss Surelee looked like she had dressed in the dark. Yikes! Okay, I wasn't looking that swank either in jeans and button down thermal beneath long-sleeved flannel but this is how I almost, always look around Boolee in the fall and winter because I am firstly, a Dodge; secondly, someone who doesn't plan to impress unless it was Billy needing the impressing. Because really, no one about this tick of a town deserved a first-class impression the way I pretentiously did back in Amarillo. Miss Surelee however, never left home without her classic, tailored, and expensive paring no matter whom she was seeing or where she was going.

"What's really going on, Miss Surelee?"

Her eyes dipped to the floor, roaming.

"Why don't you just call and cancel, then? I won't mind. Heck, I'll even dial the number". However, that wasn't what I really wanted. This double date was our chance to snoop and figure out what in the Dodge was going on around here, our escorts, unpaid and unwittingly, our bodyguards. I was positive it wouldn't rain tonight and that my date wasn't relation. Besides, the odds were looking good that Rusty wouldn't end up with another flat tire.

Miss Surelee violently shook her head no.

Okeydokey...

"Listen. You set this bizarro date up, so either you're canceling or you're riding shotgun," I said wondering why she even bothered getting to know the yokels. With her car done by this time next week, she'll have her freedom to leave and head for the big apple to begin her failure on Broadway. Broken hearts aside, she wasn't one to stay put in the hills or the swamp.

Miss Surelee continued to shake her head no.

Finished with a leftover Ordello's sub sandwich for her dinner, Laney poked her head in and asked how it was going. Miss Surelee groaned a third time, unnecessarily loud.

"Fine," I said then shuffled her puss face out of my room.

A moment later, Laney's door slammed shut followed by slapping size nines. I waited until I heard the droning sounds of a portable come to life before I closed my door and turned on Miss Surelee with a puss face special of my own.

"Look, if you don't call him back and cancel or if you bail on me..." I started, sucking air to finish my whispered threat, "...then I'm going to drive you to the pokey and make you tell Brent that you did see Dickie at the theater Wednesday afternoon."

"You wouldn't," she said clutching her cheeks.

Nice try, princess... "Oh, yes, I would," I replied with a full-on poker face. Two can play the blackmail game.

Miss Surelee glanced about and then startled. A low grumbling sound vibrated forth. Two seconds later, Miss Surelee grinned and rocked to her feet, saying, "I'm suddenly feeling better."

Uh-huh, I thought so.

Regardless, Miss Surelee refused to change her mashed-up attire or add makeup to her pallor looking face. I just shook my head and then shuttled us downstairs to begin the wait for our mystery dates.

Thirty minutes in, Bandit bounded down the stairs. A second later, Laney followed and glanced about.

"What is it now, Daughter?"

She shot Miss Surelee a worried glance then fully remembering I was her mom, puckered her lips and turned her scrunched up nose my way before saying, "There's been another fire."

No frickin' way! That's the third one this week; fourth if you factor in Junior Pensky's place Thursday last. "Who...when...where?" was all I could mutter, however.

Miss Surelee gave off another groan and started to rock.

Laney just shook her head once before saying, "East Pine and Sycamore, I think; something about an abandoned pawn shop. Same M.O.; went up about an hour ago," she said on a shudder, sounding like a Wannabe-in-training.

Shit. "Was anyone hurt?"

Laney released a huff, waving her hands up to say, "It was abandoned—hello!"

Whew, back to teenager mode.

Relieved to know that no one ended up injured or burnt to a crisp, I pressed on asking, "Hey, did they happen to say who owned that place?"

"Um...yeah...Mickey-something-or-other," she said, shot Miss Surelee a sympatric look then about-faced and headed toward the stairs, Bandit fast on her heels.

Was that Regatta Miller's husband?

Laney was half way up the stairs when I called after her saying, "You want to join us at the fairgrounds?" The only response I got was the sound of those size nines slapping wood. I guess that portable didn't make me a hero in her eyes after all. I'm only good enough to talk to when there's a firebombing reported on the seven o'clock news. I suddenly snickered. Firebomb. I couldn't help it. Three months later and that stunt I pulled on Dickie back in Amarillo, has me laughing still. No wonder Laney thinks I'm evil incarnate. Double snicker.

Miss Surelee just frowned at me.

My next thought had me going rigid: Did Derby somehow manage to escape the crazy spa? After all, she was the one who firebombed Black Beauty way back when, so I wouldn't put it past her this time, either. A moment later, gravel crunched, headlights flashed and then cut dark, shaking me free of my past worry, currently latched upon a present set of concern. I hustled up to the side window and peered out into the darkness. Doors opened then closed before our mystery dates shrouded to shadow approached the Victorian.

I opened the door in satirical greeting and welcomed them inside. My heart sank when I recognized mystery man number one, cloaked in something spicy smelling standing with his back to the yellow glow of the porch light. It was none other than Travis Jenkins. A second later, my heart beat normal because he was helping Miss Surelee into her goose down. He was closer to my age than Miss Surelee's unknown digits but closer to her in height and weight. Apparently, that wasn't one of her prerequisites for finding a date. I suppose though, she might have had second thoughts if she knew how Travis was Oscar and Karin's younger brother and second cousin to my ex-husband, Dickie Trollop. Man-o-man, where does she find these men?

My date on the other hand didn't have me seeing red, or stars or anything in between. I especially was pleased to note, he didn't bathe himself in cheap cologne or any cologne for that matter. Thank goodness, because my nose can only take in so much sneeze inducing stank.

"Sorry we're all late," said my date as he introduced himself. Charles Rayburn or Charlie Ray Watts, I think. "Gotta flat tire on the way over."

"Nothing bad, I hope," I asked remembering Rusty's twice over crap luck and then remembered something equally unlucky. "Hey, you didn't happen to see a midnight blue Ford truck drive by when the flat happened?"

"Just a lousy nail from wanna the construction sites near Sycamore, and no, I don't think so; why you all askin'?"

"No reason," I said reaching for my purse and hoodie before turning back to my date.

As far as I knew, Charlie Ray was harmless. I think we went to high school together; something about him transferring during grade school and graduated the year I skipped town, so yeah, he and I are not related. He didn't stand out then, and he didn't stand out now, at least, not in the creepy crawly affect that most of Boolee's male population did. Still, he looked somewhat familiar in a more recent kind of way. I gave him the once over, surprised I didn't spasm, dry heave or run away. A couple of months younger and nearly a foot taller than me with average looks, a medium build, and no sign of a pot belly. He still had a full head of hair, although thinning a bit on top, but no visible bald spot. He stood straight, shoulders back as if he were visiting anywhere else but Boolee. Lucky for him his face was clean-shaven as well. His eyes were hazel-brown, his hair was hazel-brown and his boots were hazel-brown. His attire of loose fitting and faded blue jeans, washed out Virginia

Tech sweatshirt, plain navy-blue scarf and brown, cowhide gloves was appropriate for tonight's haunted hayride. It also didn't scream hillbilly. He smiled at me and I noted he had all his teeth, although the bottom row a bit crooked. Huh, I'm surprised I hadn't noticed normal-man before now.

Oh crap. "You're not married, are you," I said with squinty eyes because I wasn't in the mood to enjoy tonight's festivities if that man was two-timing some unlucky woman.

"No," he said on a chuckle, helping me into my quilted, zip-up hoodie.

"Ever been," I pressed.

"Nope," he said releasing a second pleasant sounding chuckle while he held the Victorian's front door open.

Okeydokey, that was good enough for me.

I gave a quick shout out to whoever might be listening that we headed out, hiked my leather special up my shoulder and stepped beyond the front door. I waited on the porch for Charlie Ray to close the door to the Victorian (because he insisted) before he led the four of us back across the front lawn.

I gave him the twice over while I waited for Miss Surelee and Travis to climb into the back seats when I suddenly realized where I might have recognized him from: the pokey. Or, more recently, Marty's cruising partner from that unavoidable, Tuesday morning when I got, suckered into delivering petrified road kill to the treasure trap. Oh man, I think he was also the one to help break up a group of wrangled stupidity at the movie theater, Wednesday afternoon. Charlie Ray was a full fledge Wannabe, mid- or nightshift, I think. My soured thoughts roamed about a bit until they twirled in the opposite direction and I quickly perked up to my good fortune. Charlie Ray was a cop; a cop with a gun and badge; a cop that could protect me if dipshit reared his smug-ugly-mug or, possibly, he could repel certain booger picking idiots from coming within a square mile of me. Yes, finally, the angels were off potty break!

Surprise number two, Charlie Ray drove a sparkling, dent- and rust-free evergreen colored Super top Chevy truck, four doors and bucket seats all around. Things were looking up and up, I mused as he held the door for me while I hopped on up into the front passenger seat. Closing the door before he rounded the hood to slip behind the wheel, I noticed a slight aroma of cinnamon and musk about the plush cab. Nice; not overpowering, not wimpy or sugar coated either. It was manly. More importantly, it didn't make me sneeze.

I swiveled my head to see Miss Surelee and Travis buckled in and gave her a reassuring grin. She quickly averted her eyes and shrank three inches. My toothy grin dropping a notch, I turned back and buckled myself in too.

Closing his door, Charlie Ray asked, "Everythang okay?"

"Um," I cautiously began. "You're not packing, are you?"

"Nope," he said on a chuckle, "I'm off-duty."

A moment later, Chevy purring and we were on the road, headed toward the west end of town, listening to a sleep-inducing ballad, by some hillbilly country wannabe. Charlie Ray drove the same route that Miss Surelee and I had the unfortunate pleasure of escaping not more than twenty-four hours ago. The cab went eerily quiet as she and

I sucked breath, wistful to drive by the pile of ash, incident free.

No such luck. Charlie Ray couldn't resist making small talk. "Heard that was something, all right," he said, continuing a block west; Miss Surelee and I shuddered but we were breathing normal again. "Is that where you all got that shiner?"

"Uh, no," I said flatly, hoping my singed eyebrows went overlooked before I perked up; if I couldn't wrangle information out of my two favorite gossips' then third best might do. "What department are you in?"

"Crimes," he said.

"Hey, do you know if my cousin, Derby is still vacationing at the loony bin up north?"

Charlie Ray took a second to ponder my use of the English language before saying, "Yup."

"Oh, okay...so then did you happen to hear something around the pokey about who might be setting all these fires?"

Charlie Ray turned onto Joplin and headed south to the outskirts of town, fully avoiding the smoldering lot of fire number four. "Nope, 'tective is keepin' a tight lid on that one."

Sucky, my luck wasn't back in full swing after all. Not yet, anyways.

Tonight's' festivities, running an encore tomorrow and Sunday as well, is curtsey of Jerry Smucker's recently renovated stripper club, the Pink Squirrel. No doubt, you're thinking the fairgrounds, decked out with pasties and G-strings, dildo's all around with magical booths at the ready. I know—it's what I was thinking. Sorry to disappoint. The strip club only sponsored the refreshments and a couple of the gaming booths, fully clothed, not an inch of skin exposed, nothing shady or sexist going on. Good thing too, as there were families present, otherwise, some of those heavily made up faces might be, rushed over to County right now with hyperthermia or giving a private lap dance causing the strip club owner, Jerry Smucker to end up on the wrong side of a lawsuit. On the upside, he'd get to spend more time with his incarcerated brother, Terry.

They did pass out flyers at the gate entrance, however.

I noted that Charlie Ray smartly declined. Naturally, Travis stuffed one to his coat pocket.

My heart sped up to a delightful strum, warming my bones. I sniffed the air as the four of us bumped, bounced, and weaved our way through the shoulder-to-shoulder crowds about the dirt packed grounds. This is what I live and breathe for—food! Freshly grease-fried aromas of corndogs, candy bars, elephant ears, onion rings, sausages, curly fries, pizza, buttered popcorn and so much more had me turning this way and that like a hound dog delirious with several scents to choose from at once. It was intoxicating! Oh, the choices! What do I order? What do I want to gnaw on first? I settled on a deep-fried sausage on a stick and elephant ear for the warm-up. I was certain there'd be plenty time to make my way through the other fifty-plus samplings of fair-going food before the night ended.

Miss Surelee huddled to my side, clutching a basket of curly fries, eyes roaming all about as if we were cruising Stan's junkyard. Sheesh, that girl is skittish. Whom am I kidding?

Even though I have food to distract me, so was I. I couldn't help it. We were so jumpy to every shout, squeal or laugh of the crowded fairway that we looked like we were expecting something or someone to jump out at us at every turn of the cheaply erected wooden booths. We even shuddered our way past the sporadically placed oil drums, alit with a contained fire to keep partiers safely warmed. We looked ridiculous.

Charlie Ray paused at one of the booths and turned to me, eyes questioning in a playful-distracting sort of way.

"Yeah sure," I said, digging about my purse.

Charlie Ray waved me off and said, "I've got it."

I blew out a sigh of relief, hoping he didn't notice. It was a good thing he offered to pay because my secret stash was dwindling fast. Oh, my lucky day—finally, a man worth getting to know better, when I noticed him slip a wad of twenties from his pants pocket. Wannabe's in this town weren't known for their weekly paychecks.

"Um, that's not from something...*illegal*, is it?"

"Heck no," he said, chuckling. "Otherwise, Pine wouldn't a been keen on losin' it all."

"Losing, as in, gambling," I asked, swallowing a dry lump.

"Gamblin' ain't legal," he said, taking our tickets, and shuffling us forward. "But Thursday night poker is."

Swell. I guess that's okay, if Boolee's only Detective thinks it is. I nodded but didn't say anything more when he handed me the Beebe rifle. I watched as he proceeded to instruct me on how to cock it, sight, and shoot. I didn't bother stopping him or correcting him because I was having too much fun. I thought about asking Charlie Ray if he ever visited the stripper club—you know, recreationally of course—thought better of it and his sudden windfall. I didn't need to throw a wrench into the timing and screw it all up by opening my cake hole in protest. Yep. Better to keep quiet on the finer points of how, poker playing for money IS gambling speech or laden him with a lecture about my opinion of women stripping for the pleasure of beer-bellied men.

Unfortunately, Miss Surelee wasn't as lucky as I noticed her pocketing her change after paying for her and Travis' tickets for a chance to win a stuffed whatever.

"You all got me daunted," said Charlie Ray after our round of gaming, not sounding impressed, handing over a stuffed purple monkey. "But keep it up and I might think you all don't need me."

Huh? Oh right, him being a Wannabe and all. I beat him three games to one. I suppose being on the force and having firsthand knowledge of my ancestry, never mind that dipshit debacle back in July/August but he would already know I know how to shoot. Mind you, I detest killing or anything related to guns and Dodges. But it was after all, something taught since I was old enough to stand upright like a rite of passage. Still, I can't believe Charlie Ray expected me to lose to him! Sheesh, Machoism is (unfortunately) alive and well.

"Well, well, well...," came a voice of my second-hand past. I cringed and noticed Charlie Ray stiffened, "...look-e what we all have here."

"Hello *Brentwood*," I said, giving him a look that suggested I might be better off running into Red and Barbarilla at their funhouse of flames, instead.

My ex-boyfriend, Brent naturally chuckled, causing the sleeping baby bundle strapped to his chest like a backpack to gently rock up and down. I noticed the wreck about his chin recently shaved, caterpillars trimmed back to earthworms. I bit back a snicker as I gave him back a smugly grin of my own instead. I turned to his wife Sally and waved. She was clutching at two very wiggly and very curious boys, playfully slapping at helium-filled balloons, bow tied to a belt loop at the back of their pants and now eye balling the monkey. She nodded back with a quick "hello" of her own. I guess waving was out of the question. I guess waving might set loose on unsuspecting fair goers one set of wiggly and curious boys.

Brent took in the sight of Miss Surelee's date. Travis was now looking rather lost or perhaps, looking for the exit. Brent wasted no snark on those two, appropriately saving it all up for me.

"Watts," he said.

"Pine," Charlie Ray replied.

They were two grunts away from induction into the Dodge inherited hall of flames.

I smacked palm to forehead before I could stop it. Brent grinned on.

"Cheese and crackers, can't a girl enjoy one night out," I said my snap worse than Hemi's is. I'm just saying, give that girl a bone and she'll have it gnawed down to a nub in less than five minutes flat.

"Nice monkey," Brent said instead.

My response? I slipped the monkey to his youngest son. Charlie Ray furrowed his brows; I overlooked it. The boy squealed and hugged it tight while the older boy looked back at me expectantly. I shrugged, saying, "Sorry kiddo, you'll have to share."

Miss Surelee perked up and had herself a peek at the sleeping, ball of fuzz. "Oh, isn't she just precious!"

Sally, Brent, and I shushed her at once. I don't really know why considering the noise surrounding us, but I guess it was more instinctive than not.

"I'm just saying," Miss Surelee muttered then quickly averted her eyes.

Brent shot a questioning look Sally's way; she nodded once before she ushered their two boys in the direction of a cotton candy machine. He turned back to me with a nod to his left, "Got a second?"

Um... "Yeah, sure," I said, giving Charlie Ray a palms-up before I followed Brent between two gaming booths. I glanced back to where Charlie Ray lingered beside a skittish Miss Surelee and a rather bored looking Travis. Charlie Ray tightly crossed arms and kept his gaze trained on me through the passing, compacted fair goers. I turned back to Brent at once.

"What's got you constipated this time, Dicktective?"

"Harley lis'en," he began, cautiously, searching for the right words, hand cradling Jasmine's back in a protective, gentle way before saying, "I think you all should watch yourself with that one."

I stared back unblinking. Brent was suddenly protective of me?

"Who, Charlie Ray," I asked.

"Uh yep," he replied.

"Still ticked for losing money to him," I said, hands to hips, eyes narrowed.

Brent's face when through a flickering of emotions before settling on a stoic expression. He quickly ignored my jab to say instead, "There's a reason he all ain't settled down yet."

"Oh geez-louise, that's the last thing I want," I cried toward the heavens then added for his benefit without my mind filtering my mouth, "Otherwise I would have stayed with you!"

Brent flashed me a look that was a cross between anger and hurt feelings. I think. Shit. "Oh geez...(fuck)...Brent, I'm sorry...I, I didn't mean it that way."

"No, I get it. You all did me and Sal a favor, is the way I'm seein' it," he quickly said, glancing down at his daughter, still sound asleep, avoiding eye contact with me and my scrunched-up face.

I quickly recovered and lowered my voice to ask, "So, this Charlie Ray, he's not into anything shady or illegal, is he?" Considering my previous luck in that department, I had to ask.

"Ope, nope, good guy, better cop," he said, reverting to his Wannabe voice. "I 'spose all that Navy trainin' came in handy. Anyhoo...mans' missin' the husband gene; sucks at relations but other than that, notta thang wrong with that-thar-in."

"Thanks for the heads up," I said, my voice neither spiteful nor thankful. "Was that it?"

"Nope," he said, taking a deep breath, eyes roaming the fairgrounds before he finally got around to saying, "Sal wanted me to jog your memory 'bout you all invited this Tuesday for dinner. Wanted it to be Wednesday but figurin' you all'd be at the Wake and I gotta lot a paper work to sift through. It's my Sal's way of thankin' you all—for the flat tire. So, Dodge, you all gonna make it?"

Oh geeze...I purposely forgot about the flat tire not to mention, the Spigot reunion. Thanks for the reminder, *Brentwood*...

I flashed him a look that suggested he had to be kidding. Brent started to sweat, wormy mustache nervously twitching, eyes roaming about. If I didn't know any better, I'd say Sally wore the pants in that family. Surprisingly, he wore it well. However, now it looked to me like Brent had better get me to say yes or he might find himself surfing their seventies-styled sofa, permanently. I considered that scenario. Brutal, I know. I can't help it! I'm destined to do the unthinkable. Unfortunately, it was short-lived. Despite my incarcerated reunion and return to Boolee three months ago, I knew that I somehow, I couldn't make him sweat out his uncomfortableness much longer. Call me a sucker-bumper Dodge, but Brent didn't deserve more of my insubordinate behavior. It wasn't his fault I up and left him, and Boolee.

I snuck a last peek at Jasmine and haplessly shrugged my agreement. "Anything else you need me applying pressure to?"

"No," he said on a heavy output of breath as he civilly weaved us through the crowd and back to the others. He turned to my group and said, "Enjoy your all's eve'nin."

Charlie Ray gave him a stiff nod but it went overlooked because Brent had already turned back and joined his wife and sons; Travis blew out a sigh; Miss Surelee shuddered.

"So then," said Charlie Ray, taking me by the arm to say, "Everyone up for the hayride?"

A collective round of head nods, two corn dogs, cotton candy and a hot chocolate later, we were standing in line to the ticket booth.

"Can we go back to Ladybugs' when the ride is over?" asked Miss Surelee on a shuddering whisper, picking at my leftover cotton candy.

"Yeah, sure," I said, unconvincingly because I was still dreaming about those chili-cheese-fries we past two booths past. It was then, when I spotted idiot number two headed our way and thoughts of food and leaving evaporated from my present attention.

Charlie Ray noticed my cringe and asked, "You all know that loser?"

"Unfortunately," I replied, stuffing corndog to my mouth.

Charlie Ray quickly stepped between me and idiot number two. Boomer glanced up and being the idiot that he is, ignored Charlie Ray and angled his head around him to say to me, "Still lookin' for a date, babe?"

"Go away, Boomer," I said rather aggressively, corn dog waving.

Charlie Ray grasped Boomer by the upper arm and strong-armed him toward the pizza cart. I heard Charlie Ray warn idiot number two to stay clear of me or he'd have him arrested. Idiot number two stupidly shrugged at Charlie Ray, shot me a wink then headed off in the opposite direction, unaffected. I stiffened. Aunt Letty just darted from between two booths and shot me a double-handed, waving and rolling, flip of the birds before she ran off in the direction as Boomer did. My mouth fell open; corndog crumbles, tumbled loose. I think that when she was flipping me off, she was grinning. I can't be sure. Her face had been doing something that I wish I could now un-see.

"Damn idiot...no good at cards, worse with women," said Charlie Ray approaching our group, oblivious to my Aunt's sporadic bird-flipping. He shook his head once as if to shake the Boomer encounter away before saying, "You all ready to do this?"

I just shrugged. Guess idiot number two wasn't his immediate problem. It wasn't mine either because I think I just spotted dipshit slinking between shadows near the opposite end of the fairway, headed in the direction of the Gaffadee's stabled horses. Nope. Unt-uh, not this time, I thought and quickly turned away, stuffing the last of corndog to mouth, doing my best impression of someone deep in denial. If I don't acknowledge it, then it never happened, right?

Tickets in hand, Charlie Ray and I boarded the roofless, wooden wagon, stacked with bundles of hay like seat backs and hunkered in for the slowest ride around the makeshift horse track this side of boredom. I mean, don't get me wrong. It was nice having a somewhat decent looking, better than average smelling, legal job-holding man sitting next to me, keeping the chilly air off my neck. On the other hand, I wasn't looking for anything beyond one date and

Charlie Ray didn't have my libido doing back flips. Charlie Ray seemed nice, but a little bit too comfortable seeing how he just put his arm around my shoulders, protectively, or possessively. I can't be certain which.

"What," I asked fully forgetting that he just asked me a question.

He chuckled once before repeating, "You all have a date to the Ball next Friday," Charlie Ray asked, his eyes expectant.

Um...

I was about to answer when my teeth mashed together and I bit my tongue, instantly tasting metallic flood my mouth. The sudden jolt to the wagon came out of nowhere. A strangled cry wrenched its way free of my scrunched-up face. Then before I could check how much blood splattered, the wagon jolted a second and a third time, jolting be back and forth as the wagon rocked then bounced before it slowly tipped sideways. Our driver shot down from his perch of the rider lawn mower and ran off. Coward, I wanted to scream. Then Charlie Ray sprang to action by grabbing the side of the wagon before he easily leapt over it, leaving me to save my own ass. Some of the other couples jumped out just as effectively as Charlie Ray had done, clearly concerned with their own safety as well while others just stared wildly about, screaming, or shouting for help as Miss Surelee was presently doing before, she too, abandoned me. Travis had since high-tailed it for the exit.

Before the final tip, I caught movement in my peripherals. I couldn't believe it! It was my brother Rodger-Dodger along with his costumed sidekick and he just rammed our wagon with that mysterious, monster-looking Ford for the fourth and final time. I was doing my best to stand up and foolishly go after Rodger-Dodger when a flame shot from the roof of Gaffadee's stables, engulfing it within minutes. Horses whinnied; several escaped. People went running and screaming in all directions; alarms rang out; sirens wailed in the distance. It wasn't until I was, flung sideways did, I get my chance to go after a retreating brother of mine.

Okay, maybe not.

I think I must have hit my head because when I came too, I was once more staring into the clearest and sexiest eyes I'd ever known. My mind went fuzzy, my stomach bottomed out and I thought of nothing else. Not even chocolate.

A moment later Billy was helping me slowly stand up, handing me back my thrown purse and a second white, cotton hanky. I think I heard him say something as I patted at my nose, but it sounded tinny and far off. I turned slightly and saw Charlie Ray, eyes narrowed, brows furrowed as he stomped closer, hooked my arm to his, said something to Billy and shuttled us clear of the masses next to Miss Surelee huddled about a drum barrel, flapping arms to keep warm. I looked Miss Surelee over. Dang it! I want to know how she skirts the same kind of danger I find myself in but comes out looking unscathed! I was, covered head-to-toe in something squishy and the gag-inducing smell was beginning to reach my nose which coincidently, was bleeding a second time.

"What's that smell," Charlie Ray asked his voice raised an octave, concern over me misplaced. I think it sounded high-pitched. I couldn't be a hundred percent certain because, everything sounded high pitched no part in thanks to that constant ringing going on in my ears.

"Yes, I'm fine! Billy helped," I shouted back, shooting a glance over my shoulder but disappointingly, he was gone.

"Oh. *Him*," said Charlie Ray, jaw muscle twitching as he scrunched eyebrows once more when he noticed the hanky. "What's this?"

"What, you don't like him," I asked sounding appalled because the ringing was subsiding and I thought the hanky needed no explanation.

"Pine favors him," replied Charlie Ray, glancing over his shoulder before he picked at the hanky to better adjust it to my bloodied nose.

"He does," I asked, my curiosity ratcheting up two notches.

"Yeah, well, s'pose that was before he all joined us for poker night," he said.

"He plays poker with Pine and the gang?"

"It's not like he all's from around here," he said.

Neither are you, I thought but kept my mouth shut instead.

"Where all'd you all get this?" he switched his curiosity back to the hanky as he fingered that oddly shaped embroidered icon.

I just scrunched shoulders to ears. No point in reminding him further of a man he wasn't keen of remembering.

"This belongs to a SEAL," he flatly said blasting me full on with a death stare.

"Okay," I said because I had no idea what Charlie Ray was trying to say to me.

Moving on, Charlie Ray quickly said, "Looks like your friend is ready to call it a night. You all thinkin' the same?"

No goodbye kiss later, Charlie Ray dropped Miss Surelee and I off at the Victorian looking pissed off as he sped away.

Chapter Nine: Track-Ap Crazy

Apparently, I had overslept again. I could care less, it was Saturday and nothing exciting ever happened on a Saturday. Besides, after last nights' firebombing of Gaffadee's stables, the Dickie sighting, my constant near misses with Rodger-Dodger, Charlie Ray's sudden downslide in demeanor with Travis's sneaky departure and nearly a week of Miss Surelee's snoring I only had more questions on top of a Dodge pile of unanswered problems that I deserved extra sleep. I'm not even going to mention smug-mugs' untimely appearances. As sure as pinecones, if I get up, Red will corner me for another round of 'let's get Harley all fired up'. Besides, I was, still bruised and a bit sore over the hayride from hell. So, no thanks, I'm not getting up. I rolled over and tried going back to sleep.

Unfortunately, the Victorian had other plans for me.

I sat up to shouts going back and forth between Miss Surelee and Aunt Bertie, something burnt, making its way heavenward; what-in-the-world that is ...

Groaning, I flung covers, shrugged into my terry cloth robe then charged the stairs. Rounding the bend to my left, I stopped short of the kitchen entry, wincing, because I just stubbed my big toe on baseboard. After the throbbing subsided, I coughed as I waved at the cloudy room before hugging my robe closer on a shiver. I noticed the three casement windows were wide open, helping to clear out some of the smoke. My heart did a wild thump in my chest fearful the Victorian might have been the arsonists' latest victim.

Then I noticed the mindboggling mess and knew differently.

I took stock of the dismantled kitchen and of whom who might have dismantled it. The farmhouse table was, covered with flour and mixer bowls, sides dripping a sticky batter; every square inch of Aunt Bertie's laminate countertop were haphazardly awash in bread slices, butter, bacon grease, jam, peanut butter, a variety of berries, spent egg shells, splattered milk, chopped ham, cheese shavings, mushrooms, sliced peppers, wadded up paper towels and more flour. I noticed Miss Surelee still clad in an old pair of Uncle Walt's pajamas, now sprinkled and splotched with flour and pancake batter was wigless; her thinning and graying hair receding from the forehead back was a shocking site to behold. She looked naked without her usually colorful and stylish wigs and I never noticed how small her head really is wigless. What was even worse was Aunt Bertie still sporting nightgown, housecoat, and slippers and neither one of them looked especially calm. I glanced to the wall clock but the time only added to my confusion. It was half past ten in the morning.

My nose scrunched up in protest. My eyes followed the smell, over to the opposite wall. All four burners on the stovetop were pan covered, smoldering or sizzling. I quickly made my way over to the stove and snapped off all four gas burners. I'm surprised Aunt Bertie hadn't done this sooner.

Then I turned to those two jokers with a squint and sourly voice and cried, "What's going on in here."

Aunt Bertie and Miss Surelee turned on me at once, happy to snip and snarl their version of events. Laney was, perched to the far end of the table, Bandit cradled to lap, both, licking peanut butter from a spoon, taking it all in like an eager spectator. I shook my head, held up both hands, waited for the shouts to subside before I pointed to Miss Surelee and said, "Explain."

"I'd be happy to Sweetness," she said, waving a spatula. "I thought it might be a nice surprise if I helped out around here. Besides, my insides can't take another round of that pie, so I says to myself, I'll make everyone brunch."

I didn't know Miss Surelee could cook.

Laney giggled. Aunt Bertie folded her arms across chest and harrumphed. Priceless, if only she knew how eerily similar, she looks like Red when he finds himself all fired up. It runs in the family no doubt, case in point as I found myself casually unfolding mine.

Miss Surelee continued with bottom lip jutting. "Then Ladybug came in, hovering my skills and told me I was doing it wrong. I was going just fine until you butted in you know. Now it's ruined; had to dump a dozen of those chickadees."

"Tragic waste," Bertie muttered, eyes narrowed, laser locked on Miss Surelee.

Naturally, Laney chose that very moment to bring up a round of applause.

We all rounded on her with stink eyes.

She smartly stopped clapping and sucked peanut butter. Bandit smartly took off for parts unknown.

I turned to Aunt Bertie saying, "Let it go, I'll clean it up when I get back." Then I turned to both Miss Surelee and Laney and said, "Get dressed, we're going to the store."

Laney clapped and squealed then shot off to her room. A second later she doubled back, dropped the spoon she was licking a moment earlier to the sink and took off for her room once more. I gave a finger curl for Miss Surelee to follow.

"I just wanted to help," said Miss Surelee frowning, shoulders drooping.

"I know," I said, motioning us once more, toward the stairs.

Miss Surelee sighed, set the spatula down, gave my Aunt Bertie a small repentance look saying, "Sorry Ladybug, I'm not used to cooking on cast iron with flame."

Aunt Bertie nodded stiffly, acknowledging her apology and my mere presence.

Miss Surelee finally gave in, nodding as she followed me back to my room.

An hour later, showered and changed, we huddled to Rusty and headed toward the Piggly Wiggly. Naturally, Laney had Bandit hooked up to leash and dragged him, mewling and hissing along.

Despite this morning's abrupt awakening, the day was looking good. For once, the sky was free of clouds blanketing the horizon. The canvas a clear color that reminded me of Billy's baby blues. I gave in to a mental sigh with a side of drool. Although the air still crisp, trees nearly striped of leaves and looking spindly against the bright blue canvas,

I was smiling. Today I was determined to sputter along, incident free, despite my rude and smoldering awakening.

The parking lot of the Piggly Wiggly was bursting to full by the time we arrived. Five minutes of me cruising Rusty throughout the lot, I finally spotted a vacancy at the far end. Sheesh. We would have been better off parking at the Square. Laney and Miss Surelee frowned. I suppose dressing up in heels might have had something to do with their puckering. I bet you it was the passing comments Booleeites gave to Laney for dragging an unwilling cat by leash that might have had them frowning. I however, had no problem hoofing it to the automatic doors in my low-rider boots, Piggly Wiggly himself, smiling down from his perch over the doors like Agnus the 93-year-old greeter.

Once inside, Laney grabbed a cart, clipped Bandit to the kiddie seat and tottered straight toward what she thought would be the chocolate isle. I snickered but didn't rain on her parade. Management moved those goodies to the other side of the store a month ago. Oh well, she'll eventually figure it out.

I headed to my left. Miss Surelee brought up the rear in all her made-up style. She was wearing a jumpsuit, go-go boots with stacked heel and one overly teased out 24-karat golden colored afro. Several shoppers passed by with jealous stares and belittling comments. Some of those comments might have had something to do with my smelly escape from last night at the fairgrounds. Mostly I think it had to do with Miss Surelee's colorful attire. Who says you can't wear white after Labor Day? Yep, that's right haters, she's with me! Miss Surelee simply, strutted past without a blink or snip or bothered to turn their way. Man-o-man, that girl has Marty's jewels on lockdown.

Twenty minutes later, puss face found Miss Surelee and me sampling several cocktail weenies with special sauce and with no intention of buying. We unloaded the essentials of peanut butter cookies, chocolate chip cookies, chocolate ho-ho's, coconut zingers, three bags of chips, five bags each of Halloween bite sized candy bars and one box of chocolate iced, blueberry toaster tarts. Laney stared on, frowning. See? I told you she'd figure it out. Now for the replacements to Aunt Bertie's depleted refrigerator as we made our rounds past bread, dairy and pork products, amply stopping at every cheese, cracker, cookie, and ice-cream sampling stations. Last on the mental list was produce.

Up until now, Laney had been chatting away, sounding like a mosquito that just wouldn't take the hint and buzz somebody else's ear. Bandit smartly took a snoozer. Then we rounded the bananas and she clammed up, suddenly remembering she had to use the restroom. I turned and spotted the reason at once. Ah, I see. The stock boy who was adding to the overflow of pumpkins and squash must be Laney's glorified ride to and from school, Leroy Watkins. So being the momma that she wishes she didn't have, I grabbed my daughter by the arm with a wicked grin and pushed the cart closer. Laney looked terrified and tried to hide when she realized she wasn't getting out of this interesting turn of events.

"Hello, Misses Dodge," he said, startled, his voice even squeakier than Laney's is most days and cracking around the edges.

I nodded back. Why bother correcting him on the 'Misses' part when the boy was just being polite? Exactly.

"You all doin' okay?" the boy, finding his courage asked Laney as he stabbed at the bridge of his wire-rimmed eyeglasses.

Laney averted her eyes, cheeks blooming crimson over the sight of Leroy Watkins while she gave off a small nod.

I reveled in this exchange. I bet you my boots that Laney has a crush on him.

I gave the sixteen-year-old boy the once over. He was taller than me but gangly as if he were all bones and nothing else. He had teeth the size and shape of chicklets, freckles, and pimples all around. Even his hair screamed Richie Cunningham, appropriately dressed as if having been born in the fifties. I kid you not, this kid looked like Howdy Doody got his wish and came to life. All I can say is that I'm glad he's not relation and that he's lucky Laney is almost fifteen.

"Isn't he the cutest," Miss Surelee whispered to Laney causing them to break out into a fit of smothered giggles. Then they started slapping hands, trying to stop. Those two were useless.

I turned back to Leroy, his face flushed at the cheeks, eyes wide so I pumped up his uneasiness by gunning the Dodge, asking, "So Leroy, I take it you are taking my daughter to the Ball then?"

"Mom!" cried Laney, eyes bulging, cheeks puffed fuller than a chickmunk is during nut season.

Priceless.

Leroy swallowed hard; his Adams apple bobbing like a cork, eyes darting nervously about the store before he finally said, "Uh...yes ma'am."

Miss Surelee ripped open a rice crispy treat before I had time to recall us adding the box to the cart and stared on. I shook off that thought saying, "Take a breather Leroy," and fought back a grin. "I'm not here to chew you out." Leroy hissed a pent-up breath but the flushing got suddenly worse. I glanced around to see what might be causing it when I remembered it was, I causing his discomfort. I snickered inwardly and did a mental fist-pump.

"I have a question," I started to say to the background of Laney's muttering. "As a teenster, I suppose you might hear things, am I right?"

Leroy just nodded, eyes still wide, face still tomato red, searching for a way out.

"Good. So maybe you might have heard about the new construction going on around town, any thoughts?"

"MOM," Laney cried a second time, this one lacking all shock or embarrassment.

Miss Surelee ripped open a miniature chocolate bar and took a bite.

Leroy stared back, non-blinking.

Okeydokey, time for a different tactic...

"You're hip to today's latest technology, am I right?"

Leroy slowly nodded yes, looking to Laney for help.

I snapped my fingers to bring his attention back to me saying, "Suppose I get this text from someone, only I don't know who that someone is. And suppose I tried calling it back, only it went to some stupid robot machine instead.

Is there a way I could maybe find out without that person knowing?"

Leroy blinked once, nodded once, face going back to freckled normal as he reached around to his back pocket. He pulled out a smart phone that probably cost more than Miss Surelee's wigs and shoes combined and tapped at a few screens. A moment later, he was showing me something that was foreign to me.

"It's called an app, mom," said Laney sounding impatient.

"Right, but what does it do," I asked.

Laney crossed arms and rolled her eyes, embarrassment fully forgotten. Miss Surelee fished around the bag of Halloween candy, selected a chocolate covered wafer bar and ripped it open. Bandit meowed, curious as well.

Leroy glanced down to his phone as if he too was confused before he said, "It tracks summin's phone."

Hold the double espresso! "It can?"

"Uh-huh," he replied, rubbing the back of his neck, shooting nervous-looking eyes toward Laney. "It'll tell you all who all it belongs."

Oh, my lucky stars. "Where do I go to buy it," I asked, eager to learn more.

Laney and Leroy exchanged knowing glances before both broke into a round of laughter.

That was harsh.

"Just tell me!"

Leroy nodded to Laney who then grabbed at my purse and had my phone extracted, tapped, swiped, selected, installed and operational then returned to my purse before I could keep Miss Surelee from inhaling a toaster tart.

"All set up," she said smugly, giving Bandit a scratch behind his ears.

"Okay," I said, snagging the other toaster tart from Miss Surelee's grip and took a bite. "...well, Leroy, it was nice seeing you again," I mumbled between chews of blueberry jam and glazed frosting, motioning for my tagalongs to tag along toward the checkout counters, produce aptly forgotten.

Good thing Miss Surelee was feeling guilty for this morning's cooking debacle because she paid.

We exited the Piggly Wiggly when I caught a plains-clothes dressed Pine and company in my peripherals. I muttered something incoherent under my breath and quickly handed the key to Rusty over to Miss Surelee, shooing them toward the back of the lot. Miss Surelee caught sight of Brent and had her and Laney off with the cart and Bandit before Brent could catch me by the arm saying, "You all got sumpin you all wanna tell me, Dodge?"

Well good morning to you too. "Uh, nope, I don't think so, why," I said, hoping to sound oblivious, shooting a nervous look over to Sally.

He didn't buy it. "Harley," he hissed through some teeth grinding.

"I already agreed to dinner," I said, free arm flying upwards. Sheesh, he's lucky I'm keeping tight-lipped about poker night.

"Three others done-did saw Rodger-Dodger last night," he barked instead.

"Oh goodie, you found him," I said, looking for the sight of Rusty.

"Not so fast," he said, but he released my arm before he heaved a sigh. After a swipe of a hand down his ragged looking face he said, "You know sumpin, don't ya?"

Maybe. "Nope, I'm just as confused by his disappearing act as everyone else," I said then shot him squinty eyes saying, "Do you know something I should?"

Brent turned to his brood, nodding them to go on in to the Piggly Wiggly. "I'll catch up." He waited until Sally had the tethered boys and Jasmine's stroller behind the automatic doors before, he turned back to me to say, "As you all probably guessed, the Ranger is here on a tip."

I sucked air over that little ditty, "Dickie?"

"That'd be my guess, but Pinky wouldn't elaborate," he said, face and mustache frowning.

"Pinky," I questioned, brows raised, desperately trying to fight back a bark of laughter.

"Let it be, Dodge," said Brent before he lowered his voice saying, "All I can say is that he thinks it's somehow connected to all those ding-dang fires springin' up."

"Wha," I mouthed back, feeling my scalp prickle with sweat while my heart skipped a beat. Dammit, I bet anything that those fires might have something to do with a no-good, lousy, ratfink, dipshit of a man. I just have no idea why. Brent nodded as he overlooked my inner hysteria then asked me to keep it under my boots for now, further instructing me to call him without hesitation over the next Rodger-Dodger sighting.

"Is he missing on purpose or is he missing for some other reason I should know about," I asked.

Brent just gave me a, palms up saying, "Your guess is as good as mine."

No, it wasn't.

"Any word on Ginger," I asked.

Brent deadpanned, giving up nothing new there either.

"You'd let me know if you knew something, right?"

"Dodge," he said, his face sagging from the weight of trying to think. "I've got Smarty on it for now."

"Good," I said, feeling somewhat better about my missing-in-action, relation and started to turn back toward Rusty.

"Oh, and Charlie Ray's pretty pissed. What'd you all do to him?"

"What makes you think I did something," I huffed, hands to hips.

Brent flashed me a glimpse of Hell. Oh yeah. I forgot about landing in horse dung last night, the smelly truck ride home.

Dang it! He wasn't going to have the last insult—"Hey, did you tell Sally how much money you lost to him during poker night," I said with a snippy grin, my date with Charlie Ray forgotten.

Brent just shook his head saying, "Watch it, Dodge," then turned heel and headed inside the Wiggly to rejoin his growing family brood.

I take it that he hadn't.

Naturally, Miss Surelee and Laney had their faces pressed to Rusty's windows when I approached. Once they spotted me through the fogged glass, they turned back facing forward at once. But once I closed my driver side door, they turned back to me expectant for an explanation, licking cheese doodle sprinklings from their fingertips. Bandit coughed up a fur ball that smelled suspiciously pea-nuttery. I flashed Laney a mom frown. Naturally, it went overlooked as I eased Rusty back toward the Victorian.

Food safely tucked away, I divvied up chores; Miss Surelee wiping down stove, countertops, cabinet doors and table while I washed and Laney dried dishes after which, she vehemently protested as I scooted her out the door in Rusty's direction with a bucket and sponge. It was her cat's fault for why she was now cleaning up feline vomit; it was her fault for having fed him peanut butter in the first place.

Chores finished, I made up cold cut sandwiches, spruced up with mayo, cheese and hamburger dills, added a side of chips and chocolate chip cookies then poured chocolate milks all around. Bandits' bowl got white milk instead. This time, Miss Surelee devoured her food without a frown. Mr. Willoughby joined us half way through so I made him up an olive loaf with mustard and cheddar special. He thanked me by way of handing over another galvanized nail, which I took back to my room, Miss Surelee in my wake, appropriately flopping to the beanbag looking sedate. Yep, cold cuts have a way of doing that to me too.

I dropped the nail to my dresser, adding to my growing collection just as Laney appeared at my doorway, cradling Bandit.

"Who's been texting you mom?" she asked, leaning over to wedge my old Texas license plate free from behind my dresser. It was the one that formally came attached to my Bentley, Black Beauty; the one that was, firebombed three months ago. She stared at it for a heartbeat then dropped it to the top of the dresser without a second thought.

Hunh, I wondered where that had run off to... "I don't know. That's why I asked Leroy all those questions. I want to find out."

She flashed me a frown and hugged Bandit closer.

"What's wrong," I asked, my radar flicking up several notches. It wasn't like Laney to grace me without sarcastic wit.

"Nothing," she quietly said and headed back to her room, portable roaring to life, door closing with a single click, no hint of size nines slapping wood.

"Did I miss the eighth grade or is there something bothering her," I asked Miss Surelee. She just shrugged, not looking overly concerned. Then Miss Surelee gave off a powerful yawn, rocked free of the beanbag, crossed the room to settle upon the old army cot and closed her eyes.

I wasn't as tired as Miss Surelee clearly was and Laney was acting out of character. I don't think it was that time of month for her. Then again, she never needed a reason to sling snark my way. But suddenly, today, she found the need to act like the child I've always wanted. So, I went to Laney's room and knocked. I had a right to find out what in the green ackers of the hills was going on. If nothing else, I needed her help.

A moment later, she cautiously let me in, and I joined her at her bed. Laney wasn't in the mood to talk and I had no way of broaching the subject of her unusual moodiness—or lack thereof so the two of us stared off in the direction of the portable, perched to the ledge beneath the row of casement windows. Bandit fidgeted but found his snuggle spot on my lap.

Tuned to one of three channels the portable struggled to receive, we watched the snowy, black-and-white screen as the news droned on about the fairgrounds fire, the majority of Gaffadee's thoroughbreds rounded up and finding temporary boarding in Kentucky, mention of me landing in horse manure (hey, it wasn't my fault!) and several fairgoers getting flat tires after running over nails.

I suddenly had a thought, perked up, nudged Bandit to the bed and jogged back to my room. I fished my cell phone from my purse and headed back to Laney. I immediately asked her to show me how to use the track-app. She was suddenly back to her usual sour-puss-faced self, smugly showing me the ropes. Thirty minutes later, I think I finally got the hang of it, using my number as an example first, Miss Surelee's, second. Next up, was mystery texter number G.

"Well that can't be right, can it?" I frowned, holding my phone so Laney could see it was pinging right here, in the middle of Boolee, West Virginia.

"Whose number is that," she asked, interest piqued.

"I don't know," I said on a sigh. "The track-app wouldn't say".

"Try someone else's," she suggested.

So naturally, I punched in Red's number but it only showed him wandering about the Mill. I snickered. His job was his life. Then I punched in Laney's number but it wouldn't show up on planet earth. "What's up with that?"

Laney glanced at my cell then giggled. "Oh, I forgot to tell you, if a number doesn't show up, it's because they aren't broadcasting their location."

I frowned. That wouldn't do me any good if a certain slimy smug-mug was texting me from a disposable cell phone. I switched gears and after trying Brent, Barbarilla and Gladys's cell phone numbers, I was, hopelessly hooked on this tracking application. I thought about whom else I could spy on so I punched in Rodger-Dodger's number.

"Are you sure I'm doing it right," I asked rather flustered. Laney nodded. Rodger-Dodger's phone was pinging somewhere east of Blue-Veil, Kentucky. I only knew of one family that grew up around Blue-Veil and they were (definitely) not from Boolee.

But their grandson is.

I totally forgot about why I was in Laney's room, hoping to have a bonding moment, figuring out why she was previously sullen as I quickly sprang to action, waking a confused and blubbering Miss Surelee from her midday nap saying, "I think I might know what's been going on around here, want to ride shotgun?" Miss Surelee said no. I suckered her into it, none-the-less, her moaning and looking one shade short of death itself. Don't criticize; I asked Laney to tag along but she had her sights set on keeping feet firmly planted to the confines of the Victorian, without me, embarrassing the hell out of her.

No love loss there...

Twenty minutes later, Miss Surelee and I were driving west, southwest in search of Boolee's Cedar Park Trailer Community, rounding on lot number thirteen. I put Rusty in park behind a beat-up Dodge that still looked better than Rusty ever will and headed for the wooden, three-foot-by-three-foot sized, front stoop on the opposite side. We rounded the front of the faded, pumpkin colored trailer with brown trim, appropriately decked out with cheap store samplings for the Halloween season of tombstones, skeletons on sticks, witches on brooms, blood covered, boney, hands pushing dirt, cobwebbed covered windows crawling with glittery and glow-in-the-dark spiders, white sheets swinging on the breeze, fake blood splattered everywhere. At least, I hope it was fake blood.

The front door yanked open with a creak before we hit the first step. Andrea Rosenbaum greeted Miss Surelee and me with arms crossed, leg thrust forward and a mile-wide frown. Sheesh, so much for being a Dodge. Miss Surelee startled and inched back. I held my ground and took a step up. I was a Dodge after all. Lucky for Andrea though (me included), her mother, Reeva, poked her head around her daughter's shoulder with a Booleeite welcoming smile and arthritic wave, welcoming us to her home, or I might have accidentally said something I might enjoy. If her welcoming was traditional however, Andrea's frown would have paled in comparison to a shotgun's double-barreled steel. Seeing how Reeva is the dispatcher over at the lock-U-up getaway, I guess she didn't need to threaten family or visitors alike with a front row show of buckshot and steel. I guess being friends with Brent gave me a leg up in this tin can community.

The chilly air stayed at the door; the interior a hotbox and within seconds, Miss Surelee and I were shedding our jackets. Two more steps inside their mobile tin can and the aroma of dirty ashtray assaulted our delicate senses at once. Being ever the professionals, we inched our way over to the plastic, slip-covered sofa, nonetheless, breathing only when necessary. I guess it doesn't matter if you leave your husband or he ups and leaves you; the woman always ends up with the crap end of the separation. Reeva's downshift in living arrangements was a point to that testament. Just look at mine if you need more convincing.

Reeva hustled up the three steps to the adjoining kitchen, rummaging through the refrigerator for nibbles while Andrea poured us both a strong cup of coffee. Not one to turn down a cup of caffeine, I took a sip, biting back a wince. It was lacking a cup of sugar and a bottle of French vanilla cream. It was super, duper bitter.

"Well ain't this all a friendly bewilder," said Reeva, setting a plate of smelly cheese, sliced liverwurst and stale looking crackers on the dinged up wooden coffee table to our knees. Neither one of us reached out. "Don't get many callers these days," she continued to say, easing down upon a worn-down recliner, and lighting up an ultra-light, super long, sucking nicotine deep to her lungs before asking, "What can we all do ya for?"

She got straight to the point. I was glad because I wasn't in the mood to dawdle. "Well, actually, I was hoping your daughter could help us out," I said, giving Andrea a friendly smile. Andrea shot Miss Surelee daggers instead. Therefore, I leaned forward, setting my coffee mug to the table, and asked, "How close are you and Penny?"

Andrea shifted daggers my way but eventually said, "Like this," and she held up two fingers crossed to indicate just how close.

I took a deep breath, steeling myself for my next question. "Has Tucky ever been late on child support before now?"

Andrea's face went rigid and flushed fifty shades of something resembling hell. She shook her head once before saying, "That-no-good-rotten-son-of-a-bitch, cuzin' a yours! You all know he knocked up Racine, right?"

Uh...nope, I had no idea.

Reeva rocked back in her rusted-out, squeaky recliner puffing away, apparently amused.

"That little turd outta be stayin' in, not gamblin' or," she paused, sighting Miss Surelee to her icy-eyed stare before concluding with, "taken ho's out durin' daylight."

Miss Surelee stiffened but refused to do anything further to rise to Andrea's bait. Reeva let out a bark of laughter that quickly turned into a nasty fit of coughing that coincidentally, could rival Bandit's hacking balls of fuzz and gunk.

I quickly caused a diversion by asking, "Speaking of family, you guys haven't seen Rodger-Dodger around lately, have you?"

Andrea and Reeva went ridged, exchanging curious looks that gave up nothing either one of them were willing to divulge. Andrea turned back to me with another frown, shaking her head no while Reeva simply said, "Heard 'round the station he all'd been missin' a spell".

Okeydokey...

"Yep—back to Penny...was this Tucky's first late payment or has there been others," I pressed.

"No," she spat then muttered, "Lousy good for nutin turd."

"Uh-huh, say, you wouldn't happen to know why he's been late, would you...I mean, he must do all right with his landscaping business, don't you think?"

Andrea flashed me a stink eye. Oh, right. The day at the movies, I had inadvertently spoiled her and Penny's bit of fun to find that out for themselves.

I suddenly found my reason to leave this tin can and stood to leave. Miss Surelee quickly followed me to the door, jackets almost zipped to our chins when Andrea just had to go and say one more stupid thing. "Next time I see that one loiterin' I'm gonna pound it, got it?"

Nope, Miss Surelee didn't get it or take it. It surprised the hell out of me because I wanted to be the one putting Andrea in her place. But instead, in a blur, Miss Surelee hauled back an open hand then let it rip. It struck Andrea across the face like a feather. Stunned for all but two seconds. Me too. Andrea let out a roaring laugh. I quickly shuffled Miss Surelee back to the safety of Rusty, disappointed. One of these days, I'm going to teach Miss Surelee the art of cat-fighting.

I floored it out of the trailer park, not bothering to slow down for the twenty speed bumps along the way and narrowly missed sideswiping a kid on a moped. Turns out it was Boomer and I should have floored it dead ahead, pun intended.

"What'd we find out visiting that one?" asked Miss Surelee, finding her resolve, crossing arms, jutting lip, eyes narrowed and locked on her side mirror.

"Not much other than Andrea really hates Tucky. I can't say as I blame her though. All women do. Understand this now, Miss Surelee?"

She nodded slowly and said, "Yes."

"Oh, please don't tell me he's your date to the ball on Friday!"

"No," she said, disappointment ringing loud.

"Good, because he's not accepting of your lifestyle, Miss Surelee, you'll only get hurt."

Miss Surelee absently nodded before asking, "Where we off to next?"

Next up was Bubba Dennisy.

Twenty minutes later, and no closer to the mystery, because he had no idea where Ginger ran off to (and acted suspiciously unconcerned), I pulled into a vacant parking lot across from the corner of Scranton and Pine. I was thinking that Tucky connected to all that's been going on but now I had less answers than when I started out. Now what?

Miss Surelee sucked air and smacked hands to eyes. This time she didn't yell out, "monster" but I knew that's what she had seen, because I just saw Rodger-Dodger swerve to his right and around the corner of Scranton. Not one to let the competition get the drop on me, I put Rusty in drive, mashed boot to petal and hooked a left. I followed, nearly getting sideswiped by a fuming and hand-singling, Letty Dodge, peeling rubber the opposite direction. No time to reminisce about stupid, I ignored my relation and cried,

"Get my cell out—Miss Surelee—uncover your eyes and punch in Rodger-Dodger's number on that new app that Laney gave me—hurry quick—do it now!"

I was determined not to get too close and kept a block between us. This time, Rodger-Dodger wasn't swerving all about or driving ten miles over the speed limit, and traffic was especially light, only two other cars travelling this neighborhood, opposite direction. The monster Ford hooked a right, temporarily from view. It looked like he headed toward the abandoned strip malls closer to Joplin and Summit.

I urged Miss Surelee to give me an update. After fishing her eyeglasses from her purse, it took her several tries and five minutes more before she had Rodger-Dodger's number tapped in and pinging. "Says here he's idling at Blue-Veil Kentucky," she said, oblivious.

"Are you sure," I asked unconvinced.

"I think I know how to work these fancy-to-do gizmos," she said, lip jutting.

"What—no—that's not right," I cried as I noticed now that the monster Ford had vanished. "Try it again!"

Miss Surelee did and gave me the same answer once more. Crap. I idled at the intersection of Summit and squinted to my right. Not trusting the app, or Miss Surelee's skills, I made the decision and turned right regardless. Three blocks north I spotted that beast of a Ford, slowing, brake lights lighting up before it angled right and into the abandoned strip mall. Dang, it was the same place where Rusty got his first flat tire. I let off the gas, checked my mirror but traffic was nonexistent behind so I braked and eased Rusty alongside the curb, idling a block and a half south of that strip mall.

"What are we doing," asked Miss Surelee.

I reached over and yanked my phone from her hands. I cleared the last search, punched in Rodger-Dodger's phone number, and waited. Thirty seconds later, it pinged. Dang it! Miss Surelee was right. Rodger-Dodger's phone was showing up in Blue-Veil Kentucky. That can't be right!

"Uh-huh," she said.

"But that's him," I cried to no one, pointing ahead, beyond windshield, totally convinced I was right and Laney and Leroy's latest technology was W-R-O-N-G! "Blue-Veil isn't Boolee!"

I'm stumped. I'm staring out the windshield at this truck that Rodger-Dodger has been, seen, driving all around town, but not his phone. Apparently, it wasn't on him or perhaps, someone else has it. I suddenly had a thought and punched in mystery texter G. It pinged two seconds later just two and a half blocks north of my location. Craptacular, I'm beginning to see the greater picture here...

"What are we waiting for, Sweetness," Miss Surelee asked, sitting to the edge of her seat, slapping hands to the dash. The glove box sprang open at once, only this time, she ignored it.

"I'm waiting to see what he's doing, where he might go. I don't think he's spotted me, so it should be easy to do now that I know which number I'm tracking."

Miss Surelee was restless (or felt I was insane) for she plucked the phone from my hands, eager to prove me wrong. It was just our crappy luck that a fireball exploded dead center of those abandoned buildings at that exact moment, startling us both. A second later, the monster Ford peeled rubber and flew across the intersection, headed west and beyond view. Miss Surelee squealed, my phone flying, smacking the windshield, case breaking apart, innards free-falling.

"Pick it up," I cried not knowing which motor skills I should have, activated first. I wanted to race after my brother; I wanted to scoop up my phone; I wanted to flee Boolee and all said relation. I settled on multitasking, doing my best to fumble for the other two pieces while I tried hopping a U-turn to catch a different cross street west toward Joplin.

Unfortunately, we never made it. I suppose I should have had my head above the dash when I made that illegal turn in the middle of the street. Otherwise, I might have avoided getting T-boned by one of Boolee's flunkies. Neither one of us had spotted the other until it was too late.

I inched nose above dash and spotted the crumpled hood and cracked windshield of the blue and grey crossover. I foolishly grinned. A cue ball face sported a surprised look. Miss Surelee noticed him right away and gave him a goofy-faced smile with a finger wave. It was Marty Smarty and he sure looked confused. Moments later he regrouped and had the mangled crossover backed to the curb, Rusty sitting opposite without a scratch on him while I dazedly watch as a stream of fire trucks, SUV's, EMT's and one unmarked vehicle roll to a stop a block from that blaze of glory. I have to say, that I should have known this might happen. Miss Surelee's burnt toast was the premonition and I should have heeded that omen by going back to bed.

Two hours later, sun nearly set and fire now under control and soon extinguished, Miss Surelee and I were free to leave when I noticed Billy's SUV parked among the rest of the Wannabes. I glanced around and located him hovering Brent's right shoulder. I frowned. Miss Surelee was, lost to her own thoughts as was I and hadn't noticed nor responded to my angst. What is Billy doing here? I shook that side note free because my worry centered elsewhere. Why is Rodger-Dodger driving someone else's truck and why does his cell phone say he's in Kentucky? Worse of all, is Rodger-Dodger the fire bomber? I still think there's a connection between Rodger-Dodger and Tucky but I had no solid reason as to why.

"Where to next, Sweetness," Miss Surelee asked, oblivious.

"Home," I said, my voice crackling low, thoughts swimming in a thousand-and-one directions, eyes watching and wondering, all excitement fleeting like a popped balloon. "Stick a fork in me...I'm done."

Chapter Ten: Snooping on the Unsuspected

Sunday morning, Aunt Bertie and Mr. Willoughby were off to early service at the local Patriarch, Protestant/ Catholic Church while Laney went along with the Whitley girls and the Halvsies for youth group. Miss Surelee and I appropriately slept in, hogging the quiet of the Victorian all to our sleepy, overwrought selves while Bandit sneakily slinked about. At half past eleven, Miss Surelee and I stirred. I changed into jeans with flannel covered t-shirt while she wore something less conspicuous. We headed downstairs. I was the first to notice the note. Miss Surelee, the first to notice the snake, tipped to one side. I think I know what Bandit's been up to this morning.

"Your Ladybug sure got talent," said Miss Surelee on a low whistle, fingering its glistening scales, setting it upright. "She's like Martha Stewart meets the crypt keeper, you see what I'm saying?"

"Crap," I said, setting down the note. I thought Mr. Willoughby just delivered them a raccoon? I glanced to the wall clock over windows just as Miss Surelee asked what was wrong. "Another delivery, seeing how everyone else is conveniently gone, looks like we'll be doing the drop off."

"What, the snake," she asked, suddenly concerned, suddenly protective of the petrified reptile.

I nodded saying, "Family delivery."

"Are you sure about this, Sweetness?"

I nodded a second time.

A moment later, she sighed then said, "I can dig it, might be kind of fun!"

Uh-huh. Not.

At fifteen minutes to noon, travel mugs loaded with coffee we hustled to Rusty with Miss Surelee protectively hugging the snake to her lap while I pointed us toward the northwest end of town. I got goose bumps the closer I got to Joplin. Not because it was ten degrees colder than yesterday or that we headed in the direction of the interstate or out of town but because we turned north, one block shy of Joplin onto Crescent Street where only one family subsided near Boolee's Northerly outer limits. Crescent Street wasn't really a neighborhood, or anything resembling a sprawling real estate haven. It is actually no man's land, but that phrase pretty much sums up all the stupid that is Boolee so I'll just go with this: Crescent is the edge of nothing that leads to nothing except wooded mountain views of even less. And if you find yourself lost and headed nowhere fast in this deplorable direction then you should have heeded the 'DEAD-END', the 'NO TRESPASSING', 'NO HUNTING', 'PRIVATE PROPERTY' and 'EVERYONE will be SHOT ON SIGHT' with 'NO EXCEPTIONS' signs that you passed at every snaking turn several miles back. And just in case you missed those warnings, the skull and cross bones, double barrels for eyes, should have you hooking a U-turn, pronto—as in, yesterday!

Okay. That pretty much sums up Boolee as well.

Naturally, I wasn't, lost or heeded warnings and drove on up to the end of the pockmarked and weedy drive. Am I a daredevil or what?

Miss Surelee sat quietly taking it all in.

I shivered; goose bumps to the ready. I wasn't looking forward to this delivery.

Hundred-year-old Spruce, Sugar Maple, and Oak trees looking like kindling with a sprinkling of skyscraper Pine densely packed either side of Crescent Street, stretched beyond rolling hills and blended with the graying horizon. It was an allergy and asthma sufferers' worst nightmare even though most of the maple and oak leaves have since shriveled of color and fallen and lay in decaying clumps about the shaded, weedy, and muddied ground. The wind had picked up but most of the squat Spruce kept it at bay. Dead center of all that sat a lopsided redwood barn that was long since converted to housing. I think at one point, a long, long time ago, it once was, used as a Moonshiner's hidey-hole. Glad to see nothing's changed. It looked eerily vacant; no Halloween decorations clustered the stooping porch or splayed out across the untamed, mangled, trampled, yet muddied patch of lawn. Still, I knew someone lived there because that sloping shack housed family. I did an involuntary shudder. This wasn't a family visit I'd make consciously, though, and even if it was, I wouldn't be happy about it. I'd rather be making a trip to the gates of hell instead, because this house belongs to my Great Uncle Leo and Great Aunt Margret; the worst of the lot of us Dodges, because Leo is the black sheep of the family (yep, more so than me), because Leo married Margret. Margret isn't from West Virginia. Margret was a

Spigot from Kentucky. People around here didn't like people from Kentucky, which is why we never visit Kentucky and they stay clear of Boolee like avoiding the plague. Dodges around here didn't like the Spigots and vice versa. Their feud has been around since the beginning of time. I think it had something to do with a pig and a foot and someone's Dodge-sized ego. That might explain why their daughter Letty has been going out of her way to flash me a flip of the bird. Don't ask me, I'm just glad I'm not a Spigot even though most days, I wish I wasn't a Dodge.

You can see why I've got the duck bumps now, can't you?

I thought about having Miss Surelee pitch the snake out Rusty's window, onto the front walkway as we drove the turnaround but my conscience won out and I side parked Rusty on the half loop. I could have parked in the rutted out and mud packed driveway but decided that was a risk not worth taking. Besides, I think I spotted Tucky's trailer full of landscaping machinery unhitched from his truck and parked, taking up most of the dilapidated drive around the back end as an obvious deterrent. A newer mini Ford SUV backed it all in, protectively. I got a sudden spasm in my left eye. Miss Surelee hadn't noticed. I was right. This wasn't a delivery I ever wished to encounter.

All out of excuses and delay tactics, we exited Rusty and carefully made our way up the wobbly stepping stone walkway, avoiding crushed soda cans, broken beer bottles, a spattering of rusted screws and bent nails, patches of sunken ruts as we sidestepped spent condoms, a sock or two and waded-up toilet paper that was suspiciously tainted brown.

Ah, nothing says decorating the property for repelling trick-or-treaters like the way they have.

We made it two-thirds of the way up the walk when the front door creaked opened and a face like death itself glared out. Miss Surelee startled, nearly dropping the snake. I was a bit surprised too. I wasn't expecting anyone home. I was hoping to leave the snake statue on the front stoop. No such luck as the face began to pinch into a wrinkled frown. The face belonged to my Great Aunt Margret and she looked a wreck. I think that's how she always looked, though; short, squat, probably fifty pounds heavier than Miss Surelee weighed, squinty bloodshot eyes, ruddy cheeks on skin like the walking dead, silver hair chopped short, graying mustache left unchecked, appropriately dressed in moo-moo with matching slippers. I thought Great Aunt Margret would be at service or on her way home from church or with both feet in the grave. I guess she didn't feel like Sunday prayer or dying was the way to go this morning as she sneered or smiled at us from behind a haze of smoldering menthol, glued to her wrinkled lips, a shadow hugging her right shoulder that (not surprisingly), flipped me the bird. I couldn't be certain what Margret's face was doing but I did my Dodge duty by keeping my hands at my sides, smiling, and foolishly nodding back, nonetheless.

"Whadda you all want?" Margret finally croaked our way through bouts of coughing, voice husky, appropriately perturbed at having her morning ritual of sucking nicotine interrupted, even by relation, but especially by *this* Dodge relation.

"Got a delivery for Leo," I said through shaky lips, motioning to Miss Surelee, who in turn, shot Margret a look, a look to me then back to Margret, hugging the snake closer. Unbelievable, I think Miss Surelee grew attached to the stuffed copperhead.

Margret glanced to her right before saying with a hint of determination, "Leo ain't here," sucking tar without the use of fingers before she opened the door an inch wider and setting her sights on Miss Surelee.

Miss Surelee gave a squeak, nearly flinging lose that copperhead and our reason to visit their place this side of Hell.

I found my courage as I glanced back and noticed Great Aunt Margret's frown. I turned back to Miss Surelee, curious. Ah, I see. I think Miss Surelee's Princess Leia wig might have something to do with Margret's gawking. Call me Dodge crazy but I think her staring might really have had something to do with the spandex fuchsia pink ski pants and purple UGG boots that screamed look away, instead. Either way, I didn't care; I was, used to Miss Surelee's creative attire. What I wasn't accustomed to was, the funky gasoline and urine smell drifting forth from Margret's condemned looking home and it took all my doing to keep from pinching my nose with thumb and forefinger or from passing out.

I sucked a lungful of air instead and shouted, voice raised an octave, "That's fine, just doing a drop off!" I stepped closer but Miss Surelee refused to move. "Ah, Miss Surelee," I questioned.

Miss Surelee startled and looked away from the door before she finally handed me the copperhead. She must have smelt something too, for she just sucked air and began creeping back the way we just came. In turn, I rushed forward and handed the snake over to my Great Aunt Margret when I noticed the shadow had shifted left, morphed into a much younger yet equally worn-down version of Margret. It was my Aunt Letty, and she just flipped me two more birds. Ah. Now I see. I had intruded on a family reunion of sorts. So be it.

Our business concluded I quickly said, "Enjoy," and hustled Miss Surelee and I back to Rusty. We had our doors closed and locked, me breathing normal when we heard Margret's front door slam tight. I shuddered once, grateful that this side trip was over with, started up Rusty and pointed us back down the way we came, vowing never to make this trip again.

After a moment of awkward silence, I finally asked, "Did you smell something funky coming from her house?" Because trust me, that smell made Rusty's pungent aroma seem delicately tolerable by comparison.

She shook her head no, saying instead, "You're related to her?"

"Both unfortunately," I said, sounding like I was regretting the knowledge.

Miss Surelee gave me a squint before adding, "Not all that welcoming, is she."

"Nope," I said, pleased.

"She looked familiar, but that other one..." she said, voice trailing, unable to finish her thoughts.

Probably seen her around town, I thought. "We're only related because she married Leo like a hundred years ago. By the way, she's Tucky's Grandma and that other one, his momma."

Miss Surelee absently nodded, fully ignoring my jibe when a moment later, she said, "She ever do a layover in Texas?"

"Not that I know of, why," I asked.

"Must have been the trick of the light then..."

...or, the flip of the burning menthol...

Twenty minutes later and idling at Crescent and Summit, our useless errand forgotten, we both had a jolt to our tickers as we stared straight ahead. No trick of the light here. We both just spotted the mystery Ford and it headed straight for us. I don't think they noticed us so, thinking fast, I yanked the wheel to my right before Miss Surelee could smack hands to face and headed north up Summit one block then jerked it left and looped back around but I was too late. The Ford hadn't followed as I first thought and was now long gone. Nor were we able to speed around and catch him at whatever game he was playing because Rusty got a third flat.

"Un-freaking-believable," I cried to the Angels on potty break.

Five minutes later, they came to my rescue...sort of.

Big red flew around the corner, squealed past me then squelched to a stop, hooked a U-turn and parallel parked me opposite the street. The devil himself shot me a startled frown from the driver's side window. I feel the same way, Red. I overlooked our relation and clutched at the steering wheel, hoping to overlook our connection; hoping he overlooked my existance. No such luck. Red exited his truck then stomped around to the back of Rusty as I watched him in the rearview mirror, wondering what he was doing in this part of town. Red shook his head once and came to my window, saying, "You all ain't got no spare."

No kidding. "Third blowout this week," I muttered then I whipped out my cell phone. I was going to have to call Stan to come and tow me.

"Would you look at that," said Miss Surelee awestruck, pointing to the passenger side of the windshield.

As sure-as-hell is here, another fireball exploded and shot toward the heavens, several blocks south. Moments later, alarms rang out, sirens followed and Wannabes appeared around corners and beyond intersections headed right for the latest arson this week.

Red abandoned my moment of distress and slid behind the wheel of his big boy truck before I caught myself thinking my next dreaded thought. I was halfway out of Rusty to ask him for help when the angels really did come to my rescue. Miss Surelee's face flushed and she giggled. I might have flushed a little bit too, but I had the grown ass decency to keep the giggles on hold. At least until Red was beyond earshot.

Billy parked at the cross street, jogged on over, gave Red a nod and turned to me. Red shot off like the hellfire he is and I didn't watch or care. Billy flashed us a smile and I instantly melted. "Truck trouble?"

"You could say," I said, sighing, inconspicuously swiping at drool. "I was just about to call Stan for a tow. I got another flat tire."

Billy glanced at Rusty's tires and noticed the slight tilt to the driver's side. He nodded once. "Need a lift?"

Naturally, Miss Surelee said "Yes!" with a capital HELL YES! I however, knew I needed to wait for Stan before I could go anywhere truck friendly and explained this to him. Then I regrettably watched as he jogged back across the street, hopped behind the wheel of his black Chevy SUV, and headed south. I resettled myself behind the wheel of Rusty and dialed up Stan. Miss Surelee turned her frown my way.

Thirty minutes later, Stan had us hooked up and headed back toward his garage. Another thirty minutes later, he had me all set up with yet another new tire but this time, threw in an additional spare. Now I had two settled to Rusty's bed. He also reassured Miss Surelee that her car parts were due to arrive tonight and that her car would be, finished by two, tomorrow afternoon. I was about to pull out of the garage and head for the exit when Stanley stopped me. "Thaw'd you all wanna know, summin's trackin' you all."

I stared stupidly back at the pen he was holding. "Huh?"

Stan clicked the pen once and a pin spot of amber light flashed at the tip. He clicked it a second time and the light went out. "Founded wedged to ya glove box, droppin' papers."

What. The. Fuck? "Someone was tracking my movements," I cried.

Stan nodded yes.

Miss Surelee and I exchanged worried looks. I only knew of one person that had authorization to do this to me.

"Fuck," I said. It wasn't a question. It wasn't a gleeful cheer either. It was a flat-out statement of pure angst. This might seem like payback for my track-aping yesterday but this, I thought, was different. Someone purposely set out to know my whereabouts while I was driving Rusty. I suddenly realized the significance of that freakishly tall Ranger-man's fascination with Boolee, with me, or rather, my way to the highway of catching smug-mug himself. I thanked Stan, told Miss Surelee to click the pen back on and put it back in the glove box as I peeled rubber toward town, aimed right for the pokey. I nosed parked to curb, asked Miss Surelee to grab the pen and we marched up the cemented steps that housed Boolee's flunkies.

I rounded on Joe-Bob Connelly at once, nearly causing him to flat line. Good.

"Ain't nobody here," he cried, hands in the air as if I held him at gunpoint. "I swear it!"

"That's fine, we can wait," I said, refusing to move.

Miss Surelee gave him a finger wave and Connelly nearly passed out.

"I ain't kiddin', Harley, ain't nobody 'round!" he cried, mopping pudgy and shaky hand to his sallow, sunken face.

I glanced over his shoulder and noticed the graveyard of Wannabe's were MIA. Not one deterred from my hell-bent mission, I nodded Miss Surelee over to the bolted down plastic seating and settled us in for the long haul. Either Detective Pine would eventually leave to go home, or else he would be on his way back from whatever errand he was running. This spot gave us the perfect view leading in and out of the pokey, unless he took the back exit, that is.

Five minutes later, I watched as Connelly hung up his phone.

"Who'd you call," I shouted his way.

Connelly blew out a sigh but eventually said, "'tective's on his way."

Sweet!

Ten minutes later, Brent blew past the front doors and rounded on us, balled fists to his belt that looked more like an inner tube about his expanding waistline. "Christ Harley, what is it this time?"

I sprang to my feet and matched his stance by leaning in, saying, "I'm not pleased that someone is watching my every move!"

Detective Pine's face slackened, hands fell to his sides. "What?" he said.

"Exactly," I said, motioning for Miss Surelee to produce the spy pen. "See? Stan found it to my glove box. Any ideas why Ranger-man wants to track my whereabouts?"

Brent took the pen from Miss Surelee and gave it a good, long and puzzling once over before handing it back to her. "Sorry Dodge, but that ain't Pinky's," he said.

"Oh, no you don't," I said, following him to the locked door. "He's the only one authorized to do that to me!"

"Lis'en up, Dodge, real good now, 'cause I'm only gonna say this once," he fastened a hard stare my way before he concluded. "It ain't Pinky's doin' or I would a known about it, got it?"

I swallowed a dry lump suddenly looking for the exit. If Ranger-man didn't spy me, then only one other person ran through my thoughts like poison. Brent must have sensed which way my thinking headed because his eyes just went wide like saucers. We stared at each other for a heartbeat. Then Brent asked for the pen back and told us to go on home, nothing to do, don't worry, he'd figure this all out. "I gots me enough to worrah 'bout after that dang fire on Pike, so go on home, Dodge and let me do my job."

"Pike—but that's a...that's a neighborhood," I said, ignoring his suggestion.

"Yep," he said, "Skeeter's place."

I startled; does he mean Larry and Ronita's home? They lived over a coin-operated laundry. Or, they did...oh geez... "Are they," I said swallowing a lump, "Okay?"

"Yep, they all were visiting Shelly at the time," he said opening the door to the hallway. "Go on home Dodge, I mean it."

I suddenly had a different thought and hoped Brent hadn't noticed. I nodded my thanks toward Brent and shuttled Miss Surelee and I free of the Pokey and stuffed ourselves to Rusty's protective custody.

"We headed back to Ladybug's?" asked Miss Surelee.

"No. I'm going to see my Uncle Walt," I said.

"We got another delivery I should be knowing about?"

"No," I said, hooking a left toward Cutter Drive between Trout and Spruce at the southwest part of town. "He's not just my uncle; he's Boolee's fire marshal."

"Ah," she said, but sounded confused because she asked instead, "And why's that important?"

"Lots of fires are being purposely set around here. Don't you think that's strange?"

Miss Surelee stared on.

"Okay, here's what we know so far," I began. "Rodger-Dodger went missing the same week those fires started. All the fires set—minus the Ego and the stables—were at abandoned buildings. Somehow, everyone who sees the truck, ends up with a flat tire; a flat tire caused by a nail; a nail that's used in construction; construction that is getting done faster thanks to all those fires."

"What about sweet-cheeks, is he still a part of this?"

"Tucky is an idiot, knocked up four different women, possibly a fifth, is late on child support payments and Dickie attacked him at the theater." I gave Miss Surelee a hardened flat look before adding, "So yeah, need I say more?"

"No," she said, sounding like a scolded toddler, and stared on, listening, barely reacting.

"Now we have a Ranger in town, on a tip. I'm getting coded text messages from possibly dipshit and now someone is tracking me. So, what do you think, Miss Surelee? Should I be worried someone suddenly wants to know my whereabouts and do what Brent suggested and go on home or should I go ask Uncle Walt what's going on about these fires?"

"Uncle Walt, here we come."

"Exactly," I said, pulling into the drive of Uncle Walt and Aunt Doty's two-story grey painted clapboard and pink shingled home.

"Oh good, you're still here," I said as Uncle Walt opened the frosted, storm door to my knock; Miss Surelee let out a squeal and smacked hands to her eyes. I gave her a puzzling look, glanced at Uncle Walt, and instantly saw the resemblance. Although thirty years older, half a foot shorter and probably fifty pounds heavier, I can see why Miss Surelee thought Uncle Walt might be Rodger-Dodger. He too sported a head and face full of scraggly hair, although his was two shades greyer than Red's is. "Put your hands down, Miss Surelee, this isn't Rodger-Dodger."

"Sorry, habit," she said lowering hands, uncertain.

Uncle Walt gave her the once over but didn't react to all that is Miss Surelee. Instead, he opened the storm door, turned back to me asking, "What can I do ya for?"

"I see you're headed out?"

"Yep," he said, going back to the bench seat next to the wall hook of coats and scarves, sat down and pulled up a county grade, fireman's fireproof boot to foot.

"Got the call ten minnis ago," he said. "Seventh one since last week, can you all believe it?"

"Well, that's what I sort of wanted to ask you about," I said.

"I ain't really s'pose to talk it," he said, yanking on the other boot before shrugging into a fireman's jacket. "And don't you all go buggin' Woody none either."

Wasn't planning on it, but now that he mentioned it...

"Please, Uncle Walt, I think this might have something to do with Rodger-Dodger's disappearing act. So, anything you can tell me would be helpful," I said following him down the walkway toward the truck parked to the driveway.

He climbed up into the cab of his full ton, diesel fueled Dodge truck that looked ten minutes old and turned the key over. Knowing that Rusty had him and his truck blocked in, I held my ground and waited. "Dang, Harley, Derby wasn't enough?" he said.

Well that's just plain insulting. Derby caused her own doing. I just happened to blow it wide open. "Look here, Uncle Walt, I'm tired, I'm pissed and I think I'm pre-menstrual," I said, eyes narrowed with a threatening look to my taunt face. "I am not about to let this one pass! Rodger-Dodger isn't one to cause trouble, but he seems to be caught up in something and I just want to figure it all out!"

Uncle Walt gave me the once over, shook his head once then finally said, "You all needin' to worrah 'bout Bee 'cause her critters bein' the in-cin-e-airies."

Wait—what? "Someone's using Aunt Bertie's road kill as firebombs?"

Uncle Walt nodded a grim yes.

"B-but who...w-why...w-what for," I asked, stumped.

Uncle Walt just shrugged then eye-balled Rusty. I understood that look, nodded, and motioned for Miss Surelee and me to enter Rusty, fire him up and back out of my Uncle's driveway. I idled at the curb and watched as he drove away Northwest, toward the smoldering remains of Skeeter's home/business on Pike Street. The smart thing for us to have done would be to drive Rusty back to the Victorian, lock the doors and pray for an early retirement. But my Dodge roots took hold so naturally, I did the opposite, headed toward the Northeast end on town, seeking some much-needed answers of my own.

"Who lives here?" asked Miss Surelee, taking in the outdated two story, greenish-graying, half-stone, half-clapboard house with attached, two-car garage on Regal Drive.

"My brother Rodger-Dodger," I said, shutting down Rusty and exiting the cab.

"Why we here then?" she asked, following me up the cemented driveway, turning at the pathway off to the left toward the front door.

"I have questions," I said, ringing the doorbell.

"Sweetness, if Rodger-boy is missing than who do you expect to answer?"

"His wife," I said as the front door opened wide, "Shelly."

"Harley," the lackluster, plain faced, thirty-nine-year-old wife and mother of four greeted rather reluctantly with a pinch to her starched expression. We didn't exactly run in the same circles back in our youth; we didn't exactly hang out now that I think on it. So, I had no reason she'd be cordial of my unannounced visit. Then again, I was her sister-in-law. She patted once at her hot-roller styled bob of tan fluff adding, "Please tell me you all didn't come down here to bring me a sour apple."

Ah, not that I'm thinking. "I'm guessing you still haven't seen or heard from Rodger-Dodger, then."

Shelly's eyes hooded and her mouth set to a grim line. "No."

"May we come in," I asked.

She looked hesitant but seeing-as, we're relation, she'd look foolish if she declined my request. She was after all, born and raised Boolee. Not-to-mention, the wife of a Booleeite lifer. Such mannerisms expected whether you wanted to follow the rules or not. Such is my curse, but luckily, ended up in my favor.

Introductions aside and coats removed, Miss Surelee and I settled to one of the two sofas flanking a white stone fireplace where a flat screen television, rivaling that of Red's billboard sized one, tuned to the local news channel hung on the wall just above the mantle. I heard noises upstairs and glanced at the ceiling. Shelly followed my gaze, quickly saying, "The boys," before she excused herself to the kitchen to round up coffee and cake. It was her wifely duty; Boolee-duty-bound I smugly grinned to no one.

I glanced around and to my greenie-eyed vision, noticed that my brother was doing all right for himself. Not as great as Red, mind you, but better than I'll ever manage since moving back to Boolee. Even though the outside of the house looked four decades old, the inside looked recently renovated and smelled pleasantly like gardenias. There was new plush wool carpeting, the latest gaming console, that widescreen nearly rivaling that of Red and Barbarilla's technology and furniture from this decade. Shelly's decorating style was pleasing and complementary in cool tones of blues and greens. Even the casement, double hung windows looked expensive and especially clean.

Guess working for Red's recycling plant pays a pretty sum.

Shelly came back carrying a server tray loaded with tea cups, matching saucers and small plates loaded with a slice of cake, happily diverting my jealous attention. Now, knowing my sister-in-law as I do, I was one-hundred percent certain that the coffee cake made fresh, by her, this morning. I dug right on in. A moment of awkward silence later, I swiped crumbs from my mouth with the back of my hand then announced the reason for Miss Surelee and my visit.

"I keep seeing Rodger-Dodger all around town."

Shelly startled with coffee cup halfway to her perfectly lipstick covered lips and stared back at me.

Two for two, I gunned the Dodge adding, "And I'm not the only one and when we do, it's like he's trying to run away or something."

Miss Surelee kept very quiet but nodded in agreement.

Shelly set down her cup to saucer with precise movements, back to ramrod straight and stared back, face set to a sourly expression. She refused to elaborate.

Uh-huh... "Any ideas why that might be," I pressed.

Shelly's face slackened if only slight. With measured movements she smoothed out her slacks without a reason. Her cotton twill pants looked neatly pressed, the crease running the length still crisp. Then she sighed and glanced my way. I wondered if she would ever get to the talking part of our get-together when she finally said, "I don't know if this all will help, Harley, really I don't but it's the same I all told Brent when he all gave me a jingle the other day."

He did? "Okay, and?"

"Well, Rodger is Rodger, ya know? Acted like always, same routine, same old Rodger," she said, glancing inconspicuously toward her bay windows before concluding. "He went to work, then after supper he all helped the girls with their homework and the boys with their curveballs. Then we turned in.

"He did the same like he always done-did Thursday for poker night at Stan's. He mentioned sumpin 'bout the new kid in town. Now, I don't know what-cha all lookin' into but he didn't do anythang outta the ordinary; nutin' outta kink, even that mornin' when he all went down to the Piggly for the paper."

"But he didn't come back, did he," I asked.

"No," she said on another sigh, another press of her kakis and another glance toward the windows before she added. "I gave Red a jingle, askin' if he all might a called Rodger to help him with whatever it is Red always needs helpin' with."

Shelly and I nodded our heads in agreement over that. Shucks. Our one relative bond had to be our mutual understanding of Red's demands, especially on Sundays. "But he wasn't with Red," I said, not liking where this knowledge headed.

"No," she stated then stood up as if she were late for a PTA meeting and started gathering up our cups and plates.

I quickly licked at the crumbs on the plate before handing mine over to her. I stood as well to ask, "Did he happen to say anything about visiting Tucky or Margret?"

That got a flat-out stare. A breath later she said, "I don't think so, why?"

"Oh, nothing," I said, even though my thoughts were swirling with suggestions to the contrary. "Thanks, Shelly."

Coats in hand, Miss Surelee and I headed to the door. Shelly met us halfway asking, "You all think he's okay?"

I sure hope so. "He looked fine to me, Shelly but all the same, can you call me first if you do hear from him?"

"I can do that," she said, voice hallow, holding the front door for us while we stuffed ourselves to our coats, eyes wandering to the street beyond. "But it's a long shot. I keep callin' his cell but it all just goes to voice box."

"I know the feeling," I said then waved goodbye.

"That was fun," said Miss Surelee, sounding bored.

"Maybe," I said, sounding intrigued. Shelly had secrets that she wasn't keen on sharing.

Speaking of which, as I started up Rusty, I caught movements in my peripherals. I wasn't fast enough to question his presence. But I did notice who as I caught the last of Stranger-Danger man's dark-tinted SUV turn the corner from view.

...curious and curiouser...

I turned back to Miss Surelee about to ask if she too noticed Stranger-Danger's peculiar timing but she was busy filing fingernails to have noticed anything else. Without a second thought, I put Rusty in gear and floored it back to the Victorian.

I guess all that running around that we've been doing this past week has worn Miss Surelee ragged because after Sunday dinner, she fell asleep in two seconds flat, now snorting and grunting, sounding like a log-sawing lumberjack. Good thing her car should be all patched up by tomorrow afternoon because I don't think I can take one more night of her noisy sleep habits. I however tossed and turned until I couldn't stand it anymore. It might have had something to do with hearing Dick-breath's name leaving her lips that had me sneaking down to the kitchen for a three-a.m. snack. Or it could have been another text message from G that had my stomach souring because it said: U STILL HAVE WHAT I WANT. No, I didn't. I checked.

The key fob was missing from the top of my dresser. I think that's what smug-mug was after. Either way, I wasn't going back to sleep until I had my head cleared of those thoughts and my stomach filled with anything that wasn't. Good thing I found the last zinger as I rolled up a slice of bologna and cheddar forgoing bread, and just finished pouring myself a glass of milk, when Aunt Bertie joined me.

"Don't say it, please," I mumbled between bites.

"What's wrong dear?"

I hung my head. She had said it, anyways.

"Nothing," I mumbled.

"Does this have anything to do with that boy calling on you earlier tonight?"

"Wait—what boy?"

"Charles Rayburn Watts, said he was your date to the fairgrounds Friday night," she said, studying me. "Is that true?"

"Yeah, he's harmless," I said, swallowing the last of my milk, swiping coconut zinger crumbs from the table and depositing them to the sink. I rinsed my glass and pushed my chair against the table.

"That may be well and good but you know I don't like strangers calling after hours. That's not how we do things around here. Please let him know this the next time you see him." Aunt Bertie stood up to follow me to the stairs.

"He somewhat grew up here and works the graveyard shift at the station, but all the same, there won't be a next time," I said on a yawn. "Besides, I'm not so sure he's the one we need to be worrying about."

"So, there is something itching your hide, isn't there?"

I nodded but didn't say, Rodger-Dodger or bother to mention Aunt Bertie's hobby used for arson because that thinking led down a path of every Booleeite who's ever bought one of her stuffed works of art and instead found myself saying, "Billy."

"The antique shop keeper—whatever in the world has you worried about him?"

"He's not from around here, and for some reason, he keeps showing up everywhere I go," I said, climbing the stairs.

"Is this a bad thing?" asked Bertie.

"Well, no, but it's coincidental, don't you think?"

"Not if it's meant to be," she replied, optimistically.

I startled on an intake of breath. Maybe she had a point? Not likely. My luck wasn't destined in that direction.

"I don't know, Aunt Bertie, he's like this puzzle no one seems to be able to solve. Guys hate him, women adore him, but for what—for the way he looks," I said skeptically. "Nope, I'm not buying it, Aunt Bertie. That man has secrets."

"Let it be, dear," she said unencumbered, lingering at my door. "If it's meant to be un-riddled then it'll all work itself out in good time," she said then added, "Goodnight, dear."

I stared after Aunt Bertie even after she was long past the bend, settled once more to her and Mr. Willoughby's room. Let it be? But I couldn't let it be. Billy *is* a stranger. A stranger that suddenly appears out-of-the-blue when he should be snug to his junk store waiting on hot and bothered women. It's no wonder Charlie Ray wasn't happy to see him come to my rescue the other night at the fairgrounds. Not-to-mention, someone is tracking me (probably smug-mug) while another someone (possibly Rodger-Dodger) bent on setting fires for unknown, random reasons.

I swallowed hard as I closed my bedroom door and turned toward my bed, flopping to its creaking springs, finding myself feeling a little nauseous around the edges. No Aunt Bertie, I will not 'let it be', I thought, settling myself once more beneath my tangled covers to attempt round two of the nighttime blues when a beauty of an idea swam into view. Tomorrow, I gleefully thought, tomorrow I know just what Miss Surelee and I can do to make the butterflies in my stomach subside.

Chapter Eleven: Kentucky Isn't Boolee

Monday afternoon, while waiting for Miss Surelee to return with a new-and-improved, cherry-red Porsche, I was having a nice, leisurely visit with my friend, Rinna Mathers, now my relation through marriage to my cousin Mason Waverly. She stopped by the Victorian to give me the low-down of "one fine looking man". I already knew this first hand. Still, gossiping about Billy the shop owner was better than the usual fair of Harley shenanigans. She explained how his shop has been a non-stop of 'womanly activity'. I nodded, fully understanding. She added, saying how several women took it upon themselves to drop off a variety of homemade cooking with hopes of enticing Stranger-Danger to their boudoirs. That is, whenever he was around his shop long enough to accept such shameless advances.

I was, appalled! The nerve of those girls sneaking behind their hillbilly husbands' beer bellies. I snickered though. If I had legally married Dickie or was still with him, I too might find myself hunting for a fantasy check. I guess Rinna knew me better than most. I guess she had me in mind when she dropped off a sampling of her world famous seven-layered dip, with special mention that it was my idea and that I helped.

No, it wasn't and no, I didn't.

Around one-thirty, a truck roared up my Aunt Bertie's makeshift drive causing our giggles to pause long enough so we could crane our necks in that direction. We listened as it idled for a minute, door slamming before it thundered off. Thirty seconds later, Miss Surelee stormed the Victorian with the verbosity of a bear just out of hibernation. She barreled past the hallway, beyond the kitchen table and yanked the refrigerator door wide. Up to that point, Bandit sat at focused attention beneath Rinna's chair, pelting a paw through the air hoping to catch some of her son, Jud's slobbering crumbs. The moment Miss Surelee arrived however he shot off like a bullet toward parts unknown, secretive only to his fuzz ball size.

"I need me something—I need me one of them ho-ho's—I need me a hot pocket or a spritzer—I'll settle for a shot of liquor if yous got any!"

"What's going on," I asked while Rinna stared on, bouncing a slobbering blonde beach ball that is her two-year-old son on her knee who was now scrunching his face into a pout.

"My car ain't gonna be done today," she said, slamming the refrigerator door shut, eyeballing Jud's baggie of animal crackers and cheddar gold fish crackers. "Gonna be another week."

"What do you mean it's going to take another week," I joined in, shouting to the angels on potty break, swiping the sorting of mail aside in a show of frustration.

Miss Surelee glanced my way as she slumped to the chair next to me at the kitchen table, desperate to recoup her senses while Rinna handed two crackers to Jud, desperate to keep from wailing uncontrollably. He shoved both crackers and part of a hand to his drooling mouth.

I stared on Miss Surelee's way, expectant to hear out the details of her misfortune. Miss Surelee's eyes roamed all about the Victorian's kitchen before she said in a voice barely above a whisper. "The truck was jacked last night."

"Who would do such a damn fool thing?" I angrily said. But I knew it before I said it as Rinna and I exchanged secretive but knowing glances before I concluded on a half whisper that resonated with admiration saying, "Great Uncle Leo." Rinna nodded. Cousin by marriage and all, she knew of Leo's reputation too.

Leo had spent two decades in the clink for just such a foolish sideline of work. He was famous for it; admired, even. Known within a three-county radius, Leo was the man to see if you needed something expensive that came with a questionable price tag and even questionable place of origin. Mind you, he made *Amazon* look like sissies and *eBay* seem like amateurs.

"Who's this Leo," Miss Surelee wanted to know.

"Snake delivery yesterday," I explained.

Miss Surelee stiffened but nodded her understanding.

Even after I said it, I thought, no, it couldn't be Leo, seeing how he's been out of the clink for two and a half decades now, doing his best to reform to upstanding society, keeping mostly to himself and Margret, tucked to the northern patch of woods about Boolee, living the life off the welfare system.

Or was he?

I thought about whom else might have done the swiping instead. Only one thought came to mind: Tucky. He was the other logical village idiot who might have done the hijacking because he grew up, raised by the best. Then again, idiot number two might have had something to do with that bit of illegal activity as well. However, knowing idiot number one is Tucky, and idiot number two has even less going on upstairs, I thought this highly unlikely. Those two jokers couldn't mastermind a comb in a barbershop.

"*Why* would someone want to jack a truck with Porsche car parts? Especially around here, where obviously, the only Porsche belongs to Miss Surelee?"

Rinna shrugged and Miss Surelee looked ready to bolt or throw up. I couldn't be certain which. She was looking pallor around the cheeks and her eyes refused to stay focused on any one thing at any one time. My stomach soured. My thoughts squirmed about because now I have one more thing to worry about. I whipped out my cell phone and called Stanley back, demanding answers, or second-rate parts at the least, but all I got was an "Ungh," and what I think was the sound of a shrug before he hung up.

Well, hell, so much for relation.

And, so much for today's' plan of action; I was going to talk Miss Surelee into letting me test drive candy. Not only that, but I was going to wrangle Miss Surelee into helping me snoop on Billy. Because in my buckshot thinking, he was the only one not from Boolee, showed up a month and a half before all this firebombing and Rodger-Dodger trouble began. He seemed suspicious to me, disliked by all the single men, adored by all available and married women alike. I also wondered if he connected to Dickie somehow or worse, he had ties to the Giovanni family. Anything was possible in this point of my delirium.

Sensing Miss Surelee's frustration and Jud's' twisted pout, Rinna stood up, balanced the blonde beach ball on her hip and asked, "Are you free tomorrow afternoon?"

"Maybe," I said; Miss Surelee frowned.

"Great! Marnie's in town and havin' a little get-together of the discounted variety. You all wanna join?"

Family or not, it only took me two seconds to think, absolutely. Another three before I asked, "Um, don't you have one or two rug rats to look after," nodding in said beach ball's direction.

"Randy's in daycare now and I got a sitter for Jud," she said, looking desperate for a day out of the house that didn't involve wet naps or chew toys. Guess Jud was still teething. "Besides, Mason will be home to watch them if thangs run a little tardy. Come on Harley, it'll be like old times!"

Miss Surelee shot me questioning eyes. "Hold on here," she said flashing Rinna a pout. "My candy's been vandalized and here you be squawking about discounted things? What's up with that?"

Rinna and I exchanged grins before I explained. "Marnie Drexler is one of my cousins," I said to Rinna's nod and Miss Surelee's puzzled expression. "No matter, Marnie was known for a lot of things back in the day, when we were growing up. Legitimate sales weren't one of them. Her parties are famous for selling off handbags, shoes, even bling, which could almost rival Leo's infamous talents."

"Let me understand this; she jacks cargo and resells?"

Rinna and I exchanged curious looks before I corrected. "No, no, Marnie sort of...inherits these items from willing benefactors and gives us girls' first crack before they get donated to the landfill."

"She got Elsa, Bruno or Fermani?

I stared back, blank faced. I had no idea who those people were.

Miss Surelee gave off a huff and corrected saying, "Gucci, Prada or Fendi?"

"Possibly," I said. Not likely, I was thinking.

"Count me in," she said and slumped further down on the kitchen chair.

"Harley?" said Rinna, eyebrows raised expectantly.

I blew out a sigh. "Yeah sure," I said.

"Fan-tastic! See you all at one at her usual spot."

After Rinna and Jud left, Miss Surelee glanced about the kitchen looking lost and still pale around the edges of her cheeks to ask, "What am I supposed to do now?"

"I don't know," I said and went back to sifting through several envelopes that I had the lunacy to open to glance through their contents. It wasn't something bad or detrimental to my left-handed talent. Still, it just wasn't something worth reliving either.

"What's with all the cards?" said Miss Surelee, noticing, poking at the pile before she snatched at one of the cards. "I thought you said you were born around Christmas?" I sighed as I watched Miss Surelee toss the card aside and sift through several others before she plucked at one of the folded newspaper clippings. She unfolded it, glanced at the article, released a low whistle, and glanced my way. "What's this all about? Why'd they send you this?"

I gave up a second sigh before I explained. "You're right about my birthday, Miss Surelee, not until December. Look closer at the cards. They're supposed to be gestures of sympathy because of my Aunt Gladys' article about me last Tuesday, you know, at the treasure trap, and then our narrow escape from the Ego?"

"Don't look like they forgot about the galloping doodoo neither," Miss Surelee reminded, inspecting a different news clipping.

"Anyways, it's what we do around here I guess, for sport. Some communities have the phone tree; we have the *Redlight* and for some dumb reason, women around here want to make sure you know what happened in case you forgot," or, in my case, had *tried* to forget.

"Ouch. Don't they know you already know what happened? I mean, you took a dizzy-dive and bloodied your nose. Who wants to be, remembered for that, see what I mean?"

I agreed, but there was no point in trying to un-riddle this crazy, small-town gossiping phenomenon to her when they also sent clippings of our accidental bash-in with Marty's cruiser. Besides, my words would only sail off into the horizon, refusing to sink in. Therefore, I asked instead, "Want to go on a road-trip?"

Miss Surelee squinted back asking, "You trying to get rid of me, Sweetness?"

Miss Surelee may be the worst bunkmate I've ever had, which is saying a lot, considering who I shackled up to for the past fifteen and a half years. But I truly liked Miss Surelee, so she wasn't near as bad as my idiot ex-husband. I didn't want to get rid of her so much as I wanted to help her on her way. "No," I cried then released a chuckle. "It's been fun having you here, visiting, really, but aren't you sick of hanging around Boolee?" I know I am.

She flashed me a stink eye, all the same.

So, I elaborated. "I just thought since it looks like you'll be stuck here for another week or so, that we could get out of Boolee for the rest of the day. We could spend it snooping around a bit. Mind you, it's an hours' drive each way but it might prove interesting," I said, "So, you in?"

"Who you thinking about snitching," she asked, curious.

My grin drew wide before saying, "Family."

"I don't know what it is about your relation but they're interesting, so count me in," she said then headed upstairs to dress down from her dressed up attire.

Uh-huh, I thought devilishly. You might not be saying that after you meet *this* (particular) grouping of relation, Great Aunt Margret aside.

I tidied up the kitchen while I waited for Miss Surelee. Fifteen minutes later, she clomped down the stairs and rounded the kitchen. Today Miss Surelee chose to wear black spandex leggings, brown wooden clogs, and black and white checkered, long sleeved flannel over some type of stretchy yellow knit top. The only thing missing from her falsified-western ensemble was a straw hat. Thank goodness. Nevertheless, she did swap out her strawberry blonde clacking braids for a slick, neon blue bob.

So much for being sneaky...

"We're headed out for the day," I called to Aunt Bertie, who I was certain was down in the cellar, rooting about the subzero. "Probably won't be back for dinner, so don't wait up!"

She called back with, "No time," and Miss Surelee and I headed out, refusing to unriddle that dilemma.

A half hour later, we were on the road, headed past Joplin, past the curve to the left. I was doing my best to keep from ditching Rusty into the grouping of yellow colored water barrels that smug-mug left me no other choice in the matter to crash into nearly three months ago, via Derby's bad boy blue Chevy truck. I hooked the onramp and merged with light traffic and chugged North, Northwest along I-77, incident free. After my hands stopped shaking and my heart downgraded from its hammering, I settled in to driving on autopilot, sputtering along at a reasonable sixty-five, miles per hour even though everyone else around me was zinging past at a heart-stopping ninety. Let them rush their way toward an accident; Rusty and I were happy bringing up the rear with bumper still intact. Besides, I think I was already pushing Rusty to his dusty limits.

My thoughts wandered off to greener pastures as I glanced ahead at the bright horizon. The sky was sunny and clear. It was the kind of sunny and clear day that gave me sunny and clear thinking; the kind of sunny and clear day that I couldn't help but smile over. Therefore, I did. I smiled thinking today was going to be a great, sunny, and clear kind of day!

Unexpectedly, Miss Surelee gave off a high-pitched whistle. I nearly hopped the solid, yellow line to almost sideswipe a newer modeled truck. They honked and gave me the bird, then motored ahead. I smiled and waved them one of my own, happy to welcome them to my little neck-of-the-woods.

"Woo-wee, would you look how far up we are!"

"Yep," I said. It's the way of the steep, slanting hills.

"A person could go vertigo staring down there too long."

"Yep," I said then glanced to my rearview mirror once and noticed the sky, slate gray as it hovered about a receding Boolee in a depressing sort of protective way. My smile faltered as I noticed something else but was afraid to dwell on that tan colored unmarked car for fear I might be right and glanced to Rusty's dash panel instead.

I should have looked back at the sunny and clear sky instead.

I noticed Rusty's tank was idling just below half so I did a few minutes of mental math, wondering if I could make it to our destination and back without a refill. Since I nearly squeaked by in my high school math and the fact that Rusty's gas tank is questionable, even when full, I decided I'd better pull over at the next available travel station, just in case. No sense taking a chance on stranded out in the middle of the boonies with only two spare tires and no additional gas can. Kentucky isn't exactly welcoming to stragglers, let alone, a Dodge, but especially, *this* Dodge; sure-as-pinecones, they'd have Rusty stripped bare without a second glance my way.

Five miles later, I was veering right at the first travel stop exit, scoping out a vacant pump. This time of day was usually the busiest for travelers, carpoolers, and the occasional hijacker. If it were the weekend, that is. But seeing, as it was the Monday leading up to Halloween, most of the travelers and carpoolers had reached their purposed destinations, (and I'm just guessing here), accident free. And naturally, the hijacker was long gone, probably shored up at some abandoned warehouse or south of the border. Therefore, I was able to parallel park next to my pick of available pumps without having to wait my turn. I shut down Rusty and went to the panel of options. Miss Surelee was rooting about her purse when she asked, "What you needing, Sweetness, I'm buying?"

A different life or maybe a one-way ticket to the Emerald City, I thought. "Whatever you're having," I said instead as cheerily as I knew how while giving Rusty his fill, sighing inwardly doing my best to ignore the unmarked, tan car shadow. It wasn't working though as my heart hammered away over thoughts of Texas, dipshit and Arnold's brains splattered to kingdom come.

Twenty minutes later, Rusty full, pee break taken and Miss Surelee and I, loaded with drinks, chips, cellophane-wrapped hoagies and the odd assortment of travel station donuts and two dill pickles, we were back on the interstate headed for the state line. It was dumb luck, but luck no doubt that I once more, spotted the tail of an unmarked car, four car lengths back and one lane over. Nope. I wasn't imagining it. No doubt about it. That tan car was shadowing us.

Normally, driving a well-traveled interstate his shadowing would seem like typical behavior. Nevertheless, that unmark car's behavior wasn't typical. It was matching Rusty's speed to the rpm. But seeing how I saw that tan car pull into the travel stop, one minute after us, parked at the far end of the lot and sat there waiting while Miss Surelee loaded up with the essentials and I loaded up Rusty with the necessary, I couldn't help but think otherwise. The cowboy-hat-wearing person, who was driving that unmarked four-door sedan didn't even exit their car to stretch. Not wanting to be the bearer of bad news, let alone, did I wish to cause Miss Surelee's heart to reach stroke levels, I decided to keep my lips clamped tight and occasionally glanced to the rear and side windows every so often. It was better this way. Miss Surelee was smiling and sipping away on her big gulp, fiddling with the radio stations, oblivious. No sense raining on her already lousy day by alerting her to the fact that a Texas Ranger was keen on following us out of Boolee.

Dang it, how in the hell did he find me? I thought Brent kept that tracking pen of his. Ut-oh, maybe he found me by tracking my cell phone. No, that can't be it. I'd turned it off last night and kept it off ever since.

No time to dwell, my exit would be coming up in ten miles.

"Hunh, I saw an interview on Morning America before Bluebird took off for school this morning. It was about all these ways you can use Coca-Cola besides drinking. Did you know that?"

"Get out," I said, sailing along on my mental autopilot skills. "Is that true?"

"Oh, uh-huh," she said, slurping up said cola through her big-gulp straw. "Did you know you can remove grease stains with it?"

"Uh, nope," I said, hoping the tail would fall back or turn west. "What else?"

"Well, it'll clean car batteries, scrub pots, de-ice your windows, even restore coins and grout like new!"

"I'm beginning to see a wacko theme emerging here," I said, rethinking my own cup of ulcer inducing, Coca-Cola as I glanced to my side mirror.

"Are you calling Miss Lara a liar?" she asked, eyes narrowed.

"Uh, nope," I said once more keeping my focus on the car several paces behind.

"Good, 'cause you know what else you can do with it? You can ease a tummy ache or repel a skunk's stink and even jumpstart compost."

"Wow, who knew soda can do all that," I said with insincere zeal.

"Yep and know what else I didn't know soda-pop could do?" she asked, giving me a sideways glance, sucking up more of her Coca-Cola.

"No, what," I said, flicking a glance to my side mirror.

"This is the best part, and to think I should of known this," she paused, gulping more drink, eyeballing me like a steak dinner before she continued. "It'll give your hair body and bounce and," she paused once more, this time for greater effect by lightly bouncing on her side of the bench seat before concluding, "It can lighten hair-dyed hair! Is that genius or what?"

"Uh-huh," I said my eyes to rear-view mirror with thoughts on the possible tracker, four cars back.

"Okay, maybe I got me some of that wax buildup, but what's your excuse?"

"Huh?"

"Exactly," she said, glancing to her own side mirror to say, "What's got you preoccupied back there?"

"What? Oh, sorry," I said, eyes back front, noticing the sign for our exit. "I thought I saw something—nothing important—oh look, this is our exit."

"Blue-Veil, Kentucky," Miss Surelee said on a whisper, reading the exit sign before turning to me to ask, "This day trip wouldn't have something-something to do with Gee, would it?"

"Maybe," I said, but didn't elaborate. If anything, I was hoping it had *nothing* to do with mystery texter, G. However, seeing, as Ranger-man was keen on following me, my heart thumped rapidly in my chest, believing differently.

Now since I sort of knew where I headed or was somewhat familiar with that general direction at least and the fact that it was easier for Ranger-man to tail me through traffic on the interstate without my getting suspicious, I decided to give him the slip by driving the back-county roads rather than take the state route to our intended destination. It would add an additional, twenty or so minutes to our travel time but I think the detour would be worth it. These back roads went on for miles of wide-open spaces and at this time of year, fields plowed down to nothing. In addition, the roads would be free of travelers or commuters this time of day, making it more difficult to blend in. Maybe one or two tractors inching along to wrap up farming season might give Ranger-man some cover but aside from taking that chance, there would be no other way he'd be able to stay hidden from my rear view.

Yes, I'm snickering. I love any opportunity that affords me the chance of getting the upper hand, especially now. Ranger-man was the last person in the world I wanted hitching along to my spur-of-the-moment, reunion.

I exited the interstate, hopped a state route for a quarter mile, hung a sharp right at the first intersection and drove for another half mile then made another right, looped across that county road then slowed.

Miss Surelee flashed me a frown saying, "Are we headed back already?"

"No," I said, turning around before I headed back west toward my destination. My erratic driving proved accurate; I ditched the tail half a mile back. Smiling, I watched as he turned back for the interstate. "Can you please get my phone out of my purse for me?"

"Sure thing, Sweetness," she said. A moment later, she was glancing at the black screen puzzled. She turned back to me asking, "How come you never turn your phone on?"

I turned the corner and slowed to the side of the deserted, county Kentucky road. I relieved Miss Surelee of my cell phone and switched it on. It dinged twenty times and while I waited for the messages to finish loading, I lobbed back saying, "Why is it you don't want anyone knowing you saw Dickie in town?"

Miss Surelee's back went rigid and I swear she just let out another squeaker. I cracked my window two inches just in case that one too, decided to fester and reek.

"Okay, here's the thing," I said on a sigh. "I first thought those text messages were coming from Dickie."

Miss Surelee's face drained of all color and that was pretty dam talented, considering how much foundation I've seen her use.

"Miss Surelee," I asked. "Are you okay?"

A beat later, she broke free of her trance and nodded once.

"But now I'm not so sure," I continued but sounding just as realistically uncertain, "Hence my reasoning for driving here."

Miss Surelee perked up. "I'm feeling the need to go snitching. Who we gonna start with?"

"Ducky Humphrey," I said. Even after having said his name aloud, I couldn't stop the giggle that escaped. A moment later I managed to clarify for Miss Surelee's sake, "He's Tucky's first cousin on his grandmother's side of things. His momma Myra is my Great Uncle Leo and Great Aunt Margret's second or third child or maybe their fourth, I think. I'm not really sure about that side of the family tree."

"Tucky and Ducky," she said, sampling the way their names sounded on her tongue. "Hunh, sort of like Humpty and Dumpty, don't-cha think?"

Something like that...

"Crap," I said aloud before my brain registered a step behind my mouth.

"What," Miss Surelee asked.

I was staring at the screen of my cell phone in disbelief. She glanced over and read:

I'M STILL WATCHING

"Who's still watching what?" she asked.

"Me, I think," I said, looking up the Humphrey's address on one of the internet's searchable maps. A minute later, I had the directions listed from my location, put Rusty in gear, and sputtered along the county road toward the outskirts of Blue-Veil Kentucky.

"Why," she asked me.

I gave Miss Surelee a half-assed shoulder shrug because what could I say? Had she been around three months ago, she wouldn't need to ask. Then again, did I really need to remind her about Dicky?

I turned left, drove about five miles down the deserted county road before I turned right and swung Rusty underneath the wooden arch that displayed the name of the ranch. It read, SPIGOT'S STUDS. Appropriate if it described Stranger-Danger man. However, this is Ducky we're talking about and I'm pretty sure they were referring to their twenty some horses milling about the rolling acres of fenced pastures, not Ducky.

The Humphrey's lived miles away from civilization on the outskirts of Blue-Veil on a ranch the size of Boolee that makes Red and Bertie's land look miniscule by comparison. I had no idea what they ranched or farmed besides raising studs and I didn't care to know otherwise. The horses used for producing racers ran during the Triple Crown. I guess you could say this was Derby country, no pun intended.

An hour later, we were back to Rusty and headed east.

"Ducky was a bust," I said, disappointed he had nothing to add to the matter of arson. Because his story held and I didn't think that he had the brains or the motive to wrangle

Rodger-Dodger into something that was happening seventy miles away, across state lines. Besides, he had an alibi seeing that he was up to his armpits in horse manure, what with the additional housing needs for Gaffadee's stable less mares. Even his parents never left our side throughout our questions, vouching for this past week of his whereabouts.

Now Myra and Chris were somewhat better mannered than the rest of the Spigots, but I was still a Dodge after all, so they practically drilled holes into my head the whole time I poked around their ranch, seeking answers. They especially didn't appreciate me asking about Great Uncle Leo maybe being the one who might have jacked a truck last night. Then again, I'm pretty sure Myra's older sister, Letty was mostly to blame. She'd been visiting her relation all about Boolee after all, recovering and seeking sympathy over the loss of her husband; the wake and funeral set for Wednesday afternoon in Boolee of all places, but what do I really care? So, it was no surprise to see her visiting her sister in Kentucky. Unfortunately, that wasn't what had my mind and stomach doing back flips: Aunt Letty nearly went into a rampage over the sight of Miss Surelee during the last five minutes of our Spigot Stud sightseeing tour. No idea why. I loved Miss Surelee's colorful and gay ways. Apparently, Letty Spigot Dodge did not. She was one to talk, looking like a miniature version of Margret, who even on her best day couldn't rival one of Miss Surelee's worst. Not only that but I was certain Aunt Letty looked surprised, practically choking on her insults to see me snooping about Spigot's Studs. Then again, maybe not, after she flashed me a rather pathetic-looking, middle-finger salute over Aunt Myra's unsuspecting shoulder.

It was getting late in the day, the sun setting to our backs. Miss Surelee looking green aground the gills once more while my stomach grumbled right on cue but I wasn't ready to give up on the Rodger-Dodger mystery and haul us on back to Boolee just yet. Besides, I was curious why Miss Surelee shied away from Letty's insults. Just because someone looked differently than her, didn't give my Aunt Letty the right to openly sling snide jabs Miss Surelee's way. And mostly, Miss Surelee ignored anyone who did. This time however, she nearly shrunk into the ground from the humility of Letty's seething comments, especially when one of those slung my way.

I slowed at the intersection of two deserted back county roads then idled. I turned to Miss Surelee and said, "Anything you want to tell me?"

Miss Surelee squeaked to a start, smacking blue bobbed weave to window before she turned to me with a small shake of her head.

"How come you didn't say anything back there," I asked, equally wondering why I, myself stood there tongue-tied when Aunt Letty called me a "lousy gold-digger, too!"

Miss Surelee stiffened, eyes wandering away to look anywhere but at me.

Alrighty then, time for a different gear...

"Why did you really come to visit me?"

A moment of silence later, Miss Surelee finally spoke, asking instead, "You sure that was your relation?"

Um, yep; I never joke about who, just why. "Yes," I said then asked, "Is that a problem?"

"No," she said on a whisper and went back to glancing out her side of the window, desperate to keep from continuing this conversation.

Fine by me so I instead, punched in Rodger-Dodger's number on my cell phone.

"Sonofabitch," I swore the moment his number showed that it was pinging off to my left about a half mile down the road.

Miss Surelee squeaked to a start and asked, "What? What is it?"

"What are the odds," I said instead, glancing up from my phone as I squinted to our left, pointing.

Miss Surelee glanced that way, uncertain.

The plowed fields to either side of the road went on for miles. There were no houses or barns not even another vehicle. Yet somehow, Rodger-Dodger's phone was out there. I explained the track-app's apparent lack of judgment to Miss Surelee.

"Hunh," she said, squinting down the way. "I don't see a monster. Do you see his monster?"

"Nope," I said turning the wheel and pointing us down the county road, inching along, getting closer to the pinging. We were practically on top of its location when I noticed the service road off to my right.

I know I'm calling it a road even though, technically, it isn't. Keep in mind that roads back in Boolee as well as here is something of a mystery. If you can't find where you want to go, then you just make one up, hence our reasoning for driving trucks. And this one was no exception, by the looks of two, rutted out tire width tracks over patchy grass and clumping, bumpy dirt that wound further back from the road toward a cluster of woodsy trees. I put Rusty in park, jumped down from the cab and stomped around a bit, looking for that, damned cell phone of his. Miss Surelee followed.

"What we doing now?" she asked.

"I'm looking for Rodger-Dodger's phone," I said, staring about the ground, pushing aside reedy grass and weeds. "My app says we're standing right on top of it."

"Well look here what I'm holding," she said a moment later, waving a flip styled cellular my way. "Is this it?"

I snatched it up, flipped it open and scrolled through the directory noticing not one of those calls came from Shelly before the battery flashed a warning then powered itself down. Most of the numbers confused me, until I had spotted my number. It confirmed it. This was Rodger-Dodger's phone.

I pocketed the cell, motioned us back to Rusty and turned down that makeshift road headed toward the grouping of woods, black spots dancing across my vision while my heart clanged about my chest like a jackhammer worried about Rodger-Dodger's safety because nestled amongst the shadows was a dilapidated shack that was, probably once used for moon shining.

For as far back as I could remember I loved a good adventure story with my favorite story of course, being the *Wizard of OZ*. I wanted to find the wizard and have him grant me my wishes. I wanted to find the munchkins and have a party. I wanted to find the tin man, the scarecrow and cowardly lion and ask them to adopt me so we could go on a picnic or maybe gang up to steal the wizard's magic. What I really wanted most was to have a great adventure that didn't involve anyone getting hurt or firebombed or kidnapped.

Unfortunately, that is the type of adventure my life has found as I swerved, slammed brakes, and skidded to a sideways stop. I stared dumbly, blindly through the cloud of dust and nearly swallowed the steering wheel because I couldn't believe what I was seeing. With hands and mouth duck taped, staring back at me as if I were the Devil himself was my cousin, Ginger Dodge.

Chapter Twelve: Poker-Faced

"What the hell," I cried to the angels on intermission when I spotted my cousin Ginger Dennisy emerge through the billowing dust like a swamp creature.

Miss Surelee slapped hands to eyes and moaned out a rather weak cry of, "monster."

I ignored Miss Surelee, put rusty in park, shut him down, swung out of the cab and ran to my cousin. "What are you doing here? How'd you get here? Do you know who did this," I said to the heavens, fully forgetting that Ginger was still duck taped up. "Are you okay?"

Miss Surelee eventually recouped her senses and joined us. She gave Ginger the once over, stuffed the last donut from the travel station box to her mouth and bobbed her head in acknowledgement of my thousand-and-one-questions, equally wanting answers.

When we stumbled across Ginger, she was, bruised and banged up but no broken bones, very dehydrated, shivering, and hungry. Unfortunately, she wasn't exactly grateful of her rescue.

Good thing Miss Surelee ate that last donut.

Good thing I finally realized Ginger was, kidnapped and sprang to action. "Stop moving around," I cried, trying to get the tape peeled away from her mouth. "We're here to help!"

Miss Surelee was even less helpful, darting around Ginger like a grasshopper with a nervous disorder. Was she trying to help me out or not?

"Ginger," I cautiously began, once Miss Surelee had the last of the duct tape removed from Ginger's hands and we had her reluctantly settled on the cracked, faded, vinyl bench seat between us within Rusty's swank and sweaty-smelling interior. "Do you know who did this to you?"

"Get me the hell outta here!" she cried instead.

I took a breath and placed a hand on her knee. With as best a motherly look I knew how, I said, "It's me, Ginger. It's Harley, your safe now." Then I repeated my question.

Her eyes refocused my way before she shook her head no. Then, remembering the shock of her recent situation, she went back to staring beyond the windshield's view, eyes darting about like an induced seizure.

No time for stalling, I re-fired Rusty, quickly put him in gear and floored us back to hillbilly country, headed straight for the weekend lock-U-up getaway that is Detective Pine's second home.

Ginger remained quiet as I focused on the interstate while Miss Surelee rooted about her purse. A moment later, she gave off a huff then snagged mine off the dash and gave it a search. A second later she was holding something up and asking, "What kind of lipstick is this?" She poked a finger at a tube of lipstick that looked like it could double as a prop for a third-grader.

"Uh, that's not mine," I said; because I no longer owned a single tube after they all melted when someone allegedly crammed them into the roaring HVAC system back in Amarillo, Texas.

Ginger stared on.

Miss Surelee stiffened, saying, "Ut-oh."

I knew just where her thinking headed and I clenched the steering wheel for different reasons yet similar all the same. Ten miles north of Boolee, I had picked up the unmarked tan car. Go ahead. See if I care that you found a second way of tracking me. It won't do him any good once we make it over state lines. "Put it back in my purse, Miss Surelee," I said, exiting the interstate, flooring it for the pokey. "I'll give that one to Brent too."

Ginger just gave me a puzzling look before going back to her self-centered thoughts.

We continued to drive in eerily silence, all three of us holding breaths until we crossed the county line and into the safety of Boolee's limits. It's a good thing Ranger-man fell off the pace five minutes ago, or things might have ended up differently. Pent up breaths and thoughts relaxed, I decided to press on with more curious thoughts before Detective Pine had his way with twenty questions of his own boggled mind.

"Ah, Ginger, that day, we showed up for costumes at the Ego?" Startled from her own set of worry, she nodded hesitantly; I took a breath and gunned the pedal. "What did Boomer want with you?"

She relaxed, fully forgetting that we just rescued her from her kidnapped state saying, "That all idiot had the damn nerve to think he all could get me to pay up Bubba's marker!"

"Marker," I asked, uncertain.

"You all know—his loss in poker last week."

"Oh, okay, but why you?"

She shrugged once then said, "I dunno, I guess he all thought I would be stupid enough to oblige."

"Do you think Boomer was the one who kidnapped you?"

Ginger gave me a look that crossed between frustration and curiosity before she shook her head no. "Damn idiot couldn't figure out his all butt in a butt-kickin' contest."

I snickered, fully agreeing as I nosed Rusty to park in front of the pokey. Ginger stiffened at once, looking ready to dart. "This will be over in a flash," I reassured but held tight to Ginger's arm and urged her beyond Rusty's protection, nonetheless. You know, just in case Detective Pine refused to believe my wild tale of locating a one, kidnapped Ginger; I had her live and in person to prove I wasn't making it up, or, that I wasn't the one who had kidnapped her. Miss Surelee brought up the rear of our group, keeping Ginger from running off as she followed us on up the steps and into the Wannabes hidey-hole.

Spotting us at once, Officer Connelly gave a start, eyes darting, hands uncertain what to do but eventually swiped at the back of his pudgy neck, toady face flushing before eyes came back to focus on our little group meeting to ask, "What's goin' on?"

"Buzz us back, Cuz," I said, leaving the explanation of Ginger's reappearance left unsaid.

The door clicked open at once. I guess Connelly would rather catch hell for giving us a free pass than having to deal with me for one more miserable second. Good, because I wasn't in the mood to deal either.

Brent glanced up from the growing mound of Wannabe paperwork atop his metal desk. His mouth fell open the second Miss Surelee and I escorted Ginger beyond his frosted paned door. He shifted looks between the three of us, mouth still catching flies. A second later, he startled free of his shock, stood up, clamping lips into a frown, came around his desk and closed his office door. He turned back to me, hands to belt demanding, "Frick-a-see-sake Dodge, What's goin' on?"

Oh yeah, right. Like I'm going to latch onto that one and get this party started. So, I crossed arms and stared back, not willing to do my Dodge duty by gracing him with my backfired wit. Luckily, Miss Surelee interrupted our staring contest when she plopped to the pleather seat closest to the file cabinets.

"Whew, what a rush, I'm torn in!" She proceeded to fan her sallow looking face, now dotted with sweat.

Brent turned his focus upon Miss Surelee, same threatening stance, same look to his unattractive face and steely eyes before he cast a glance Ginger's way. Ginger hugged herself and looked at me instead with a regrettable longing to be anywhere else but here. I know the feeling cousin. But knowing that the whole reason we showed up at this ungodly place of torture was because of her, I didn't hesitate to thrust her in the spotlight.

Unfolding my arms with a sigh I nodded her toward the vacant and only other pleather seating this shoebox size of an office cared to provide. Then I said, "Go on Ginger, tell him what happened."

Ginger hesitated but gave in with a sluggish start, sagged all her weight as if she was shedding the world from her shoulders.

Brent cut her off at once.

Sheesh, was he trying to outshine Red or what?

Then he cast me another frown, small shake of his buzzed cut head before going back to his desk and sank to his wooden, banker styled chair. It creaked (possibly moaned) to the shift of his sudden, unforgiving weight. Looks to me like ever since Jasmine came along, she wasn't the only one getting (over)fed.

I stifled a giggle, hoping he hadn't noticed, or overlooked me and my many flaws.

Brent shot me a stink eye, nonetheless.

Five minutes of tension-filled silence later, Brent started up our reason to visit the pokey this side of incompressible.

"Got my hands full of them ding-dang farer's springin' up, you all minds tellin' me why you all buggin' Letty?"

Miss Surelee moaned, started to rock while a squeaker escaped to the oblivion.

Say what? How did he know about that? We just left her an hour-and-a-half ago. Oh. Aunt Letty probably telephoned. But wait one frick-and-fracking minute—she insulted *us*! I crossed arms, narrowed lids, and frowned. "I had no idea she was visiting the Humphrey's!" There. That'll show him.

He wasn't buying it and continued with, "Christ Harley, she's been grumblin' 'bout you all followin' her 'bout town—why's that?"

Nope. Unt-uh, that's not my version of things as my mind twirled back in time, remembering, wondering...*fuming*. "My run-ins with her were all accidental," I cried for all that is Boolee to hear. "It's not my fault Letty was born a Spigot."

Brent flashed me a funny little look of confusion or possibly he looked startled, earthworms beneath nose following suit before he cleared his worthless thoughts to say, "Not yoot—her!"

My gaze went from his extended pudgy finger to where it pointed, landing on Miss Surelee. She glanced up once then fainted. Miss Surelee's quick thinking had me stunned then staring for all to see. A second later, I barked laughter that could almost rival Rusty's getaway. I couldn't help it! Now, why couldn't I think of such things rather than snip and snarl my way through one of Detective Pine's twenty-question-sessions, squirming? Truly, though, I thought it was genius of her, figuring a way out of Brent's interrogation by fainting. No man was susceptible and usually lost coherent thinking altogether in the presence of a fainting woman. Then again, Miss Surelee is a he, which, I suppose is why Brent's' frown deepened, eyes darkened and rounded upon me with one of Red's infamous, hellfire expressions.

But hold the phone here, why would Detective Pine think Miss Surelee has been out to harass Letty Spigot Dodge?

Nope, unt-uh, I'm not going to stand for Brent dragging me into that argument so I gave up a shoulder shrug to that worthless ploy of his and ten minutes later, had Miss Surelee semi-conscious and settled to that pleather once more. Realizing she was awake and still in Detective Pine's presence, she hugged her self and started to rock once more, humming a worthless moan even louder than before.

I however found my tenacity and cut Brent off at the pass saying, "Forget Letty, are you going to help Ginger out or what?"

Brent finally downgraded his scowl to something resembling a pent up, frustrated expression to say towards Ginger, "You all ain't missin'."

Well, duh, not anymore.

Ginger merely stared back.

Detective Pine glanced to me. Okay, right. Dodge duty time. I gave up another sigh, this one rather exaggerated to say, "We found her. You're welcome." Then we spent the next hour, explaining how it was, that we came across Ginger. Naturally Brent blasted me with several scowls, raised eyebrows and downturned 'stash before he quizzed me about my need to go sticking my nose where it didn't belong. Now I truly am, insulted. Has he forgotten I'm still a Dodge? I know I keep trying to forget but what's his excuse?

After some urging on his part, not mine, Brent finally got Ginger to explain her account of the day that she was, jumped in the alleyway on her way to the back, parking lot of the Alter Ego. As added insult, she explained how her kidnappers always dressed in costume (one, conveniently dressed up like Batman) and never spoke. Ginger had no idea she was even in Kentucky until Miss Surelee and I stumbled upon her by sheer dumb luck.

"I had one a them grocery sacks over my head," she said. "Next thang I knew I was wakin' up in a closet, all of me trundled like a Christmas goose." She further explained how earlier today before we stumbled upon her that her kidnappers scrambled from the shack, doors slamming, engines roaring to life when she decided to make her escape. She had managed to undo the duct tape on her legs and given the opportunity to run, she forgot all about stopping to undo her mouth or wrists.

Brent's soured expression immediately shifted back to cop-mode when he dialed up a station in Blue-Veil, Kentucky to relay this bit of criminal information but by the time they showed up to investigate, the kidnappers had long since abandoned the dilapidated shack, showing no signs of returning anytime soon. Seeing, as the shack wasn't, registered to anyone now living, the authorities there or Brent couldn't catch a lead on who might have snatched Ginger. Detective Pine was also pessimistic about narrowing down the list of suspects because one, every Booleeite got their grocery bags from the Piggly Wiggly and two, just about every other resident owned a roll of duct tape. It was the given go-too emergency staple for just about everything around here, kidnapping including. And three, costumes were a popular sight all over America given the fact that Halloween was four days away.

Ginger also, had no idea the Alter Ego had burnt to a crisp until Brent disclosed that bit of shocking news. She looked confused at first before her face relaxed into a look of relief. I wondered why but didn't think fast enough to ask her this aloud. But Brent managed to question, remembering my near-death experience saying, "Why'd you all leave? Why didn't you all just close up?"

Ginger rung her freckled hands, flicked her eyes about before she finally said, "Harley had her girl there shoppin'. Besides, I needed to warn Bubba before Boomer showed up."

I already knew this. Ginger had somewhat explained this to me on the drive back from Kentucky to Boolee's station what Boomer had wanted with her the day she disappeared. She pinched her lips into a frown saying that it was nothing worth explaining in detail, which is why she was trying to give him that portable black and white in lieu of Bubba's marker. He wasn't having it; otherwise, I wouldn't have ended up with it.

Satisfied with her answer, Brent moved on saying how she was fortunate enough when Miss Surelee and I came across her when we did, even though he grilled me for twenty minutes about why I suddenly found the need to go visiting Kentucky, what with Letty in a fired-up tizzy about little old me and my side kick of crazy following her all about town. I shrugged my way through that mind-numbing drill, refusing to elaborate on my need to go snooping and track-aping or that we had found Rodger-Dodger's cell phone. He finally gave up and allowed Miss Surelee and I to go our merry way...

...but not before adding, "And stay clear a Letty. Woman's got a 'nuf to worrah 'bout over losin' her ol' man."

No need telling me twice. But someone other than me ought to clarify for Letty's sake the meaning of staying clear of one, Harley Dodge.

Tuesday morning started out on a depressingly slow note. Because even though we found Ginger the night before, we still couldn't locate Rodger-Dodger or understand what was going on around town with all those fires. Lucky for me, Brent had reminded me about our dinner date, for later tonight. Even luckier, I had somehow, *stupidly* agreed to be Charlie Ray's date to the Boolee Ball this coming Friday while I was attempting to shuttle Miss Surelee and I free of the pokey last night. Naturally, Miss Surelee was happy I accepted under the guise of duress. Go figure.

With Ginger resting at county hospital under guard (I guess in case the kidnappers reappeared) and Laney safely tucked away at school, Miss Surelee and I cowered (yet again) to the Victorian for most of Tuesday morning, Aunt Bertie working away at stuffed road kill still oblivious that someone is using them to start fires while Mr. Willoughby ran errands in the mint green Ford, returning promptly around one o'clock.

I had inexplicably found myself bored, lounged across my lumpy bed perusing back issues of the *Redlight* hoping someone around Boolee might find the desperate need to hire me for employment. I think I was down to my last twenty-bucks. It was another one of those déjà vu moments that I just didn't wish to relive because the previous incident had ended badly. So, I did my best to pretend I still had credit left on my over-extended credit card instead. Deep to my own personal denial, I almost forgot Miss Surelee was still here when she startled awake and yanked me free of my daydreaming. Then she had to go and remind me about my agreement to go discounted shopping by answering my cell phone on my behalf. Miss Surelee flashed me a frown and handed me my phone. Immediately, I regretted answering.

"Where the heck you all at," cried Rinna.

"Home, hiding, whining, why," I said.

"You all recall...Marnie Drexler's at one?"

Dang, I'd forgotten all about Marnie's party. My silence should have been the hint, but Rinna kept at her insistence until I finally caved. I thought it over for about two seconds when I realized, I'd be better off going, showing my face for five minutes then hightailing it back to the Victorian before tonight's' double-dating pleasure at the Pines' family-hood. If I didn't, I'd never hear the end of it from Rinna.

"We gonna do that shopping spree or what," Miss Surelee asked on her way to the bathroom the moment I disconnected Rinna's phone call.

"Yep," I called back, slipping on boots.

Miss Surelee and I quickly scrambled to Rusty's chilled interior, buckled in then sputtered off toward the drive-in at the west end of town, five miles north of the fairground and two miles north of the Pink Squirrel, nestled behind abandon row houses that once doubled as temporary housing for families when coal mining was a booming business. Later, it became a rent-by-the-hour motel before the owner up and died, leaving it condemned and rotting and overran by the likes of Boolee's wild vegetation and overly populated, squirrel population. This time of year, the

Barclay's closed down the graveled lot to movie-goers so they could vacation in style, at their secluded log cabin a few miles south of Route fifty-two, returning only long enough for the birds and the bees to do their spring and summer fling. This also provided Marnie a perfect place for all her customers to park and shop in one conveniently-located spot. It was easy for her because before she was known as Marnie Drexler, she was born Marnie Barclay, youngest of three and hell-bent on being the odd person out. Sort of like me! So, being related to owners of a drive-in was luck on her part as well as mine, I suppose. Being related to owners of a drive-in closed during off seasons was her biggest reason for throwing these discounted parties of hers in the first place; no one would question why. More importantly, no Wannabe would find the need to go and tag a bunch of chintzy women as criminals after the fact.

The party was in full swing by the time I swung Rusty next to a pole with speaker box, suggesting a parking spot that wasn't really a noticeable spot, overran with weeds. Four rows up filled with every make and modeled truck, SUV or crossover known to Detroit city and just beyond, a faded, whitewashed billboard now blank that doubled as the movie screen. Milling about between parked vehicles and billboard was the gathering of goodies and women who forgot all about Billy. This one-hour flash sale was about scoring a deal, not a man.

I shut Rusty down, glancing to the horizon, praying the puffy and rolling grey clouds would hold off for an hour or quickly scoot on by. I wasn't in the mood for any more unexpected showers.

Shivering, I hiked my purse up my shoulder then motioned Miss Surelee toward the gathering. She quietly followed, which surprised me. Miss Surelee usually has something to say about most things. This time, however, she didn't. I think this is the first time she ever shopped outside of four walls and for items with questionable origins and purchased with cash only, receipt suspiciously, not an option. I think it left her curiously awestruck as I watched her take it all in like an eager spectator until we drew closer.

"What's that there?"

"Hotdogs," I said with a side of drool.

"Is that chocolate I smell?"

Yep, sure is, I thought while nodding to say, "Hot chocolate," and I led the way over to Gary Wilkinson's hot dog cart for sustenance. It was his side hustle, sort to speak, because firstly, Gary was a volunteer fireman. Secondly, he had almost the same desire as me to do little else.

"Dang Harley, I'm surprised I'd be seein' you all here after what you all done-did to Pine," Gary said on a pleasing smile as he loaded up a steamed hotdog to bun. "What'll it be?"

He just had to go there, didn't he? I knew my past would come back to haunt me, I just didn't think it would be about the part involving my ex-boyfriend Brent. I shuddered inwardly and focused on the meal at hand, instead. Now, seeing how my Aunt Bertie's cooking has been on hiatus and that I'm not one to worry about spoiling a meal, I held up two fingers and said, "My usual, chili and cheese, please."

Gary gave off a bob of his ball cap covered head, smothered the two hotdogs with steaming sauce, sprinkled them with a handful of shredded cheddar and passed them over. I didn't hesitate and dug in. Miss Surelee had only one, plain. Sheesh, live a little, girlfriend and dabble on some hot mustard!

Now seeing, as we just had the unfortunate lecture via Detective Pine yesterday and that I'm one for not listening or remembering, I went ahead and stuck my nose in and fished around for some gossip. I'm certain Gary worked those fires that have been springing up like competing weeds. Maybe he knew more than what my Uncle Walt was willing to let on. "You have any idea who's been setting all these fires around town?"

Gary gave a start. Guess he wasn't expecting me to be so forward with my curiosity. "We all ain't s'pose to chat it."

Right, "But what do you think?"

He puzzled that over for a millisecond before saying, "I don't."

Thanks, smart ass. "No really, do you have any idea who?"

"Nope," he said then changed the subject asking, "You all figured on what all Rodger-Dodger's been carryin' on 'bout?"

I shook my head no then mumbled between chews, "Do you?"

Gary only chuckled.

Was that a yes or a no? I swallowed then asked him to explain, for my sake, seeing how I was just as clueless as the Wannabes are most days.

"I just thought it was all Shelly's doin' is all."

Huh? "Why would you think that," I asked.

"Dang Harley, don't you all chat up your relation?" he bantered.

Not if I can help it. "Explain, Gary," I hissed out rather impatiently.

Gary grinned wide, a slow shake of his head before saying, "You all can thank me later Harley; Shelly learnt how much moolah he all lost poker night."

Oh. Well. I had nothing to say to that except, "Seems to be a lot of that going around." I smiled to myself. As far as I knew, Sally still didn't know about Brent's financial lost to Charlie Ray either. And I knew it wasn't going to be me spilling the cargo hold of that secret to her. I chewed down the second chili dog and pondered what Gary had said for two seconds. Nope. It didn't add up. Why would Shelly be the one forcing Rodger-Dodger to drive all around town, in a truck that wasn't his and possibly stolen, causing anyone who gets near him to get a flat tire all the while, fire's spring up with no one the wiser and, all because he lost money during poker night? Nope, it doesn't add up.

Hotdogs finished and hot chocolates to hand I thanked Gary for the food, silently thanked him for the Rodger-Dodger revelation and then motioned Miss Surelee and I toward the goodies. We ambled between the upturned, cardboard boxes, piled up with all of Marnie Drexler's discounted wares and began our perusal, Miss Surelee to my shadow, quiet as a mouse.

"There you all are," Rinna cried, making her way toward us, arms loaded with two purses, three pair of shoes, a bracelet and one cashmere looking scarf.

Miss Surelee gave off a low whistle. "You weren't kiddy when you said this stuff is jacked. It's sort of like a garage sale without the garage."

"I think you mean, wacked," I corrected then said, "no matter. Hey Rinna, sorry we're late."

"All the good stuff's gone, but I see you got something to eat."

I glanced down. Sure, as pinecones, I had a chili cheese splotch on the front of my zip up hoodie. I just shrugged. Stained clothing was my norm and never my main concern. "I'm here, that's what counts."

Without warning, Aunt Letty popped up between parked vehicles and flashed me a double flip of the bird. So, I flipped her back.

"What the heck was that 'bout?" asked Rinna.

"Letty," I said without further explanation, because honestly, what was there to explain?

"Ah," Rinna replied, knowingly, agreeing with what was, left unsaid about my curious relation.

Miss Surelee however looked like she had something to say on the matter but simply farted instead.

Seeing how I was beyond broke, Miss Surelee looking one shade short of death itself and Rinna satisfied that I at least showed up, I muttered some worthless apologies that we were, needed back at the Victorian and scooted Miss Surelee and I free of that useless pastime.

"Wasn't what I expected," she mumbled on the drive home.

"No, don't suppose it was, Miss Surelee. See, you can afford to buy, top of the line merchandise," I said. "I, like the rest of Boolee, cannot."

Miss Surelee plastered on a scowl, opened her mouth to say something but thought better of it. I happily overlooked it and kept Rusty sputtering along the hills.

We made it back to the Victorian shortly before three and collapsed to my hide-away room, hoping to scrub our miserable boredom from our existence when an hour later, sour puss strolled and poked her face beyond my breathing with a surprise inquiry about dinner.

"You're not ordering from that pizza place again," said Laney, gracing me exclusively with puckered frown.

I glanced up from the menu that I had memorized sometime back in the eighth grade. How could she say such a thing? Ordello's was the best! "Not unless you want fried sammies," I replied, lacking enthusiasm. "By the way, how was practice?"

"MOM—we're supposed to meet over at the Pine's'!"

I'd nearly forgotten our invite to Detective Pine and company. A tumbling of mixed emotions assaulted my delicate nature at once. On the one hand, it was free food, seeing how Aunt Bertie has been slacking in that department of her domesticated duties. On the other, it meant us having to endure a couple of hours stuck inside the family-hood with a one, Detective Pine and company. See my dilemma? Laney brought me clarity, however with another one of her famous hand-perched-to-hip-rocketed-led-stance and stare. I guess she was looking forward to this invite. Okeydokey I thought then kept going by thinking, why not bring a plus one?

I glanced over to where Miss Surelee, splayed over the bean bag, had her nose stuck between pages of another one of Laney's teen magazines and said, "Miss Surelee, you in?"

She glanced up, took in both Laney and me before asking, "She gonna serve us hotdog's too?"

Hotdog's was a possibility having sampled Sally's cooking firsthand, several months back. Hotdogs would be an upgrade from her crispy-fried, blackened roast chicken. "Not likely," I said, uncertain.

"Count me in," she said, flinging the magazine aside and struggled to stand up.

Fifteen minutes later, I snickered inwardly as I drove Laney and Miss Surelee toward Pineville's unsuspecting brood. I know, I'm devious—I mean, dangerously stupid—for having invited Miss Surelee along. I'm pretty sure the invite didn't include her fancy ways, seeing how everyone thought she would have her car fixed and settled to the big apple by now. Yep, they looked unprepared for an extra place setting. You're welcome, Brent.

Once dinner concluded incident free, Miss Surelee, Brent and I took our coffees and pie and adjourned to the living room for some light banter while Laney graciously followed Sally to the kitchen to help clean up. Oh sure, *now* she wants to look like she's a keeper! I waited two seconds before I asked Brent, "What do you know so far?"

Brent took a sip of his coffee, did a mental tally before his stoic expression sagged. "I cannot believe it, but thangs are lookin' mighty gloom for your Aunt Bee," he said.

"You can't be serious," I cried for all to hear, pie crust crumbs tumbling loose of my flapper.

"I know," he said on a sigh, hand scratching at the five o'clock stubble about his cheek. "I told Walt to look into it deeper."

"Good," I said then asked, "And Rodger-Dodger?"

"It's lookin' worse for him," he said.

I set empty pie plate aside, took a sip of coffee then nodded, agreeing before I said, "But I don't think it's by choice."

"How's that, Dodge?"

"If he's the one doing this—which there's no solid proof that he is—why are the places around town so random and what's in it for him?" I said. Then for added emphasis, I set coffee mug aside so I could produce Rodger-Dodger's missing cell phone from my purse, happily explaining when and where Miss Surelee and I had found it. Brent went livid over that omission yesterday, when we strolled on in to the lock-U-up station with a presumably, missing, Ginger Dodge. I smugly shrugged.

Recouped from my little surprise he went on to say, "Thunk-it up myself, too. I ain't gotta clue why he'd be the one doin' this."

We thought on this for a moment or two, sipping coffee. Huh, nothing. I had nothing to go on either so, I wrangled up the list of victims, muttering them aloud; Brent paying close attention; Miss Surelee slurping coffee, keeping suspiciously quiet.

"Old man Johnson's place was the EconLodge; the second fire was at Bubba and Ginger's costume shop where we nearly escaped; the third was Mickey and Regatta's pawn shop; the fourth was the Gaffadee's stables, where once again, we almost became road kill."

Brent released a low chuckle over that statement.

Sheesh, not funny...

I pressed on, saying, "The fifth was Tom Pullins' and Harriet Peck's strip malls and the sixth was Larry and Ronita's laundry. So, do you have any idea as to the connection with all those places?"

"Ain't none, other than they all'd been purposely set by summin other than them-thar owners," he said before adding, "You all forgot one; Junior Pensky's lube and tires, went up Thursday last."

Oh man, he was right. I did forget reading about that in the *Redlight* last week when I was eager to forget about my Aunt Letty's unfortunate and untimely induction into the widowers' club. Hey wait a minute! "That makes seven fires in nearly two weeks!" Sheesh, Uncle Walt was right.

"Yup," Brent said with a nod.

"Wait, how do you know it wasn't any one of them setting the fires," I asked, unconvinced.

He nodded a second time, adding, "They all'd been ver-i-fied and they all had alibis bein' elsewhere at the time of all them ding-dang farers."

"So, then, the owners, they're going to get paid by the insurance company," I asked.

Brent flashed me a curious look before he nodded a third, 'yes' my way, adding, "Providin' them all gots them-thar insurance."

"What does Pinky think," I had to ask.

Miss Surelee had dozed up to that point and startled, pie crumbs tumbling to shag carpeting, her oblivious while she questioned, "Who-dat?"

"Ranger-man," I explained.

Miss Surelee suddenly farted, unusually loud.

Brent and I did our best to ignore it, before he said, "He's bent on you all-know-who bein' the ring-leader."

Ah dipshit. I'd nearly scrubbed my lousy, no-good ex-husband from my unpleasant memories when Brent had to go and remind me of my connection to that three-timing, lousy excuse for a man. I gave in to a nonchalant nod.

"You know who's this 'you-know' he's talking about?" asked Miss Surelee.

"Uh-huh...*Dickie*," I said with a venom-laced tongue.

Miss Surelee stiffened, sneezed once while simultaneously farting. That was talented. Does she need to make an appointment for a coloscopy? But I was suddenly coming to terms with her intestinal problems as being more nervous-related than food-induced. Sally's peanut butter pie and hamburger with corn-chip casserole had my stomach setting off to dreamland instead. "What's wrong, Miss Surelee?"

"Nothing," she muttered and adverted her gaze to settle about Brent's psychedelic colored living room.

Detective Pine stared on, not convincingly, I might add. He looked like he was fighting back several questions at once.

So, I beat him to the punch line of his bewilderment by saying, "I don't want to say this, or admit under false assumptions, but I think Great-Uncle Leo and Tucky are involved somehow."

That got me a flat-out stare.

So, I gunned the metal and slammed the petal to add, "I ran into Gary today, and before you say it, he mentioned something about this might be Shelly's doing. Now, I don't know about you but I can't see her being the mastermind to arson."

"Why you all tellin' me this, Dodge?"

"Because he mentioned something that Shelly found out about my brother losing money on poker night and that might be why he's running all around town like an escaped convict."

Detective Pine flashed me a peculiar look for all but ten seconds before his face flickered into a look of startled curiosity. He quickly abandoned his coffee mug to end table then scrambled to his feet and went to the built-ins along the far wall. He rooted around some then came up with a mini address book. I asked what he was doing when he shushed me. Sheesh, I was only trying to be helpful. A moment later, wormy mustache at attention, he glanced my way with a startling revelation that only his riddled mind was privy to.

"What," I cried, equally standing, causing Laney to rush into the den followed by Sally cradling a sleeping Jasmine; two wiggly boys bounded in a moment later; everyone curiously staring our way.

Brent ignored them, putting on coat while saying to me, "I think I might know what's been goin' on around here."

Miss Surelee and I grabbed coats and hustled right on up those three steps and out the front door in Brent's wake.

Laney caught up, huddled next to Miss Surelee at the sidewalk while Sally lingered at the open doorway on the stoop, protective of her brood and home, watching on. Brent gave Sally a nod and climbed into his county issued V-8 truck and sparked it to life.

Unt-uh, no way, he's not going to drop that little revelation at my boots then drive away without explanation. I was a Dodge after all; I deserved to know first-and-foremost the latest-and-greatest of anything, gossip worthy. I hustled up to his driver's side window and pounded at it with balled fist asking, or rather, demanding, "What'd you figure out, Brentwood?"

Brent gave me a flat out, double barreled stink eye before shooting a glance Sally's way. Then he gave me a second stink eye.

"Just say it, Dick-tective," I shouted through the glass, lacking charm, or excitement. "I have a right to know too."

Once more he shot a look from Sally, then back to me, but this time he pressed the button and lowered his window partway. Then he held up that little black book for only me to see as he said on a whisper, "Poker night."

I felt a flash of hellfire shoot through me all at once. I stood aside as Brent peeled rubber, headed in the direction of the pokey. His words felt like lava, stirring up our recent conversation for me to suddenly put the pieces together. I understood where he was going with his accusation and if so, he might be right. I wanted him to be wrong. Because if he was right, then my brother, Rodger-Dodger might want to consider driving that monster truck all the way to Mexico and never come back.

Chapter Thirteen: Texas Two-Stepping

I didn't hesitate to chase down Detective Pine's getaway.

I had the key to Rusty, shoved to ignition, engine sputtering before I had my door shut or before I remembered my two tagalongs. Laney and Miss Surelee barely made it upon the bench seat as I had Rusty in gear and flooring it north out of the family-hood and toward the lock-U-up in Brent's V-8 trucks' speedily wake. My tagalongs flashed me frowns and worried looks. No time for explaining to those two, who held on with death grips, my reason for peeling rubber and chasing down Detective Pine as I managed to blow past five of the twenty-some stop signs along the way. I needed some answers, and Brent's two-word explanation didn't explain all that much.

At least, not in the way I think he was figuring.

Especially now since he turned east, one block shy of the pokey, then hooked a left one block later and continued north along Regal Drive instead.

I squelched a stop at the curb beneath the only street lamp now glowing. Slightly peeved, slightly worried, I threw Rusty into park, shut him down then bounded the driveway, hot on Brent's heels who neared the front porch, appropriately decorated for the upcoming spooky holiday with carved pumpkins, bed sheets for ghosts and an oversized, glittery black spider. All of it was awash in a yellowish glow from the bug light to the right of the front door. Miss Surelee and Laney finally realized I had stopped driving as they too scrambled after us. Brent shook his head my way and thundered the rest of the way up the front walk, scattering dry, crinkly leaves in his wake. I hustled close to his shadow, undeterred by his wrinkled frown, worms following suit.

"So, you're going to ask Shelly about poker night," I asked, not sure where his thinking was leading him. Brent shook his head no. I didn't buy it because he was clenching teeth. "But isn't that the reason why you're here," I asked. "So, you can find out which buddy is holding his marker?"

Brent turned his back on me to ring Shelly's doorbell, turned back and flashed me a deepened frown and a wag of his finger saying, "Just let me do the talkin', Dodge, I mean it."

So long as I got to tag along, then fine by me. I just shrugged my reply, not promising anything.

Shelly flashed hooded eyes the moment she spotted me hugging Brent's left shoulder aptly ignoring my tagalong shadows then settled last looks Detective Pine's way. I think she first thought we might be early trick-or-treaters, or possibly, big man Red, himself as she flashed everyone a perturbed expression.

"Eve'nin, Shelly," said Detective Pine.

Shelly kept her look of contempt about her face, forgoing pleasantries to huffily ask, "Is this a social visit, 'tective?"

"'Fraid not, Shelly," he replied. "May we all come in?"

Shelly glanced to the group of us, considering Brent's proposal for all but two seconds. Seeing how only one of us was law enforcement, Shelly must have sensed this unannounced visit wasn't congenial and the fact that Detective Pine was sporting his on-duty handgun, she'd look the fool if she declined now, or offered him a candy bar. Instead, her shoulders sagged as she nodded once and then stepped aside, parting the door wider to allow the four of us entry, past the foyer and rounding the living room to our right, all without a fight or a click of her tongue.

With me right on his heels, Detective Pine suddenly came to a squelchy shoe stop, mouth catching flies. I instantly bounced off his saggy butt, unprepared once more for the sudden braking habit he was, accustomed to doing whenever I was nearby. I collected myself from the floor then poked my head around his shoulder, curious to know what caused him to yank on the emergency brake this time. Miss Surelee glanced around his right, curious as well then smacked hands to eyes with a whimpering cry of, "Monster," while Laney sucked air.

What. The. Hell? "What the heck, Shelly," I cried to the heavens. So much for me keeping my mouth shut. The second I spotted Detective Pines' reason for annoying me this fine evening was all it took to unlock my snark.

Detective Pine sprang from his stupor and put balled fists to belt, glaring in the direction of the soft blue colored sofa centered about Shelly's living room, muttering, "Christ, almighty, what in the blazes is goin' on?"

I followed suit of Detective Pine and put hands to hips yelling to no one, "Yeah, what's going on?"

Shelly however, did her wifely duties by ignoring Detective Pine and my outburst, turned back toward her kitchen, and rounded up mugs of coffee and a plate of cookies.

Brent and I continued to stare on at the reedy silhouette, slouched to the sofa. He was looking up from the hunting and fishing magazine he'd been reading, staring back with equal amounts of alarm and frustration. Five minutes later, our staring contest was looking ridiculous so I dropped hands to side and came over to the sofa and leaned in with a wag of my finger. "You do know Red's going to blame me for this, don't you?"

Damn brother of mine had to go and toss me back a shrug. Sheesh.

Yep, you guess it, I was staring back at the troublesome person I sometimes call relation, my brother, Rodger-Dodger, and the reason Red's been hell-bent on catching me off my game. Sheesh, my brother sure didn't look missing to me.

Shelly returned with coffee and cookies all around, a glass of milk for Laney. Laney hugged Miss Surelee's side before each sank to one of the two arm chairs flanking the sofa and stared on hesitant to do anything else. Not me, I snagged two cookies for possibly later.

Detective Pine turned back to Shelly equally ignoring a mug of coffee to bark, "Why in the hellcats' fire and damnation, dint you all call me and tell me he all done-did come back?"

"Yeah," I agreed, stuffing cookie to mouth. Okay, maybe they won't make it for a midnight snack after all. "Why didn't you call *me* and tell *me* you heard from *him*?"

Brent flashed me a frown. I ignored him because even though Sally's pie was 'delish', Shelly's cookies were pure, chocolate euphoria. Not only that, but their four children, ages from five through twelve just bounded down the stairs, curious to know what the stink was all about too.

Shelly's eyes went all misty. She shot a look to my brother, a look to me, then to Brent then back to her husband before she slipped to the spot next to Rodger-Dodger and hugged her youngest daughter to her lap. The other one rounded on Laney with a happy, oblivious grin. The two oldest twin boys took a stance behind the sofa where their parents sat, practicing to take over Red's hell someday. Detective Pine hesitated before he turned back to Rodger-Dodger with the same amount of buckshot vocabulary, repeating his question, albeit, this one G-rated for the sake of children's innocent hearing.

Not me.

"Yeah," I double agreed, stuffing cookie number two to my overworked, cakehole. "You could have frickin' called someone, other than me! Red's been wondering where you frickin' took off to and blabbing to anyone who frickin' cares to listen!"

Rodger-Dodger shook his head once and said, "Get on back home, siscer, this ain't your concern."

Nope, unt-uh, no fricking way! "It's too late for that, brother, besides, I'm not going anywhere until you tell Brent what's been going on," I said. So that way, I could be the first one to beat Red to the checker flag.

Rodger-Dodger glanced once Shelly's way then turned back to me with a look of confusion. "And tell-em what, that I was snatched by Batman?"

"You were kidnapped," I asked, mouth yawing wide as I snuck a glance toward the plate of melt-in-your-mouth, chocolate chip cookies wondering if it would be rude of me to snatch up two more.

"Sure, don't look kidnapped to me," Miss Surelee whispered to Laney who was rather preoccupied playing a hand clapping game of patty cake with a miniature version of Shelly to comment back.

I had enough of this three-ringed circus and knowing I was about to blow a gasket or stuff a third cookie down my gullet I perched hands to hips, leaned in, eyes narrowed my brother's way, voice shaky, yet laced with a threatening calm I mostly reserve for Laney and said, "Maybe we should make a stop at the pokey."

Brent caught up saying, "Shelly, you all mind?"

Shelly nodded once, equally understanding and five minutes later, had her brood rounded up and secured to their respective rooms once more, upstairs. Good. That interlude gave me just enough time to snag two more cookies for the Rusty ride home.

Brent finally found his reason, why he was a detective and asked, "Rodger-Dodger, do you all know who all kidnapped ya?"

"Nope, 'cause everah wanna them dang yarhoo's was prancin' 'round in costumes."

I gave a start, stiffened, and shot Miss Surelee a worried glance. Ah. That explains the Batman sighting as his passenger. I turned back to my brother and snickered; Brent didn't. Guess he overlooked my inside joke or my need to nibble away at cookie number three.

"Do you all know why they all kidnapped ya," Brent asked, continuing to overlook my need to diffuse a stressful situation with laughter and chocolate chips.

Rodger-Dodger glanced to Shelly as she rounded the stairs and returned to her seat next to him. They exchanged curious glances before my brother replied with, "Maybe."

Maybe? Oh, I'm going to slap the stupid right off him if he doesn't start playing nice. "Well *maybe* you might want to clue us in on that one," I shouted rather unnecessarily, cookie crumbs tumbling loose.

Detective Pine grunted. Guess he wasn't pleased my mouth kept flapping wind or that I tend to eat at every opportunity, stressful, highly charged situations included. Brent continued to overlook my troublesome need to be troublesome and asked my brother, "Why they all wantin' you all tearin' up the town?"

"Dunno," Rodger-Dodger replied.

I saw a jaw muscle twitch on Brent's face and it took all my doing as a Dodge to stifle a snigger because let's face it I wasn't the only Dodge to cause him heartburn on an ongoing basis.

Brent hadn't noticed my smug look because I think he was more preoccupied with acid reflux and pressed on. "Dint any wanna them-thar yahoo's say anythang worth rememberin'?"

"Nope, notta wanna them dang jokers talked. They all done-did wrote every ding-dang thang down!"

If I wasn't in such a tizzy over finding my brother suddenly not missing, squatting at his own home, Shelly clearly in on this fact, then I would have laughed; Brent just scrubbed a hand down his face and hung his head. I think maybe he was counting to three. I, however, stuffed another cookie to my mouth instead, not about to let loose that it was exactly how Ginger described her kidnappers.

After a collective breath, Brent looked up to ask, "Anywhere else besides town they all made ya drive?"

"Nope," he said.

"And you all been back here, each night?"

"Yep," he replied.

Brent's face hardened as he overlooked that omission before he asked, "Any idea whose truck you all been drivin'?"

"Nope," he replied.

"Maybe it belongs to Ducky and his parents," I said as an afterthought, because I was all out of cookie. "Their farm was just down the road from where we found your cell phone and Ginger; she was kidnapped too, by the way."

Brent flashed me a frown. Oops. I guess he didn't want that catnap out of the bag just yet. Too late!

Rodger-Dodger ignored me and Brent's staring contest to snappily reply with, "I would a recalled that yarhoo the minna he walked!"

"Who-dat," said Miss Surelee, clearly feeling left out of my unhappy family reunion.

Oh, I forgot. "Pigeon toed, limp; Ducky Humphrey," I said, explaining for Miss Surelee's sake just in case she might have overlooked it from yesterday's visit to Spigot Studs. She absently nodded. I turned back to Rodger-Dodger. "Like I said, that's where we found Ginger, in Blue-Veil."

"So," he replied, equally unfazed.

"So? But she was, kidnapped too, possibly from the same ones that took you, and *probably* for the same reasons!"

Brent flashed me a double-barreled stink eye. I smartly overlooked it.

"Yeah, what'd that be, if you all so dang smarty?" said Rodger-Dodger, crossing arms across his bony chest.

Oh, that's it! I dug wildly about my pockets. I'm going to call up Red right now if my brother didn't wipe that smirk from his scraggly bearded face! I gave up two seconds later. Realizing my phone was in my leather special and the special edition was still sitting to Rusty's vinyl bench seat. I took a mental pause then flashed him my best, go-to stink eye, taking a breath to say, "Because, *Brother*, someone was trying to get her to pay up Bubba's marker!"

"Wha," he uttered.

"Yeah, that's right, brother of mine, we know all about you losing on poker night!"

Shelly began sniffling and foolishly blubbering. Their brood hovered at the top of the stairs, whispering, equally sniffing and blubbering. Rodger-Dodger just shook his scraggly head, blasting me full on with a murderous look. So was Brent. So, I gunned the pedal and sarcastically added, "What—not too sure about that one either?"

"That's the only dang thang I'm sure of," he said with a better-looking stink eye than I've seen Red give my way.

"Is that why they're making you set all those fires," I asked, totally stunned I said this out loud before my thoughts caught up with my mouth; because I was totally stunned that I had thought it in the first place and now I was feeling insulted; Shelly just collected the cookies and coffee back to the kitchen. Whatever... Okay, no, I'm not sorry. I turned my squinty eyes back to my brother and glared on. He shouldn't have pushed my buttons. He shouldn't have forced my mouth to operate without a cookie or me thinking first.

"What in the sandbox of hell gots you all thinkin' that?" Rodger-Dodger finally spat back.

"Because—"

Detective Pine held up a hand my way, forcing my mouth to clamp shut. Sheesh, I was on-a-roll here. Lucky for him, I did pinch lips tight. So, I crossed arms and whistled steam, waiting for Brent to get to the punch-drunk line of his reasoning.

"You all gots ya any idea who'd a might a been settin' all those ding-dang farers," asked Brent.

"Dunno," Rodger-Dodger said on a shake of his scraggly faced head. "But I ain't the one doin' it."

"Aaaand," I pressed on. I couldn't help it. I needed a reason to breathe.

"Cheese-it, sis, let it alone, will ya?"

"No fricking or fracking way, Rodger-Dodger! Buildings are blowing up around town and someone's following me around like I was a treasure chest filled with doubloons. Don't get me started about Red!"

"Don't forget about Gee," added Miss Surelee.

That comment sent me over the edge causing my voice to hover just above high C when I said, "That slime ball! He says I still have something he wants but I don't, not after Derby and Newbie blew up Black Beauty!" Miss Surelee sucked air. It was the first time since hearing about my Bentley's demise. Glad to see she cared.

"Geez siscer, I'm sorrah," said Rodger-Dodger. And for a second there, he meant it.

"Are you truly, sorry, because if you are, I'd like to know what in the green acres is going on around *here*!"

Rodger-Dodger sighed. His face and shoulders going slack, Shelly returned, nudging him on, swiping at her teary eyes. A minute later, he finally gave in and spilled the doo-doo.

"It was poker night at Stan's garage, we all were doin' good. Next thang I know I'm down next months' mortgage. Never saw it comin," he said.

"Who did you lose the money to," I asked, stunned. Shelly wasn't going to like me hearing about that.

"It ain't that simple, sis. Being, broke sort of temps a man so I gotta get my balls back, ya know?"

Miss Surelee nodded her understanding. I stared at her speechless. If I had balls needing back, it wouldn't be for that reason. I turned back to my brother. "No, I don't know," I said flatly. "Who'd you lose the money to?"

"So, Uncle Leo tells me about the track..."

I put my finger to my twitchy eye and sighed before asking, "How much more did you lose to him?"

"Twenty-grand in all," he said.

"What were you thinking, Rodger-Dodger?"

He just shrugs. Shelly sniffed.

"Tell him to give it back," I cried.

"Yep, talked to him," he said then added, "It ain't like I actually paid-em. You all think I gots me that kind a dough lyin' 'round?"

"So, what, he just lets you go your merry way...no harm done," I asked.

"Nope, Leo ain't gonna go for nutin short a the greenback."

"What are you going to do," I asked, swallowing a lump in my throat.

"So, Leo tells me about a job he needs doin', gonna clean the slate, make us even."

"Shit," I said hissing air, "Why?"

"'Cause it's Leo," he said with a huff, hands paying homage to the angels on potty break as he concluded, "Can't exactly go 'round jackin' goods no more, now can-e?"

This wasn't good. Shelly was palling over this omission. "So, it's Leo who has you driving around setting fires?"

"No," he said, pausing before he added, "I ain't never gotta chance doin' what Leo wanted me doin'."

"Wait one dang minute," Brent interrupted with a huff. "What exactly are you all doin'?"

"Keepin' you all from gettin' blown up," he said as if he was casually explaining how to sight up a deer during hunting season.

Fat lot of good it did us at the Ego...

"What," I said, hearing the same thought echo off Brent's lips. "Why?"

Rodger-Dodger only shrugged. I guess he wasn't privy to accessory after the fact.

"Fine, whatever," I said. "But you need to get Leo to drop your debt; wipe out your marker!" So, Shelly doesn't go postal and backhands him in the presence of Detective Pine. Actually...I'm all for the pleasure of doing it myself if she chicken's out.

"No can do, Leo's in worse shape than me."

"Preach to the hand brother," I said, but seeing the look on Shelly's face I just had to keep going and asked, "Why's that?"

"Welp, he all went missin' the night before they all snagged me."

Craptacular.

"So, what you're telling me is this: whoever took Leo, probably took you and for the same reason they took him?"

"I dunno, maybe," he said, "Can't see it being so."

"Why's that," asked Detective Pine.

"Game set up like always at seven at Stan's place. Stan, me, Leo and Joe-Bob, ain't nobody else in on it after Junior backed out."

Brent gave a start before he and I exchanged curious thoughts, nodding our unspoken agreement. Neither one of us could see either Stan or Job-Bob wrangling my brother into crimes against nature. However, Job-Bob had a son. A son that somehow was besties with idiot number one and that idiot was grandson to my Great Uncle Leo. I regrouped my thoughts to ask my brother, "Okay, so whoever took you was because you owe Leo money, right?"

Rodger-Dodger gave me a, palms up with a two-shoulder shrug.

"That could be it...," I said, turning to Brent. "Put him under protective custody."

Before Brent could agree with me Rodger-Dodger sprang to his feet saying, "I can't leave—not gonna let them all hurt my Shelly and the girls and me boys if I don't cooper-ate. And so, should yoot, go on and git outta here!"

"Brent can protect them too, right," I said.

Miss Surelee nodded in agreement, as if she had first-hand experience. She was probably thinking more about Joe-Bob than anything else. Shelly only pursed lips my way. Rodger-Dodger deadpanned then said, "You all mean like he all done-did for you back-a-ways? Nope, ain't gonna chance it."

Lovely, bring that up now, why don't you.

Brent whistled steam beyond worms and disagreed barking about the room saying, "Harley's right, you all need to come in where we all can keep an eye on you all."

"What—no! Not gonna let you all get my girls hurt!"

"Fuck Robert, what other choice do you have?"

After five minutes of my stellar persuasive attitude and a crisp, twenty-dollar bill he relented.

Once Detective Pine had my brother's family settled, I finally remembered the fake tube of lipstick, handed that and my brother's cell phone over to Brent and shuttled Miss Surelee and Laney free of the pokey. Brent didn't seem bothered by the fact that someone is going out of their way to shadow my whereabouts, insisting once more, that it wasn't Pinky's doing.

I adamantly disagreed.

Another twenty minutes later I was shuttling my tag-along's back to the seclusion of the Victorian, knowing that my brother and his family were safely behind bars at the weekend vacay, all expenses paid, curtsey of me and my big mouth.

You're welcome.

As an added insult of stupid, Charlie Ray dialed up the Victorian to remind me about Friday, wondering what costume I'd be wearing. I only shrugged my reply then reminded him to stop calling after hours.

Here's hoping the fires too, will stop.

Wednesday began with the usual fanfare of Leroy chauffeuring him and Laney off to school, Aunt Bertie elbow deep to petrified critters, Mr. Willoughby beginning deliveries and the phone ringing off the hook. Because as everyone around here knows, the second they catch wind of gossip, they latch on to it with a death grip and refuse to let it die until they've had their say. Especially since it centered on me and my brother, Rodger-Dodger, and their misguided thinking that he was the one setting all those fires these past couple of weeks.

Nope. I'm not even going to defend that mangled truth.

I noticed Miss Surelee still fast asleep. Hunh, for once, I beat her to the bathroom. Good thing, because I think the hot water was running a bit low.

Lucky for me and my thoughts Aunt Bertie kept at my frustration and upped it with a side of sour by reminding me of the wake and service for Aunt Letty's husband and his ashes, beginning promptly at two. Good thing Miss Surelee and I had slept in and caught up on our sleep deprivation, otherwise, I might head on over to Red's funhouse of flames for some heart attack fun with an early exit from this spinning ball of fire. To my scrunched-up nose, Miss Surelee had slipped away two seconds earlier.

"I'm not going," I said with a side of protest.

Aunt Bertie planted a hard stare, pursed lips my way before saying, "Don't you think for one minute I can explain away your absence. Especially, not after what's been going on with Rodger."

Leave it to her to resurrect Red's one-track way of thinking and snag me into the heart of blame. I suddenly startled and glanced about. It would be my luck to have Red storming the Victorian with buckshot's of insults flung my way. I turned back to Aunt Bertie. Nope. I'm not going to rise to her trickery. So, I just shrugged, hoping but not caring if she took the hint. I also didn't care what lies she wanted to say about me, I still was not attending.

"They're family," Bertie added, overlooking all that is me.

"So, you say," I replied instead.

Aunt Bertie harrumphed, dug about her purse then pushed on with a green bribe.

Now seeing how I'm not one to follow the crowd, or that Laney is in constant state of wondering why I'm her mom or that Miss Surelee has a way of blackmailing me into worse situations, I thought this was below the fan belt of my Aunt's moral compass and did my best at looking appalled. The nerve of her trying to bribe me into attending!

I let her wave that twenty-dollar bill for ten seconds before I snatched it right up. Besides, it helped me break even after last nights' truth and dare session at my brother's house.

"Good, now go get presentable," she said with a smug look to her face. "We're pulling out in ten minutes."

I cringed inwardly with a sigh. Yep, so not looking forward to this outing as I muttered my dislike all the way back upstairs.

Miss Surelee startled upon the beanbag the moment I entered my room away from abnormal, asking, "You're not really gonna attend, are you?"

"I have no choice," I said, slipping on boots over jeans. "Not unless I want to find myself sleeping in Rusty."

Miss Surelee shook her head once and shifted upon the beanbag chair; Bandit poked his head up from his snuggle spot atop my pillow. Miss Surelee overlooked the sneaky little feline and said, moaning, her voice cracking around the edges, "You go on without me, Sweetness. I'll be just fine holding down the farm."

Nope. "Not going to happen, Miss Surelee," I said, shrugging into my hoodie over long-sleeved thermal. Do I know how to dress for a wake or what? "If *I* have, to go, then *you* have to go. Besides, it'll be over before you know it."

Miss Surelee gave off a low groan, while a grumbling deep from her belly rumbled away. "I'm feeling the need for Pepto."

"Bathroom," I flatly said, as I snagged my purse off my dresser and headed for the stairs.

Aunt Bertie gave me the once over the second I joined her at the front door. Dressed in her funeral best of black, ankle-length dress, matching jacket and daisy covered, pillbox hat, she cradled a cellophane covered platter of her famous crumb cake, blasting me an unholy expression. Oh sure. Now she has time to bake for afternoon mourners while the rest of us go malnourished each night. Sheesh. Aunt Bertie continued to blast a stern expression my way. Because I looked the same way I did when she had suckered me into a petrified delivery a week ago, Tuesday. Now I may have trashed all my expensive, department store labeled attire back in Amarillo, leaving me to dress casually for all that is Boolee. And, not-to-mention, that I owned only one dressy black dress good only for showing off during funerals, that coincidently, Aunt Bertie had purchased for me back in August for Newbie's funeral. Still, that doesn't mean I care to dress to impress for the Spigots, especially after the way Aunt Letty has been treating me since her unannounced visit back. Goodie, now Aunt Bertie is puckering her lips into a frown. I don't know why's she's upset over my choice of attire because this is what twenty dollars' worth of a bribe will get you. She should have given me a fifty instead. Lucky for me her staring and frowning suddenly redirected elsewhere.

Miss Surelee joined me by the front door, looking tired and skittish, or worse—looking like she might have the flu—equally dressed to not impress in polka dotted moo-moo of black and white, yellow vinyl platform rocker boots and a spiky, universal-type mullet and oversized, black, beetle-like, overly-priced sunglasses covering most of her face. Naturally, my Aunt's frown shifted from me to her the moment she shrugged into her lime green goose down, sleeveless jacket. Otherwise, I might have found the need for a snarky retort as I settled on a snigger instead.

Mr. Willoughby scooted in from the kitchen looking spiffy in his charcoal grey suit and blueberry colored tie, wisps of white hair slicked over his liver spotted dome while his hearing aid was suspiciously missing. He gave me a goofy-looking grin, easing my giggles back a notch because even though he chose to go without his hearing he did however, decide that today was a good day to sport a full set of dentures. Spoil sport. I gave a small head shake, not trying to hide a scowling frown as he accepted the small, platter of crumb cake to in turn, hand a folded-up umbrella back before he followed Aunt Bertie out the door and to her mint green colored Ford that looked better and ran better than Rusty ever will.

Normally, funerals around here held at the Patriarch church on the corner of Main and Spruce, a block west of the town Square. But apparently, Letty's husband wasn't Catholic or Protestant nor did he need burying as she had decided to have the wake/funeral services for his ashes at the VFW hall on the southeast side of town, nestled amid clapboard homes, some of which, converted to apartments. I guess her husband was a veteran and belonged to his chapter in the state they were residing. I've never been to the VFW hall before and since I never served in the military, I had no reason to visit its walls before today. I wish I had paid attention a week ago, last Tuesday during the delivery from hell to the treasure trap or I would have realized that I had, or rather, visited its parking lot. The VFW conveniently sat across the street from Stranger-Danger's recently acquired shop. Yikes.

I eased Rusty alongside the curb and parked along the street, illegally, because one, the whole of Boolee showed up for the wake and the macadam lot was bursting to full of every known Dodge, make and model, one Ford and two Chevy's. Two, I just didn't care if someone towed Rusty or worse if one of Boolee's flunkies decided to give me a ticket. Personally, I think if either scenario happened, I would expect Brent to wrangle me free of those charges, being that I would hope that he and the Wannabes have better things to be doing than hassling me, Harley Dodge.

I glanced to the sky and shuddered. It was gunmetal gray, threatening rain once more or possibly, snow. I just mentally shook my head over my crap luck, shut down Rusty, pocketed the key and slid a glance towards Miss Surelee. She had her eyes locked to the hand painted sign over the front door of the treasure trap. Her pallor was degrading from yellow to green with a hint of something sour hovering. I hiked purse to shoulder and motioned to Miss Surelee as I quickly exited Rusty just in case her intestines were ready to explode or the skies parted and rained forth.

Miss Surelee joined my side with a measly, overly imagined groan before she shifted gears and gave off a hand-covered giggle. "Shoot, Sweetness, I'm gonna dizzy-dive in five."

My eyes flew across the street at the same time Billy opened the front door of his shop. He nodded once over his shoulder, then closed the door and jogged our way. I gave myself a mental hand fan of face to keep from doing a 'dizzy-dive' of my own. Because, Billy has that effect on me as well as, every living creature within a three-hundred-mile radius with no one the exception to his hypnotic ways. Watching him jog was like watching an episode of *Bay Watch*, without the hassle of sun, surf, sand, or those itty, bitty red shorts. Not that I'm complaining though because the sight of him fully clothed was just as gloriously gratifying.

"Thought that was you," he said, leaning in with a heavenly grin.

"Wha," I said with a side of drool then repeated saying, "What?"

"Your truck, it's unmistakable," he explained.

Oh right. I cringed inwardly. "Thanks," I muttered then asked with a wave over my shoulder, "Um, are you attending Letty's thing?"

"I was thinking I should show my respects," he said. "That okay with you Boots?"

Hell-fricking-yes, it's fine! "Yeah, sure," I said on a shrug, keeping my thoughts and body cool like that as I turned on wobbling knees toward the oak doors of the VFW hall.

Miss Surelee shamelessly fanned herself as she followed.

We made it to the outer set of doors just as a light mist began to settle, causing my split ends to poof.

I'd like to say, we made our rounds of condolences with as little fuss or fan-fare possible with, no one on the Spigot side of things the wiser. Nope. That'd be a lie, otherwise.

But it will be what I choose to say in court.

Because after Red had his misguided say about Rodger-Dodger's incarceration, my entire relation stood as witness the moment Miss Surelee shoved me aside and went Looney Tunes, ballistic about the VFW's heavily polished, parquet wood floors, causing Red to continue to shoot his hellfire my way, rather than referee. Billy remained, suspiciously calm off to one side, taking it all in. So, nope, I'm not going to make excuses for Miss Surelee's unusual ways or stop her, because I've been known on occasion to react in a similar fashion. But more importantly, I think Miss Surelee had a right to act like a chicken with his head cut off especially now, seeing that Letty's deceased husband was none other than Arnold Hibbard and she was charging the two of us. I just wasn't sure of, why.

See, the thing is, no one about Boolee who wasn't a Spigot, a Harley, or a Detective Pine, had firsthand knowledge that Arnold was Dickie's secretive partner back in Amarillo. No one about Boolee, who wasn't a Spigot or a Miss Surelee, knew that Letty Spigot Dodge was really Loretta Hibbard.

Until now, that is.

In two seconds flat, I had recouped from my stupor and found myself chasing after Aunt Letty who was now chasing down Miss Surelee, plastic butter knife to one hand, cheese ball to the other, screaming or choking on insults Miss Surelee's way. Margret, Tucky, the Humphrey's, several other Spigots and Boomer, hot on our heels because they were feeling left out of this kind of stupid. I had no reasonable understanding of why the Spigot's chased after Miss Surelee. I just didn't care. But I did care about her delicate nature and the fact I thought it just, plain rude otherwise, that I felt compelled to protect her. Besides, no one else stepped up to intercept on her behalf.

That was a mistake I won't be making twice. Aunt Letty just cheese balled me. So naturally, the rest of her immediate family (and possibly one or two of my own) got in on the action and hurled cookies, crumb cake, pie, crackers, spaghetti bake, crust-less sandwiches, pickles, chocolate cake and chili-cheese dip my way. You know, just in case they too, were feeling left out of the food-throwing-fun. I suddenly flashed back to my senior year in high school. That day didn't end well for me either.

While I picked at mangled food about my hair, face, and clothes, I noticed Letty now had Miss Surelee in a headlock, Miss Surelee squeaking her alarm, a pinch of Letty's hair to her right hand in a sort of death grip. I almost forgot I was trying to help Miss Surelee because the sight of those two was belly-gripping funny. Then my conscious jumpstarted my molasses like limbs and I sprang to action...almost...

Brent and the rest of the Wannabes crashed the party and put the brakes on this round-up rodeo with a click of his handgun. No one was, shot. I think. Yep, Brent wasn't foolish enough to disinherit me from that side of the family tree, but he was foolish enough to aim his issued, handgun overhead and squeeze the trigger.

After the sprinkling of asbestos sifted away, he turned his frown my way, saying, "Christ, Harley, what'd I done-did tell you all 'bout buggin' Letty?"

Chapter Fourteen: You Can't Fix Stupid

I glared back at Detective Brentwood Lewis Pine through slitty eyes before I shifted my under-fueled hellfire about the VFW hall, glowing eyes landing over every one of my dang Dodge and Spigot relation. All motion ceased; all jibber-jabber snuffed. Except for Mr. Willoughby who stuffed cheese ball covered cracker to mouth then gave off another one of his goofy-looking, toothy grins with a thumbs up my way, clearly oblivious; Aunt Bertie stood hands perched to hips, frowning, or fuming at me, I think. I noticed Marty Smarty had Miss Surelee off to one side, furthest away from any-and-all Spigot retaliation, protectively. Sheesh, why hadn't Billy sprung to action and come to my rescue? Otherwise, I wouldn't be the only one food-bombed and looking the fool because it was just my dumb luck that Brent thought this was my doing. Not-to-mention, Red agreed. The rest of the appalling or frustrated and snarky faces (perhaps, one or two looking curious) gawked at me as I mulled over Brent's unnecessary accusation.

Now, I know I didn't cause this mess; at least, not the initial stages, you know. So why automatically blame me for this rounded up disaster? Okay, maybe I am partly to blame for the food fight, but I refuse to accept ninety-nine percent of the assumption that this was one-hundred percent my doing or the fact that Brent seems to think I came here on purpose to purposely bother Letty. Besides I didn't plan on attending. My attendance is all Aunt Bertie's twenty-dollar-doing, I thought, narrowing lids her way. But even if I hadn't shown up at all, locked myself to the Victorian and feigned a coma, somehow, some way, someone would figure out a way to blame me because this is my life; a life with lousy luck that usually ends badly. Need I mention what happened to me back in July/August over my Bentley and with my ex-husband? Or the fact that, twenty minutes ago, Red had blamed me of causing Rodger-Dodger's recent lockdown at the Pokey?

Nope. I didn't think so.

While I continued fuming his way, Brent turned to the uniformed Wannabes and motioned for them to wrangle up the Spigots, Miss Surelee and of course, me off to one side while the rest of our relation and lingering guests watched on hoping to get first scoop for my Aunt Gladys' *Redlight's* gossip-mongering pages, with a possible, front page exposé. It was a shocker she wasn't still here because she had left five minutes before my arrival. Brent gave a hard stare about our group, blasting last looks my way. Hands to belt he once more, asked for me to explain.

What could I honestly say? This wasn't my doing because I was an innocent bystander in all of this! Besides, the Spigots needed a lengthier explanation than I was capable in providing but more importantly, I was sorry Red had witnessed my stellar unpopularity, first hand. Nope. I couldn't think of anything to say that would make me come out of this mess smelling like Laney's fruity-smelling shampoo. So, I scooped chili dip from my shirt and licked fingers instead.

Brent's wormy mustache did a funny little twitch before he gave up on me and moved on to Letty asking, "You all mind explainin'?"

Naturally, she was all for it and sprang into her twisted-up version of how this party crashed spectacularly downhill to a grinding halt.

"What'd all I'd been tellin' y'all sheriff?" she cried. I snickered to my hand; Brent stiffened over that hiccup and I'm pretty sure I heard him mutter "Detective" through his clenched and coffee stained teeth. "That one's been nothin' but a pain in my ass!"

Brent glanced over his shoulder to see where Letty was pointing. I startled, surprised because she wasn't pointing my way. Finally! Someone took up my side of things because Letty was pointing in the direction of a polka dotted moo-moo.

"Miss Surelee?" he asked, sounding equally surprised. "I done-did thought you all was kiddin'."

Letty nodded and swiped at her tear-stained and ruddy cheeks.

Brent glanced back my way, questioning. Again, what could I say: *I told you so?* So, I flashed him a smirk and gave him a palms-up before I licked chocolate icing from my sleeve. Brent turned back to Letty, hand to forehead, eyes pinched shut before he glanced up and asked, "You all wanna let me in on that?"

Letty frowned, her face turning three shades of that chili dip over in the corner. Remind me later to get a cup to go, it was delicious!

Naturally, Red took this opportunity to butt in on our little circus act because he was feeling neglected. "What in jee-zus H Christmas you all gone and done-did this time?" he cried my way.

Yep, I know. He can't let me go. I ignored him as best I could and the fact that he had married Barbarilla, spawned twin daughters or that he was still breathing to say to Brent instead, "Maybe you might want to move this over to the pokey?"

Aunt Letty went, ballistic while Tucky tried restraining her from charging me and my big mouth.

To my surprise, Brent agreed.

The remaining Spigots kept Arnold's wake going strong with a couple of Wannabes staying behind while Marty and Brent had Letty, Margret, Miss Surelee, and I shuttled off to the lock-U-up station for a round of some twenty-question fun.

Naturally, Red protested over Brent's refusal of him following behind.

Believe me Miss Surelee wasn't thrilled about it either.

Joe-Bob Connelly nearly passed out over the sight of us but quickly buzzed our group beyond bulletproof glass. A second later, I noticed he slipped away to the bathroom.

Letty's eyes went wide as she gave off a garbled cry and charged the graveyard of off-duty desks the moment she spotted Rodger-Dodger, reclining to one of the Wannabes' desk chairs, left hand holding a fanned grouping of playing cards while his poker-playing partner and security detail, Charlie Ray glanced up with an encouraging grin my way, oblivious to our reason to visit the pokey this side of never. Rodger-Dodger looked at us unfazed. Brent pondered Letty's moment of stupid for two seconds before he sprang to action and had her by the crook of her arm, wrestled beyond the grave yard and back to his office, protectively.

I dragged boots behind the wide birth that is my Great Aunt Margret while Marty and Miss Surelee brought up the rear with Marty standing guard to this claustrophobic room. No one moved toward those twin pleather seats. I frowned. I thought the only one missing from this round-up rodeo to give me a distraction (or an alibi) was Billy, who decided that (to my sagging shoulders and drooping libido) he needed to return to his shop when our group left the VFW hall, via a parade of blue and grey crossovers complete with siren and flashing lights. I was hoping someone might wish to take up my side of things, because someone else had decided to join in on the fun instead. Ranger-man just shadowed Marty's right shoulder, leaving me suspiciously concerned, Miss Surelee swaying and moaning while Letty and Margret remained distracted with their own scheming thoughts.

Left unimpressed by the interruption, Brent turned and sank to his creaky chair, shuffled papers about his desk before he pushed this after party into overdrive. "Gots me 'nuf to figure over them dang farers springin' up," he said, (rather unnecessarily because as far as I knew, the firebombs went on hiatus the second Rodger-Dodger and his family were put in protective custody upstairs). As an added insult, Brent went on to blast each of us with a fully loaded stink eye before adding, "So, you all gots ya one second to start talkin' before I start arrestin' each wanna you all!"

Naturally, I protested, his threats bouncing off me forgotten as I proceeded to cross arms over chest while I kept to the far wall that housed file cabinets, simmering with soured thoughts wishing Marty wasn't between me and my reason to leave this tick of a town.

Right on cue, Miss Surelee farted then had a 'dizzy-dive'. Sheesh.

Poor Marty looked on with a nervous flush to his cleanly shaven, Gerber-baby looking head and face, hands doing the hokey-pokey, uncertain what he should do or do it to.

Good thing my Aunt Letty lacked all subtly or concern, crying, "Y'all see sheriff? I've been doin' nothin' but tryin' to tell y'all it's all that skank-ho's fault!"

All eyes rounded her way at once, curious to hear more. Or, at least, I was the most expectant.

Not missing a beat, Brent kept this party, a-pumping saying, "Elaborate, Loretta."

She swiped at tears finding their way loose of her leaky eyes to shout, "Arnold was mine, we had a good life until that one came along and turned his head on backwards!"

All eyes rounded toward the spot on the blue and white floor at Marty Smarty's feet; the spot where Letty was pointing; the spot where Miss Surelee remained, passed out.

Brent flashed steely eyes toward Ranger-man before he gave Letty his full focus quizzing, "Miss Surelee shot Arnold?"

"Now why y'all gotta go and sip a can a nitrous, sheriff? I said that fruity-tooty gone and 'ticed my old man away. I didn't say no nothin' about no killin'!"

I barked laughter. I couldn't help it. Aunt Letty was starting to sound like fun.

Now, don't get me wrong, I wasn't laughing because of Letty's colorful choice of words, describing Miss Surelee. I love the gays; hell, I'm all for their fun-tastic, creative and courageous style of dressing, walking, and talking. I think they're no different than most the woman here, on plant, earth and (hands-down) a thousand percent more interesting than all the heterosexual men about Boolee (Billy, possibly, the only exception). Yep, I absolutely love them because they make some of the best platonic, honest, and trustworthy friends a man-less woman could ask for, this one, especially. Not-to-mention lightly, but they sure can cook up a killer spread so I don't have to. And I do love Miss Surelee for other reasons and mostly, because she is my friend but especially because she was a wizard with my ratty to-do, up do I sometimes refer to as hair. But I had trouble wrapping my noodle around Letty's accusations: Miss Surelee and Arnold—Letty Spigot's husband—together? As in, they were an intimate couple? Without me ever finding out? Nope. I'm not buying it. I'm not going to foolishly jinx my friendship by believing the wild tales of family, especially from the likes of that side of my family roots.

Exactly and now you know why I was laughing.

Letty just flashed me an expression that eerily resembled Tucky's wandering expressionless, expression.

I suddenly stopped laughing.

Her expression had me realizing with a jolt to my ticker why Miss Surelee was questioning me about that side of my relation and if they had ever visited Texas or why her attraction to Tucky was prominent in the first place and for some dang reason that eluded me my whole life, is how Tucky resembled Arnold. Sheesh, how did I manage to overlook that or the fact that possibly, Letty was telling the truth?

Nope, unt-uh, I needed to hear Miss Surelee's side of defense before I did the unthinkable and sided with Aunt Letty.

With Brent, Letty and Margret still glaring my way, I hitched my pride to bra strap and with the help of Marty, had Miss Surelee conscious and back on shaky feet once more. Naturally she paled to her surroundings as she hugged her shoulders tight, eyes wandering like the beginning stages of a seizure.

Letty tossed out a smug-ugly smirk.

Miss Surelee continued to squirm as she sucked air. Brent heaved a heavy sigh before he relayed Letty's accusation for Miss Surelee to clarify. Miss Surelee's eyes slid Ranger-man's way once before she inevitably gave up a sheepish nod my way in agreement.

Unbelievable, Aunt Letty was right! I shouldn't have been surprised, but surprisingly I was. I suddenly realized something else: "So that's why you've been flipping me off all over town."

Letty just glared back; Margret crossed arms; Miss Surelee squeaked; Ranger-man, suspiciously, quietly, taking it all in; Brent, however, turned his frown my way.

"Oh, right, you were flipping off Miss Surelee."

Letty gave off a stiff nod and one-finger salute toward Miss Surelee; Margret harrumphed; Marty chuckled while Miss Surelee sank in on herself. Talented.

Brent scrubbed hands, down his scruffy face before redirecting to ask, "That it? That why'd you all been slingin' mud her way?"

Letty and Margret exchanged curious looks and that's all. Not good enough, I thought and found myself hissing air while I rocked a leg and perched hand to hip. Oh, if Laney could see me now; she'd be proud enough to say I was her mom. "Spill it Letty so I can get a shower in before Christmas!"

Well, that comment of mine managed to return my Aunt Letty to her normal, Dodge-hating self while she wagged a finger my way saying, "Oh! Like, y'all ain't gotta finger in the pie too!"

Huh? "What in the green acres are you crowing on about now?"

"Like I gotta s'plain myself to the likes a *yoot*," she replied with a glance her mother's way before adding, "That lousy, no-good, rotten husband a yours, that's what I'm talkin' 'bout!"

How dare she—"Dickie and I weren't legally married!" Brent flashed me a look that on any other day might make me wish I was dancing away, inebriated at Red's funhouse of flames. Nope. Not today. I was all petered out of excuses on his behalf. Therefore, I sucked the last of the breathable air about Brent's office to shout back adding, "I have nothing to do with that dipshit!"

Not anymore.

Aunt Letty wasn't buying it. "Oh yeah, then how come he all drove all the way back here to get what all Arnold promised them-thar other men? Huh? Tell me that so I can get the hell outta here!"

I stiffened. I suddenly found my reason to wrap up this party with one of Barbarilla's glittery pink bows. "Hey, where's Leo?"

That did it, I think.

Beads of sweat dotted Letty's face while Margret shot me dangerous daggers. Brent looked on clueless. I pressed on.

"Like Brentwood said, someone had better start explaining," I shouted, just in case my relation decided to go deaf.

And that's when Aunt Letty finally broke down, half choking on her sobs to say, "Why can't y'all do anythin' normal-like? I leave here all thinkin' I don't gotta be around none a that stupid no more, but no! Y'all had to go and drag me right on back!"

I know the feeling...

"What does any of that have to do with Great Uncle Leo," I asked.

My Great Aunt Margret gave off a throaty sigh before she finally joined the party to elaborate saying, "My Leo's been reformed. Sheriff, I want it on a recordin' before-in we all go and s'plain the rest." Brent hesitated. I think he looked bewildered but eventually gave up a small nod, perhaps more to encourage her to keep talking instead of what Margret thought he was agreeing. My Great Aunt Margret took a deep wheezy breath and continued. "If I'd a known that my baby was wrapped up in somethang a *that* one's doin' I'd a put the brakes on it ages ago. Seein' as it got outta hand, I had Loretta fly home the minna she told me 'bout them hooligans."

"Those hooligans, being who, the Giovanni's," I asked, taking a stab in the dark, ignoring her jab my way.

Letty stiffened, Miss Surelee farted.

"Yep," said Margret on a tight nod. "I was thinkin', havin' Loretta near relation so she wouldn't be in a kind a danger."

"Until someone decided to kill Arnold," I said.

"Yep," said Margret, this time with a frown my way. "You all gots some nerve holdin' out on relation."

Here we go again, putting me center stage of a Dodge wreck. But she had a point; a point that led directly toward Dickie and his trolling ways. Frowning, I glanced Miss Surelee's way. Then I rounded Miss Surelee with a full-on stare. Although decked out in shiny yellow rocker, platform boots, polka dotted moo-moo with lime green goose down jacket and brunette mullet, wig now askew I wasn't staring because of that. Like I've said before, I love Miss Surelee's ways. But I had noticed something else that took precedence; something unusual and highly suspicious, given the state of things. I noticed her stomach pouch had shifted sideways and that the coloring between neck and chest were slightly two different shades. For as far back as I've known Miss Surelee, I was certain of three things: She was really a He; two, she loved wearing wigs, makeup, and all things girly and three, Miss Surelee had always been slim. So, hold the, everything with everything—what's got her body all twisted up like a soggy pretzel? "Okay, what in the heck that is Boolee is going on around, here?"

Miss Surelee overlooked or possibly, ignored my blabbering cry.

So, I redirected, stomped closer while cautiously saying, "Um, Miss Surelee, you care to add to this?"

"Uh-hum," she replied, paying me no attention or to the fact I was now inches from one of those spiky hairs.

Within seconds, I had the wig snatched free, startling Marty to foolishly chuckle. While Miss Surelee was groping for the wig in my left hand, I snatched at the rubber latex that had begun to peel itself free of her slender neck. Miss Surelee threw back a shriek, Ranger-man taking it all in with a slight curl to his upper lip. "That's it—start talking! What is going on with you?" I was staring back as if I were gawking at a Dodge wreck, fully forgetting our locked-down at the pokey or that I had relation ready to snuff me from existence.

Miss Surelee slapped at the wig in my hand then sighed. She glanced once to everyone staring back, suspiciously curious, suspiciously awestruck; but Miss Surelee didn't seem bothered by any of it. She did however look eerily spooked enough to keep from elaborating.

I plied her with a slitty-eyed look, daring her to clam up now. Just in case my eyeballing went overlooked, I added, "I'll squeal about you knowing about the Dickie sighting if you don't just get it over with and tell me." Oops. Too late, I thought with a sleazy grin. One second later, I startled to attention over my thought saying, "Oh-m-gee, Dickie wasn't attacking Tucky; he was going after you!"

Miss Surelee glanced once Brent's way then sighed a second time, picked at her mangled attire with a nod before she finally explained, saying, "I'm in disguise."

Obviously... "But why?" was all I could manage to say dropping wig to floor.

"Because of my honey-boo," she said on another deflating sigh.

Aunt Letty released a garbled cry.

I ignored her to ask, "Do you mean Arnold, about him getting shot?"

Miss Surelee looked away, gave off a small nod before she went into her version of that night. "Me and honey-boo go way back. Long before your beau and him took up partnering," she said, slumping back against the wall, peeling away at some of that cosmetic enhancement. "Long before I met you, Sweetness, or before he could tell *her*."

"Tell her what," I asked, indicating toward Letty.

"My honey-boo ain't one for women," she said, adding, "Well, real woman, know what I'm saying?"

I did but I think Letty just found a set of claws, ready to drag them pointy-side-down Miss Surelee's wigless face eager to show her the real meaning of a real woman. I quickly diffused that by asking, "Did you know about Arnold's, uh...extra circular activities?"

"Yes, because he was my sugar-daddy," she said on a definitive nod. "But it wasn't something that interfered with our romance, see, so I looked away, never gave it a second thought."

Letty threw out a huff of disgust.

Ah. Now I see how Miss Surelee afforded three cars, a rack of couture with wigs, shoes, and purses to match. "When did you become involved enough to want to hide out here, in Boolee of all places," I said on a mere whisper, hoping I wouldn't spook Miss Surelee into clamming up now.

"On the night he was shot," she said, casting a nervous looking glance Ranger-man's way.

My eyes bugged out and my hands flew to my mouth before I could stop them. "You didn't...*did* you?"

"No," she said on another shudder, this time, hugging herself, glancing about Detective Pine's office.

Aunt Letty harrumphed in agreement adding a smug look to her face.

I ignored the withering branch of my family tree and swallowed hard; my next question needed said aloud. "Do you know who shot him?"

Miss Surelee eyed me square on, non-blinking and half shrugged, half-nodded.

I gasped on a rather loud intake of breath, caught myself and waved her on to keep going.

Miss Surelee glanced away as she rubbed nervously at her arm. Brent's office went eerily quiet. The only sound aside from my pounding heart was the steady ticking of the battery-operated clock on the spot above the frosted paned door. So, I held my breath and waited. I didn't want to push my luck.

Miss Surelee's wandering eyes eventually landed on me once more. She took a breath and finally told me the rest of her story; the whole, ugly, dirty, dangerous truth.

After having explained how his wife, Loretta, a.k.a., Letty was out of town visiting relation (to which, Aunt Letty chocked out another mangled cry), Arnold called and set up their date for later that night, meeting up at his home office. She said it wasn't anything new; done it before, where they decided to diddle around (again, causing Letty to spit and sputter her angst); something about Arnold having a fantasy he wanted to play out because he was going away on business and didn't know for how long. Unfortunately, this time, is when the gunman entered. (Upon hearing this, Aunt Letty clammed up). Miss Surelee continued, explaining how the gunman caught Arnold seated behind his desk with his pants down around his ankles, Miss Surelee hidden on hands and knees underneath that oversized mahogany carved wooden desk. The gunman approached. Apparently, not close enough to notice Arnold's state of undress to realize Miss Surelee's hidden presence.

"My honey-boo recognized him at once," she said. "And he weren't all that happy about it being him showing up like he did. He went limp in two seconds."

Ewe, I didn't need to know that last part. Because I had already known, from my left-handed talent that collided with a wooden, horse stature last Tuesday morning. I never realized Miss Surelee was the other woman. I guess Letty didn't need to be, clued in on that scandalous bit of information either. I stayed focused and maintained being a human wall between Miss Surelee and my Aunt Letty. It was necessary because my next question was going to be a doozy. "Was it, Dickie?"

Miss Surelee gave me a squint of an eye before she shook her head no. "It wasn't like I'd seen his face, but that voice wasn't his."

"But you know who's it was," I asked.

"No, Sweetness, can't say that for sure either," she said, glancing away. "But I saw his loafers—armadillo—they ain't exactly cheap and they definitely weren't knockoffs because I'd swear I'd seen them somewheres before."

I noticed my Aunt Letty nodding so I asked her instead, "Do you know who they belong to?"

Letty let out a mangled choke of, "Those dang men who was after your lousy husband!"

Ah yep, she must be talking about the Giovanni's. I turned back to Miss Surelee asking, "What did he want from Arnold?" I had my own set of suspicions as to why but I was more curious to know if she knew the same thing I was thinking.

"Well, my honey-boo wasn't alarmed seeing loafers but he wasn't happy having him show up like that, 'after hours' neither...said it was up to my beau to represent."

"Do you know what that was all about," I asked, barely able to move, let alone force the words spoken aloud.

Miss Surelee frowned. "Shoot Sweetness, that's why I waited 'til loafers left so I could high-tail it over here!"

"But you must have heard something that guy was after, right?"

"No. Like I said, loafers weren't speaking my language, see what I'm sayin'? Anyhow, I think he tossed something to my beau only I couldn't see up top of his desk so I didn't know what it was right away. I couldn't move, no-how. Yous know how delicate I am. That's when loafers reminded him of what needed done.

"My honey-boo waved him off, refusing to do anything, yelling for loafers to get the hell out because Dickie left him 'high and dry back in some hick town'. Sorry Sweetness, that's what my beau said, and ... and he also told him about you having something that Dickie was trying to get back."

I spasmed all that is me and I think my blood left my body for dead.

Miss Surelee must have noticed too, for she leaned forward to add, "It wasn't what loafers wanted to hear. That's when he laughed like one of them silly balloons before he shot my beau!"

Oh, fuck. I was right. It was the Giovanni's and I suddenly remembered that I had met them once, years prior before I had decided to trash my things back in Amarillo and come crawling back to Boolee. Because that laugh Miss Surelee described was unmistakable.

Aunt Letty let out a strangled cry.

"Oh my God, Miss Surelee," I said, finding my blood supply and my strength as my hands flew to my mouth a second time. "What did you do?"

"Nothing at first...felt like hours I waited there. It wasn't the best spot you know. My honey-boo peed himself after he got his brains rearranged."

Letty released another mangled cry.

"I'm sorry, Miss Surelee, I didn't know Arnold was your man," I said; she waved me off as if it were an everyday, occurrence. It didn't occur to me to ask if she was upset over losing Arnold or that she was two-timing about Letty's marriage. It especially didn't occur to me to mention that troublesome statue. "Did anyone see you leave?"

"No, but I wasn't taking any chances and next thing I knew I flew from his house, hightailed it back to my condo, cleaned out what I could stuff to candy and bee-lined it here."

"But why here? I thought you were headed to New York," I asked, riddled.

"Oh, um-hum, that's what I told the girls at the salon in case any of them came asking about me."

"How did you...you know, figure on that fat suit?"

Miss Surelee flashed me a huge smile, teeth, and all, despite what she just confessed to me and glanced once to Ranger-man. I noticed he nodded back, encouragingly.

"That's my ingenious thinking, see. I detoured to one of my clients' homes. He's a make-up artist for one of them science fiction shows. Well, bless him when he saw the state of me and after I explained my honey-boo was dead he said, 'Miss Surelee, ain't no one gonna spot a two-ton diva!' Swear it, that's what he said, and hooked me up."

I stared back, struck speechless, momentarily. Wouldn't they already recognize Miss Surelee by her wigs, let alone candy? Dickie and I both had.

Ranger-man took that moment to nod once in Brent's direction; Brent returned a stiff nod; Ranger-man then turned and left the sight of us, fully forgotten, fully ignored on my part because I was suddenly concerned about something, much more important than Miss Surelee's financial loss. "Wait-a-minute," I turned on Margret at once. "I still don't see why you think Leo need's protection? Remind me again what he has to do with all of this?"

Brent finally caught up to my stellar thinking and nodded in agreement.

Margret gave a huff before she said, "Well hell, ain't it obvious? Damn idiots came after me old man the minna they found out 'bout *you all*!"

Oh. But wait-a-minute, "What has my brother got to do with Great Uncle Leo missing?"

Ut-oh...

Brent finally realized he was a detective after all and stood up, came around his desk to ask Letty, "Please don't tell me you all been the ones settin' all those ding-dang farers?"

Aunt Letty instantly paled.

My Great Aunt Margret however managed to pull her three-hundred pounds of flesh taller, pushing her face inches from Brent's, threateningly to say, "It ain't like we all gotta choice, sheriff, now do we?"

"It was you; you kidnapped my brother?"

Margret shot me a nasty look before saying, "You all think I enjoyed that part? Hell no. That was that one's kin a doin'. Damn grandkid a mine ain't worth the ground he pees all over."

I did a mental snicker. Glad to see I wasn't the only one who thought Tucky was an idiot.

"Tucky did the kidnappin'," said Brent, his voice and face reflecting his awe as he finally caught up to the rest of us.

Margret nodded; Letty heaved a sigh, hanging head before she said, "Yep, sure did. It was his idea, seein' how those other men had gone and snatched up daddy, holding him for ransom to *that* one's stupidity."

You may call me Dodge, but I'm pretty sure that I'm not the ring-leader of stupid about this shoebox sized room. Nope. I've been known on occasion to follow stupid, stupidly without thought, but that doesn't mean I'll stupidly fix it or cause it.

"Explain," said Brent, leaning forward, a pinch to his left eye.

"Gladly," said Letty as if the burden of carrying around arson was too much a secret to maintain. "Those men, those Gio guys said that if we all wanted to see daddy alive then we all had two weeks to give them all the money Arnold's partner owed them. They also wanted us to give them *that* one so they all could take back what she all had. Well I had no idea what they all were talkin' about but seein' as I had no choice, I told my relation."

"Ah, so Tucky thought this up all by himself," I asked.

"Now why y'all gotta go and say it like that? A course it was his thinkin'!" cried Letty.

Brent redirected so Letty wouldn't sidetrack with a fist my way and asked, "What was his thinkin'?"

Margret shook her head and snatched one long and slim menthol cigarette to pinched lips; Brent flashed a frown. She didn't light it up, but she didn't put it back to her cigarette case either. Letty shot Brent a stink eye before saying, "Dang sheriff, how in the hell was I s'pose to wrangle up half a million bucks in two weeks? Huh, Y'all gots ya any bright ideas to that one? Dint think so, but my Tucky did, and it was genius, if y'all asks me."

Ah, we were asking, but not because we thought he was a mastermind.

Letty concluded saying, "He got everyone a those dang idiots to lose at poker, hand over them all deeds to them all's property. Then when the coast was clear, he and that udder one got that one's relation to haul them all on over there and burn it all to the ground."

I started on my own realization to shout, "Next time you want to know my whereabouts, just ask. Tracking me was pretty low."

Letty frowned; Margret squinted my way.

Okeydokey... "You weren't tracking me?"

They both shook their heads no.

"Does that mean you weren't texting me either," I asked.

Letty continued to frown and Margret tossed out a grunt.

My body did a dangerous spasm. I suddenly realized that the track-app only showed in proximity of where mystery texter was. Those thoughts too, connected the dots of all those dang slimy sighting. I glanced over to Brent. He too thought this one through to its only, three-timing, and smug-ugly-mug conclusion: Dickie Trollop. I quickly diverted my thoughts to ask, "Okay...but why my brother? Why threaten his family if he didn't go along with your plan?" Unfortunately, I knew the answer before the last word flew wildly from my flapping gums.

Miss Surelee slapped hands to eyes.

"'Cause I already done-did told you all why," said Rodger-Dodger from just behind Marty Smarty's left shoulder.

"Oh right, the twenty-grand you lost to Leo," I said, to the collective nods of Letty, Margret, and Brent.

Brent then gave Marty a wave of his hand. He in turn, turned on rubber sole and returned to the graveyard.

Naturally I was curious. "What's going on Brent?"

"Nutin for you all to be nosin' in on," he said, but sensing I wasn't letting go he elaborated on a sigh, "He's roundin' up Tucky and Boomer."

"Oh, now I get it," I said, really wishing I had figured this out a week ago. "You used Boomer's truck to do the driving."

Margaret harrumphed while Letty nodded.

I guess that explains those two idiots using costumes.

"Okay, so let me get this straight," I began to everyone's muttering dislike, Miss Surelee going back to a weak moan while my brother returned to his card game with Charlie Ray. "The Giovanni's killed Arnold then kidnapped Leo, held him as ransom to get Letty to pay up Arnolds share in what he and Dickie were doing." I waited for the collective nods to stop nodding. "So Tucky thought he could collect on the insurance money after Uncle Walt did his reports to pay the Giovanni's and get Leo back?" Again, more head bobs with one or two puckered frowns. "But my brother didn't own enough to collect on so you decided to make him the patsy?" This time, blank stares. Oh-kay... "But that still leaves the problem about Ginger; why did you kidnap her too?"

This time Margret charged me and shoved an unlit cigarette clutched between two gnarled and wrinkled fingers to my face saying, "Damn idiot snatched the wrong one!"

Oh. My body sagged before I slowly turned back to Brent with a two-shoulder shrug and weak smile. How lucky can one girl get?

Brent went to his desk, picked up the handheld, stabbed a pudgy finger at one of the non-blinking buttons, waited a heartbeat before saying, "Get the welcome wagon ready, I've gots me two more on their way in." After hanging up he turned back to Letty and Margret saying, "I can keep you all here if ya don't wanna chance it on a count a Leo's still missin."

Letty and Margret exchanged curious glances.

"How we gonna get him back, sheriff?" asked Margret.

"I'm workin' on it," Brent said on a huff, a flick of his steely eyes my way before adding, "I can't make you all any promises, but I gots me an idea."

I'm pretty sure his idea involved a one, Harley Dodge.

My Aunt Letty and my Great-Aunt Margret exchanged another glance between them before they gave in, nodding their agreement of being, placed under Detective Pine's protective custody and followed Joe-Bob Connelly to the second floor of the pokey.

Now, I don't know about you, but I'm pretty sure even Detective Pine can't fix this kind of stupid with all the Dodges in the world.

Chapter Fifteen: Stranger-Danger, Stranger-Danger!

After Brent dropped Miss Surelee and me off at the VFW hall, we collected Rusty and shamefully yet cautiously trudged back to the Victorian feeling a bit skittish but mostly, pissed-off. At least, I know I was, because we had an escort of the Wannabe kind.

Not only had I learned who was causing the fires and why but I finally understood why Tucky was late with his child support payments to Penny: he was trying to help his mother round up a half-a-million-dollars for ransom to the Giovanni's who incidentally, may or may not be hovering the outskirts of Boolee hoping to snag me so they can off dipshit. Not that I care what happens to that lousy, rotten excuse for a man, but I would prefer it if everyone left me out of the Dodge loop of that disaster. So, being the adult that I pretend I'll become someday, I found the nerve to flaunt my snark by accusing my Great Uncle Leo as the one who jacked a truck. Aunt Letty and Great Aunt Margret shot me murderous looks for reasons other than us being related. Unfortunately, Detective Pine blocked my sourpuss face from souring further by vehemently affirming to the contrary, telling me I had better let that one go.

Not in this lifetime.

I slammed all kinds of doors in protest.

I entered the Victorian and did my best to ignore the constantly ringing rotary styled telephone on the stand next to the stairs but it wasn't working. Therefore, I thought about unplugging it. Then I thought about what Aunt Bertie might say and redirected my thoughts by going back to my original mood as the devil's spawn. See, I was red engine mad and maybe just a little spooked to have found myself agreeing with Brent's wonder-boy plot. With my brother's family, all known Spigot relation and Boomer safely vacationing away at the pokey, Brent made it known what he had in store for me and my not-so-innocent butt: he had the stupid idea to want to use me as bait.

And stupid me, I stupidly agreed.

I know, right?

Actually...it was Charlie Rays' half-assed idea that had Brent mulling over before he took up the thought and ran with the lunacy to use me like a dangling carrot, the Boolee Ball the stage and all its patrons, witness to something Dodge and delirious. All because I had something the Giovanni's wanted back from my lousy ex, Dickie Trollop. I might have also tried wrangling myself free of being Charlie Ray's plus one for five, cranky minutes until my stupid luck kicked in and Brent decided I should have a Wannabe tagalong to keep me out of harms' way until that dreaded night I was to prance around in a Hostess Twinkie costume. So, no, I didn't get out of being Charlie Ray's date for Friday either.

"At least no one gonna know it's you, Sweetness," said Miss Surelee on an airy chuckle.

Yep. She's the first one I'm going to throw in cow dung the second the opportunity presented itself. Friend or no friend, she could have snagged a cat suit or a bozo the clown costume on our way out of a firebombed building. Lucky for me her and Laney even bothered with the thought to grab that fake looking, Hostess Twinkie costume on their way scrambling free of a burning Alter Ego last week.

I rounded the kitchen, slapped key and purse to counter and realized I had something much more immediate to stress over that was going to cause me to stroke out for good. Aunt Bertie decided I would be earning my keep another way that had nothing to do with petrified deliveries or funeral attendance. I guess it's her way of letting me know that she wasn't pleased with my behavior at the wake a couple of hours ago. Not my fault, I reasoned on puckered frown; I had tried to wrangle my way free of attending that debacle in the first place.

Laney sat at the far end of the farmhouse styled table, sucking peanut butter from a spoon while doing her homework, ignoring my need to punch something smug-ugly that is her father. When we stomped in, she overlooked my mangled and food covered state and shot me a grin with an unnecessary remark that there was a Taco Shell at the Square and we should do carry-out. See, having arrived home before us because today she didn't have volleyball practice, she already knew that all of us were at Letty Spigot Dodge/Hibbard's wake and funeral. Only, (I hope) she didn't know Letty was the one married to Dickie's partner, Arnold or that Miss Surelee was secretly having an affair with him...or had, when he was still breathing normally, that is.

"Nana called," she said with a smug-mug that mirrored you-know-slimy-who's.

I guess she found out after all and knew what awaited our return. And I wasn't looking forward to any of it.

Aunt Bertie had decided I should try my hand at being domestic, asking Laney to leave out a recipe card for homemade mac and cheese and fried ham steak with a side of her canned green beans and instructions for us to have it and the table set by six. It was half-past four already. I guess she had planned on my leaving the wake early. Joke's on her though, because I think she hadn't planned on the way Miss Surelee and I left via a police escort. Or, maybe, the joke was on me, because she did or she wouldn't have foolishly asked me to cook.

Overlooking my spawn, I turned from the kitchen and headed for the steam room hoping to wipe fifteen and a half years' worth of misery and angst from my weary bones. I only managed to wash away the rest of that chili dip instead. Feeling recharged and smelling much, much better than earlier, dressed in sweats and long-sleeved t-shirt I went downstairs, pausing at the front door and gave a glance beyond the side windows then shuddered. Miss Surelee was traipsing back up the porch steps.

"What's going on," I asked with a puss-face special of my own after she had the door closed.

"Thought maybe he might be needing some coffee," she said then rounded the kitchen.

I thought he might need a change of zip codes as I glanced back to where Charlie Ray was still sitting to his personal super top Chevy truck, parked to Aunt Bertie's patch of lawn, protecting—or rather, guarding—an investment. I shuddered a second time. If Brent's plan worked out in his favor, he'd be the hero, and me? Well, let's just say, it wasn't looking too favorable of me coming out smelling like a peach covered rose. I turned away and headed toward the kitchen, fuming, dragging a raincloud overhead.

I slumped to a chair opposite Laney. Bandit slunk in a moment later, cast me a glance with a light mewl before he pounced to Laney's lap. Not missing a beat, I noticed Miss Surelee had gladly dove in, hands first and got us somewhat organized for making that edible meal. I think it gave her something to do. Seriously though, I think it gave her mind something to think about other than my Aunt Letty's sudden and unnecessary attack on her, earlier at the wake. Or the fact, the Giovanni's are after something they think I now have.

"You're not going to burn any of that, right," I asked, unsure, lacking all subtly.

Miss Surelee spun on me and shot me squinty eyes, saying, "I know what I'm doing now, Sweetness." Waving food smeared spatula she concluded with, "I just had to figure out this type of antique is all."

"We can do carry out," I suggested, hopefully.

Laney perked up and clapped; Miss Surelee shook her head no, saying, "Got it nearly done, Sweetness."

I can't say for sure if I cooked or baked, but it sure was fun thinking I helped without speed dialing or paying as

Laney and I watched from the kitchen table. "Where'd you learn to cook," I absently asked. I wasn't sure if I was intrigued enough to learn the answer or not, but I had to ask and fill my spiraling thoughts with something that didn't center on dipshit.

"Shoot, didn't you ever take, Home Eck in school?"

"No," I said. At least, I don't remember doing so.

"Didn't your momma ever teach you how?"

"No," I said on a frown. "She tried once or twice, but she got sick then died my senior year of High School."

"Didn't you ever get inquisitive to know how?"

"No," I said on a shrug.

"Mom prefers speed dialing," said Laney not glancing up from her schoolbooks. I nodded. She was right, after all.

"Shoot Sweetness, by the time I was eight I learned how to bake a Chicago styled cheesecake," she said in a way that made it sound like a household staple while she slipped the casserole dish to the oven before I even knew she had fried the ham. Because really, my mind went all fuzzy and stopped functioning the moment I heard the word cheesecake. I love cheesecake!

But then my mind went into freefall the moment I backpedaled and connected to something else that she absently said to all that's been going on because I think maybe it connected back to the Giovanni's, to someone's coincidental run-ins with me and possibly, how it connected back to that statue I inadvertently, without warning and against my better judgment, had touched. Thanks a lot, Miss Surelee, I thought, eyes narrowed, sending subliminal messages of stomach cramps her way before I nose-dived into denial. Besides, it was late and I just didn't have the need or strength to go traipsing around where I wasn't, wanted or needed. There will be enough of that on Friday. Because, as if I needed to remind anyone...look how well earlier today dismantled in on itself?

Exactly.

Thursday morning, I was up before Miss Surelee once more and fully rested, thoughts at ease, Bandit licking my cheek. Go figure. With Laney at school, Aunt Bertie and Mr. Willoughby taking a breather from her critter craze to help the Spigots clean up the VFW hall I decided to remain in my sweats and do as little as possible. I was growing a mile-wide frown and a suspiciously looking, nervous eye twitch to my left eye over the constant, non-stop ringing of Aunt Bertie's telephone, and not-to-mention, that Miss Surelee and I were under Wannabe custody/surveillance or the unfortunate fact that tomorrow was do or die time. Nope, I'm not going to pull the pin on any of that and did my best to ignore all that is my crap luck by putting fingers in ears and gritting and grinding my teeth. Not only that, but I was growing weak and worried, wondering when or if my Aunt would ever start cooking again.

I kept at my sour mood and puttered around the Victorian when I heard Miss Surelee's movements above. I climbed the stairs and rounded on my room away from reality, startled to see Miss Surelee was looking ten carbs short of her usual spunky self. At least she was, dressed, fat suit still in place. She had swapped out the foam roller wig for a tone-downed honey-hued, pony-tailed one and re-glued the neck piece in place looking like a stitched-up

Frankenstein. She paired her look with matching colored heels and handbag to a glitzy, golden looking spandex sweater over white leggings, twenty bangle bracelets to both wrists and gold looped earrings and she was ready to face all that is Boolee or rather, our lockdown at the Victorian. Sheesh, you'd think after yesterday's exposure, she would have ditched that fat suit altogether.

On a curious squint towards all that is Miss Surelee, I asked if she wanted breakfast, ala Harley style. It was the best I could do being that we were under house arrest, Aunt Bertie on strike and Miss Surelee unable to continue with our old-style way of cooking. She shrugged. I took it as a yes, so I motioned us downstairs to the kitchen, pausing long enough to glance beyond the Victorian. Miss Surelee gave off a wild giggle and gave a finger wave in the direction of the parked Wannabe. It was Marty Smarty, taking over the day shift for Charlie Ray. Ignoring that, I turned us toward the kitchen then I hunted around the refrigerator for something I didn't have to attempt to cook or possibly, reheat via the older than dirt porcelain oven. We took our sandwiches, milk, coffee, chips, and zingers for desert to the table and dug in. Do I know how to do breakfast lickity-split or what? Besides, there weren't any leftovers from last night's dinner.

While I was chewing, I was thinking, which is the perfect, time to be thinking as I was already just sitting there doing next to nothing. My thoughts, fully rested from all that's been hampering my employment search, wandered around about Ginger's recovery which only wormed their way back to Rodger-Dodger and of course, the Spigot's and then naturally, dead-ending on Dickie. Try as I did, I couldn't figure a way out of tomorrow nights' wackadoo plan. "What am I going to do," I said, once Miss Surelee came back inside from delivering a jumbo-sized mug of freshly brewed coffee to Marty Smarty. For a second there, I considered inviting him in. Then the second passed.

"Uh-huh," Miss Surelee muttered, slipping to a ladder-back chair next to me.

"Why do I have to be the bait in all this," I said, trying to figure this all out as I finished my sandwich. "All because they think I have something they want," because at one point I did. Still I wasn't happy that everyone was after it. It's not like I really wanted to hand it over to the FBI the second I had found it.

Or did I?

I suddenly had a thought and ran for the stairs.

I just finished yanking dresser from wall when Miss Surelee entered, cautiously, curious when she spotted me about my dresser and flashed me a fully rested, smile. "What you doing there, Sweetness," she asked, waving the newer, cleaner second handkerchief I got from Billy about the air. "Is that some new-fangled, fancy-to-do game with Midnight?"

"I thought I lost something," I said, shoving my dresser back against the wall. "I mean, I did lose something, but I thought it might have fallen behind, on the floor like my license plate did." Then I gave in to the mystery of it all and slumped to the edge of my bed. "Speaking of, where is Bandit?"

Miss Surelee only shrugged before plopping to beanbag. A moment later she perked up asking, "Was it the key to Beauty?"

"What," I cried.

"That thing you was looking for, was it the key," she asked.

I nodded my reply.

"Shoot, Sweetness, I put it in your purse last week," she said nonchalantly then splayed about like an overturned water bug, concluding, "Thought it deserved a proper burial then on the floor."

I stared back flabbergasted. What could I say? I had been looking for it since last month, although, not as diligently as I've been trying to figure out Rodger-Dodger's bizarre game of cat and mouse via one dusty, Rusty Dodge and a mysteriously owned, monster Ford. But so, what? Then I realized, so was everyone else. "Uh, Miss Surelee," I said, carefully rooting about my leather special, coming up with that elusive, troublesome key fob to Black Beauty.

"Uh-huh," Miss Surelee muttered my way, looking sedate.

"Do you realize that everyone's been after this key?"

Miss Surelee startled. "Why's that, Sweetness?"

"Because," I said, slumping to bed, facing Miss Surelee, concluding with, "Dickie told me something about it opening a security box full of diamonds."

Miss Surelee flew hands to the heavens, releasing that hanky to the tune of a squeal.

"Dang, why me," I too, cried to the angels on potty break.

Miss Surelee stared back looking concerned or frightened.

So, I redirected, picking up the handkerchief. "Charlie Ray said something about this belonging to a seal," I said, fingering the elusive embroidered icon.

Miss Surelee squinted back. "Say what?"

"I know, right? It doesn't make much sense," I said.

"Don't need no sense telling you got the green clover where it concerns dream-team."

I perked up. She was right. It seemed that Billy only had eyes for me and my destructive-like powers. Ut-oh! "You don't think he's one of them, do you?"

"Who," she asked, equally puzzled.

"Them—the Giovanni's," I said.

Miss Surelee gave off a squeaker of a fart as her only response. I shoved the hanky and key fob to my purse and redirected saying instead, "You know...that thing with Letty was a kick in the butt." Still nothing from Miss Surelee so I asked, "When you were seeing Arnold did you know that he was married to her?"

"Uh-huh," Miss Surelee finally muttered.

I stared back blank faced. She did? Well, I guess so, now that I think on it, but why? "Hey," I had a sudden thought. "If the Spigot's weren't the ones tracking me, and Brent swears up and down it wasn't Ranger-man's doing and I can't see Dickie having the brains to pull that off either," I paused for after affect. "Do you think maybe it was the Giovanni's who have been tracking me?"

"Uh-huh," Miss Surelee muttered a second time.

To my dismay, I wasn't sure if she was agreeing with me or not and decided to go for broke. "I found a hundred-dollar bill on the floor, is it yours?"

"Uh-huh," Miss Surelee muttered right on cue. I hadn't found any money and I was certain Miss Surelee only carried plastic.

"Miss Surelee," I cried just for her sake.

Miss Surelee startled on a frown my way. "Sorry Sweetness, I just miss my honey-boo is all."

Oh, right, the reason for all that is my hell. Then I downshifted; I felt bad for her, even if it was Arnold. "So, did you ever find out what the shooter gave to Arnold?"

"Oh, yes," she said. "It was a woody replica of Silent Night. I think he was in the running for the triple-loop tiara."

"Ah, I'm going to go out on a limb here, but do you mean the *Kentucky Derby*'s *Triple Crown*?"

"That's what I said," said Miss Surelee on a huff of breath. "Besides, he didn't give it to him, I said he tossed it my honey-boo's way; it belonged to my beau, see what I'm saying?"

Craptacular, it was that horse statue that I had inadvertently touched with my freakish ability nearly two weeks ago. I perked up, sullen however; my thoughts needed said aloud. "If it's any help, Arnold's last thoughts were of you."

Miss Surelee startled then blushed.

Then I had another thought. I know I was going to regret it but I had to ask, "Do you have any idea why?"

"I don't know but as I was scrambling out from underneath my beau's legs, I remembered you telling me once about your dizzy-dives and I thought you could do your voodoo thing on it, so I pried that sucker loose of my honey-boo's fingers then got outta there."

Swell. That explains why I mistakenly saw Dickie go after Tucky; he was instead, aiming for Miss Surelee and something he presumably thought she had too. Ut-oh, I had yet another thought that I know I was going to regret and asked aloud, "Do you still have it?"

Miss Surelee shook her head no.

"Do you know where it is?"

Miss Surelee nodded yes.

"You want to expand on that?"

Miss Surelee sighed before saying, "I might of sorta left it back at the old-fashioned store."

"How could you leave it behind," I cried to the Angels not caring if they were on potty break or not.

"I didn't plan on it," she replied on a huff. "Not at first. I was distracted by dream-team and before I could tells you all about it you had yourself flattened on Billy-boy's floor doing an impression of a snow angel that got beat up by frosty himself."

Thanks for the reminder. "Why didn't you just go back and get it," I asked.

"I really am thinking you're needing one of them earwax specials, Sweetness, 'cause I tried, but it wasn't where you dropped it."

Oh, right. "So, it could still be inside the antique store."

Miss Surelee nodded hopefully.

"And you never thought to go back the next day or any day since?"

"I'm sorry, Sweetness, I just forgot," she said, shifting on that beanbag with little progress. "I didn't mean to make a mess of things."

"No, Miss Surelee, it's not your fault! Heck, it's definitely not our fault that Arnold is dead and Dickie is the way he is, because this is all his rotten doing, I just know it!" Oh wait...I suddenly had an even worse thought: "You don't think Billy found it, do you?"

Miss Surelee only shrugged, still rattled and clearly out of guesses or ideas, "Don't think so, why?"

"Well, that does it then," I said on a sigh. "We need to make a trip to the treasure trap without anyone the wiser."

"Are you sure about this, Sweetness?"

"Yes," I said, slipping on boots.

Miss Surelee gave me a squint. "You wanna clue me in there, Sweetness?"

"Don't you think it's strange that Billy showed up a month before all this business with Arnold came about?"

"No," she replied.

"Well, don't you think it's strange how he said he was originally from Chicago?"

"No," she replied once more.

"Think, Miss Surelee, where do you think the Giovanni's might be from?"

Miss Surelee squinted off to the wild oblivion before she gave me a two-shoulder shrug.

"*Chicago*," I cried.

Miss Surelee squeaked to a start, causing her prefabricated ways to shift sideways on the beanbag.

"See, the way I'm thinking is, I need that statue to tell me what got Arnold shot and why." And my thinking isn't usually all that great because right now, it has me thinking of doing the very last thing I thought I would ever be thinking of daring.

Miss Surelee scrunched sideways, startled, eyes the size and shape of cartoon eyes, bugging out to ask, "You sure about that, Sweetness?"

Not really. "Yeah," I said. "It's possible that Billy is involved."

"Not mocha latte!" she cried, hands clutching unshaven cheeks, twenty bracelets jingling to the sudden movement.

"Afraid so," I said. "Um, I'm not a miracle worker but I can do my best to help patch you up, but honestly, I think the cat's out of the bag, sort to speak," I said with a wave toward all of her. "I really think it's time for you to ditch that getup." The fat suit that is.

Miss Surelee vehemently shook her head no.

Okay then. "Your call, but you are riding shotgun on this one—no arguments—I need a second set of eyes."

"I think you're wrong about dream-team," she said, blowing out a sigh.

"I think I'm right," I said, even though I had no solid proof. Well, not yet anyways...

Miss Surelee eventually conceded to my goading with a small nod and gathered up her wits and that prefabricated bodysuit.

"Good, meet me on the back porch while I give a call to Rinna".

Ten minutes later, plan in place I waited on the porch, nervously glancing about the bordering pine. Miss Surelee pushed past screen door a moment later.

"What we looking for back here, Sweetness?"

"Rinna," I said, hiking purse higher on shoulder, nodding toward the grouping of densely packed pine and the hand that was waving us her way. "She's our way there and back without a Wannabe being the wiser."

"You sure that's what we want to be doing?"

"Maybe," I said and jogged us on over. "But all the same, it's too late to back out now."

Miss Surelee only groaned.

"This is so cool, I feel like I'm in a episode of *Charlie's Angels*—come on," said Rinna on a puff of breath, clearly excited to be doing something that didn't revolve around wet naps. "I got Jud in the back."

We made our way through the thicket, past the clearing to where Rinna's SUV sat idling along the dirt packed road of route fifty-two then climbed aboard. This was the long winding and hilly way back into town and rarely traveled but seeing, as we were under Wannabe surveillance it was worth the extra ten minutes out of our way to go snooping.

"We're looking for a marbled based, carved wooden statue of a Triple Crown horse, got it?"

Nods all around, Rinna floored it for the treasure trap.

I don't know what I was thinking about entering the antique shop on a rouge mission when she parked the van across the street. Miss Surelee was adamant about not getting hog-tied into tagging along beside me or that we should have told Marty. I on the other hand, was vehemently protesting, saying someone had to keep company with Jud in the car. Rinna and Miss Surelee weren't buying it. Yep, I caved and entered that little shop of horrors with my side kick of crazy, my childhood friend and a slobbering, teething, two-year-old, blond beach ball hoping to get in and out without Stranger-Danger or any of Boolee the wiser.

"Everything okay, Boots," asked said 'dream-team', spotting us at once.

My heart leapt to my throat.

Sheesh, so much for us being sneaky...

Miss Surelee giggled to her hand while Rinna grinned back. I considered doing the same but opted for a flushed face, instead, mentally downgrading my rapidly thumping heartbeat before I quickly—awkwardly—waved nonchalantly saying, "Um...just looking." I then hustled Miss Surelee and Rinna off around one of the shelving units and let out a rush of breath.

Miss Surelee fanned herself whispering, "He's so steamy-fine, he is!"

Yep, Rinna and I agreed on a nod.

Now, down to business...

Thirty minutes later, Miss Surelee, Rinna and I regrouped at the door, statue less. I think Billy noticed something was wrong with us because he just strutted our way once more, ignoring the overheated stares of loitering women.

"Can I help you with something explicitly?" he asked.

Rinna and Miss Surelee huddled closer and giggled.

"Um, yes," I said, perking up to my instant bravado and asked, "You wouldn't happen to sell anything that didn't originate from your store, right?"

Miss Surelee sucked air; Rinna shoved gram cracker to Jud's slobbery face and stared on.

"That's not our usual way of doing business, but if there's something we don't stock, I might be able to call around. Why, is there something you had in mind?"

Oh, yes...oh yes, oh yes, oh yes! "No, not really," I said then quickly sprang to action saying, "Um, can we use the bathroom?"

Billy cast a glance Miss Surelee and Rinna's way.

"Oh, right," Rinna said, perky-like, fully catching on to add, "I think Jud need's changin'."

Billy mulled that over for a nanosecond, nodded once then turned us past the back counter along the hall, first door on the right. We quickly followed, jockeying for position. The three of us then huddled to the interior of the refrigerator sized bathroom, looking foolish, hoping to look innocently inconspicuous.

"Let me know if you need anything else, Boots," he said with a flash of his knee-weakening grin before he turned back along the hallway and resumed his attention amidst the tittering and gushing customers.

I quickly closed the door, leaned against it, and let out a hissing breath.

"What's really goin' on?" asked Rinna.

"Yeah, Sweetness," said Miss Surelee. "What we gonna do now?"

"We're going snooping," I said then quickly explained, "You know how Billy cleaned his shop up by himself that day you came to town?"

"Uh-huh," said Miss Surelee while Rinna juggled a squirmy pudge from one hip to the next.

"Well, like I just asked and he just said there's a good chance he locked it to his office if he noticed that statue didn't belong to his inventory."

"Oh, I get it," said Miss Surelee, looking uncertain. "What we doing again?"

"We're going snooping," I repeated then turned to Rinna saying, "You're the lookout. Buzz me on my cell if he comes back then distract him so we can slip back here. Okay, everyone ready?"

"Yep," said Rinna, eager for some adventure in her life that didn't involve cheese nips or wet naps.

Miss Surelee gave off a small nod even though her face scrunched into a frown.

Rinna slipped out of the bathroom first, waited a breath before she gave a rap at the door. I led Miss Surelee and I further back along the hallway to the last door on the right and slipped inside. I closed the door, waited for the florescent to flicker to life, then hustled up to the wooden desk. Miss Surelee the second lookout while she filed fingernails.

Ten minutes later I was at a loss.

"We ready to go?" she asked.

"I don't get it," I said, frowning, turning off the lights and leading us back out into the hallway. "I thought for sure he would have set it here if he knew it wasn't his."

"What's up there?" asked Miss Surelee, eyes pointed heavenward.

That's it! "His apartment," I think.

"I'm game," she said, reading my mind or the fact I was already three steps up.

When we reached the landing at the top of the stairs, I held a breath and leaned in, pressing ear to door, hopeful to hear nothing of the slobbering, snarling, barking type of home deterrent-like alarms. A beat later, I released breath and tried the door knob. Luckily for me it wasn't locked. Luckily for Miss Surelee it wasn't or she might have had the notion to go high-tailing it down the stairs and out the front door.

"You sure you want to be doing this, Sweetness?"

"I know what you're thinking," I said, hand still to knob, door only an inch wide. "But if that statue can tell me who killed Arnold and why, then yes, I think we need to be doing this."

"But what if dream team comes up here?" she said.

"Rinna will buzz me long before that happens," I replied with a wave of my cell phone.

"Okay, but what if we don't find it up here," she continued. "Can we go on back to Ladybugs?"

"Yeah sure," I said. Unlikely, I thought.

Miss Surelee gave off a shudder but followed me inside Stranger-Danger's apartment none-the-less to do a little recon.

It was nothing either of us could have prepared for.

It smelled like someone threw a party a week ago and quickly abandoned. Rather than seeing cardboard boxes, furniture, possibly a television screen we saw two card tables with folding chairs flanking the front windows that faced northward. The wooden floors were bare and the wallpapered walls left peeling, fading and undecorated. There were empty pizza boxes from Ordello's stacked to one corner of this room, empty donut boxes from the Piggly Wiggly scattered to the tops of those card tables with a sprinkling of chip bags and emptied soda cans here or there. I snickered. It reminded me of home-away-from-home. However, the most troubling of this view came when I focused on the computers atop the card tables because one of the flat screen monitors had a picture of me taken from my drivers' license staring back at us. The other two computer monitors were beeping and flickering with dots about a map—a map of Boolee, West Virginia.

Okay, I know I should be a little freaked out that Stranger-Danger man has secrets he's not sharing or the fact that one of those secrets revolves around me, but to learn that someone managed to have the entire town of Boolee plotted out like a double-dare because last I knew, Boolee didn't show up on any search engines, had me seeing red. Plotted as if it were a maze to someone's secretive game of cat and mouse. Did I mention someone from my past thinks I should be the cheese?

"What the freak," I hoarsely cried, darting toward the computer that displayed my mug shot.

"I'm not feeling too good," moaned Miss Surelee as she hugged body suit and refused to move away from the door.

I ignored Miss Surelee's weakened cry and focused on pressing matters. That mug shot was a clear violation of boundaries! Not only that but if he had wanted my picture, then all he had to do was to ask me, or at the very least, waited until I had time to retake my drivers' license photo. Sheesh. So, I did the first thing that came to mind: I started pecking and poking at the keyboards, hoping to delete that photo for good.

I only made matters worse.

"Get over here and help me figure this out," I cried back to Miss Surelee.

She only moaned back her reply.

I kept at my useless attempt to delete my picture when bells and whirring noises sounded from the other monitors, clicking noises began to stutter from the computers beneath the tables, lights flashed, monitors flickered before I felt something sting me on my neck. Five seconds later, I slipped to dreamland.

When I came too some twenty minutes later, I was once more, staring up into the clearest, sexiest yet secretive eyes known to desperately lonely women around.

"Wasn't planning on us meeting like this, Boots," he said.

I felt my cheeks grow warm and prayed to the angels on potty break that I hadn't peed in my denims.

"Me either," I finally said before I melted into the floorboards.

Chapter Sixteen: Over-and-Out

Stranger-Danger man wasn't such a stranger or a danger after all.

To me, that is.

"I apologize for the cloak and dagger," he said while he helped me to a folding chair. "I was just following orders."

"That's okay," I said patting at my neck, my thoughts latched on to the complete opposite meaning of 'okay'. Zapping me with a stun-gun was unnecessary.

I glanced about and saw two men hovering the perimeter and door of the room. They both looked like bouncers for the Pink Squirrel but I didn't recognize them and knew they weren't from around here either. They had darkly tanned muscles that'd give Marty Smarty tears of jealousy and were both a foot taller than Billy.

He must have noticed my look of concern when he said, "They're with me."

Okay. Then I noticed that my crazy half was long gone.

Figures.

Billy must have noticed my pouty curiosity because he quickly added, "I had Ryely take Miss Surelee downstairs to wait for Marty to drive her back to Miss Beatrice's."

Okay, but...

"That other one left twenty minutes ago," he added.

Naturally.

Thanks for nothing, Rinna.

Good thing he explained the rest of my troublesome, curious thoughts so I didn't have to resurrect my reserve of snark I mostly save up for Brentwood Lewis Pine. Introductions aside, Billy wasn't his real name after all. His real-real name is Jesse James Huntley and his real-real profession is retired Navy SEAL and currently an FBI agent. Now I understood Charlie Ray's curiosity over Billy—I mean, Jesse—and his hanky or the fact he only held daggers whenever Jesse came to view. I guess that explains a lot of what's been going on around town with the men, the women and especially a one, Harley Dodge.

"It was necessary to keep you in the dark, Boots," he explained while handing me a half-mangled jelly.

I didn't, I thought, stuffing donut to mouth.

As it turned out, headquarters had called Jesse in on special assignment, having worked under Agent Gruber's department, both he and Detective Pine thought it a good idea they set up this little rouse of a trap in hopes of catching Dickie Trollop, but more importantly, so he could lead them to the ring leaders themselves, the Giovanni's. Uh-huh. I only shuddered over that admission of secrets because it only reminded me of tomorrow nights' pre-planned truckload of fun at the Boolee Ball. Okay, so pity party aside it was Jesse after all who had planted the tracking devices on Rusty and my purse, for obvious reasons. Since it was Jesse's first sting operation, which, in mutual reasoning all around, everyone thought he'd be the best choice, seeing how he'd be the *obvious* choice of getting the closest to me. Sheesh, am I really that transparent?

Obviously, I am; obviously, it worked.

But that still left me questioning the secretive text messages. It wasn't the Spigots; it wasn't Brentwood and it sure-as-hell wasn't Ranger-man, but especially, I was relieved to learn it wasn't Jesse's doing either. No doubt left, I was certain it was dipshit.

And I was freaking back to square one.

"You mind explaining all this?" he asked, breaking me free of my dreaded thoughts, motioning about his fake accommodations, indicating heavily about Miss Surelee and my earlier, B and E.

Not really. But he just flashed me a superman grin, so I buckled and spilled my dirty little secrets, none-the-less.

What? You would have done the same.

"I lost something that I needed back," I said then explained how the statue that Miss Surelee brought with her from Amarillo belonged to Arnold and how I might fully understand what is so special about it. He grinned on. So, I had to further explain my freak talent. His grin got bigger but lucky for him he kept his personal opinions locked down tight. "So that's why we came here hoping to find it."

"I think I sold it last week," he said.

"Oh, my, gawd—*Dickie*," I said.

"No, a girl with blonde braids, I believe," he said.

Not good. I knew exactly who he meant. Only one person with a heart for a dotted 'I' did I know had reason to be slinking about Boolee and that only solidified my thoughts that Dickie was after me and Beauty's key fob all along. Only one thing left to do: I dug about my purse, hesitated but eventually with sinking heart did I finally hand the key fob over to Jesse fully explaining all I learned from Dickie about its purpose. "Does this mean I don't have to show up tomorrow night?"

Jesse looked uncertain but lucky for him Detective Pine reared his wormy nose past the door, hands to belt and nodded once to solidify my need to flee all that is Boolee.

After all, we still needed to get Great Uncle Leo back.

The day I had been dreading since twelfth grade arrived. The "moment a truth", is how Brent described it. The moment of setting Harley up for a ride of her life, is how I preferred to endure the Boolee Ball this fine, cloud-free Friday evening.

Boots in place over jeans I had managed both legs through the bottom half of that golden, spongy, outer foamed shell of my Twinkie costume. The top half hung limp from the front of my thermal covered waist because the top half was heavier than the bottom half and I had given up trying to reach the zipper twenty minutes ago. Whoever thought a costume deserved a zipper down the back was on drugs; it's the worst place to be putting anything that arms just weren't, designed to go. I thought about leaving the costume unzipped and limp when Laney reared her puss face past my bedroom door and barked laughter.

That's so degrading.

Her laughter might have had something to do with my explanation about Billy the Huntley after Brent gave me and Miss Surelee a Wannabe escort to the Victorian yesterday. Or the fact he wasn't as interested in me in the way I presumably thought. Then again, I'm sure her laughing has to do with tonight's trick or treating kind of delirium.

Time to shut down the Dodge.

Hands to Twinkie-free hips, I narrowed lids her way. She overlooked our blood connection and kept right on laughing.

Curiously, with little surprise, Laney was dressed-to-break-hearts in a cutesy little 'goth' number straight out of Tim Burton's daydreaming nightmare, complete with blackened and smudged eye shadow, brownish rouge, and plum lipstick. And without explanation on her part, it was no surprise to see her handling a leash that hooked up to harness now snuggly attached to Bandit, whom I might add, was sporting glittery devil horns. I could tell he too wasn't looking forward to prancing about the Boolee Ball either.

I can't say as I blame him.

I shot Laney a fully loaded stink eye for reasons other than our relation. Still, she didn't stop laughing nor collect her snark until the moment Miss Surelee pumped the fun up twelve more notches when she too, entered my room, decked out in full twinkling Tinkerbelle replica, minus one prefabricated fat suit, complete with glittery wings, beehive sporting tiara and waving about a magic wand. I know just where she can stick it, too. They instantly gushed over each other's choice of Halloween/Alter Ego costumed fun before they glanced my way, expectant.

I stared back stalling. Two seconds later, shoulders sagging, I heaved a sigh and barked orders. Laney came around to the back of me, Miss Surelee to the front as those two jokers wrangled me the rest of the way into that coffin-like Twinkie costume, zipped and adjusted, arms poking out like twigs, head completely covered and heavier than the rest. I spun wide to Laney's giggles and toppled sideways at once. I sighed and tried to sit up. With no luck left, I flapped arms and legs about, managed to rock back and forth several times before I realized I looked ridiculous, that Bandit thought I was a game and that I wasn't making any progress. Now I know how Miss Surelee felt as she wrestled with the beanbag. I was beginning to sweat in this suffocating, steam bath and suddenly felt my throat seize. What if this happens to me at the ball? After five more minutes of me struggling, I gave up, shouted something Miss Surelee's way before she and Laney helped me to my feet.

"See here, Sweetness, ain't nobody gonna know it's you in there."

Yeah, right. I rounded on Miss Surelee with a fully loaded mouthful of stark and toppled a second time. Two more tries later, I gave up and shouted back, "Just grab hold of something and lead on!"

Twenty minutes of one blind and agonizing step after another, they had me down the stairs and near the front door, my escape from the Victorian almost at hand when someone knocked, jumpstarting Aunt Bertie from the kitchen, camera to hand to intercept my need to flee, indefinitely. Laney or possibly Miss Surelee had opened the door to more party goers and ushered them in from the settling chill of Halloween night. I peered through the mesh window that gave me a shadowed, baseball sized view of whatever was directly in front of me and frowned. I know, don't say it. No one noticed my heavy breathing either because the amount of a near six-foot Twinkie took a curious center stage. I did notice Aunt Bertie's half crooked grin while she was fussing with the cube-like flash bulb about her seventies-styled camera. She was (not surprisingly) dressed in overalls and rubber boots, hair braided like the Swiss Miss girl and covered with straw hat, a corsage neatly pinned to one blue jean strap. This was her go-to costume every year for the past thirty or so years. A moment later, Mr. Willoughby shuffled in behind her with bed sheet covering all of him, eye holes cut out while a permanent black marker smudged below to indicate a crooked (or spirited) smile. I gave off a huff that went overlooked, possibly overheard from all this muffled padding. Mr. Willoughby's costume was genius! Now why didn't I think to go as a ghost instead of stuffing myself to this loony-bin, lockdown getup? Sheesh! I put hand to where I thought my head was before I could stop myself and toppled backwards yet again. Good thing this costume came with extra padding.

I felt hands scramble about me, helping me to my feet. When I managed to blink the sweat from my eyes, I found myself staring back at Batman. My heart leapt to my throat and my stomach did a dizzy-dive and I nearly tumbled to the floor once more. Did Stranger-Danger man Billy, a.k.a., Jesse really invite me as his date to the ball after all? Then Stranger-Danger Batman spoke and my heart sank twenty notches past my booted toes. Oh. I forgot...purposely. Because, it was Charlie Ray and just my dumb, blind luck, he too decided to dress up as Batman.

Lovely.

I almost backed out of this stupid ploy to dangle me as bait when I noticed Miss Surelee's date was none other than Marty Smarty and he dressed like a strip-o-gram copper ready to cruise the beach, practically stretching that stretchy, glittery fabric to the brink of its double stitching. Then he did something that made me change my mind and want to attend the Ball after all: he leaned down and gave Miss Surelee a peck on the cheek before he handed her a wrist corsage of orange blossoms and baby's breath. I perked up to Miss Surelee's good fortune and suddenly realized why she was fascinated with Marty, why he never had my stomach doing summersaults and why he never outgrew a Bruit-smelling wardrobe. Marty too must be gay! After all these years, who knew? Well, good for them!

Miss Surelee and Laney started giggling suspiciously, as if those two jokers had known all along. After Laney helped adjust the corsage about Miss Surelee's wrist, she glanced up and sucked air. I moved slower than a slug this time so I could stay upright and peered across the drive but it wasn't until Laney sucked air a second time then giggled Miss Surelee's way before I knew it was Leroy Watkins. When he stepped beyond the porch, I could just barely make out his matching zombie-goth-whatever-costume as he scanned our group then waved once Laney's way before he proceeded to slip a death bloom array of black roses to Laney's wrist with shaky hands. I grinned then frowned and slowly glanced toward Batman expectant but Charlie Ray stared on, empty handed. Sheesh, my crap luck was back in full swing. Miss Surelee and Laney did some more foolish giggling and hand-slapping while this party headed outside to the setting sun for photo opportunities.

Good thing that Twinkie encased me head to knee because I can and will, deny ever being the one inside. Unfortunately, I once again, toppled sideways down the porch steps because everyone forgot I was the only idiot dressed to treat rather than trick.

After a roll of film snapped up on Aunt Bertie's antique camera everyone headed to their respective trucks. It took me five tries but I finally got all that yardage of sponge on up into Rusty and stuffed up under the steering wheel when I remembered my date. He was staring at me with this weird expression. I couldn't tell if it was confusion, jovial or contempt. Whatever it was, it wasn't becoming of Batman's reputation or codpiece. Oh, right, it was Charlie Ray and he wants to drive. Whatever... I blew out a sigh that went both overlooked and unheard, tumbled down from Rusty and allowed Charlie Ray to help me waddle over to his super top Chevy. Good thing I forgot to snag Rusty's key, or the fact I couldn't see too well out of this death suit or I might have found the need to give him a lecture on feminism and equal rights.

Naturally, we were the last to pull out of the drive and headed toward the fairgrounds for tonight's game of cat and mouse with Harley Dodge as the cheese.

We slowly made our way past the deserted fairway where rides and gaming booths once stood, now packed away for next year's round of fun, and headed toward the track. Good thing Charlie Ray paid as well as, kept my arm in his to keep me from toppling as he led us beyond the gates and out onto the central area of the packed dirt arena or I might have found the need to tell him how disappointed I was being the only one without flowers. Or, felt the need to drag him down to my low-down, dirty level.

The live band, courtesy of my twenty something cousins was set up to the far side, up on platform a foot above the ground and was pumping away and getting the crazy started. Lights strung overhead with candle-lit pumpkins and a variety of Aunt Bertie's stuffed critters lining the perimeter of the makeshift dance floor like starlight. I shuddered over that lousy memory and glanced to my right. There were several chairs and bistro type tables for loiters while on the left, long folding tables loaded with party favors and my favorite sampling of all things edible.

I started in that direction at once, made it two steps then stopped, Charlie Ray oblivious of my reason, why. My own need to play keep-away with food was ironic because I'm never one to keep away from all things delectable. Not ever. But I suddenly realized, I did, or rather, had no other choice in the matter. My smile slid from my face but you wouldn't know that, what with it encased in Twinkie costume. Now I am super steamed, literally, and figuratively speaking. There is absolutely no way in Red's hell I'll be able to eat any of that glorious goodie spread without unzipping. I think...or maybe not. Yes, I think maybe I can slip one of those brownies through an arm hole if I angle it just right... Charlie Ray must have just figured out what I was thinking too, because he redirected us right on out to the dance floor instead.

Thanks for nothing.

The slow song finally ended and I was feeling lightheaded. This costume needs better air circulation and

I could feel my hair starting to melt against my cheeks. I wanted to sit down or burn this costume when Charlie Ray excused himself. I slowly turned but I lost sight of him to the rest of the dancing couples. This is bad, I thought, as I foolishly stood still, not wishing to topple backwards, here of all places when the angels came to my rescue.

"Looking good, Boots," said Billy, a.k.a., Jesse.

I slowly turned and stared into a cool looking Batman and foolishly grinned. Because trust me, had I realized my face was incognito, I would have licked my lips instead, knowing full well, he wouldn't have seen me do that either. I quailed and nearly toppled. I frowned his way, suddenly realizing; how did he know it was me? "How did you know it was me," I blurted rather unnecessarily.

He glanced down to my boot covered feet then back to me, his eyes and grin, ending with a twinkle.

Oh crap. I did a mental head slap because doing it for real would have caused me to topple without question. So much for no one noticing it was me hidden beneath fifty yards of foam enhanced sponge.

"May I," he asked, indicating a chance at a slow dance.

Oh hello! Sprinkle me with chocolate, I'm going to faint! "Yeah, sure," I said.

Half way through the song my aching smile turned upside down; Batman number one was tapping at Batman number two's shoulder, asking to cut in. Naturally, Batman number two being the gentleman he is and much better at everything else, conceded and gave me a nod before he slipped amongst the crowd of partiers.

"Nice going, Charlie," I huffed, feeling perturbed. "It wasn't even a full song." Batman number one just pulled me painfully tighter. I tried squirming but it only caused the sweat to run down my face faster while Batman number one gripped me even tighter. "Let up, Charlie," I managed to say because he hadn't heard my complaint the first time around. "That's too tight!"

Batman number one wasn't having it, cocked his head, leaned in with a jeer and said through minty-smelling breath, "That's not what you used to say."

Oh. Fuck-a-doodle-doo!

I did my best to remain calm but every fiber of my being was protesting Batman's hold on me, desperate to have me wrangle free and drive the Dodge to Canada. But my struggling was useless and pointless because this Batman only gripped me like superglue as I realized to my panic it was my ex-dipshit, Dickie Trollop. As if I didn't have enough to worry about, I was suddenly concerned that all three Batman's' were of similar height and build. This only added to the confusion of me trying to figure out which was who and who was which slimy witch. Okay, so Billy/Jesse might be an inch or two taller than the other two and the fact that he was, hands-down, the best looking of the three, but all the same, he too was, covered in black foam enhancement. So, how was I supposed to know this was Dickie?

I gave Batman number three a second look, curiously wondering. Was it really him? Then he did the unthinkable that solidified my belief that this really was Dickie: he slipped a corsage of pink roses to my left wrist. They were my favorite flower and only smug-mug would know or realize that I would remember that he only treated me nicely like this when he was feeling guilty or in the case of today: if he was after something. All the same though, his gesture left me dumbstruck and I missed my opportunity to run away or knee him in his cod piece. He was after all, the love of my life, the reason I chucked my heritage and all that is Boolee to follow him to the ends of the earth. Because, back then, he was ever the charmer no matter what his devious thinking was thinking which only turned my constipated thoughts to mush. Until, that is, when his thinking turned into scheming and caused my own thoughts to jumpstart into scheming which prompted me to up and leave his sorry, three-timing, slimy ass and run for the hills of holler.

I realized now I should be trying to struggle my way free instead of reminiscing about lousy times, but I couldn't stop. I may have had the courage to run from him once but look where that got me? Then my thoughts did the driving for me as I feared that running from him now would have ended up with me toppling into the crowd of dancing couples no thanks in part, to this damn Twinkie costume. Besides, I once again, remembered that we needed this lousy idiot so we could rescue my criminally idiotic, Great Uncle Leo.

With that visual flooding my thoughts, I finally ditched my nostalgic brain fart and tried slapping at his hand instead, shouting, "Let go of me, Dickie!"

"Not so fast, my love," he said in that smug-ugly voice of his as he pulled me even closer, breathing his mentholated, tobacco tainted breath all up in my Twinkie covered face. Ugh. I'm going to pass out, I just know it.

"Come on, Dickie, just let me go," I snapped. "The FBI put out a bounty out on your lousy ass."

"Fuck," he hissed then said, "But I'm not about to blow town until y'all hand it over. Y'all still got somethin' I need."

Figures, do I know dumbass or what?

"Not anymore," I huffed; this Twinkie encasement may be stifling my words but not my thoughts or snark.

"I know that ain't true, darlin'," he said with a side of a smug grin. "Y'all'd never part with what's left of Black Beauty."

How-the-hell does he know that? I only just found the key fob today! I flinched, frowning. Miss Surelee. Dammit, she must have told him, but wait—why? Dang it, now I'm going to have to burn that fat suit into oblivion for her dragging me back under Dickie's slime.

Dickie took me on a twirl around the dance floor, leading me further away from everyone else at the edge of the makeshift area. When I stopped spinning to catch my breath I asked, "Why now? Why not move on to something else and leave me the hell alone!"

"Because," he began in that ever so stupid charmer voice he thinks he has. "We both know that's not what you really want."

Ugh, wrong-oh.

"What happened to Brandi," I redirected. I didn't really want to know or care what happened to his jail-baited girlfriend but I couldn't help it; I had to ask.

Dickie twirled me a second time before answering with, "History, my love."

I stiffened. Did he mean she was dead too?

Dickie must have sensed where my thoughts landed—which, was annoying to me now more than ever because he was so good at reading me back then—because he just flashed me a darkened stink eye saying, "Nothin' to fret about, darlin', she's takin' a breather in the Caymans' with someone much more suited to her braids."

Ah. Now I see. Jailbait Brandi up and left him for a man younger than him. It'd be funny if he were talking about anyone other than him. Nope, on second thought, it was pretty, fucking funny; he deserved payback in the form of a karmic bitch. I couldn't help it and said, "What comes around goes around."

Dickie just flashed me a smug grin, my words rolling off his steely, foam enhanced hide like water droplets.

So, I switched into high gear and an even higher voice saying, "You need to stop texting me!"

"I think it's fun," he replied, edging me ever closer to the exit.

"Tell that to Laney the next time you're feeling restless, dumbass!"

"How is my baby girl doing?" he asked.

As if he really cared. But my body suddenly went stiff with momma bear mode. "Crap Dickie, what do you care? It's not like you were ever there for her?"

"She'll always be my baby girl," he replied.

"Then why weren't you there for the birth," I said, feeling the pain resurface after all these years.

"I'm here now," he replied instead.

"You know, once the FBI snags your lousy butt and throw away the key, she'll be a distant memory on your one-track mind."

"Enough with the foreplay, darlin'," he said on a sneer, snatching me tight against his codpiece. "I've business to conclude."

Ugh. Not if you were the last man on earth...

"Sorry to disappoint, but I already gave the key over to Brent," I said, feeling pleased with myself that he couldn't see my poker face to know I was wildly bluffing...er, sort of. I had in fact, given it over to the FBI, a.k.a., Jesse James Huntley.

"Dammit Harley, I need them both," he said, twirling me once again.

The Twinkie costume, the dancing and dipshit were making me nauseous and lightheaded. If he didn't let go of me in the next thirty seconds, I was certain I was going to pass out. But not before I figured out what he was truly after. "There's another key?"

He stared at me for a heartbeat before saying, "I need them both to open the safe!"

Oh. Well. He had me there.

Good thing for me, Dickie wasn't about to clam up now. "That damn twink of Arnold's went and stole it after Lemmie plugged up that leak!"

Oh crap. "Um, I'm pretty sure that Miss Surelee doesn't have it either."

"Save that shit for your boyfriend," he said. "I know what he stole from his desk."

Double crap, she did have it, or rather, had; it was that troublesome horse statue now lost about all the stupid that

is Boolee in the fall. Then I had an implosion: According to
Jesse, Brandi now had it and according to dipshit, she was
resting easy somewhere in the tropics. I suddenly found the
funny and choked out my amusement.

Dickie blasted me with a death stare before saying,
"Where the hell is it, my love?"

I found my resolve, choked back another round of
laughter by asking, "If I give it to you, will you leave Boolee
and me forever?"

"Perhaps," he said, sounding devious, totally lying.

Uh-huh. Two can play that game. So, I gave him a smirk
that went overlooked for obvious reasons and said, "Not
until you call up the Giovanni's and have them hand over
Leo."

Plan in place, Dickie had me stuffed to a plain looking
truck (a Dodge no less) and driving us on back to that
dreaded trap of a fake antique store. Well, at least, *I* knew
it was a fake and only *I* knew who awaited our presence.
Yes, I'm laughing inwardly to my devious thoughts. I'm also
shaking like a leaf in the wind because Dickie refused to help
me peel out of that stupid costume.

It took Dickie five seconds to pick the front door lock
of the fake antique store. Ten seconds later, someone giggled
followed by two more, equally-looking, dirty-dealing goons
otherwise known as the Giovanni's. Related or not, all three
dressed themselves as if they shopped from the same
department store of uppity, cologne-soaked, millionaires.
My heart sped up beyond stroke levels and I thought now
would be a great time to pass out. After all, I still had that
stupid Twinkie costume entombing my entire existance so

it made perfect sense to me. Unfortunately, Dickie had a death grip of my arm the other clutching that troublesome peashooter once belonging to the late, officer Newbie and now aimed in the direction of the Giovanni's. Or, more importantly, toward the one wearing armadillo loafers; the one with the high-pitched voice that sounded like he sucked helium; the one he referred to as Lemmie.

I peered about and wondered where Great Uncle Leo was.

"Hand it over," said giggles. "Boss ain't got all day."

"Where's Leo?" someone shouted back.

Oh. Whoops. That was me.

Giggles and his shadowy goons removed handguns of their very own from their doubled breasted suit jackets and aimed them my way. "Who's the bitch?" said Giggles with the same sort of annoyance I hold near and dear whenever I find myself caught to Red's buckshot of vocabulary. I think the sight of a six-footer Twinkie might have disoriented them a bit. I know I was.

I flinched while Dickie shifted us backwards into the shop before saying, "No one y'all need to worry about. So, like the lady said—where's he at?"

"Where's the key?" said Giggles, flanked by the goon squad where they continued to look unfazed, or worse—like they were just itching to flex their trigger fingers.

"Leo for the key you fuckin' lackey!" shouted Dickie.

I wonder if now would be a good time to topple backwards?

Giggles gave back a squint before he turned to the goon on his right, nodded once and we all got to wait out an excruciating five seconds of strenuous silence before the goon returned, marching a shaky, handcuffed, and delirious looking Leo beyond the front doors of the treasure trap.

Okay, now would be a great time to do a swan dive or for Jesse's backup upstairs to come charging to the rescue. I held a breath and waited two heartbeats before I realized they weren't saving the day. Then I panicked: what if they had stopped tracking me? It's possible. I think that might have had something to do with me and my stupid thinking when I was hoping to delete a less-than-pleasing image of me on their tracking equipment upstairs.

Sheesh, I hadn't thought any of this through...

"Now hand it over," said Giggles.

I couldn't help my uncontrollable, reflective outburst and started to giggle. Giggles' voice was infectious. I mean, here was this six-footed man dressed in a thousand-dollar silk suit with yellow hair so white it could almost pass for tagging him as an Albino, and who spoke like a third-grader on a sugar high. Guess the nickname suited him. Guess he wasn't impressed with my misplaced observations because he turned his gun on me saying, "Shut the fuck up, sweetie-pie."

Nope.

"Brandi has it," I cried out, unable to keep this tangled web from strangling me further. "Dickie said she's in the Caymans!"

There. That'll do it, I think.

Everything was a blur of shouts and gunfire after that.

Somehow, I managed to duck before I toppled. Somehow, someone had managed a pot shot off my way before the government woke from their stupor and came to my rescue...sort of...

I felt hands under armpits lift me to my feet. I managed to right that uncomfortable, oversized costume and peer out into the crowd. If I didn't plan on living like a Dodge, I might have had myself a toppling, dizzy-dive. Instead, I let out a strangled, garbled cry. All three faces staring back belonged to Batman and one of them had yelled out that he was special Agent, FBI. Naturally, Dickie wasn't among them. Turns out, Ranger-man had chosen to don a Batman costume as well. Obviously. I also learned that Ranger-man was the one who finagled the truck heist so that Miss Surelee would have to stay in Boolee until he had 'captured his man'. Naturally, my cousin Stan was in on the secret, housing those supposedly stolen car parts about his junk yard until Ranger-man gave him the, go-ahead.

Too bad his 'man' eluded him too as I watched from Jesse's shop while he stuffed one of the handcuffed goons to the back seat of that unmarked, tan car. Unfortunately, Giggles and the other goon hightailed to parts unknown shortly after everyone's guns discharged, eluding Ranger-man, the FBI, and Boolee's Wannabes. And (no surprise here), Dickie had fled first, saving his hide like always, leaving the rest of us to ponder that.

Brent shuttled an uninjured Leo back to the lock-U-up tourist trap while Jesse helped me out of that troublesome Twinkie costume. I couldn't stop staring at the bullet hole; it was twelve inches above my naturally placed head to shoot clean through Twinkie's eyes and exit through the back. In hindsight, I should have been more worried over the fact I looked like a drowned cat when Jesse leaned in and... and...

Forget it. He didn't kiss me as my thoughts had dreamily demanded. He hugged me for reasons unknown to my shaky self and nothing more. Sheesh, he sure picked a fine time to be all professionally, professional.

A week later, after Jesse's squad packed up and high-tailed it back to wherever they usually reside, I settled to Aunt Bertie's kitchen table within the cocoon of the Victorian, hunched over a steaming cup of Javalot's coffee, doing my best to block out the previous two weeks, thinking maybe I might change my mailing address to no-man's-land when I heard gravel crunch. I perked up, went to the windows that overlooked my Aunt Bertie's makeshift drive and smiled. I watched as that cherry red beauty of a car zip up Aunt Bertie's makeshift drive, stop, pause, door open and a thin wisp of a man exit. He made it half way across the lawn before I charged the front door, flinging it open to shout, "Who are you?"

"Shoot Sweetness, it's me, Miss Surelee!" a familiar voice cried.

I tried to place the voice to the face, but my eyes were pranking me. I stared upon a little sprite of a graying headed man, dressed in bland colored V-neck cashmere sweater over button down shirt, instead. Shiny penny loafers, peeking from the cuffed edge of his belted faded dungarees. A gust of wind could topple his trim little body if he didn't anchor down.

Seeing my glossy-eyed stare, Miss Surelee pursed his lips, perched a neatly clipped, unpolished hand to his bony hip and snapped the other twice across his face. "What up, girlfriend, I look svelte, right?"

"Miss Surelee, you're not wearing a dress," I whispered in awe.

"Not anymore, I'm done with all those sweat suits and those heels gave me corns," he said.

Turns out, he was only sporting couture, getting into character, as it were for his honey-boo, Arnold Hibbard. I'd forgotten all about his little Dickie mix-up and his need to go incognito with the fat-suit. I just never knew it was temporary until that spilled out. I just assumed after we got my Great Uncle Leo back and unharmed, he'd be on his way to New York, or possibly, back to his life in Amarillo. I hadn't planned on the unexpected fact that Marty had a way of bringing out Lee Harvey DúVough's natural personality and blonde highlights, however.

"You look fabulous," I said, fanning my face.

"Thanks, darlin'," said Miss Surelee, cheeks flushing a bright pink.

Turns out, Mr. Lee Harvey DúVough wasn't interested in Broadway any more. Not since he met Marty, or Boolee or the fact that he caught a deal on Billy/Jesse's store-fronted cover, once Stranger-Danger man's cover was blown, that is. Here I thought Billy/Jesse was gay or working with the Giovanni's to catch me off guard. Who knew he was FBI? Everyone knew Miss Surelee was gay, however. I just never suspected that Marty Smarty was lingering in the closet until the right woman came along, or rather, the right *man*.

Well hell, good for them!

Parting aside, Miss Surelee nodded over his shoulder saying, "Looks like mocha latte is still interested Sweetness."

I watched as Miss Surelee turned heel, sank behind wheel, and drove off toward his newly found, hillbilly abode before I finally let out a breath and swiped at some drool. I stood rooted to screen door and watched as Jesse James Huntley shut down his SUV, strutted up the drive then grinned before he said, "You ready to do this, Boots?"

ABSO-FREAKIN-LUTELY!

"Rodger-Dodger, over and out," I said with a mile-wide smirk.

THE END.
I Think.
Maybe.

Don't miss out!

Visit the website below and you can sign up to receive emails whenever K. L. Metzger publishes a new book. There's no charge and no obligation.

https://books2read.com/r/B-A-ZBLL-LFHHB

BOOKS 2 READ

Connecting independent readers to independent writers.

About the Author

Kathie Metzger is an American writer of contemporary, chick-lit mystery with a humorous bent. With an affinity for all things quirky and out-of-character, Ms. Metzger resides in the multicultural coastal city of Virginia Beach where she spends her free time making waves, grilling out and tending to her gardens and margaritas.

Read more at https://kathiemetzger.wixsite.com/klmetzgerauthor.

CPSIA information can be obtained
at www.ICGtesting.com
Printed in the USA
LVHW051106291020
670168LV00002B/350